WITHOUT
A WORD

WITHOUT A WORD

E.C. SHEEDY

BRAVA

KENSINGTON PUBLISHING CORP.

http://www.kensingtonbooks.com

BRAVA BOOKS are published by

Kensington Publishing Corp.
850 Third Avenue
New York, NY 10022

All Kensington titles, imprints and distributed lines are available at special quantity discounts for bulk purchases for sales promotion, premiums, fund-raising, educational or institutional use.

Special book excerpts or customized printings can also be created to fit specific needs. For details, write or phone the office of the Kensington Special Sales Manager: Kensington Publishing Corp., 850 Third Avenue, New York, NY 10022. Attn. Special Sales Department. Phone: 1-800-221-2647.

Brava and the B logo Reg. U.S. Pat. & TM Off.

ISBN-13: 978-0-7582-1561-1
ISBN-10: 0-7582-1561-4

First Kensington Trade Paperback Printing: March 2007
10 9 8 7 6 5 4 3 2 1

Printed in the United States of America

To Tim. Always and beyond.

And, with a smile and much appreciation,
to my Nanoose Bay readership: Phyllis Downing,
Betsy Millar, Rhonda Lott, and Margaret Johnson.

And to those talented Red Door crazies,
fellow writers and friends.
Thank you for your insights, advice, and comic relief.

Chapter 1

The quilt, that inflexible weave of vinyl and recycled cardboard common to cheap motels, gave in to Dan's final kick and collapsed to the floor at the base of the bed, leaving him to battle the sheet binding his hips like a shroud.

Not that any part of his lower anatomy was even close to being dead.

Must have been some dream.

He extricated himself from the bed linen, sat on the edge of the bed, and took a couple of deep pulls of air. His mouth was dry and his face rough with a two-day growth of beard, and his pounding head reminded him of what a sorry asshole he'd been in the bar earlier.

The numbers on the bedside clock, 2:21 A.M., glowed red enough and bright enough to stop traffic.

He closed his eyes, concentrated on his most predictable body part.

The part wanting sex.

Trouble was, he didn't know who he wanted it with—but it was for damn sure it wasn't himself.

"Shit!" This time he voiced the word, while trying to remember the last time he'd gone this long without a woman. He couldn't, so he stood, then padded across the room toward the bathroom and the Questor Inn's third-rate shower.

A soft rap on the door stopped him halfway to the bathroom.

"Dan, baby, you in there?" The voice was female, the whisper was loud, and the tone was raspy.

As usual, sexy as hell. Her low, dark voice went right to a man's groin, exactly where Belinda Diamond aimed it.

And it was exactly what he didn't need right now. He quickened his bare-assed walk to the bathroom, flicked on the light, grabbed a towel, and secured it low over his hips. Motel-cheap and the victim of harsh laundry soaps in a thousand washes, it wasn't up to the job.

He opened the door.

Tall, dark, and beautiful, she smiled up at him and waved an amber-colored bottle in his face. It would be scotch, very good scotch. Which meant Belinda was here to party. The half-light from the hall seeped into his room along with her gravelly voice and the words "I brought you a nightcap." She stared at the excuse for a towel he'd slung around his hips and smiled. "Looks like you've got one for me, too."

"You shouldn't be here, Belinda." He closed the door a fraction, but the fraction wasn't big enough. She stepped around him and into the room.

"I shouldn't do a lot of things." She touched his bicep and walked her fingers to his shoulder. "But I do." She went to the old Formica-topped table by the window. On the table was a tray holding glasses, an ice bucket, and the makings for morning coffee. "Perfect." She turned two glasses upright.

Dan closed the door but kept his distance; Belinda on the prowl meant trouble—trouble he didn't need.

The line of light in the room switched from a shaft of hallway yellow to a triangle of bathroom white, enough to illuminate a torn seam in the worn jungle-patterned carpet. He rubbed his stubbled jaw, wondered what he'd done to piss off whoever up there was in charge of the bad-luck department. One quick trip out of camp to pick up his client, his mind fogged with too much booze, his body seriously sex-deprived, and he had to deal with his ex-lover, now the wife of said client. A very hot wife, as he knew all too well.

"Where's Barry?" he asked.

"Asleep." She poured him two fingers of scotch and brought it to him, her denim-painted hips an easy sway, her gaze fixed to his. "Where all good husbands should be during the wicked midnight hours." She wiggled the glass close to his face. "How else would a woman have her fun?" She dropped her eyes to his crotch and sighed. "I remember"— she ran the tips of her fingers along the hard jut in the towel—"one of these waking me up; you pressed so tight to my ass, you felt like part of me. Me turning. You going in long and slow. . . . Those were good times." Her gaze was heavy-lidded and smoky. "I mean, really, baby . . . you don't want to waste this, do you?" She gave him another stroke, this one slower, with a pause at the tip and some added pressure.

When he jerked against her hand, she tongued her lower lip, smiled at him.

"Jesus, Belinda." He sucked in a breath, stepped away, and headed for the jeans he'd tossed on the chair before he'd zonked out two hours earlier.

The room wasn't big enough, and she was damn fast. One tug and the towel was off; one toss and it joined the quilt and tangle of sheets at the base of the bed. When he turned toward her, she was unbuttoning her shirt, staring at him openly, avidly.

She'd come prepared, because she wasn't wearing a bra. In two seconds the shirt joined his towel on the floor, and she was cupping her breasts, offering them up like ripe melons.

Damn, she had magnificent breasts.

"Let's fuck, Dan," she said. "Like there's no tomorrow. Like we used to. Remember that layover in London. Or

Cairo . . . You can't have forgotten Cairo." She unzipped her jeans.

"That was a long time ago. Another lifetime." But he remembered all right; they'd stayed in their hotel room for days. And he'd been *in* Belinda for most of them.

She let out a long breath, touched a nipple with one finger, and slipped her other hand into her jeans. "You were the best I ever had." He caught sight of her black silk panties and watched her hand move under the silk and denim, watched her play with herself, heard her breathing turn ragged. Her tongue circled her lips; her eyes, greedy and dark with sex, met his. "C'mon, baby. Do me. I want you to do me."

His own breathing was hard now, along with the rest of him, and the way he saw it, any man who didn't want to look at Belinda Diamond's breasts while she fingered herself had an empty crater for a brain.

Dan Lambert didn't have a crater.

What he had was miserable hard-on.

And a wife.

"Get out of here, Belinda." He turned his back on her, pulled on his jeans, and tucked himself in. Carefully. "I'm a married man." *And a father.* Okay, so he sounded like a retired church deacon. It was the truth. More or less.

"Yeah, you're married all right. To an unfaithful and very"—she walked up to him, placed her palms on his bare chest—"ungrateful bitch." She circled her hand on his chest, and he felt his nipples harden. "She still seeing that guy? You know who it is yet?"

The room suddenly darkened, as did his mood, and he didn't answer. He had no idea how Belinda came by information about his personal business, and he sure as hell wasn't about to add to her meager store of knowledge—or admit to her he didn't have any.

"Come on, Dan," she cajoled. "It's the twenty-first century. Everybody has a little bit on the side. Monogamy's dead, don'tcha know? Even your dear little wife's picked up on that. So why not a little tit for tat?" She cocked her head and a brow, gave him a slow smile. "My tits, your tat."

His gut clenched, and he strode to the door and opened it. Wide. "I repeat, get the hell out of here. And don't come back."

She eyed him for a few seconds, then shrugged and bent to pick up her shirt. She put it on—slow as hell—and ambled toward the door, where she turned to look back at him. "Your loss, big man. But if you change your mind, you know where to find me." She gave him the once-over, then a perplexed look. "That wife of yours? Holly? Must be dumb as a brick. Because she sure as hell doesn't know a good thing when she's sleeping with it."

When she was gone, Dan headed for the shower. He wanted to wash Belinda away, and if he were lucky, the mess he was in with Holly would wash away with her. He knew he wasn't the first man to have married the wrong woman, but he hadn't expected her to screw around on him.

He shoved thoughts of Holly and her lover—whoever the hell he was—off the backside of his brain. He and Holly would settle that issue when he got home. That's what they'd agreed when he'd left for this job, and that's how it would play out. In the end he was determined they'd do what was best for Kylie. But for now he'd taken on this security project in the Alberta tar sands, so like it or not, he'd have to manage being a daddy by phone for a while. God, he missed that kid. The two, maybe three months ahead of him were going to be tough.

Maybe he'd manage a couple of flights out somewhere along the line—if only to see Kylie.

Neither he nor Holly and her stupid affair mattered. Only Kylie did. If he got nothing else from his marriage to Holly, he had Kylie. She was a gift, and she deserved a home with both a mother and a father. He intended to give her that.

He didn't plan on having more kids, but he'd damn well look out for this one.

He'd already lost one child. He would *not* lose another.

Chapter 2

Camryn Bruce kicked off her shoes at the door, dropped her keys on the hall stand, and set the nineteenth-century cranberry-colored glass sugar sifter carefully beside them. She had precisely the buyer for it. All-around, she thought, a very good day, businesswise at least, and she was home earlier than expected.

Blessedly, the house was quiet. No TV, thanks to her father being away on one of his short trips. She immediately felt a stab of guilt and reminded herself he wouldn't be staying much longer—or so he said. She was glad to help him out. . . . Okay, not glad exactly, but at least okay with it. You didn't need a perfect child-parent relationship to do the right thing.

Although with the way things were between Craig and her . . . To hell with it!

She wouldn't think about Craig, at least not in a negative way, and she wouldn't think about her father, his odd comings and goings, his endless financial problems.

She padded barefoot toward the stairs. She wasn't going to flash up the worry machine and ruin an otherwise okay day.

Craig wouldn't be here for at least an hour. Not only did she have time to change before dinner, she had time to actually *cook* dinner—something other than the grill-and-greens fare they'd been eating for the past month.

With her father away, she and Craig would enjoy a quiet dinner for two.

She paused mid-staircase on her way up to the bedroom, ran her hand over the smooth oak of the railing. Not that either of them would say much. It seemed as though both of them were living in their own heads these days. When she thought about it—and she tried not to—what troubled her most was that the mist, the coolness between them, didn't bother her enough. It should, damn it, it should bother her. But somehow her mind wouldn't focus on it.

Maybe after the baby is born . . .

She patted her flat stomach and continued up the stairs, anxious to get out of her suit and get started. She'd make a great dinner, light some candles, put on soft music, the whole enchilada. Then she and Craig would make lo—

Inside the bedroom door, she froze, stared, and blinked.

Craig, who'd been shoving clothes into a gigantic red sports bag, straightened, and his gaze shot to hers. Equally as fast, it slid away. In his hand were two freshly laundered and folded white shirts.

"Craig? What are you doing?" Monumentally dumb question, but all she had.

Instead of answering, he cursed, took in a noisy breath, and crammed the white shirts into the gaping canvas bag. He stood looking down at it, his chest heaving.

Camryn scanned the room. The closet door was open, as was every drawer in Craig's highboy. Clothes from both lay spread over the bed. A box and two large suitcases, closed—and she presumed packed—sat at the base of the bed. Her mind processed what she was seeing in a series of stops and starts. Her heart drummed in her chest. Understanding didn't dawn—it lumbered in methodically, stolid and surefooted.

So this was how it happened. This was how five years of marriage ended—stuffed haphazardly into a red sports bag.

Craig finally faced her, his hands on his hips, his expression both guilty and boyishly defiant. "You're home early. I wasn't expecting you."

"I can see that." She pressed her hand hard against her stomach.

The air in the room lay flat, fatally quiet. His mouth worked silently, and his eyes scanned the room before at last settling on her face. "I'm leaving, Camryn."

His words slapped her, and she balled the hand she was holding to her stomach. "I get that, too." Questions, too many of them, backed up in her brain; she couldn't find one to start with.

His eyes shifted away from her, but his voice softened. "I tried to tell you, Cammie. I'm sorry."

Sorry. A glib, soft-in-the-mouth word intended to mollify, instantly wash away all sins, either heinous or venial, and assuage all hurts. It was like using a silk scarf to suffocate a fire. Not enough. Not nearly enough. "This isn't about 'sorry' or what you 'tried' to do. This is about sneaking out the back door. This is about deception." The words came before her feelings, feelings too varied and coming too fast to make sense of. "What in hell were you planning, Craig? To send me a postcard?"

"No, I—" He rubbed his neck.

"What, then?"

"I tried to tell you," he repeated, his voice low. "But, damn it, there's never a moment in this house since your dad landed in on us, when he isn't hanging around, looking over our shoulders."

"He's only been here for a month. You're using him as an excuse." Her father's sudden arrival, after virtually no contact in years, had shocked even her, but she wasn't about to turn him away. She didn't know how.

"It's almost two months! And he's in our face, day in, day out. And it doesn't look as if that's going to change anytime soon."

"He's having a hard time right now." A weak defense, but the best Camryn could offer when it came to her father.

"He's the goddamn master of hard times, Camryn, and you know it." He stopped, let out a noisy breath, and looked upward, like he always did when he was trying to settle his anger. "But you're right, he's not the reason I'm leaving. Not all of it, anyway. But him coming here? Living here? It took up what was left of the space in our lives. And that makes him the last straw."

Camryn rubbed a knuckle along her lower lip. What was happening here had nothing to do with her father. This was about—her face heated as her heart tumbled—something else entirely, something . . . irreconcilable. "If you wanted to talk," she said, "we could've talked. We sleep together, remember? Right here in this room, all alone, not a father in sight." She waved a hand, buying time, ignoring her own insincerity, not wanting to go where the real problem sat poised like a scorpion.

"Yeah." He looked at the bed she'd waved her hand over, and his expression turned rueful. "I guess you could call it sleeping together." He shook his head as if to clear it. "And if you'll check your memory banks, you'll remember my pitiful male effort at telling you how I felt about the way things were going between us. That I wanted to . . . ease up on things for a while."

Ease up on things . . . Oh, yes, she remembered. She remembered that exact and terrifying phrase. And she remembered brushing his words aside, not wanting to hear them, certain he'd come around to her way of thinking as he'd always done. Guilt struck a glancing blow, then another, this one sharp with accusations of her selfishness, her blindness. She'd known his feelings, and she'd ignored them. Now she was watching him pack a red bag. Watching him leave. Watching her dream leave with him.

"You don't have a stupid bone in your body, Camryn. You had to see this coming. You *had* to."

When she didn't answer, because she had none to give, he took a few steps away. "Your dad showing up? Hell, he was just the icing on a fallen cake."

"It's about the . . . baby, isn't it?" The words tumbled out on a rush of breath and honesty in a question that frightened her more than losing her husband.

"The baby . . ." he repeated, and again shook his head. "*Jesus.*"

"The truth, Craig. You owe it to me." Even as the words escaped her, she wanted them back. Truths were unpredictable and fearsome, like snakes, venom-packed and lethal. Truths were turning points.

He hesitated, then put his hands back on his hips and faced her, but he didn't speak right away. He seemed to be looking for the right words. "Okay. . . . It's about *the baby*—the one we don't have, can't have. The whole getting-pregnant thing you're into—"

"I thought you were with me on that. We talked about it."

"It was the *only* thing we talked about. *Ad nauseum!* "And I was with you at the beginning. But I didn't think we'd be selling our souls to the fertility industry."

"Then this is about money?"

He shook a negative. "No. Money's the least of it. It's about . . . this drug, that drug, this clinic, that clinic, this test, that procedure. We've been on the get-a-baby treadmill since we got married, with absolutely nothing to show for it."

"I just need to know—"

"You *do* know. But you refuse to accept it. You've had four doctors tell you the same thing. The last one, what's his name? Andrews. Only last week, for God's sake."

She had the insane urge to cover her ears. Dr. Andrews,

yet another reproductive endocrinologist, had been the frankest and most direct of all of them. He'd put her chances of conceiving at "around minus zero."

"That doctor was—"

"*Right,* Camryn. That doctor was *right.* Confirmed to the letter everything you'd heard before."

"There's still a chance." She had to say those words, had to, even while hating the sliver of doubt embedded in them.

Craig shook his head. "You won't let go. You'll never let go. You're obsessed, Cammie." He paused. "And I'm . . . not."

Camryn unclenched her hands, forced herself to calm. He was right. She was determined, and focused. She didn't know any other way to get what she wanted, what she needed from life. "I see." Somehow, hearing the utter blandness of her response brought some degree of acceptance to her mind. Craig was leaving. She'd survive.

Craig shook his head. "You still believe it will happen, don't you?"

"Whether I do or don't doesn't matter." She took a step toward him. "There's more, isn't there?" She wanted it out, all of it. It was the only way she could deal with it.

After a long silence, he said, "Yeah, there's more, and it shouldn't matter—me being such a caring, contemporary kind of guy." He took a breath, then his eyes met hers directly. "It's the sex. Maybe you don't remember, but we used to make love. And afterwards we held each other . . . touched each other, laughed with each other. We didn't have intercourse on the clock and by the book, and we didn't spend an hour after sex—very *tense* sex—reviewing the odds of my sperm meeting up with your egg and heading upstream from there." He hesitated. "Lately? I guess you could say the sex is running ninety-percent procreation and ten-percent masturbation." He shouldered the sports bag and picked up the suitcases. "I'm done, Camryn. I'm gone."

She swallowed, knew his words came from justified frustration, knew they were true. But, still, they cut deep.

Yet, sadly, not deep enough to bleed.

"Then there's nothing more to say." Her words were stiff and tight, but all she had. She suddenly wanted him gone, wanted the emptiness of the house, an endless silence to paw through her mess of feelings. Dear God, there was actually relief in there, a weird warmth that had no place in the chill of a marriage failure.

When he reached the bedroom door, he looked back at her. "You know, I didn't figure you'd try too hard to stop me, and it looks as though I was right." His own words seemed to hurt him. "The truth is I think you stopped thinking of me as anything more than a sperm donor a long time ago." He dropped his head a moment, then straightened. "I'll get the rest of my things later."

She nodded. "I'll have them packed for you."

"And there's something else you need to know. There's no other woman, Camryn. Never has been. I didn't cheat on you. You're better than that. I'm better than that."

He walked out and silence entered.

Camryn sat stone-still on the edge of the bed. For a moment, she had the insane wish there had been another woman, some noxious female she could call nasty names and hate. It would be easier to take than losing your husband because you were lousy in bed and your womb was a black hole. A vacuum.

Nothing grew in a vacuum.

She covered her mouth, stayed a sick laugh edged with hysteria.

Craig was right. She was obsessed, deaf to the countless doctors who'd told her she'd never conceive a child of her own. She'd refused to believe them, because hope was all she had, hope and the entrenched notion that if you wanted something badly enough, you didn't quit. Ever.

Maybe she'd been wrong. . . . Even her mother had told her to let go, to accept her infertility and move on.

But more than anything else in the world, Camryn wanted a child. When she'd attended Kylie's delivery, watched that precious new life jerk and cry in the doctor's hands before being placed in Holly's arms, her heart had filled with a longing so intense her knees had weakened.

Call her obsessive, call her fixated, call her plain crazy; none of the tags mattered, because somewhere deep inside, there was a pool of love, a very special love meant for a child. Her child.

Or so I always thought. . . .

It wasn't as if she couldn't carry on, keep trying. She didn't need Craig . . . or any man. There were other options. Options that offered a world of waiting, a world of disappointments. The idea of them weighed on her, exhausted her.

She stood, walked to the window overlooking Lake Washington, and leaned her forehead against the cool glass, hurt and weariness sapping her resources, making her feel lost, outside herself.

"You had to try, Camryn Bruce, you had to travel that road. You had to take it as far as it would go." She blinked, then blinked again, feeling no regret, only emptiness. "But now you'll have to travel another . . ." She lifted her head, stared vacantly at the still autumn waters of the lake, and let the tears flow.

The trouble was she had no idea what road it would be.

For the first time in months, Holly Lambert felt free. Free of worry. Free of guilt. Free of her rotten decisions.

Closing her eyes, she savored the peace that came with visualizing her future without him. Finally and forever, the mess she called a life was cleaned up. Purged. If she were any happier she'd break apart, the pieces of her floating away like butterflies. She almost laughed at her own silliness, but smiled instead. She'd save the laughter . . . for when she could share it, when she'd told him her decision.

It's over. Done. At last. Irrevocably done.

She'd done what she had to do. She had a second chance—or sure as heck hoped she had—and she didn't intend to mess it up. There'd be no more stupid mistakes. She'd get it right if it killed her.

Pulling her long auburn hair into a hasty ponytail, she breathed deeply.

The morning air was autumn sweet, scented with pine and rain-dampened moss. The sun sent shafts of light through the trees to kiss the cool earth. Mist rose lazily from the ground, curled around the trunks of maple and birch, then disappeared. Its time spent.

She stretched, first one long tanned leg, then another, and rolled her head, circling her strong, straight shoulders. Impatient to get started, she took a drink of water and another lung-expanding breath.

Shifting her gaze to the path in front of her, she happily anticipated the five miles of running-high and heart-pumping solitude that lay ahead. The narrow lane, dense with brush and trees on either side, was soft-packed earth, bare and inviting—a commercial for Nike or New Balance.

Before tugging her T-shirt down, she patted the words scrawled in bold blue italics across its front. LIFE IS GOOD. She ran, gained speed and ease with each stride, thinking of all the good things that would flow from her finally having made the right decision for her and Kylie. Now all she had to do was convince Dan. . . .

Yes! For the first time in years her shapeless old running tee had it right. Life *was* good. Damn good!

A mile down the trail, she learned something else.

Life was short. . . .

"Hi." Surprise made her stop abruptly. "What are you do—"

Falling . . .
One last, searing thought. Kylie!
One last desperate breath . . .
One last beat of her healthy heart.

A person clad in coveralls and wearing a hairnet and rubber gloves stares down at her through eyes shot through with shock and fear.

The lithe, strong body lay sprawled on a mat of fallen leaves, arms flung outward, one knee bent. Her head, which the bullet had cratered deeply on the left temple, is clotted with hair, filling up with blood and brain fluids; it rests on a bed of stones at the side of the path at an angle only death allows. A stream of red flows from her ear.

Even in death she's beautiful . . . always so beautiful.

When the tears start, a blood-spattered gloved hand brushes them away.

One shot, thank God. Only one shot.

The incongruity of thanking God for assisting in a murder is lost in the mind static, the after-blur of violence. The first cloud of sorrow.

A leaf, bright copper under a solitary ray of sunlight, adheres to the spittle and blood oozing from the corner of Holly's mouth. Her eyes, shocked open by sudden death, stare upward, then inward to . . .

My soul! She sees my sick soul. A miserable, frightened soul repulsed by what its body has done.

The body's heart pounds, threatens to burst with its pounding.

Had to do it, had to do it. . . . No choice.

As a last act of kindness, the soul within yearns to close those damning eyes, but the body is repelled, immobile, unable to touch the blood and death it rendered.

There was love in life, laughter and shared history, but in the sin of killing, there is only cold fear and the void of death.

It's done, finally, irrevocably done. I can never go back.

The end of Holly's untroubled, privileged life brought a new beginning and a last chance to make things right . . . finally.

The soul wants to weep and beg forgiveness; the body puts the gun in a pocket, steps into the trees flanking the running trail, and disappears, more silently than it had come.

Chapter 3

Dan Lambert heard the phone while he was in the bathroom shaving. He ignored it, lifted his chin, and removed the last of his beard, going with the grain, taking his time.

When he was done, he slapped on aftershave and grimaced against the burn. But he liked the scent, kind of a citrus-and-musk thing that Kylie had given him for his last birthday. "Picked it myself, Daddy. Isn't it pithy?"

He grinned. The scent wasn't exactly "pretty," thank God, but it did remind him of home, and it went a long way in negating the lingering smell of oil-field smut, a vaporous stew of mud, grease, sweat, and sludge that took three showers to get rid of.

It had been a long three months.

Tonight, a steak as big as Idaho, and a beer as cold as the country he was in. And tomorrow the company plane and home.

Home. The thought of it took the frost out of the cold-beer idea.

He had no idea what to expect when he got there. During his and Holly's last uncomfortable conversation—at least four days ago now—before she'd put Kylie on the phone, they had, as usual, avoided talking about their wreckage of a marriage—until she'd blurted out that she'd "been thinking" while she was in Boston and had made a decision. One she hoped he'd be okay with, and be able to handle.

She'd sounded nervous and shaky, and they'd left things right there, which was fine with him. To his way of thinking, any discussion of their fractured marriage required a face-to-face, even if he did feel lukewarm going into it. The good thing was, she'd made a decision. One way or another, they'd take it from there.

He stepped out of the bathroom, wiped the last of the moisture from his jaw, and headed for the clean shirt he'd tossed on the bed. The phone rang again. He'd let it ring, let the desk take a message.

It had to be Plitski, wanting him to stay another few days and work up a preliminary security report on Burgeen Oil's new site. *Not going to happen.* He'd gone as far north and as deep into Alberta's Athabaska oil sands as he was going to on this trip, and the security was solid: surveillance was in place, the computer control center was operational, and every last man and his dog working the site had security clearance.

He shrugged into his shirt, grateful to be leaving and even more grateful he wouldn't have to come back for one final security sweep until early February. The sites would be going flat-out then, the ground frozen hard enough to take the heavy equipment required to carry 400 tons of tar sands at a go. Fifty-below time, when the north wind peeled back your skin and freeze-dried your eyeballs. No way around it. That 300 billion barrels of oil, with another trillion soaking in sand and shale, wouldn't be ignored and was always at risk, which made good business for Hoyle and Lambert, his security company.

He started on his shirt buttons. Yeah, February was his last trip. From that point on, he was staying close to home.

His hands stilled. For all his grand words about getting past it with Holly, doing what had to be done to make

things work between them, her cheating on him bubbled in
his gut like dirty crude.

If it weren't for Kylie . . .

Damn phone kept on yelling at him. He finished buttoning his shirt and picked up the black phone's receiver.
"Yeah."

"Dan? Dan Lambert?"

Not Plitski, thank God. "You got him."

"I have some . . . news."

When the voice registered, his eyebrows shot up. "Paul?"
What the hell . . . ?

"Yes."

Paul Grantman was Holly's father, and given he'd never
approved of Holly marrying Dan, his call was singular, a
real snowstorm in the Sahara kind of event. Dan's gut
balled. He and Paul had only two things in common, Holly
and Kylie. And trouble with either was the only reason Paul
would call. "What's wrong?"

"It's about . . . Holly."

Dan's hand tightened on the phone, something in him
icing up, something in him willing the silence coming down
the line to stretch out, never end. Although if there was one
thing Dan knew, all the wishing in the world wouldn't stop
bad news. He'd learned that from Holly.

"She's dead." Paul's words were flat, clipped, and bound
in control. "Killed, as the police put it, by an unknown as-
sailant."

"Jesus!" Dan's muscles jellied, and he sat like spent rubber on the edge of the bed. He shoved a hand through his
still shower-damp hair, while his mind took him to their last
good-bye, her forced smile when he'd left for this job, the
sour ache in his gut when he'd looked out from the backseat of the cab taking him to the airport, her waving at him
from the porch. He'd waved back but quickly turned away,
unable to look at her. What she'd told him about her . . . in-

fidelity too recent, and his promise to think things over feeling like a tumor on the brain.

"Dan? Are you there?"

"How? When?" He forced himself back to the phone call, his brain still not processing, not accepting, the information.

"Yesterday. It took me a while to find you." Paul paused. "She was running. God, I begged her to stop going out like that, running alone—"

"Where? Where did it happen? And for God's sake, what happened?" Dan wanted details, not regrets and recriminations. Hell, there'd be plenty of time for those.

Dan could hear Paul's heavy breathing, then the slosh of liquid courage in what he knew would be a fine crystal glass. "On the running track in the park behind us. Less than a mile from the house. She was found by another runner—a doctor, as it turns out. He said she was still . . . warm, so it couldn't have happened very long before he found her. I talked to him, and he said she'd died quickly." A pause. "She looks bad . . . really bad."

Dan's mind played a sick and violent movie. "Jesus," he said again, while trying to fill his lungs with air and block the images boiling in his head.

"The detective I spoke to said she was shot with a small-caliber gun at close range. That's it. They think it's probably a random killing. Said some pretty bad kids have been seen in the park lately, but they're questioning everyone. They don't seem to know anything, and if they do, they're not talking. They just keep saying they're looking into it. Like goddamn robots!" His voice rose.

"Where is she now?" Dan said, keeping his tone even.

"The morgue. They'll release her in a couple of days."

He saw her. In one of those stainless-steel drawers, with a tag on her toe, a white sheet covering her naked body. He closed his eyes, remembered her plans to redo the kitchen.

"Everything stainless steel, Dan. Fridge, stove, counters . . . everything. It'll be cool." As cool as it gets.

"Who in hell would want to kill her?" Paul said, his voice quiet and tremulous.

"I don't know."

"It doesn't make sense."

"No." Dan rubbed his forehead. Making sense of things wasn't possible right now. Sense didn't thrive in a brain fog as dense as pitch. "Kylie," he said. "Who's got Kylie?"

"Erin and I. She's all right. Too young to understand, of course, which is a blessing." Paul stopped. "Although this morning she asked where her mama was. . . ." He coughed as if to clear his throat, added, "We're keeping her busy."

"Good." Dan nodded to the empty room, glanced at the clock. Needing to move, to do something, anything, he stood and took the two steps away from the bed the twisted phone cord allowed. "With luck and decent connections, I'll be in Boston by morning." Christ, his voice was cracking. He leveled himself off, ignored the sharp stones in his chest. "And, Paul, I'm sorry. I know how much she meant to you."

"I loved her, Lambert. She was my only child." His voice was a bit steadier, and Dan knew he'd reached for this final store of strength. "I'm sure you'll miss her, too." The last words were added in the cool tone more characteristic of their strained relationship. "Call us when you arrive. There will be arrangements to make. And, as her husband, it's necessary you be part of them." A thought that obviously didn't please him.

The soft disconnect of the phone left Dan alone with thoughts of his murdered wife and now motherless three-year-old daughter, a daughter suddenly left in the sole care of a father who'd spent far too much time north of north, the twilight zone of Mother Earth—enough time to cost

him his marriage. What he had to do now was make sure it
didn't cost him his daughter.

He hit zero on the phone pad and waited for the front
desk. By the time they picked up, he was brushing at his
eyes. He coughed to loosen his tight throat, ordered what
was probably the only cab in town, hung up, and packed
with deft but hurried movements. What passed for an
airstrip was maybe a half hour away. If he could get a char-
ter to Edmonton, getting stateside from there wouldn't be a
problem.

He brushed at his eyes again. *Tears, for God's sake.* Too
damn little and too damn late. He had a kid to take care of,
and he intended to do it right, give her everything in him he
had to give. Tears wouldn't help the cause.

He might have failed Holly; he didn't intend to repeat
the mistake with Kylie.

When the phone rang, despite its being a mere arm's
length away, Camryn ignored it. Slumped on the sofa, a pillow clasped to her belly, she stared blank-faced at the TV,
specifically at an ancient black-and-white movie where
every man wore a tuxedo, none of the women had pores,
and both drank endless martinis while adrift in a wavy sea
of cigarette smoke.

The martinis were the most appealing. There were only
two problems with acting on that thought: it was barely
noon, and she hated martinis. She pulled the pillow closer.

"You doing okay?" her father asked, coming in from the
kitchen with two sandwiches and two glasses of milk. He'd
been away on one of his short trips until yesterday. When
she'd asked him where he'd gone, all he'd said was "business." His answer brought some relief, because she'd worried that it might be some medical problem he wasn't telling
her about, but when she asked, he'd denied it, told her he'd

never felt better. He set a plate in front of her and sat down in Craig's chair.

Craig would hate that, she thought, but she didn't care, couldn't think why she should. All she felt was flat, gray, and eerily disconnected.

Here she was, her life sinking to toilet level, and all she could summon up was a moody stew, equal parts despair, relief, and inertia. Either she was a damn strange woman, who could watch her husband walk out without a whimper, or she was slow on the uptake and a tsunami of emotions would hit when she least expected it.

"I asked you a question, Cammie. You okay?"

"Fine." She picked up her sandwich, put it down. Craig had been gone for three months. It felt like two years, and worse yet, it felt irritatingly . . . right. The problem was, she was *fine,* and she shouldn't be. She should be in the throes of a mental breakdown, her pillow should be soaked with tears, her heart should have a crack in it Grand Canyon–wide. He had been her best friend. . . .

Maybe that's all he ever was—a friend. Maybe I just glommed onto him when my bio-clock ticked toward midnight. Maybe I married him because he was my friend, because he was there and no one else was. If that were true, she didn't like herself very much for it, because decent people didn't go around messing up their friends' lives.

"You don't look fine." Her dad took a bite of his sandwich and reached for the TV remote control at the same time. "You look like you want to drink blood. Try that instead." He nodded absently at the glass of milk, then looked at the TV screen.

Flick.

Gone were the women without pores, the handsome men in tuxedos, the perfectly chilled martinis, replaced with burly men and a ball which they pursued with bloodlust and would apparently die to defend. She turned away from the screen. Was this her life now? Watching daytime sports with her dad?

She shot him a glance, suddenly irritated.

When he'd arrived home the morning after Craig left, she'd been in the kitchen, sobbing like an idiot. In much worse shape than she was in now. But when she told him Craig had walked out, all he'd said was, "Not surprised." Then, as if sensing more words were necessary, he'd added, "You'll be fine. Right?"

When she'd nodded through her tears, he'd looked re- lieved, trotted himself off to the den, stayed there, and avoided her for the rest of day. Not that she expected hugs and assurances. That had never been her taciturn father's style—not before he lost his fortune, and certainly not after.

When Trent Derne, a man who'd had it all, a man who drank thousand-dollar bottles of wine, flew in his own pri- vate jet, and smoked a million Cuban cigars, lost it all, he'd lost himself. He'd been forty-two, now he was sixty-three, and he'd spent the last third of his life dreaming and schem- ing how to get it all back. The process of stumbling from one get-rich-quick idea to the next, each effort more desper- ate, more costly, than the last had cost him his first wife, Camryn's mother, Rosalie, and two more after that.

Now he was living in his daughter's house. The one paid for by a small trust fund he'd set up for her at the insistence of her mother when Camryn was ten years old. It was all that remained of a fortune in the tens of millions.

So here he was in front of her TV, pretending this was a day like any other, pretending they had a normal father- daughter relationship. Pretending Camryn's husband hadn't walked out on her. . . .

If her mother weren't somewhere in Europe on her first real vacation in years, Camryn would have called her to talk about Craig's leaving. But there was no reason to ruin her mom's holiday. Camryn also knew, that if she did connect with her mother, they'd end up arguing about her father. Rosalie had been dead against her letting Trent stay with them, convinced it would cause trouble. Way too much room in there for I-told-you-so's, which made calling her mother another bad idea in a landslide of them. She'd get through this, and she'd get through it alone.

She thought about calling Holly again, but once was enough for that moan. Holly was so distracted these past few months, it was like talking to a stranger rather than your best friend. Something was bugging Holly, but whatever it was, she refused to talk about it. Whenever Camryn asked her what was wrong, all she'd say was "man problems" and insist she was close to working them out. No, she wouldn't call Holly—or Gina. Because if Holly was standoffish of late, Gina was all the way *off,* and she'd never liked Craig, anyway. When Camryn told her he'd walked out, Gina's only comment as "I always thought he was kind of weak." No, definitely not Gina.

Restless, she got to her feet. "I'm going for a walk."

Trent didn't take his eyes from the game on the television. "Want me to wrap up that sandwich for later?"

"Sure." She was at the door when the phone rang.

She picked up, and listened. "Oh my God. No!" Her legs turned rubbery and she placed a hand on the table for balance. "Oh, dear God . . ." She let the words trail off, her lungs pumping crazily. "Oh, Paul . . ."

Her dad looked up, his expression flatly curious. "What—?"

She lifted a hand, staying his question, and closed her eyes against the shock and disbelief warring in her head. She concentrated, tried to assimilate what she was hearing. Her breath jammed in her throat as she listened.

Shot! Died instantly. Funeral in a day or two . . . when they release the body. No idea who did it.

"And Kylie?" she said, when she found her voice. "How's

Kylie? . . . Good. . . . Yes. Of course, Boston. Right. I'll be there. . . . No, don't worry. I'll call Gina. . . . Oh my God, Paul, I'm so very, very sorry."

She clicked off, let the hand holding the phone drop to her side, and stood like a wax figure, incapable of movement.

"Was that Paul Grantman?"

She nodded dumbly. "Holly. Holly's dead." The words felt flat and cool on her tongue, unreal.

"My God. When?"

"The day before yesterday." She stared at him, her eyes unseeing through a wash of tears. "She was . . . murdered. In the park. Shot to death." Camryn took a faltering step away from the telephone table, sat on the edge of the chair she'd just left.

"Did they get the guy? Have a line on him?"

She shook her head. "No. Not yet." She couldn't think about justice, about *getting* anyone. Not yet. Holly was gone. Justice might, or might not, come later, but either way it wouldn't bring back her childhood friend.

Standing, she brushed at her eyes, rubbed them, and took a couple of deep breaths. "I've got to pack. Call Gina. Make arrangements. The funeral's in Boston."

Trent nodded, knowing the Grantman family well enough to understand the reason for Boston. "Where her mom's buried."

"Yes." She stopped, memories shooting through her, hurting her mind. She let the tears fall. "I can't believe she's gone. Holly's been part of my life forever. Her and Gina. Always there." She gulped in some air, tried not to think about Gina, how she'd take this news. But, then, these days she didn't know how Gina would take anything. She hoped it wouldn't be this horrible news that would bring them together again, close the distance Gina had kept from her since returning to the lake. To Delores.

"Since you were eight. When we moved in across the street from the Grantmans. About the time Grantman and I became partners." His face went tight.

She let the Grantman remark pass, having learned long ago not to go there. "Six. Holly and I since we were six. We started school together. Gina came later. First year of high school."

Her father nodded, then raised his pale eyes to hers. "Remember the time the two of you went to that dude ranch in Arizona? Holly tried to help you up on that horse . . . sent you flying off on the other side." He stopped. "I think you were maybe twelve or so." He paused, and his voice cracked when he added, "She was a nice little girl. Those were good days."

Camryn nodded, surprised by her father's clear memory of that time—a time she barely saw him. She quelled the lump in her throat and pulled his memory close, tried to hold on to it instead of the agony in her heart. "I broke my little finger." They'd lived two houses apart then, went to the same school, the same camps. Like sisters. Their fathers were in business together. "Yes," she said. "They were good days."

Through her tears, she looked at her dad. "Shall I make the reservations for two?"

She could see his withdrawal, his face turning sullen. "No."

"This is about Holly, Dad. It's not about Paul. Surely you can put that . . . business behind you long enough to attend her funeral."

"Doesn't work that way. Not for me, and not for Grantman. That man ruined me and enjoyed doing it. Nothing will clean away the bad blood between us. Even looking at his smug, rich face would make me puke. I won't be a hypocrite, Camryn."

"Dad . . ."

He shook his head, looked away from her, back to the TV wasteland. "You run along, call Gina. Make your arrangements. I'm sorry about Holly—for your sake. Sorry you lost a friend. But when it comes to that bastard Grantman, I don't give a rat's ass what he feels."

Chapter 4

Gina Solari said good-bye to Camryn, set the phone down, and put her hand over her mouth. *Holly dead . . . murdered!*

It was as if her world had tilted.

Strange, thinking about Holly being gone. For good.

When she'd talked to her last, Holly had been full of plans for her time in Boston. All happy and excited. But, then, Holly was always happy. Always beautiful, always rich, always thin, always . . . everything. Now she'd be always dead.

Gina's heart jumped, then beat unevenly for a few minutes; she pressed her hand against her chest. A chill gripped her, as if a window had opened to winter.

Then, as they inevitably did, her blurred, stormy thoughts turned to Adam, what he'd think, how he'd feel, what he'd do now that Holly was dead—gone forever. Holly had told her it was over between them, but Gina didn't believe her. What was between Holly and Adam never ended, it simply ebbed and flowed; cold, then torrid; white-hot, then frigid— but always there. Always pulsing. No one knew that better than Gina.

Now death had ended that hellish bond once and for all. A dark smile twisted Gina's lips when she thought of Adam in a world without Holly.

She prayed he'd hurt, that Holly's death would be cold steel in his bloodless chest, plunging, twisting, turning. . . . She hoped he'd *feel* for the first time in his sex-driven, selfish, charmed life.

Sighing, she pushed thoughts of Adam aside, as she would a thousand times more before the day was done. She hated the way he stayed with her, infested her mind, gnawed on her heart. She hated him. Craved him. And it sickened her.

Taking her hand from her chest, she filled her lungs. The usual dust-laden scent of the house assailed her nose. There were no tears, nothing resembling grief for her *friend*. No, it was more like the dank cavern inside her had warmed, lightened, and in an odd way settled. She blinked her eyes. Definitely no tears.

Camryn wouldn't understand, would think her mad or cruel—and maybe she was. But Camryn didn't know everything, and Gina had no intention of telling her. Too late for that, not to mention pointless—like everything else in Gina's life. Let Camryn go on thinking Gina loved Holly as much as she did. Gina would not cry over Holly's dead body.

It was Adam's turn to grieve, and there was a pitifully small amount of justice in that.

"Who was that? What did they want? If it was one of those awful telemarketer people, I hope you gave them what-for." The loud, deep voice came from the room at the top of the stairs, the room that sat house-center, like the crux of a spider web, the place of alertness, of sentry. Possession. It was the voice of her mother, Delores Maria Solari.

"It was Camryn." Gina spoke from the bottom of the stairs, her hand fused to the newel.

"What did *she* want? Still looking to buy my Waterford for nothing, I'll bet."

"It wasn't about your crystal." Gina sucked up her annoyance, the heat of her frustration. Delores was her penance. Her chosen punishment. You didn't talk back to your punisher: you either bore them or killed them. Or you punished back by never letting them get under your skin, no matter how sharp their scalpel.

"Good, because it's not for sale."

No, Gina thought, better they sink under the weight of the dust accumulating on them. She rubbed the newel. Hard. "You've made that clear, more than once. I'm sure she's got the message." Delores had been suspicious of Camryn since her last visit, when she'd made the mistake of praising her extensive Waterford collection.

Camryn ran Glass Finders, a company that specialized in locating rare china, glass, and crystal. She'd started it herself and now worked through a network of women who lived in just about every large city in the country. She called them "tracers." When a customer wanted something, Camryn put out the word, and between their efforts and contacts, plus her own inventory and network, even the rarest pieces could be found. She shipped worldwide and worked from home, like she'd always planned to, so she'd be around for her kids.

Gina knew Camryn wasn't getting rich, but she was doing well enough. Her heart kicked at her again. Like Holly, Camryn always did well, albeit for different reasons: Holly because she was born beautiful and rich with a daddy who took care of her, and Camryn because she had smarts and the energy to match. Yes, everything came up roses for Camryn, too, although she wasn't as showy about it. But she didn't get those kids she wanted, and her marriage to the boring Craig Bruce was a disaster. Gina took solace in that.

"And she'd better not be angling for another damned visit. I'm not ready for that. Not ready at all." Her mother's comments were followed by the sound of her wheelchair bumping over the raised sill at her door, then its squeak as it rolled over the scarred oak floor, stopping at the top of the stairs. "Well, what *did* she want?"

Gina took her hand from the stair post and looked up the stairs; Delores glared down at her, her expression sour. "A friend of ours was . . . killed." She knew it irritated Delores when she wasn't specific, so it was natural to withhold information. "Camryn phoned to tell me about the funeral arrangements. The service is in Boston."

"You're not going." It wasn't a question.

"No."

"Who got killed? Ah, Boston. Has to be that stupid Holly Grantman girl. Always was a brainless wonder." Delores fired down her vitriol, her face pale and tight with distaste, and rolled her chair onto the lift. She cursed when it did its usual getting-started lurch.

The lift carried her down, snagging and bumping on the fourth stair from the top as it always did, then complaining the closer it came to the last. Her mother wasn't overweight, but she was tall, close to six feet, and large-boned. She descended slowly, drifting down like a giant crow. Gina stepped away from the stairs, away from the clank and whir of the chairlift.

Delores rolled herself off the lift, straight toward Gina. "So . . . was it Holly?"

She wasn't surprised her mother had guessed correctly. Delores didn't miss much, and her sixth sense was second to none, except maybe Camryn's. Gina's senses, sixth and otherwise, shut down months ago. Now it took all her effort to look and act normal while her insides housed snakes, pain, and bleakness.

"Yes, it was Holly. She was out for a run and—"

"Spare me the details. I'd prefer lunch."

Gina clenched her jaw. "Fine." Delores Solari, with her height, broad shoulders, and straight bearing, used to be imposing, regal. Until a badly aimed bullet grazed her spine during an argument with one of her lovers over which of them was the most unfaithful; it was the night *imposing* became cruel and *regal* became dictatorial.

"I should send a card, I suppose." She frowned as if annoyed. "Paul will be a damned wreck. That spoiled girl had the wool pulled over his eyes well enough, even if she did have the brains of a rutabaga." Her mother went on, setting her mouth into a mean line. "Running alone, no doubt." She snorted. "No surprise she got herself killed. Just asking for trouble."

The front door creaked open behind Gina.

"No one asks to die, mother dearest," Sebastian, Gina's brother, said from the doorway. "Except maybe you, by being your constantly sweet and endearing self." He turned to Gina. "Who's she talking about?"

Delores didn't give her time to answer. "What are you doing here?" She curled her lip. "That tramp you're living with turn you out? You should start having them take a number, boy, or you're going to lose track." She sneered. "Why don't you come back here, sponge off me? I could vet your lady friends. Save you a lot of false starts. Be like old times."

"I'd rather chew dead snakes, Delores."

"My, my, we're sharp today, aren't we? Make another million on the market yesterday, did we? While your sister and I live here in abject poverty."

Sebastian snorted, looked as though he'd laugh in her face, but said nothing. *Thank God!* Gina hated when they went at it. Her stomach was a stone for a week after one of their arguments. And while Sebastian did manage to make a living as a day trader, Gina knew right now things weren't going well. But that was something he'd never tell Delores.

"Gina needed some things," he said, turning away from his mother. "I brought them."

"Gina, Gina, Gina. What about me? I'm the one in the goddamned wheelchair."

He set the bags he'd carried in on a side table near the entryway to the kitchen, then walked over to Gina and kissed her cheek. "Another day in paradise?" he whispered in her ear. She sensed his grim smile and felt his hair, as usual an inch or so too long, brush over her cheek. Their coloring—olive skin and deep black hair—was a gift from their Italian grandparents. Delores's hair was equally as dark, although now shot with gray.

"Not so bad," she whispered back. She squeezed his strong arm, had the urge to not let go, hold him here with her. She knew he only came because she was here, but even so, Sebastian never stayed long. If anything his relationship with Delores was more circuitous and confusing than her own. And while he said he hated her—even more than Gina did—she never quite believed him. There was something of the faithful dog about Sebastian, both to Gina and Delores.

"I'm not deaf, you two," Delores muttered, rolling herself toward the table with the groceries. "And in case you haven't noticed, I don't give a shit what either of you say. So have at me." She dug into a bag, pulled out an apple, and took a bite, eyeing them over the top of her reading glasses. "Jesus, what a pair. A daughter who shot her own mother—"

"I didn't—" Gina started.

"And a son who spends his life fucking stupid women. When he should be here helping his crippled mother." She shook her head in disgust, spun the chair, and headed into the cluttered room at the front of the house she insisted on calling the parlor. Gina thought of it as the smoking room because it was there, during the day, where Delores spent her time, dragging on cigarettes while she read endless biographies and listened to long-dead composers. Delores hated television and refused to have one in the house.

She was halfway to the parlor when Sebastian said, "You're

as crippled as you want to be, Delores, so why not get out of that chair? Give Gina her life back." His words were as soft as the disturbed dust swirling in the light coming from the stained-glass window above the front door. Gina knew the restraint was costing him. "You could at least try," he urged.

Delores acknowledged his statement with a dismissive wave of her hand before she disappeared into the parlor and slammed the door. Sebastian moved to follow her.

"Sebastian, don't." Gina grabbed his arm. "You know it won't do any good."

He turned on her, his eyes fiery. "You're not a cripple either, Gina, so why the hell don't you walk out of here? Today. My car is outside."

Gina looked at the doorway her mother had rolled through. "I owe her. You know that." *And I have no place to go and no will to find one.*

He snorted. "You saved her life—such as it is. She's the one who owes."

"If I hadn't picked up that gun—"

"That loser boyfriend of hers would've shot her in the heart. She'd be dead, and so would you, and you damn well know that. I can't believe you've bought her crap about it being your fault." His strikingly handsome face was a study in disapproval.

Oh, Sebastian, if you only knew . . .

When she didn't answer, he turned abruptly, grabbed the sacks of groceries, and headed for the kitchen.

Gina trailed after him. She didn't want to talk about the shooting again, but she did want him to stay. He never stayed. No one ever stayed. Except Delores. Day by day, this horrid old house, all thirty thousand musty square feet of it, tightened around her like a dying fist. "How about a cup of coffee?" she said.

"Can we have it outside on the porch?" He shot her a challenging glance.

She glanced toward the window above the stained porce-

lain sink. The pale gray day and the lake beyond were ob-
scured by the silver curtain of rain coursing down the window. "It's not very nice out there."

He watched her, his brow furrowed with half concern,
half frustration. "It's warm enough, and I suggested the
porch, remember? It's covered. You can at least do that,
can't you?"

"Of course I can," she said, careful not to snap. "But not
in this weather." She could go outside . . . if she wanted to.

"Are you still seeing Doctor Ren?"

Doctor Ren was a psychiatrist, and a friend of Sebastian's. "Yes, we've had three sessions." She tried to sound serious, committed. Rational. And it was true enough. She
was holding her own, and would as long as she kept her
world tight and close. "I like him, Sebastian," she lied.
Well, almost lied. She didn't dislike him exactly, just viewed
him as a waste of her time. But if talking to Dr. Ren made
Sebastian feel better, she'd go along with it.

"What did he say?"

"He says I'm a bit depressed." *More than a bit, and not
exactly breaking news.* But who cared? What difference did
it make if she'd rather stay in than go out? There was nothing
out there she needed. "He gave me some pills. And he's coming again next week."

"Good. That's good."

"Yes." She got lost for a moment, trying to think where
she'd left the pills. "Everything's good."

"And what about Mother? How's she taking your seeing
a 'nut doctor'? Isn't that what she called him?"

"The first day he came she cursed him from the top of the
stairs, called him a two-bit quack—among other things—
and told him to get out of her house."

"But she didn't come down."

"No."

"I didn't think she would. Probably afraid he'd reserve
her a padded room somewhere." He didn't smile.

Gina did, briefly. "Ever since that first day, if she knows he's coming, she doesn't come near the stairs. Just stays in her room."

"I'm telling you, she's afraid of him."

"Maybe." Gina had a hard time seeing Delores afraid of anything. In that way she and her mother were alike.

"Doesn't matter. What matters is that you keep seeing him. Promise? Because whatever the hell is going on with you, it isn't right."

Her stomach knotted. She didn't like him saying she wasn't "right."

"I said I'd see him, Seb, and I will."

"Good." He studied her a moment longer, then started digging into the bags. In minutes he'd be gone.

She hurried to the cupboard. "I've got cake. I made it yesterday. Chocolate. Your favorite."

"Okay," he muttered without enthusiasm. "Coffee and cake, then I'm out of here."

Gina started to make the coffee, then she remembered . . . Her heart missed a couple of beats. She hadn't told Sebastian about Holly. *Oh God! Poor Sebastian.* He'd feel everything she didn't. *Damn you, Holly. Damn you!* Something hot and hard settled in her stomach, and she worked to steady her hands, pick up the knife to cut the cake.

Seb sat at the table, drumming his fingers, a nervous cat, ready to spring for the nearest exit.

"Seb, what Mother and I were talking about . . . when you walked in?" She hesitated. "It was about Holly."

His eyes, until now dull with boredom, shot to hers, brightening with interest, then quickly darkening. "What about Holly?"

"She's dead, Sebastian. Someone . . . killed her."

He gaped at her, his face a blank. Then he frowned and looked away. Either he couldn't take it in or had no idea what to say.

She left him to a long silence.

He got to his feet, looking stunned and awkward. Seb was never awkward; he was innately graceful, like a shiny black panther. Gina was the awkward one.

"I spoke to her a couple of weeks before she left for Boston," he said. "We made arrangements to meet there, have dinner."

"You flew to Boston? To have dinner with Holly?" She barely masked her surprise. Seb hated flying.

He nodded. "She asked me to, but—"

"She didn't show."

He dropped his eyes, shrugged.

Gina sealed her lips before she said more and cut into the cake with more force than necessary. No point in reminding him that not showing up was a habit of Holly's. That, and telling people what they wanted to hear, then blowing them off—everyone except Adam. There was a . . . bond between Holly and Adam. Always had been. She remembered Holly telling her years ago how they fought, how they made love, how their "bodies and souls" had a "devil's craving" for each other.

Gina wanted to throw up. She swallowed her bile.

Seb didn't need to hear any of this. He'd been in love with Holly since he was sixteen years old; nothing she said would make him stop now. She wiped the cake crumbs from the knife, kept wiping until its sharp edge gleamed under the harsh kitchen light.

"Who told you?"

"Camryn. She's going to the funeral."

He shoved a hand through his hair. "Tell me exactly what she said. Everything you know."

She told him what Camryn had told her, which wasn't much.

"Running alone in a park? That's Holly, all right, but Jesus! Where the hell was her damn husband?"

"I don't know." She went to touch him, but he pulled away.

He gave her his back for moment. When he turned back to her, his deep brown eyes were black. "She was seeing Dunn again, Did you know *that?*"

He knew! Barely hiding her shock, Gina hesitated. "I knew he was back, but I don't think she was seeing him." She managed the lie, though it burned her mouth. She watched his face, saw his desire to believe her, saw it fail.

"Fuck!" He let out a harsh breath.

"She was over him, Seb. Through," she added. 'Absolutely and once and for all,' those were her very words." The trouble was that Holly's pronouncements on her chaotic on-again, off-again relationship with Adam were notoriously unreliable.

"And you believed her." He shook his head, cursed again. "Not that any of it matters now. She wanted Dunn. She got him. Her choice. Hell, you all wanted him. None of you could see what an opportunistic bastard he was."

Irritation surged in Gina, along with her pain. "Nor could you see Holly for what she was."

"Which was?" His face was tight.

"A . . . dream, a terrible, terrible dream." *Like Adam was for me.* "And a married woman, whose husband's name was *Dan*—not Sebastian and not Adam. *Dan!*" She wrestled with her anger, tempered it, and added, "Whatever your imagination conjured, Sebastian, she wasn't yours, she was never yours."

And Adam was never mine.

"That was going to change. We talked. Made plans. If that asshole Dunn had stayed away . . ."

It struck Gina how inane this conversation was. Holly was dead. Holly wasn't going to be any man's, ever again. Not her husband's, not Sebastian's, and not Adam's. "Let it go. Holly's gone. Nothing will change that." Relief hovered over the thought, making her breathing quiet, as if Holly not being alive would make her life—and Sebastian's—less troubled.

He lifted a hand. "I'm leaving." He stopped at the door, and when he looked back at her, his eyes were moist, ruined. "I loved her, Gina. I always loved her. If I could change that I would—God knows it's done nothing but fuck up my life—but I can't."

He couldn't see, wouldn't see Holly for what she was. He needed to understand. "She played with you. Then she broke your heart, Sebastian—and you let her."

He said nothing, shook his head, and walked out the door.

Breaking hearts. With her lustrous deep red hair; heart-shaped face; tall, athletic body; and endless bank account, breaking hearts was what Holly did best.

It's what Adam did, too. Break hearts. Camryn's, hers—even Holly's. They'd all been drawn to his flame, and Adam had burned them all, *screwed them all,* literally and figuratively. He was handsome, charming, intelligent, smooth, and despicable.

And utterly faithless. Exactly like Holly.

Yet Gina craved him with every beat of her traitorous heart.

Bitterness, hot and acidic, rose in her throat and was instantly displaced by a sick self-loathing. Every woman craved Adam—even Camryn. It was Camryn the bastard started with. Then he met Holly. Adam Dunn was hazardous to her mental health, Holly had said once. In Gina's case he was fatal.

Adam wasn't only a home-wrecker, he was a life-wrecker.

She had the torn womb to prove it.

Chapter 5

Dan watched Paul Grantman pace the luxuriously appointed study from fireplace to window and back again. Window to fireplace . . .

The man was giving him whiplash.

Dan hadn't seen Grantman in over a year, damn near enough time to forget how much he disliked him. He cut him slack because he was grieving, and because he agreed with him about finding out who killed Holly and hanging the bastard by his balls. Dan had his problems with Holly, but her senseless death, both ugly and cruel, made his stomach hard and his brain mean.

Paul finally stopped pacing. Hands clasped behind him, he said, "We need to talk about Kylie." He met Dan's eyes, his own fixed in a hard stare. "I don't want you to see her. I'll be keeping her here with Erin and me, and as I expect you'll be gone right after the funeral, I think seeing her now would only upset her."

Dan's gut twisted, but he wasn't surprised. He'd expected a fight over Kylie. It was a fight he'd win.

"That so?" he said, careful to keep his voice low. He set his drink on the polished cherrywood surface of the coffee table and straightened. Paul Grantman stood maybe five-ten, giving Dan a height advantage of three inches. And with Grantman, he needed it. The man hadn't made mega-billions by being anyone's pussy. Holly's father hated to lose. A trait he shared with Dan. When Grantman wanted something, he generally got it, using cash or coercion. Charm wasn't in his arsenal.

And now he wanted Kylie.

"She's my granddaughter, Lambert. My blood. You didn't think for a moment I'd let her go with you, did you? A stepfather—of little more than two years." He came close to spitting out the last words.

"Yes, I'm her stepfather, but I'm also her daddy, the only one she's ever known. Holly and I talked about it and agreed on it. It's what she wanted." *And it's what I want.*

Grantman gave him a half-smile. "Then you're in for a surprise," Grantman said. "Because when Kylie was three months old, I insisted Holly make out a proper will and organize guardianship. I put her in touch with Bernes, Wallace, and Freed, and she named me—and Erin—as Kylie's guardians in the event of her . . ." He stopped, tensed up, as though the reality of Holly's murder had just leapfrogged the easy legal steps of years ago. He went doggedly on. "We talked about it again when she arrived in Boston a couple of weeks ago. I'd made some new financial arrangements for her and Kylie involving a considerable sum of money, and Jason Wallace suggested Holly review and update her will and the necessary guardianship documents. I set up the appointment myself. She made no mention of a change in her preference."

Dan kept his mouth shut. He was tired, and now he was pissed off. Both good reasons not to argue with Paul Grantman. If he did that, they'd both lose. And with Holly's service in a couple of days—if the coroner released the body as scheduled—it wasn't the time to lock horns over who would make the best father to Kylie. Dan knew one truth: the last thing Holly had wanted for Kylie was for her to be "owned by her father and mothered by his loser wife." Her words, not his. Finally, he said, as evenly as he could, "You got a copy of that new will?"

"No, but—"

Dan stood, cut him off. "Then it looks like it'll be dueling lawyers at sunrise." His bet? Holly never kept that appointment with her father's lawyer. He knew how she operated. She never confronted her father, just agreed with him, then did whatever the hell she wanted—her way of driving him crazy. Right now it seemed to be working. "But you should know, Grantman, that Holly was specific about what she wanted. And like it or not, she wanted me to be Kylie's dad." He paused. "If it makes you feel any better, it's a responsibility I'm proud to take on. Kylie's been my daughter from day one, and I'm happy to keep it that way."

Paul snorted, took a step closer to Dan. "Holly was never 'specific' about anything. I loved her, but you and I both know she was both capricious and careless about details—"

"Except when it came to Kylie," Dan interrupted. "But I'll leave the proof of that to Holly's lawyer."

Paul ignored him. "Kylie is my granddaughter and my responsibility, so don't try anything with me, Lambert. You'll lose."

"I'm not 'trying anything,' I'm telling you what your daughter wanted. I don't give a damn whether you agree or not." He rubbed at his bristled jaw. He not only needed sleep, he needed a shave. "So if it's all the same to you, I'll take my daughter and go."

"You'll go, but without Kylie."

Dan chewed on his own frustration, tamped down his growing anger. "She isn't here, is she?"

"No."

"Where then, and with who?"

"Outside the city, with Erin and the new nanny we've hired."

New fucking nanny! Like Grantman's having Kylie was

a done deal. Dan ignored the burn in his chest, but his words came out in a tough string. "You're ahead of yourself, Grantman. Way ahead."

"I'm ahead of most people, including you." He looked so goddamned pleased with himself, it was all Dan could do not to wipe the smirk off his face with his fist.

Telling himself, again, this was neither the time nor the place to pop Kylie's granddad, he strode across the study toward its exit, crossing two Persian rugs along the way. He stopped at the ceiling-height doors which he knew led to the marble-floored hall and grand staircase. And gilt, lots of gilt. Paul and Erin knew how to live—or at least thought they did.

"I came here directly from the airport," Dan said, "to pay my respects and pick up Kylie. Seems I've failed on both counts. We'll talk again, after the service." He paused. "Holly wouldn't want us at odds over this. She'd want what's best for Kylie. And"—he again rubbed his unshaven jaw—"while I might not look the part, that little girl has called me Daddy for two years now. I don't intend for that to change." He lifted the ornate bronzed latch, opened the door a couple of inches, then decided on some conciliation. "I don't intend to keep her from you. You care about her, I know that. So there'll be no problem on that score."

"Who the hell do you think you are? Granting *me* favors," Paul snapped, his expression flat. "I was against her marrying you, you know."

"I'd say you made that plain. Like I made it plain I didn't give a good goddamn what you thought. Still don't." Dan looked across the spacious room to where his father-in-law stood by the fireplace. Its mantel was too high for him to rest an arm on, and he looked minimized and bleak in front of its carved oak facade, dwarfed by his possessions—and maybe by the death of the daughter he loved, in his own possessive way.

"You weren't the man for her," he said. "Always gone, never there for her. Holly hated being alone. You must have known that."

Dan took a couple of seconds to conquer his unquiet breathing. He didn't take his hand from the latch, thoughts of Holly, her cheating, and her mystery lover heating his mind. None of it anything Grantman needed to know.

It wasn't the first time Dan had accepted his part in her infidelity; he had left her alone. It didn't matter that she'd been the one pushing him to go this past year, didn't matter that he'd tightened his schedule, shortened his times away by living on goddamn planes. He done that for Holly and for Kylie. Turned out Holly hated his impromptu arrivals home, and it was during one of them he'd found out why. His gut knotted. "As it turned out, you were right. I wasn't the man for Holly. But I'm the father for Kylie. The only one." He opened the door and walked out, his eyes dry, the knot in his gut barely perceptible now, probably because he'd been living with the damn thing for so goddamn long it was starting to feel natural. *Shit!*

In the cab taking him to his hotel, Dan put his head back, stared at two burn holes in the cab's gray fabric head liner. Surprisingly, his eyes moistened with tears. He closed his lids against them, not sure what the hell he was feeling so rotten about, Holly's death or his own guilt that the emptiness created by her death was only an enlargement of the wound her cheating had torn into his chest months before.

Paul was right. Dan wasn't the man for Holly, and she wasn't the woman for him.

They'd married, in a blur of lust and laughter, too damn fast. Dan thought she was the most beautiful woman he'd ever seen. He liked her lighthearted view of life, her great sense of humor, and he admired what a great mother she was. Not a believer in love, he'd figured he'd come as close to it as he was ever going to get with Holly Grantman. He was thirty-five, thought it was time to settle down. One woman. One man. Holly wanted stability for Kylie, or so she'd said. Honesty on both parts, he'd thought. Lots of liking. Lots of smart, logical talk. It all worked for him.

Looking back, he wondered now if maybe Holly hadn't used him from the beginning. Maybe she married him to escape her father's control. "Capricious" Paul had called Holly. Dan would grant him that.

He pressed the heels of his palms against his hot eyes before opening them to look out the cab window. They were passing Harvard Square. Except for the yellow leaves shifting along the gutters and between the benches, the day was dismal shades of gray.

A band was setting up in the street, getting ready for the evening crowd, and two well-dressed couples met and greeted each other with hugs outside a restaurant, its glass doors already warmly lit from within.

Dan closed his eyes again. He wasn't interested in the tidy, organized street scene; he was interested in getting his daughter and getting on a plane for the west coast, burying what regrets he had for his marriage along with his wife. He'd come close to loving Holly, or thought he had, but he'd lost her months before her death.

He did not plan on losing Kylie.

Light from the bedroom window streamed in and hit Adam Dunn's closed eyelids with the heat and intensity of halogen.

Today is Holly's funeral.

He risked opening an eye, took a direct thousand-kilowatt hit, and closed it again. He turned his head from the light, but his naked body was tangled in sheets and a woman.

He yawned, ran his free hand over her ass. Good ass. Almost as good this morning as last night. But, then, his ass was always primo; he made sure of it. Grade A or nothing, that was his rule, and he stuck to it. He'd fucked the occasional ugly when he had to, but he'd hated every minute of it.

He squeezed the well-toned buttock under his hand and gave the woman a gentle shove, hoping she'd roll enough for him to extricate himself, but not wake up herself.

He wasn't in the mood for talk.

Sitting on the edge of the bed, he shoved his hair back from his face. Thick, straight, and cut to ear-lobe length, his dark chestnut hair, shot through with natural blond streaks, was tangled but shiny-clean. Women said they could never figure out whether he was more pirate or poet, but it didn't matter to Adam what they thought. All he knew was that his hair was a hell of an asset.

That and a cock that had given him serious locker-room bragging rights.

When he'd discovered women went for both, he'd learned to let them have it—if there was something in it for him. When he was younger, sex, and lots of it, was enough of a payoff; now it was more complicated, his needs more material.

Still the whole business was getting predictable, and the time lapse between a woman stroking his hair to her stroking his dick, shorter.

"What time is it?" Her voice came from behind him, low and sleep-filled.

"Almost ten," he said, getting up. "Which means I've got to go, baby."

She pulled herself up, did a cat stretch, and put her back against the headboard. Her hair was a blur of dark blond tumbling to the rosy tips of her nipples. He studied her, let his gaze linger on her breasts. Nice. Very nice. And a first-class fuck.

"I'll make you breakfast." She pushed the sheet down,

touched her pussy and smiled at him. "All this, and I can cook, too."

Shit! Here we go . . .

"Awful tempting." He put one knee on the bed, leaned down, and kissed her forehead, as patiently and as gently as possible. They always loved this morning-after crap. "And you're beyond beautiful. But—" Something sharp moved in his chest, stopped his breath, damn near stopped his heart.

But you're not Holly.

Holly is dead. He hated thinking about that, because no matter how many women he'd married—two; lived with— maybe a half dozen; or fucked—uncountable, Holly was his touchstone. Losing her was like losing home base. Whatever the explosive compulsion between them, it kept them both coming back for more. More fights, more making up, more vows never to see each other again, more I-love-you's . . . Marriages and other women put a few obstacles in the way of their hooking up, but despite these occasional snags, they hadn't spent more than ten, eleven months away from each other since college. They always found each other. And now he'd never see her again. His breathing cratered as if he'd been sucker-punched in the chest. Not fair.

Because with her dead, the damn wedding was off.

But at least she'd finally told the truth, and that truth would do two things: in the short term it would get Lando Means off his ass, and in the long term—if he played it right—it would set him up for the rest of his life. He wanted to smile but couldn't when he thought of Holly. He'd have preferred her being part of that life—her working Grantman instead of him—but that wasn't to be. All he had now was the name of the lawyer he'd taken her to last week, and Holly's word that she'd done the "right thing."

Not that Holly always did what she said she'd do. He ignored the prickly sensation on his nape.

That goddamn lawyer was his first stop.

Maybe things weren't going to be as neat and tidy as they would have been if Holly had gotten rid of her husband and married him like they'd planned, but that paper at the lawyers with his name on it would have to do.

Damn you, Holly, you'd better have come through.

"Hello? Anybody there?" The blonde waved a hand in front of his face and gave him a puzzled look.

He refocused, smiled into her eyes, and made a circle around her nipple with his index finger. "Sorry, but a man looks at you, at this"—he pressed her nipple—"he can't think straight." He met her eyes, saw the sexual mist in them, noted her sharp intake of breath. She was hot, this one. Easy. They were all easy—if you did things right. "But much as I'd love to stay, I've got to go, sweetheart." He grinned. "I take it I'm welcome back?"

She touched his face while her own turned serious. "You were . . . fabulous last night, Adam. You did things—made me feel things—I've never felt before." Running her index finger along his jaw, she added, "So the answer to your question is yes. You're welcome back . . . anytime, anytime at all."

"I wish that time was now, Lisa. I really do," he added, careful to use her name, lace his tone with regret. The morning after with a woman was as important as the night before, and considering the crumbs it took to make them happy, the effort was worth it. It didn't pay to piss them off; what paid was to keep them needy and dangling. A guy never knew when he might want to come back. He brushed his lips over hers.

"What's so important, anyway?" She reached down and cupped his balls, played with them.

He let her, enjoying the touch of her soft, deft hands on his scrotum. Then he moved his knee off the bed, stood beside it, and smiled down at her. "Hey, you don't play fair." He picked up his jeans, glanced around, but couldn't see his briefs, so he pulled cool morning denim over what was now a semihard-on, and shrugged into his shirt.

She slid to the edge of the bed, spread her legs. "I repeat, what's so important?"

He weakened, then shook his head in regret. "A funeral, baby. Anything less and I'd be right there." He nodded appreciatively at her open legs, the curls at their apex, then buttoned his shirt, and stepped into his shoes. He gave her his best lingering kiss good-bye—because he wanted to borrow her car. But it wasn't Holly's funeral he was going to. Hell, Grantman would have apoplexy if he came within a mile of it.

No, the funeral he was going to was the one where he buried his debt.

He was outta here.

Lisa's new Saab Aero was in the bowels of the dimly lit parking lot. Jangling the keys, Adam rounded the cement pillar her car was parked behind.

"Hey, lover boy, we've been waiting for you."

Although Adam hadn't had breakfast yet, something in his stomach that felt like a bag of bricks dropped and rolled. His first instinct was to cut and run, but one look at the two goons leaning against Lisa's car, and given that there wasn't anywhere to run to, convinced him he had no choice but to stand where he was—three feet from the biggest trouble he'd ever been in. Two poster boys for Steroids-R-Us.

"And you are?" he said, trying like hell not to have his voice sound like a goddamn frog.

"Name's Bob, and this here"—the man jerked his head toward his companion, who, wearing a white tee and black jeans, made a pro-wrestler look malnourished—"is Bill."

"Bob and Bill. Catchy."

"We think so." Bob pushed away from the car, took a

step toward Adam, and without a word, drove a right fist into his gut with the force of a wrecking ball.

Doubled over, gasping for breath, Adam stumbled back. He'd have hit the concrete floor if his shoulder hadn't connected with the pillar he'd just rounded. He propped himself against it, tried to breathe.

"You okay?" Bill asked. "Bob didn't hit you too hard, did he?"

"What . . . do you want?" Adam clutched his gut, fought a wave of nausea.

"Us?" Bob said and shook his head. "We don't want nothing. Now our friend Lando, he wants his mommy's money back."

"I'll get it. I told him that." Adam knew damn well they were Lando's boys, had to be, but hearing the name nearly had him filling his pants.

"And when exactly might that be?" Bob, who was wearing a suit and tie and looked more as if he were planning a day in church than a parking-lot roust, or worse, leaned against the Saab with his arms crossed.

"Soon. Real soon." *And goddamn you for dying, Holly!*

"Soon?" Bob looked at Bill, made a big thing out of frowning. "You think that's a good answer, Bill? You think Lando will go for 'soon'?"

Bill moved like a snake on speed, grabbed a fistful of Adam's hair, yanked it, then rammed his head against the pillar. Adam didn't see stars; he saw the whole fuckin' universe. When he started to drop, Bill held him by his hair and set his face less than an inch from Adam's; the scent of last night's garlic floated up Adam's nose.

"Lando is fresh out of patience. He says he's screwed with you long enough. He wants his mother's money." Bob spoke while Bill held him. "Now if it were up to us, we'd have some fun making porridge of that pretty face of yours, but Lando says no. Says you need that face for all those pussies you work on. Says you'll need it to get his money."

Bob looked at Bill and jerked his head.

In turn, Bill twisted his fingers deeper into Adam's hair and yanked, fast and hard, then let him go. Adam sagged against the pillar, stars spinning, bile rising.

"Lando says you've got a month to make things right for his mama or you'll be—how'd he say it now?—oh, yeah, eating your own balls for breakfast. Bill and I, we'll help with that." Bob, scratching his jaw, looked at Bill. "You got any ideas on how this piece of crap here"—he nodded at Adam—"is going to come up with a half mil in four weeks?"

Bill shook his head.

Bob smiled at Adam. "Maybe him and me are going to get to make that porridge after all." Again, he drove his fist into Adam's stomach, and this time they let him fall to the concrete floor. "See you around." They walked to a car a couple of spaces down, got in, and screeched off.

Adam curled into a ball, sealed his eyes shut, and moaned. "Damn you, Holly . . ."

Chapter 6

Camryn sat quietly in the rental car's passenger seat while a morose and brooding Sebastian Solari slowed for the final turn into the cemetery. They drove through an ornate pair of wrought-iron gates.

If there was such a thing as a perfect day for a funeral, this was it: a pale sun, billowy gray clouds spotting a soft blue sky, and barely breeze enough to stir or loosen the summer-burnt leaves still clinging to the trees scattered among the gravesites. Sad and unlucky trees, Camryn thought, to seed in a burial ground, their twisted roots going ever deeper into the soil, curling into old bones, new deaths.

"You okay?" Sebastian asked, driving at a snail's pace along the road taking them to Holly's service.

"Been better. You?"

"I'll make it."

The conversation faltered, so Camryn changed course. "How's Delores these days. Any change?"

He slanted her a glance. "Delores? Change? You're kidding, right?"

Okay, wrong course. "I talked to Gina the other day. I wanted to visit, but she—"

When Sebastian's jaw set hard, she stopped midsentence.

"She put you off, didn't she?" he said. "Made some lame excuse about her being too busy." His hands clenched and unclenched on the steering wheel. "She's bad, you know, and getting worse every day." He glanced out the driver's-side window. "Makes me nervous as hell."

"How so?"

"Like mother, like daughter?"

Camryn shuddered at the thought. "What about the doctor you found for her? Isn't he helping?"

"Same old story. Can't help people who won't help themselves. I think she's playing him. And me." Irritation replaced concern, but he still looked like a man dangling from the end of a frayed rope. It struck Camryn there was something dark and dire about all the Solaris, as if they'd all eaten too much bitter pie. Or someone had thrown acid in their gene pool.

"If there's anything I can do, Seb, you only have to ask. You know that."

If anyone could *play* a psychiatrist, Camryn thought, it would be Gina. She was sharp, clever, intuitive—and a brilliant lawyer, or had been until, inexplicably, she walked out on her firm and what Camryn had thought was a stellar career and returned to the lake to live with Delores. Which, knowing Gina's feelings toward her mother, had shocked Camryn senseless. Then, less than a month after her coming home, there'd been that awful shooting that left Delores in a wheelchair.

The Solaris weren't only dark; it seemed they were also doomed.

"Thanks, but my family is my problem." His answer was curt, and he went back to staring at the road ahead.

Camryn resisted the urge to, not so gently, remind him Gina was also her friend and instead said, "You look tired." The truth. His eyes were ringed, hollow, and he was too pale.

He shrugged.

Camryn knew Seb had flown all night and that his insides were as knotted as hers. She also knew nothing in the world would have kept him from Holly's funeral.

Unlike Gina. Thinking of her friend brought a surge of

irritation along with worry. When she got back to Seattle, she'd march over there, welcome or not, and have a talk with her. There had to be some way of getting her out of that horrific house, getting her to live again. But she'd save those thoughts and plans for later; today was about Holly.

Her stomach rolled, and she again looked at Sebastian's sad face. "Seb?" She touched his arm.

"Uh-huh?"

"Stay close, okay?" She told herself she was saying this for his sake, to give him something to focus on, but that was only half true. This was a day when a strong arm would be very welcome.

"Count on it, Cammie." He squeezed her knee, then bent his head slightly to catch a directional sign.

Silence filled the car, and Camryn stared unseeing out the window, trying not to think, not to cry.

"Did you ever meet her husband?" she asked. Camryn had, but only once, when Holly, Dan, and she had crossed paths briefly at the airport. There'd been barely enough time to shake hands. She remembered Dan Lambert as a tall, lean, good-looking man with strong features—interesting, very sultry green eyes. *Holly's type,* she'd thought at the time.

"No."

"You think he'll be here?"

His expression tightened. "Wouldn't be much of a husband if he wasn't."

"Yeah, I guess." Camryn turned back to the scene outside the car window, this time paying attention. The Forest Hills Cemetery, Holly's final home, was beautiful, an unusual and intriguing mixture of serene and lively. There were people walking the paths, studying the gravestones. A young man sat under a tree, reading. An elderly couple stood looking over a pond, holding hands. Holly wouldn't be alone here.

But the beauty of the place didn't lighten her mood or

ease her sorrow, because at the end of the drive, she and Sebastian would stop at the crematorium where she would say good-bye to her oldest and dearest friend.

They'd been friends since first grade, and until Holly's sudden marriage and her move to L.A. a couple of years ago, there wasn't a time they weren't together; through their parents' divorces, their fathers' bitter business breakup, the death of Holly's mother, Kylie's magical birth. . . .

Like Holly had said, when you share Barbie-doll clothes, there's no going back; you're friends forever. She'd named them the Barbie Doll Club. When Gina came along that first year of high school, the club added its only other member—Gina Solari. When Holly and Camryn each gave Gina a Barbie doll for her fourteenth birthday, they'd all laughed, but Gina knew the doll made it official; they were a team, able to survive anything. It was Camryn, Holly, Gina—and Barbie—against the world.

And Adam, of course. They'd all had to survive Adam.

Camryn swallowed, refusing to cry. She wished Gina were here, that she hadn't turned into a weird, frightened woman she barely knew anymore.

Damn it, they'd all become weird: Camryn with her single-minded baby quest, Gina with her sudden and inexplicable depression that brought her home to live with a mother she detested, Holly with her impotent but ongoing defiance of her father, her hasty marriage. . . .

Camryn swallowed, wiped her eyes, wishing regrets were tears that could be so easily swept away.

She'd barely seen Holly since she'd married and moved to L.A. Even their phone calls had become less frequent. Camryn sensed there was trouble in the marriage, but when she'd asked, Holly always cut her off. They'd make the usual arrangements for Camryn to see Kylie, then talk about nothing for a time before hanging up. Nothing went as planned for any of them.

They'd grown apart, and Camryn had no idea why. *But I'll miss you, my friend, miss what we once had.*

A few errant red and yellow leaves dusted the orderly driving path as Camryn and Sebastian entered Forest Hills through the gate that would take them to the crematorium. When they neared the circular driveway fronting the building, Camryn looked over at Sebastian.

Despite his perfectly tailored gray suit, close shave, and pristine white shirt, he looked ruined—like a man who'd been kicked while he was down. When he pulled the car into the last parking spot and pushed the gear shift to PARK, she put a hand on his arm. "She loved you, Sebastian. Don't ever doubt that."

He turned off the ignition, sat for what seemed an eternity. "Yeah, she loved me, all right—just not the same way I loved her." He shot her a glance, his face hard. "The truth is, in a sick, twisted way, I'm glad she's dead, that it's finally over between us. Maybe tomorrow I won't get up thinking about her . . . wanting her. Wondering who the hell she's with—"

"Don't! Don't go there."

"I'm not a fool, Camryn." He shook his head, opened the car door a couple of inches and looked back at her, his expression flint-hard. "It was always Adam. I knew that, and I'm guessing Lambert knew it, too."

Camryn frowned, confused. "Adam was old news, Seb." So old she couldn't believe his name had even come up. But then Sebastian—all the Solaris—had long memories. But, God, this was reaching back to college. Ridiculous.

He gave her an impatient, pitying look, then snorted. "God, you're naïve, Camryn." He opened the door and stepped out.

She had a mouthful of words, and her door halfway open by the time he got around to her side of the car. He left her no time to say them. Taking her arm firmly, he led her toward the two Ionic pillars fronting the entrance to the crematorium.

Camryn pushed Sebastian's odd statement aside. Now wasn't the time to think about Adam Dunn.

Today was all about Holly.

Dan sat alone in the first pew on one side of the Lucy Stone Chapel. Paul and Erin Grantman sat across the aisle. An organ played quietly in the background as the pews filled up, and everyone waited for the service to begin.

With well over a hundred people in attendance, the chapel was full—mostly with Grantman's business associates. It looked to Dan as if only a handful of mourners were under sixty. Other than her father, Holly had few ties to Boston since her mother died. Boston was always more her mother's town than hers—or Paul's. Both of them spent most of their time on the West Coast at the home Paul had built on Lake Washington when Holly was a child. It was where Kylie was born.

Dan had considered taking her cremains back to Seattle, having the service there, but decided Holly would prefer it here, her ashes in an urn next to her mother's. So he'd let Paul's arrangements stand.

He heard carpet-muffled footsteps coming down the aisle from his left and glanced over his shoulder to see a man and woman walking down the aisle, obviously in search of a seat. He knew the woman instantly. It was Camryn Bruce, Holly's friend. He remembered meeting her briefly at the airport, and seeing her face in a thousand of Holly's photographs. He didn't know the man but assumed he was her husband. As they drew closer, he stood, stepped into the aisle—as did Paul Grantman.

The woman went directly to Paul and hugged him fiercely. Dan heard her whisper something, but he couldn't make out the words. The dark-haired man shook Paul's hand but said nothing.

Camryn looked back at him, then crossed the aisle to

where he stood. "You're Dan. We met once," she said in a muted voice. "I'm Camryn, Holly's friend."

He nodded. "Yes, I remember you." And he did, particularly her deep blue eyes. Eyes now silvered with unshed tears.

She took his hand in both of hers, moved closer. "I'm so terribly sorry," she whispered, her hands cold, her gaze fierce with pain.

"Thank you." He gestured to the empty pew he'd stood from. "Please."

The man with Camryn gave him a cold look before touching Camryn's elbow and gently urging her into the pew. She took the seat between them.

When the minister entered to begin the short service, she clasped Dan's hand again, squeezed it, and gave him a sad, quick smile. Releasing his hand, she clasped her husband's, and fixed her gaze on the minister, who was relating the story of Holly, age three, telling her mother she was going to the "Holy Woods" to make "mooies."

Dan saw Paul Grantman straighten in his seat, saw the line of his mouth tighten as he reached into his pocket and pulled out a large white hanky.

Dan did not follow suit. He was done with crying, and a public show of it wasn't his way. He swallowed and brushed his hair back. Sitting back in the pew, he listened stoically as the minister touched on Holly's life from preschool to her tragic final moments.

Camryn Bruce wept openly but quietly beside him, shedding tears enough for both of them.

There was to be a short reception at the Grantman home after the service, and Dan didn't intend to miss it. Finally, a chance to see Kylie.

When the last of the mourners headed for their cars, Dan stood with the Grantmans, Camryn, and Sebastian outside the chapel. Paul turned to Camryn. "You'll stay at the house, dear. I insist. So does Erin." He glanced at his attractive but oddly lifeless wife. "Don't we, Erin?"

"Of course. We have lots of room." Her pale blue eyes emitted neither welcome nor displeasure. Languid described Erin Grantman, Dan decided. Or better yet, lethargic.

"Thanks, Paul. Erin," Camryn said, giving Erin a quick smile. "But Sebastian and I are fine at the hotel. We'll come by tomorrow when—"

"I said, I insist." Paul paused. "And I have some things of Holly's there. I think she'd like you to have them." He looked up at Sebastian Solari—whom Dan now knew wasn't Camryn's husband—and his expression became momentarily confused. "Your, uh, friend is welcome as well."

"Thank you, but my flight leaves this afternoon," Sebastian said, then added, "You don't remember me, do you?" The fact didn't seem to bother him a hell of lot, but then he'd been stone-faced since he'd slipped into the pew an hour ago.

Paul studied him, shook his head. "I'm sorry. No."

"I dated Holly in high school. Final year."

"Sorry," Paul said again. "Holly dated a lot of young men. Too many." He glanced at Dan, obviously lumping him in the "too-many" category.

Sebastian's mouth tightened and he directed a dark glare at Dan. "Yes, she did," he agreed. Turned back to Grantman, he said, "Maybe this will jog your memory—I'm Gina's brother. Delores's son? Sebastian Solari."

"Ah . . . yes." The older man looked as if the memory had the taste of a bad oyster, but he rallied. "You're welcome to stay—at least for the weekend. I'll send Maury to the hotel to pick up your things."

"No, thanks," Sebastian said. "Like I said, I have a plane to catch."

"As you like." Looking relieved, Paul turned to Dan, gave him the usual cold stare, and said, "You'll stay. It'll give us a chance to straighten things out between us. Be easier if you were close by."

"Fine by me." Dan would take any opportunity to see Kylie—and make damn sure he didn't leave without her.

"Tell Maury where you're staying. He'll get your and Camryn's things." At that Paul glanced at his watch, then took Erin's arm. "We'd better get going. We can't leave our guests too long." Erin did her slo-mo blink, smiled, and nodded. Together they walked to the black Mercedes limo.

Sebastian shot another cold glance at Dan, before saying to Camryn, "I'll get the car, drop you at Paul's before I leave." He strode off, leaving them alone on the shallow steps.

She lifted her eyes to meet his. "Paul doesn't like you," she said.

Her directness stymied him for a second. Then he shrugged. "No."

"He never liked any of Holly's boyfriends. Not one. So you shouldn't take it personally." Her still tear-bright eyes looked amused.

Dan didn't bother to say he'd been a bit more than a boyfriend. "I don't."

"Good." She glanced in Sebastian's direction, and Dan followed her gaze, saw the man get in the car and put his cell phone to his ear. Camryn looked back at him, annoyance creasing her brow. "You know, Sebastian dated Holly for two years in high school. They went to the prom together. They were absolutely inseparable. No way would Paul not remember him. Sebastian didn't deserve that slight." She shook her head, her eyes still fixed on the man in the car, filled with concern and frustration. "I know Paul adored Holly, but damned if he can't be a real son of a bitch sometimes."

Dan felt his lips twitch.

Camryn put a hand to her mouth, looked up at him.

"Sorry, I shouldn't have said that. Foot-in-mouth disease. It's chronic."

"I don't know. That's what Holly called him from time to time. Said the description fit real well, considering his mother."

Camryn took her hand from her mouth. "Oh God, I'd forgotten. Granny . . . Gertrude Penelope Grantman. Holly called her a 'certified nasty' and took off every time she showed up at the lake. We spent a lot of time hiding in my closet, as I remember."

"Where's Granny Grantman now?"

"Dead." She came near to smiling. "Gone, as Holly used to say, in full drama-queen mode, to justice and her everlasting reward, a universe where everyone wore bigger diamonds, everyone drove a newer car, and everyone called her Gertie, a name she hated. So you're right, Holly didn't like her." She looked up at him, and her tentative smile wobbled as a wash of tears filled her eyes. She closed her eyes against them. "I'm sorry," she mumbled. "I'm finding this harder than I imagined. She was my friend, and I loved her."

"As did I," he said, He wasn't lying. There had been love, just not enough of it.

She gave him a quick glance, then dropped her eyes. "Yes, this must be hard for you."

He had the sure sense she didn't believe him, and for the first time he had the urge to defend his feelings for Holly, and would have if he knew what the hell they were. Luckily, Solari brought the car to within a few feet of the stairs in time to stop him from stepping into that quagmire.

Sebastian got out of the car and walked to them. "Ready?" he said to Camryn, his voice brusque. She nodded, and as she turned toward the car, Sebastian gave his attention to Dan, his expression unreadable. "I'm sure I should say something about your loss, Lambert, but I figure I'd be wading in a bit late. Unless I miss my guess, your real loss was months ago . . . about the time Adam Dunn started fucking your wife."

Dan took the hit—the equivalent of a sucker punch from Muhammad Ali wearing an iron glove—but it knocked out his word-making ability.

Camryn spun to face them both, her eyes wide with shock.

Solari's expression was unrepentant. "You going to tell me you didn't know?"

Dan leveled off his breathing. "I'm telling you you're out of line. Way, way out of line."

He snorted. "Yeah, well when it came to Holly and Adam, there *were* no lines. They never could keep their hands off one another. They've been on again, off again since college. And lately very much on. Which makes you a . . . what's that word? Cuckold. Yeah, that's it."

Dan took a step forward, his chest heaving with the effort to stop himself from taking a piece out of the asshole's jaw. "Get the hell away from me Solari. *Now!*"

Camryn pulled on Sebastian's arm, but he yanked it from her grasp. "I'm going, but before I do, I'll tell you this. Holly didn't love you, Lambert, and she sure as hell didn't love Dunn—no matter how many times he fucked her. She loved me. She was set to leave you both—for me." He poked his own chest, his eyes strangely bright, then said again. "*Me!* You got that?"

"Stop!" Camryn said. "Are you crazy?" She towed Solari back, out of fist range. Her eyes, when they met Dan's, pleaded for understanding. "Please," she said. "He's . . . grieving."

Strangest goddamn grief Dan had ever seen.

"I'm not the crazy one, Camryn." Solari's eyes narrowed, fixed on Dan like fetid lasers. "The crazy one is either Lambert or Dunn. Because one or the other of them killed Holly when he found out about us. And Dunn being nothing but a cowardly opportunistic bastard, my money's on Lambert here."

"Now you're accusing me of killing my wife?" *Who the hell was this guy!*

"I'm saying you're prime suspect material."

"Sebastian! Shut up, for God's sake! You don't know what you're talking about." Camryn sounded panicked now, again tried to pull him away. He refused to budge.

Dan fisted his hands at his sides, all too aware of where he was—steps away from his wife's ashes, not the place to beat a man senseless. His eyes on Solari, he said to Camryn. "Seeing that you can't get him the hell out of here, I'll have to." He stepped into Solari's face. "Move on, Solari. And do it now."

Solari fell back a couple of steps. "I'm going—but you can take this to the goddamn bank, Lambert. If you killed Holly, you're going to pay. I'll see to it." He shrugged free of Camryn's grip and glared at her. "You coming?"

When she didn't move immediately, he said, "Suit yourself." He left her standing like a stick figure, got in the car, and drove off.

"Son of a bitch . . ." Dan stared at the backside of Solari's car, breathing like a horse after a training run. Hell, he'd had trouble enough accepting Holly had taken one lover. But two . . .

Chapter 7

Camryn couldn't get her bearings. She was standing on the cemetery grounds, having said good-bye to her best friend only minutes ago, trying to digest another friend's words—words that accused Holly of being an adulteress and her husband—or lover—of killing her.

Nothing clicked into place. Except a name she'd never forget but had hoped she'd never hear again: Adam Dunn. And it was that name that made her certain Sebastian was wrong. Holly hated Adam.

Silence rested between Dan and her, until he took her arm and made a move toward the last car still remaining in the row of parking stalls near the chapel. His grip was firm, and his gaze was straight ahead.

"You have any idea where all that shit came from?"

Still stunned, she shook her head.

"You believe it?"

"Believe Seb?" She stopped and tugged her arm from his grasp a few steps from a midsize Buick with a rental sticker on the bumper. "I still can't believe Holly's dead—that someone killed her. I don't have room in my brain for a list of suspects."

"You know this Adam guy?"

She hesitated. She really did not want to go in the direction any conversation about Adam would take them. She also couldn't lie. "Yes. I know him." The words came out edged with defensiveness, her own history with Adam inevitably tingeing them with bitterness . . . and hurt.

"Get in the car." He took the few steps to the passenger side of the Buick and opened the door.

His tone was brusque, and under normal circumstances, she'd have called him on it. But not today. Not after Sebastian's stunning accusations, and not with Adam Dunn's name again polluting her universe.

They drove for a time before Dan spoke again. "Tell me about him," he ordered, staring straight ahead.

She knew he meant Adam, but not being in the mood for another of his crisp instructions, Camryn turned in the car seat and took a good look at him. His face was lean, clean-shaven, and grim. His jaw clenched and unclenched as if in a battle for control, yet he didn't look angry. He looked shell-shocked and ruthlessly determined.

When she didn't answer, he cast her a sideways glance, his intelligent green eyes icy and unforthcoming. "You second-guessing yourself? Thinking maybe you're riding with a man who killed his wife?"

"I don't know how to answer that."

"You don't have to. You already did."

"How so?"

"You got in the car, didn't you?"

"So?"

"Holly always said you were the smartest person she ever knew, that you had great instincts. Scary instincts, she said. So the way I figure it, your getting into this car with me says you know damn well Solari's full of shit." He set his gaze back on the road ahead. "But I'll say this once, so you're sure. I did not kill my wife."

Camryn let that statement hover over those instincts he'd referred to, watched him go back to exercising his jaw. "I believe you," she said.

Another glance shot her way. "Thank you."

"Of course, it helps your case that you were out of town at the time."

"How do you know that?"

"I spoke to Holly before she left for Boston. I was hoping to see Kylie. . . . Anyway, she said you were working in northern Canada and wouldn't be back for a couple of weeks."

He nodded, left the car to silence for a time. "What else did she say?"

"Not much more than that. I wanted us to get together before she and Kylie left, but she . . . put me off, said she didn't have time. That we'd do it when she got back." Camryn remembered the conversation, how evasive Holly was, and how she'd resisted their getting together, as she'd been doing for months.

"We were separated. Did she tell you that?"

"I knew you were having some kind of problem. Holly wouldn't talk about it, but she did say it was one of the reasons she was taking Kylie and going to Boston for a while."

"Yeah, there was a problem, all right. And thanks to your friend, that problem now has a name. Adam Dunn."

When the breeze coming off Lake Washington turned cold, Gina came in from the porch. She went immediately to the phone. Called again. Still no answer. She'd thought surely either Camryn or Seb would be back at the hotel by now, and she wanted to know how the funeral went. She was curious enough for that.

She went to the window and stared out. Perhaps she should have gone to the service, if only to keep up appearances. A thought that made her laugh. She'd given up caring about appearances when she'd knocked on Delores's door months ago. The darkening world outside this ugly house held nothing for her other than broken dreams and missed chances: a ruined career, a lost child, and the man who'd caused it all.

She dropped the curtain she'd been holding back, wondered idly if Adam had attended his lover's funeral—even from a safe distance. Wondered if he mourned his one true love.

"Gina!" her mother called from upstairs.

Gina went to the bottom of the stairs. "I'm here."

"Bring me that bottle of brandy you've been hiding above the fridge. I need a nightcap."

"How about some tea instead? I made a pie." The kitchen was filled with bread, cakes, cookies. When she couldn't sleep, which was most nights, baking filled her hours from darkness to light.

"If I wanted fucking tea and pie, I'd have said so."

"You know you're not supposed to be drinking while you're taking Demerol. The doctor was clear about that."

"Fuck the doctor. He's not the one in pain." Pause. "Besides, I haven't had a pill in hours. So bring the brandy, and cut back on the give-a-damn attitude. You'll live longer."

But you won't . . .

"Fine by me. If you want to kill yourself," Gina muttered the last as she moved away from the stairs toward the kitchen. To reach the brandy in the cupboard above the refrigerator, Gina had to stand on a stool. As she did so, the thought about how Delores even knew it was there. She hadn't seen her put it there; Gina was certain of that, which meant she was getting the bottle herself when Gina wasn't around to do it for her. "Sneaky bitch," she murmured, shaking her head, and reaching for the brandy. She wasn't surprised, or even angry, knowing damn well Delores was getting out of her wheelchair more and more. She was just keeping her increased mobility to herself, because it suited her to play the invalid.

If Sebastian knew, he'd be livid, she thought, taking a

glass from the lower cupboard. Not that she was going to tell him. It would only upset things. Delores had her deceptions, and Gina had hers. So what? For now the days went by well enough.

She cleared the top step and opened the door to her mother's room. As usual, the door was ajar, allowing Delores to hear what was going on in the house.

The older woman was sitting in her wheelchair listening to Brahms and gave Gina the barest of glances. "About bloody time," she said, as Gina set the bottle down on the walnut table beside her chair. The table was littered with pill bottles, soft-drink cans, papers and pens, and an overflowing ashtray that dribbled ash and cigarette butts onto the coffee-stained doily it sat on. The room smelled of stale cigarettes, soiled laundry, and gardenia, the scent Delores sprayed on herself liberally and often.

Gina poured her mother a shot of brandy, without thanks, and looked around the large bedroom, then up at the cobwebs festooning the high corners, hanging from the antler chandelier in the ceiling. It must be getting close to the time when Delores would demand that Gina come and clean up, which she would do while her mother railed at her for ignoring her, for letting her live in a pigsty. She also knew that until Delores did issue the instruction, she wasn't to touch anything or she'd be screamed at for "poking her skinny nose" in where it wasn't wanted.

Thinking about Delores, her irrational demands, Gina worked to suppress the rage and confusion that threatened her life here. The grayness inside her deepened and her breathing turned choppy. Unbidden, ugly thoughts rose from the murky pool that had become her mind—monster thoughts that terrified her with their urgings and gravelly voices.

"What are you doing down there, anyway?" Delores asked, taking a good swig of the brandy.

"Nothing." She gestured at the filthy ashtray. "Can I?"

Delores frowned, then gave a curt nod. Gina picked up the ashtray, walked to the chrome trash can in the bathroom, and emptied it. She didn't risk washing it, because she didn't want to push her luck. What she wanted to do was get out of this room, go to bed, and sink into a mind-deadening sleep.

"Nobody does 'nothing.' Not even your crippled mother. So, I'll ask you again. What the hell are you doing down there?"

Dear God, the woman wanted to talk. "Dishes, reading the newspaper," Gina lied, not about to tell her mother she'd been sitting on the back porch, staring at the lake, thinking about Holly's death, imagining her slide into 2,000 degrees of crematory heat, seeing her skin bubbling and peeling, lifting off to float like dust motes in the oven, tossed and buffeted by boiling air and licking flames.

Holly would be ugly, her flesh heat-warped and black, before she sank, finally and forever, into the anonymity of the flame, nothing but ash and bone fragments. Her urn would be beautiful, of course. Paul would have nothing but the best for Holly. Probably gold and jewel-encrusted, garish even. She'd nearly smiled at the thought, knowing how little that would mean to Holly, but the smile felt more like pain feeding on envy. Holly always had the best.

Holly always had Adam.

"The Grantman girl's service was today, wasn't it?"

"Yes." She headed for the door. Trust Delores to pick up her thoughts. Camryn did that, too. It was like they were tuned in on some special frequency. It scared her, angered her. No one should be allowed in someone else's head, especially hers. Especially now.

"Sit, for God's sake. I could use the company . . . such as it is." Delores turned off the stereo, and the messy room sank into old-house silence.

Gina sat, her hands limply in her lap, and waited for her mother to speak.

"Paul Grantman still with that brainless slut he married a few years ago? What's her name . . ."

"Erin. And, yes, they're still together."

Delores shook her head. "Never would have thought it. What's she? Twenty-five, thirty years younger than him?"

"Something like that."

Delores went silent then, and Gina hoped she wasn't remembering her own short-lived affair with Paul. It had cost him his second wife and created a delicious scandal that everyone in her school heard about. Not only did Delores become an institutionalized joke for the remainder of high school, Holly didn't speak to her for a year—as if it were her fault. As a mother-embarrassing-her-teenage-daughter event, it had no peer. Back then she'd thought Holly a friend, cared what she thought.

"That man always was an easy mark. A damn gold-digger's wet dream." Delores shook her head again. "I slept with him a couple of times . . . I ever tell you that?"

"Yes." She stood. The list of men Delores *didn't* sleep with would be more interesting—and much shorter. "Is there anything else I can get you? I'm tired. I think I'll go to my room, read for a while." She picked up the bottle of brandy.

"Leave it." Delores wrapped her fingers around Gina's wrist, to stop her hand. One of her long nails scraped the underside of her wrist.

"Fine." *Let her drink herself to death—who cares*. She released her hold on the bottle, but Delores didn't let go.

"You in hurry?" she said. "You don't want to talk to your dear old mother? The mother you put in a wheelchair?"

Anger curled low in Gina's belly. "I did not put you in that wheelchair. I saved your life. Franco would have killed you."

"Bullshit!"

"I aimed at . . . his thigh. You know that." She pulled her wrist from her mother's grasp, massaged it.

"You're a liar, Gina. You wanted to pay me back. You wanted to get even. I know you've never forgiven me. And that night? I saw your eyes when you pointed that gun. It was the same look you had when you walked in on me and your precious Adam. You aimed that gun at me. You wanted me dead, daughter dearest."

"What happened that night between you and Franco had nothing to do with Adam." Her neck stiffened, and her head started to ache. She refused to think about Delores and Adam. She'd put that away. Hadn't she? Her vision blurred.

"Yeah . . ." Delores scoffed. "As if every night of your life hasn't been about that scummy bastard in one way or another since the day you met him. Miracle he didn't knock you up." She stopped, seemed to look past Gina. "He was a hot lay, though, I grant you that." Her eyes came back to Gina. "But him and I? Only a test run. A couple of times, that was all. I was doing you a favor, showing you what a greedy low-life he really was."

Gina stood over her mother. She would not talk about Adam, not with Delores. Never with Delores. It would be like having her bones removed without anesthetic. "You're welcome to your opinion," she said, sounding as stiff as a gun stock.

"That I am." Her mother settled back in her chair, glass in one hand, brandy bottle in the other, her expression smug. "And my opinion is my loving daughter wanted revenge because I had sex with her boyfriend, and decided to get it by putting a bullet in me."

Gina fisted her hands. "Get this straight, once and for all—for both our sakes, because we can't go on living with this . . . elephant in the room. Read my lips. That night had nothing to do with Adam. You and Franco were drunk. He was hitting you over and over—with a closed fist. He would have beaten you to death."

Delores lifted her glass and took a drink. "As if I couldn't have handled him! Instead you arrive at the door like some kind of back-country militia reject. Jesus, girl, do you think I'm a fool? You think I don't know you saw an opportunity—and took it?"

"I aimed for his leg," Gina repeated, defending the indefensible. "But you stepped in front of him, threw your arms around him . . ." She stopped, bile rising at the thought of that night, when her life, already in a miserable place, sank to a lower one. "It was an accident. You either start believing that or I can't go on living here." Her stomach churned at the thought of moving. Where would she go? What would she do? She had no job, no money, no energy . . .

The room went quiet. Delores drained her brandy glass in one swallow and set it on the messy table beside her. "I loved Franco, you know," she said. "Maybe he was too young for me. Maybe he did only want my money, but he made me feel good again. Like I was a real woman—not just an *old* woman."

"Don't . . ."

"The way he looked at me, touched me . . . He set me on fire. I felt . . . alive." She raised her eyes to Gina's, and for the first time in a year, there was softness in them. "It's hell, Gina, to think I'm never going to feel those things again—that no one cares. Like I'm dead."

The moment bound them, deepened the silence in the room and the cold stillness in the reaches of Gina's heart. She knew this loss, felt the emptiness of it, and the terrifying certainty that she, like her mother, would never feel truly alive again.

Delores poured herself another glass of brandy, took a drink. "Now get out of here, will you? Go back to the kitchen or wherever the hell you were, and leave me alone."

She shifted her chair, showed Gina her back. "Or better yet, get yourself laid. It'll take that pinched look away from your mouth." She shot her a cold look from over her shoulder. "It's what I'd do—if my daughter hadn't turned me into a cripple. Hey, here's a better idea." She narrowed her eyes, watched Gina closely. "Why not call that Adam character, ask him to come by and make us both happy? Hell, I'll bet he'd do it—if the price was right. Just like you'll stay here and look after me for as long as it suits me." She paused. "You shouldn't have missed, sweetheart, because it's going to take a lifetime for you to make up for this." She gripped the handrails on her wheelchair, shook them violently, and glared at Gina.

Gina, her hands shaking, her mind red-hot with rage, ran from the room. She went back to the porch, sat staring at the lake, barely blinking, until the night was dark enough to take a long walk along the lakeshore. She walked until the night grew blacker, the trees denser, her mind heavier, collapsing under the weight of her anger and resentment, her murderous thoughts.

Her life was hell, hopeless. . . .

Delores deserved to die.

It would be so easy . . .

The moon disappeared behind a cloud, leaving the path ink-black and treacherous. She stumbled, scraped her knee on a stone, then sat cold-eyed in the middle of the path, her bitterness acid-sharp in her dry mouth, her heart a stone in her chest.

When the pale moon reappeared, Gina looked up at it, stared herself into a eerie calm. "She was right, you know. I did aim the gun at her. I hadn't planned to. I . . . just did." She blinked, then added, "But I was afraid."

By the time she got back to the house, her cut knee was bleeding steadily, and slender streams of blood trickled down the front of her leg.

Gina didn't like blood. It made her remember that day—the day she'd lost Adam's baby. The blood had coursed down her thighs, thick and dark. Unstoppable. She'd called Adam in terror, expecting him to be upset. Expecting him to care.

Instead she found silence, then, "I have to be honest, Gina, in a way it's kind of a relief," he'd said. "Better for you and better for me. I've been meaning to call you." He'd hesitated, but barely, adding, "Holly and I have hooked up again, and we've made some plans, and the truth is you having my kid right now would be damned awkward for both of us. But I'm sorry, babe. Really."

Sorry, babe. Sorry babe. Sorry, babe . . .

She covered her ears with her palms, pressed hard. It was the last time she'd heard his voice.

She'd given him all her money, and when her own cash ran out, she'd stolen from the firm's trust account. If the senior partners hadn't covered the loss to avoid publicity, she'd be in prison. She'd given him her body in a hundred different ways—and, oh God, how she'd hungered for his. She'd carried his child. Lost his child . . . alone.

Sorry, babe. Sorry babe. Sorry, babe . . .

She closed her eyes, never wanted to open them again, not on a world without Adam. He was a fever in her blood, and he'd taken everything. He'd taken her *goddamn life!* Used her until she was dark and empty.

And now Delores was going to use her, because she'd been too stupid to aim a gun.

She touched her gashed knee, raised a bloodied finger to her mouth and licked it; she savored the saltiness of it, tasted the death in it.

She licked some more, smeared it over her lips, and looked out at the vaporous, ghostly moon, vowing never, never to be stupid again.

Chapter 8

Camryn looked up to see Dan Lambert standing in the hall outside Holly's bedroom door.

Damn it, he must have heard her crying, or laughing, depending on what memory of Holly came to mind. She brushed at her damp cheeks, oddly embarrassed, as if she'd been caught playing in her mother's jewel box.

"You're not here to talk about what Sebastian said, are you?" She hoped her expression told him that if that were his plan, he'd be wasting his time. "Sebastian was upset. We all are." She lifted her chin. "Besides, there's nothing I can tell you."

"And very little I can't find out for myself. But, no, I'm not here to talk about your friend. I'll wait on that." He stepped into the open doorway and gestured with his chin to the two dolls that Camryn, who sat cross-legged in the middle of Holly's old room, held in her hands. "That's what she wanted you to have?"

"Yes." Camryn, relieved at not having to deal with Sebastian's strange and grossly ill-timed outburst, turned back to memory lane—It was a more comfortable place than the one Sebastian created with his insane accusations. The idea of Holly and Adam together again—after everything that had happened—was inconceivable. Just as the idea that Sebastian was still obsessed enough, after all these years, to follow Holly to Boston was nothing short of tragic.

She gave a little rub to her chest, wondering at its tightness.

"Dolls?" His words were low, his gaze curious. He stood tall and still, his hands in his pockets, his head cocked.

"Not just any dolls. Barbie dolls."

"I bought Kylie one of those, but hers has the legs off." The smile he gave her was brief, but it warmed his austere face. She guessed austere made sense, given he'd just buried his wife, then had to withstand—as she had—the tedious gathering in Paul and Erin's living room immediately after the service. Not to mention Sebastian's rant.

"A little too young then. To appreciate them," she said, risking a smile back.

"Maybe. But she wanted one. . . ." He shrugged.

The floor around her was littered with doll clothes, doll furniture, and other bright plastic artifacts of Holly's twenty-five-year-old Barbie collection. Every item a memory. Again, Camryn brushed at her cheeks, even though they were dry now, and tight from her salty tears. She'd had a lovely cry—her and the Barbies. Gently, she put the two dolls back in their velvet box, again wondering how Holly had kept them so nice. There was even a Barbie suitcase with clothes—and matching shoes!—neatly placed inside.

Camryn still had her three dolls, but of the two of them that still had their heads, one had ended up on the wrong side of the scissors, her glorious, flowing blond hair now an uneven buzz cut. And the other, after she'd spent a long, rainy afternoon applying makeup with colorful felt-pen markers, looked like an untreated burn victim. Holly's dolls looked as beautiful and untouched as the day they'd come out of their boxes. Obviously, Kylie was following in Camryn's more careless footsteps.

Camryn got to her feet, box in hand. "These dolls, all legs intact, come with history and a . . . long story."

"You and Holly?"

She nodded. "And later our friend Gina. The Barbies were like our mascots. Paul built a house on Lake Washington before Holly started school—that's when we met—but Holly's mother loved this house, loved Boston, so they came back here often. A lot of the time, I came back with them. When we met Gina in high school, she joined the club. Every summer for three weeks . . . " She let out a long breath. "It was magical." She thought it best not to mention that Gina was Sebastian's sister. "One long sleepover, wearing each other's clothes, drinking too many colas, playing with makeup. A big O.D. on everything girly."

"I see."

She laughed. "I doubt it." She took a step back from him and sat on the edge of Holly's bed. "What are you doing here, anyway?"

He walked into the room, across to the window, then sat on its padded bench and looked around. He was wearing a pristine white shirt, a tie, but no jacket. His slacks, topped by a soft leather belt, were black. And he was even more attractive than she'd remembered. "I've never been here before," he said. "Not this house, not this room."

She twisted her lips thoughtfully. "Paul *really* doesn't like you, does he?" Not that it seemed to bother him. She had the impression very little bothered Dan Lambert. He had both an easy grace and deep coolness about him. She'd admired his restraint earlier today, in the face of Sebastian's stupid, misguided accusations.

"I think we covered that." He arched a brow.

"Yet he invited you here. That's not like him."

"We have business."

Camryn cocked her head in question.

"Kylie business." He pushed away from the windowsill and walked to a bookshelf on the adjacent wall. He fingered some of the books that sat like obedient soldiers on the tidy shelves, then ran his index finger along their multicolored spines. "He doesn't like the idea of my being her father, step- or otherwise."

"He wants Kylie?" Camryn stilled where she sat. She wasn't surprised, only saddened.

"Yes."

"You want Kylie."

"Absolutely yes. She's my daughter."

"And she's my goddaughter. Did you know that?"

"Yes, Holly told me. Kylie's Aunt Cammie." He studied her. "You're close, you and my daughter."

Camryn dipped her chin. "I was there when she was born."

"Yes. I know that, too."

"I know Holly talked about guardianship. Did she—" Camryn stopped when his dark green eyes settled on her. Okay, none of this was her business, but Kylie sure was. She had to ask. "Holly told me she was planning on changing her, uh, guardianship arrangements for Kylie. Did she?" She waited for his answer and tried to ignore the growing patch of emptiness in her heart.

"Yes. Thank God."

Camryn nodded back, tried to hide her flash of disappointment. Things would have been different if Holly hadn't married Dan, but she was relieved all the same, even though she knew a legal abyss when she saw one. Paul would fight. Paul always fought. And he always fought dirty. Her heart ached for Kylie, losing her mother, then becoming legal sport for two stubborn men.

If only Holly hadn't married Dan. If only things had stayed as they were....

Determined not to slide heart-first into her personal pity party, she stared hard at the serious man now walking the room.

He ambled around the room, looking at the pictures on the wall, the girly doodads on the dresser, the fancy custom-made crate in the corner. Painted red with gold bars, it looked as if it belonged in a thirties' traveling circus. It held Holly's childhood collection of stuffed animals.

Dan pulled a rhinoceros from the mix, tugged its ear, and grinned. "Kylie would like this. She'd rename it though. A 'nosheris' would be my bet." He put the stuffed animal back in the crate.

Camryn frowned. "Where is Kylie, anyway? I expected to see her." Actually Kylie was the reason she'd accepted Paul's invitation to stay in the first place. A lump grew in her throat when she thought this visit could be her last for a long time.

His face tightened. "Paul and Erin sent her to stay with her new nanny . . . until we settle the custody issue."

"There is no 'issue,' " Paul Grantman strode through the open doorway and stopped in the center of the room. "She's *my* granddaughter, Camryn." Although he spoke to her, his gaze veered toward Dan, who was back at the window, leaning lazily against its sill. "Erin and I will raise her."

Dan said nothing, but if eyes could chill a room, his would have done it.

Camryn touched her stomach, which had gone odd and heavy. She wished she could sympathize with Paul; she knew he loved Holly in his way and that he doted on Kylie, but she knew, too, that his determination to gain custody of Kylie had another motivation. He wanted her for Erin.

Erin, Holly had said, "totally creeped her out." Camryn knew her reasons and agreed with them. If Kylie were her child, she'd feel exactly the same; she would not want Erin raising Kylie. What amazed her was Paul being such a blind fool.

"Dan says Holly made him Kylie's guardian, Paul, so maybe—"

"So he tells me," Paul said. "I say, show me the papers."

"Which I intend to do." Dan looked relaxed. "They'll be here tomorrow. Along with my lawyer."

Camryn shot her gaze between the two men, decided Dan wasn't as relaxed as he looked. His eyes were narrowed, and she saw the hands he had stuffed in his pockets were fisted.

Paul's eyes blazed with scorn. "Good. He can meet mine, and we can start the countdown."

"Holly wouldn't like you two being . . . at odds like this." Camryn said. "She hated fights and disagreements. She'd do anything to avoid them. All she ever wanted was to be happy, and make Kylie happy. You have to think about that, Paul. Think about what Holly wanted."

Dan Lambert briefly met her gaze, his own angry, concerned expression softening as if in gratitude.

The lines around Paul's mouth loosened, and he looked at Camryn. "That may be so, Camryn, but Holly didn't always know what was best for her. She was too easily influenced." He shot a glance toward Dan, but at least his tone was less confrontational.

"What I know"—Camryn glanced at both men again, knew her face was stern—"is that the day of her funeral is *not* the time for this conversation."

"Hear, hear," Dan muttered.

Silence claimed the room for a moment, then Paul nodded. "You're right. We'll let the lawyers duke it out." Paul took an obviously deep breath, then gestured at the dolls in her hand. "I see you found them. Those are what she wanted you to have." He smiled lightly. "She even made a will—"

"A will about dolls?"

"When she was little girl, I tried to teach Holly to take responsibility for what she cared about. To think long-term. I guess this was her take on that." He shrugged. "The housekeeper found it years ago. I left it where it was, and so did Holly." He nodded toward the bureau. "In the top drawer."

Camryn withdrew a rolled piece of paper tied with pink ribbon. Unfurling it, she held it flat on top of the bureau. Along the top of the paper was a continuous row of Xs and Os: kisses and hugs. Camryn's eyes, a well she'd thought dry an hour ago, filled with moisture.

"Read it aloud, Cammie," Paul said. It was the first time he'd called her that for a long while.

Camryn read:

"XXX OOO XXX OOO XXX OOO
XXX OOO XXX

The last will and testimant of
Holly Michaela Grantman.

Dear Cammie, if your reading this, I hope your a hundred years old, because I'll be dead. And if your a hundred that means I probibly lived a long time to. Rite now I'm eight and thinking about Kelin and Ryley my 2 favarite doll babys in the whole world. If I get hit by a car or drown in the pool or get kidnaped or maybe even murdared, I need someone WHO CARES to look out for them That's you, Cammie, because your my best friend ever!! Somebodys always in my drawers, cleaning and stuff, so I'm pretty sure you'll get this and I can stopp worring.

And now I can sleep.

P.S. Take all there stuff too, okay? Ryley likes her pillows and beds and Kelin likes thc shoes and pink sweater. And tell Dad to give you the Barbie suitcase, the realy big one, it hols everything.

Signed:

Holly Michaela Grantman.

XXX OOO XXX OOO XXX OOO
XXX OOO XXX"

Camryn lifted her hands from the flattened paper, let it roll closed, and slipped the pink ribbon back into place. Her hands shook with the effort to hold it carefully, not crush it to her breast. "Thank you for this, Paul, but, dear God, . . . what will we do without her?"

"I don't know," he said, his expression strained, his hands locking and unlocking at his sides. "I just don't know." He headed for the door. "There are people leaving downstairs. I'd like you both to come and say good-bye." He left the room.

Camryn looked at Dan, whose eyes were on the empty doorway Paul had passed through. His expression gave away nothing. When he said, "Hard to get it right—the love thing. He tried to hold her too close, and I didn't hold her close enough." He strode toward the door. "See you downstairs."

Adam Dunn stood outside the Federal Reserve Building in downtown Boston in a state of stunned disbelief. Telling himself to calm down and think, he took out a cigarette, lit it, and inhaled deeply. Shit, even his lungs hurt, thanks to his parking-lot meeting with Bill and Bob. Gingerly, he touched the bowling-ball-sized lump on the back of his head. He was damned lucky he didn't have a concussion.

He took another drag on his smoke. If there was a way out of this mess, he needed to find it—and fast.

He stretched his neck, blew a wind of smoke, and looked up at the building he'd come from. The tallest building in Boston, its facade resembled a giant slatted blind.

Ignoring the dirty looks tossed his way by a pair of up-tight suits as they passed him, he took another pull on the cigarette, dropped it at his feet, and stubbed it out. Two seconds later he was walking down Summer Street toward the Saab, no calmer post-cigarette than he'd been pre-.

Holly had lied to him. Flat-out lied! Hadn't shown up for the appointment. Hadn't done a goddamn thing she'd promised.

He got into the car, put down the window, and rested his head on the headrest. *Damn!* He quickly sat upright, again touched his aching head.

Thumping head and aching brain or not, he had to do some figuring, and given that Holly hadn't changed the guardianship, he had no idea where to start. He needed help. He needed control of his kid. She was the only thing that would save his ass—the only way into Grantman's bank account.

He was running out of time—given he had a pair of gorilla boys on his tail. All because of a fuckin' woman. . . .

His mood darkened when he thought about what that ancient bitch might cost him—after him making her so happy. It sure as hell was no cakewalk, working on that old body night after night. Damn it, he'd earned every cent of the money she'd given him. Not a chance she'd miss it. Sunny had buckets of the stuff. He rubbed his tender gut. Unfortunately, she also had a son, Lando Means, one of the biggest, most vicious drug lords on the southeast coast, who'd paid a personal visit to Adam months after the stupid affair was over to, as he put it, explain his position, which was that Adam pay his mother back every cent he owed her or be prepared to chew on his own balls.

Those "cents," according to Lando, totaled a half a million dollars. The amount froze Adam's brain. Jesus, a few designer suits, cars, a few trips . . . Who'd have thought it would add up to that. But then who the hell was counting?

And who'd have thought a man like Lando would give a rat's ass who his mother slept with or what she did with her money? The whole thing was one big screwup, and the only way out was money.

He lit another cigarette. *Goddamn you, Holly!* Now he

had no easy way into Grantman, no quick negotiating weight. And time was running out.

Unless . . .

Adam flicked the lit cigarette out the window.

He fished his cell from his pocket, and in less than ten minutes had a flight booked for Seattle. Then he turned the key in the ignition and eased his way into the crush of late-afternoon traffic.

Maybe he didn't have Kylie, or enough to settle his hotel bill, but he had Gina Solari—or could with a minimum of effort.

Hell, if Gina was nothing else, she was a hot bitch in bed. On the dark side, too—if he asked for it; ever-ready, ultra-able, and always willing. He'd never met a woman who got off on sex like Gina. More than a little nympho there, he figured—at least when it came to him. Probably got it from her mother.

She was a goddamned lawyer, to boot! He smiled. It didn't get any better than this. It had been a bit dicey there for a time. Getting her pregnant wasn't his best move, and maybe he wasn't . . . solicitous enough when she lost the kid, but she'd be over all that by now. If not—his smile deepened— he'd have to distract her. If there was one thing he knew how to do, it was distract a woman.

For a second his smile slipped. He'd have to be careful with Delores. Never knew what the hell was going on with that one. He shook off the concern. She was female, wasn't she? He'd handle her, like he'd handle Gina. No sweat.

Gina would give him exactly what he needed: cool, logical legal advice—and a nice hot bed.

Chapter 9

The next day Grantman's attorney arrived shortly before the 2:00 P.M. meeting Dan and Paul had arranged. Maury, Paul's man-about-the-house and whose last name Dan hadn't yet heard, led him into Paul's study.

When Paul's lawyer stood to greet him, Dan gave him a quick scan. Jason Wallace was a tall, fit, neat-as-a-pin Bostonian blue blood, with eyes the color of his flint-gray suit, and a smile that looked practiced and overused. Instead of the classic legal briefcase, he carried a thin leather attaché case that looked soft enough to sleep on. His handshake was firm and brief. Dan put him at fifty, but figured he could be off by five years either way.

About the time ice was clattering into their crystal glasses, and the scotch was being poured, Holly's legal wizard, Edwin Maddox, arrived windblown, flustered, and apologetic. While Wallace gleamed with his years of legal polish, Eddie Maddox—maybe thirty, maybe less—looked as if he'd just been shot out of a cannon—and liked it.

More ice hit the glass on his behalf, and the four men sat down to business.

The business of Kylie.

Dan hadn't spoken more than a dozen words to Paul since yesterday, and right now, looking at his granite face, he was glad of it. All he wanted was for this legal farce to be played out quickly, so he could catch a plane home—with Kylie. He had the next six weeks free, plenty of time to spend with her and find a good nanny. He and Kylie were going to do fine. Better than fine.

"Let's get this over with." Paul nodded toward the two long sofas in front of the fireplace. Edwin and Dan took one of them; he and Jason took the other. Set up like chess pieces, Dan thought, as he settled into the rich leather.

Jason Wallace calmly pulled a document from his slim leather case. "This document negates Mr. Lambert's claim to Kylie and shows clearly his wife's intentions in the matter of her daughter." He passed the papers to Eddie Maddox, sat back, and glanced at his watch. Dan had the impression he was in a hurry—or perhaps unused to making house calls.

Dan's stomach did a minor pitch-and-roll. He didn't like the look of those papers or the too-confident lawyer presenting them. And then there was Holly. Hell, you never knew what the hell Holly might have done—or not done. For the first time his confidence faltered.

Jesus, if he lost Kylie . . .

Maddox flipped through the pages and said, "I don't think so." He took a solid swig of what Dan knew was the best liquor he'd ever tasted, set the proffered papers aside, and dug into his own briefcase. Unlike Wallace's, his bulged to ripping point. When he had the papers he wanted flattened precariously on his knees, he took another drink, looked around, and said, "Where is Mrs. Bruce?" He looked at the documents, narrowed his eyes. "Camryn Angela Bruce."

Paul frowned, Dan set his drink on the table, and Wallace had no reaction at all, other than the barest raise of a brow.

What the hell . . . ?

"What are you talking about?" Paul said, cocking his head.

"According to the dates on each of the documents, these"—
Maddox tapped a finger on the pages resting on his knees—
"supersede those of Mister Wallace and designate Camryn
Angela Bruce as guardian."

Both Dan and Paul shot to their feet in unison.

Dan stared at Maddox, still trying to make sense of what
he'd said. "What the hell are you talking about? I'm Kylie's
guardian."

"Over my dead body," Paul said, adding, "and about a
hundred years after that!" He looked at Wallace. "Talk to
this idiot, will you, Jason?" He glared at Maddox.

Wallace set his drink on the table, untouched, and reached
for the document Eddie Maddox now held out to him. He
quickly scanned it, stopping at the signatory page. "He's right,
Paul. This supersedes the prior guardianship arrangement.
It appears genuine."

Eddie took instant affront. "Of course it's genuine!"

Paul looked at Jason Wallace. "What the hell happened?
She saw you less than two weeks ago."

"If you're referring to the appointment you set up, she
called and cancelled. When I attempted to reschedule, she
said she'd call after she'd talked to her husband, who
was"—he glanced at Dan—"apparently due back any day."

"Why didn't you call me, let me know?" Paul said.

Wallace gave a spare shrug. "Why would I? Holly wasn't
the first person to delay an appointment, and the issue wasn't
pressing. I assumed you knew about it."

Maddox again dug into his case. "There's a letter. It's
sealed and addressed to Mr. Grantman. It was in trust with
the guardianship. Same date—three months after the one
shown on your document." He looked at Wallace, not
above showing relish at his legal victory.

Paul tore the envelope from Maddox's hand, ripped it
open. His hands started shaking even before he flipped to
the second and last page. "Jesus," he muttered. When he'd

finished reading, his face was ashen, and the hand holding the letter dropped to his side like a dead thing.

Dan figured he knew what was in that letter—a whole lot of words a father would not want to hear. The only problem was he expected it to be attached to papers naming him, not some goddamned stranger as guardian to Kylie. "Let me see that document," he said, sure his face was as devoid of color as Paul's. Hell, it felt as if his blood had iced up in his veins, and reading the legalese, checking the document dates, did nothing to warm it.

Kylie was going to Camryn Bruce. His mind black and thick, Dan tossed the document on the coffee table. "This is bullshit," he said.

"Maybe so." Maddox drained his glass. "But unfortunately for you, Mr. Lambert, it's legal bullshit—and as such documents go, this one is clear and without ambiguity." He hesitated. "When she came to me to prepare them, she advised me there was another document, one that she'd felt"—he looked at Paul—"coerced into signing shortly after the child was born. She said she'd talked about her daughter with her friend, and her friend had agreed to be her daughter's guardian. It was what she wanted, and I—to steal a quote from *Star Trek*—'made it so.' I'm sorry, Mister Grantman, if this distresses you, but her wishes were very clear. She did not want either you or your wife—Erin, is it?—to raise her child."

"This is outrageous," Paul sputtered. "I won't stand for it. If there's a legal course to take, you can bet I'll be on it. Jason?" He shot a hard glance toward his lawyer.

"We have some moves," he replied, his tone low and, Dan thought, his words purposely vague.

Maddox shrugged. "In this profession, there's always a 'course' to take. Although in this situation, my legal opinion"—he looked at Jason Wallace—"tells me it would be costly and ultimately fruitless." He shrugged again. "But, of course, what you do is your decision."

"Damn straight," Paul said.

Maddox shifted his attention to Dan. "Not that it affects things, Mr. Lambert, but I think it's only fair you know that Holly did call me recently. She told me you and she had had a 'rough spot'—her words—but that you'd worked things out." He paused. "She wanted to come in, she said, after her time in Boston and talk over some changes with regard to her will and the guardianship arrangements. Unfortunately, she offered no specifics regarding either issue." He stood, a small man, probably a head shorter than Dan. "That appointment was for next week." He stopped again, looked uncomfortable for the first time since he'd blasted into the room. "I'm very sorry."

"Not as goddamn sorry as I am." Dan felt dim, as if his brain had gone out. He decided to keep his mouth shut until he'd figured things out. He'd expected to fight Grantman, but the idea of squaring off in a custody battle with Camryn Bruce, a woman he barely knew, was too fresh in his head to make sense of it.

Maddox asked calmly, "Is the child here?"

Grantman, looking as if he were chewing bullets, glared at the sturdy young lawyer and said nothing.

Maddox was unmoved. "Mister Grantman, there's really no purpose to be served by delaying the inevitable."

Grantman glanced at Jason Wallace, raised a brow as if demanding a legal leg to stand on.

Jason shook his head.

"She's with my wife," Paul said through a jaw so tight it looked painful.

Maddox waited, arched a brow.

"About an hour outside of Boston."

"Fine. Now I'd like to speak to Mrs. Bruce, please." Maddox met Jason's flat gaze and added, "You and your client can remain if you wish."

"I have no intention of involving myself in this charade—particularly as there is no way Camryn will retain custody of my granddaughter."

"Then perhaps you can fill your time by calling your wife and instructing her to bring the child home as quickly as possible."

"Jesus, I'm her grandfather, for God's sake! What's the hurry?"

"I have a plane to catch, and before I leave, I mean to ensure that my client's wishes have been seen to, and those wishes were that all parties be properly apprised of their positions in regard to the custody issue." He raised his hands, half smiled. "The sooner that's done, the sooner I'm gone, and you may initiate any action you wish."

"Fine by me," Grantman said through gritted teeth. He headed for the door and without looking back said, "Jason, come with me."

Maddox watched them go, shook his head, and looked at Dan. "You're staying, I presume."

"Wouldn't miss it for the world."

"I know this comes as a surprise, Mr. Lambert. Not at all what you expected when you asked me to fly down here."

"Surprised, yes. But pissed is more accurate."

For a moment Maddox looked uncomfortable. "I hope you understand there was nothing I could do. My instructions were clear." He paused. "And, truth be told, I feel sorry for Camryn Bruce."

"Why? It looks to me as if she's the clear winner in all this."

Maddox raised his calm gaze to what Dan knew would be his turbulent one. "Grantman won't let go, and I suspect neither will you. The woman is in for a very rough time. Legally speaking."

"I'd say you're right." Dan knew that Grantman wasn't going down without a fight, and neither would he. Although his methods might be considerably more . . . personal than

Paul's. Dan intended to look out for, and be part of his daughter's future, and he'd do whatever was necessary to ensure that.

Not everything had to be legal.

Camryn poked her head in the door, her expression quizzical. "Paul said there was someone here to see me." She stepped into the room. "I remember you. You're Holly's lawyer. We met when—" She stopped.

"Yes. Edwin Maddox, in case you've forgotten."

"I haven't forgotten, but I'm curious about why you're here in Boston."

"Mr. Lambert asked me to come—although I'm not sure the outcome was what he expected."

She glanced at Dan. "Which makes me even more curious."

Maddox handed her the guardianship document. "Holly wants *you* to care for her child." He nodded at the papers in her hand. "It's all in there, just as you and she agreed two-and-a-half years ago. "

Her mouth slackened, and her shocked gaze lifted to Dan's, then flew back to Maddox. "But this isn't—"

"Right?" Dan finished for her.

She closed her mouth. "I don't understand."

"It's all in there."

"Yes, but—" Again her eyes met Dan's. He hoped his gave away nothing.

Maddox bent to the sofa, gathered up a stray paper, and stuffed it into his case. "Everything's in order. Mr. Grantman will have Kylie here shortly." He handed her his card. "I have a plane to catch. If you have any further questions, call me when you get back to Seattle." He glanced at Dan. "There's a chance you'll need someone in your corner." He walked out.

When they were alone, Dan walked the few steps it took to bring them face to face. The woman looked shell-shocked.

The papers, which she hadn't so far even glanced at, hung from her hands like limp pennants.

When he stood in front of her, she looked through him rather than at him. "I don't know what to say," she said, her voice barely a whisper.

"I'd say congratulations are in order." He lifted her chin, looked into eyes that were confused and unfocused; he knew his own gaze would cause freezer burn. "It appears you've just given legal birth, Camryn—to my daughter. Instant motherhood. You might want to remember the feeling, because it sure as hell won't last."

Chapter 10

Adam didn't bother calling ahead to let Gina know he was coming, deciding in this case surprise was his best move. He had no doubt she was pissed at him, and the phone made it too easy for her to say no. But him, in her face? No contest.

"Where to?" the cabbie asked, stowing Adam's case in the trunk.

Adam gave him the address. The Solari estate was on Lake Washington—within running distance of Camryn and her dorky husband.

The cabbie shrugged. "That's aways away. It'll cost ya."

The jerk didn't wait for an answer, so Adam didn't offer one. He opened the back door and got in the cab. Settled into the backseat, he slicked his hair back, loosened his jacket, and pulled out his cigarettes.

"No smokin'," the cabbie said. "Sorry."

Shit! He shoved the pack back in his jacket pocket. He should quit, anyway. Save a fortune on breath mints.

"How long until we get there?" he asked the cab driver.

"This traffic? Forty—forty-five."

Adam resigned himself to staring out the window. The drive would give him time to think about how he was going to handle Gina—and that bitch of a mother of hers.

He rested his head against the seat and closed his eyes, but it wasn't Gina he thought about; it was Holly.

Damned if he didn't miss her—hated the thought of a world without her in it. Even if she had lied to him, deceived him. Hell, he shouldn't be surprised. Lies and deceit were Holly's style. His style.

But this time he'd thought things were different, that Holly was different. Looking back, he should have known. Seen the signs.

How edgy she'd been when he mentioned guardianship—their getting married. He'd put it down to her not wanting to lock horns with Grantman. She never minded getting under his skin, but she hated face-to-face confrontations with him.

"Let's see how things go between us, Adam," she'd said the first time he'd suggested she get rid of Lambert and marry him.

For a while they'd gone along damn fine. Every time Lambert went out of town it was a fuck-fest. He'd done nothing but suck up to her—and on her—for months. He got hard thinking about it, and damned if she didn't enjoy it as much as he did. When his chest tightened, he looked out the window, tried to focus on the city flashing by the speeding cab.

He remembered the day it all went wrong. It was right after that goddamn shock of a visit from Lando. He'd been scared stupid. Made some bad moves. For one he'd pushed her to set a firm date on dumping Lambert—getting the legal work done. Pushing Holly was always a bad idea.

They were in bed. Hell, they were always in bed. She was spread under him like a feast . . .

"Hm-m, that feels good," she murmured.

He added another finger, bent his head to tongue her. When she quivered and squirmed, he kissed her nub, pushed his fingers deeper inside her, and lifted his mouth from her clit. "And it's going to get better. Tell me what you want, baby, and I'll give it to you."

"Hm-m . . ."

"You want me to lick you, don't you? Take that hot little nub of yours into my mouth."

Her breathing, already quick and harsh, turned ragged.

He shifted up, looked into her sex-misted eyes, using his thumb as his place holder. *"You want that, you've got to tell me."* He smiled down at her, tried to sound a whole lot cooler than he felt. He had a hard time being cool around Holly.

"I want it, Adam." She trailed her fingers along his cheek, down his neck. *"I definitely want it."* Her eyes were slits, and her tongue came out to dampen her lips.

"Then you'll have to promise me something."

She lifted to his hand, rolled her hips. *"Anything."*

He circled her clit, bent to blow on it, then lifted his head. *"I want you to marry me, Holly. I want you. I want our kid. I want us to be a family. And I want it now. No more delays."* He pulled his fingers out, spread her legs, then clasped her ass in both hands—lifted her to him. *"Then we can do this"*—he gave her one long stroke of his tongue—*"twenty-four seven."*

She'd groaned and tossed her head back. *"Oh God . . ."*

"Say yes, Holly. You know it's what you want. What we both want."

She'd lifted her head, her face flushed, and he could feel the heat of her skin against his palms. *"You're a bastard, Adam Dunn."*

He tongued her again—stopped—arched a brow. *"You want me to finish what I've started?"*

"Tomorrow, baby. I'll do it tomorrow."

"Tomorrow you leave for Boston." He kissed her flat belly, moved his hand from her mound.

"I'll do it there . . ." she'd gasped. *"Just . . . finish me, Adam. Please . . ."*

*　　*　　*

He didn't remember saying anything after that. What he remembered was slamming into her so deep, he'd rooted there.

The next day she'd left for Boston. Three days after that he followed.

The cab pulled to a stop outside a gated driveway. "You want I should buzz us in?" the cabbie asked.

"No. This is good enough." Adam fumbled for his wallet, handed the driver his credit card, and said a short prayer it would take one more hit. It did, and two seconds later the cab drove off, and he was standing like goddamn Little Orphan Annie outside the dilapidated Solari mansion.

He craned his head and looked through the rusted wrought-iron gate at the sprawling three-story house. What a mess. Peeling paint. Roof tiles missing. One of the windows in the top floor broken and boarded up. A lawn high enough to hide a pride of hunting lions, and a tangle of shrubs that hadn't seen a shave and haircut for years.

Across the lake the sun was sinking below the horizon, casting the West-side grounds of the house into heavy shadow. A set of sorry-looking lawn furniture sat on a patio covered in leaves.

All of it was far worse than he remembered.

He lit his long-overdue cigarette, took a couple of deep drags, and stared at the gate phone. Hell, he'd be lucky if the damn thing even worked. He hesitated, rolled his banged-up head to loosen the tension in his shoulders.

This Gina thing wouldn't be easy. He had to play it right.

Dropping the cigarette on the driveway in front of the gate, he stubbed it out. *Do it, Dunn. Just damn well do it.*

He pushed the button.

"Yes?"

He sucked up some air. "Gina, it's Adam."

Silence. Total and absolute. But the line was open. She hadn't clicked off. His breath lightened. "I've missed you."

More silence.

"You still there?"

"You're a son of a bitch, Adam Dunn, and I never wanted to see you again."

He didn't miss her use of past tense, and put his mouth closer to the speaker, lowered his voice. "You don't mean that."

"I've never meant anything more seriously in my life. You're the worst thing that ever happened to me." Her voice rose slightly, unusual for Gina, who didn't often let that hot Italian ancestry show anywhere other than the bedroom. Not as good as Holly, but . . .

She went on. "Come to think of it, you're the worst thing that could happen to any woman who gets within ten feet of you."

"You and I got a lot closer than ten feet, baby. And I loved every minute of it."

"Something I'll regret forever. And I am not your baby. Not anymore, Adam. If I ever was."

And you're not clicking off.

Adam smiled, but didn't let it show in his voice; it dripped a soft sincerity. "I hurt you. I know that, and I'm sorry, and I'll go if that's what you want." He paused, not above a little emotional muscle-flexing before lobbing his ace. "The thing is, Gina . . . I need you. I never thought I'd say that to any woman, but I'm saying it to you. I'm in trouble, and I really need you." He paused. "Open the gate, baby . . . please."

The following morning, Camryn found Paul outside on the back patio. The day was bright and flavored with soft gusts of wind, cool and autumn-scented.

He was leaning against one of the white columns that flanked the stairs leading to a lower terrace, looking preoccupied and deeply thoughtful. Her father would say he was probably plotting how he could take her down, how he'd do it without a flinch. According to her father, Paul was heartless, greedy, and a merciless enemy. He might be right, but at this moment, he looked . . . sad.

Beyond the terrace, a magnificent linden tree dripped yellow leaves onto the lawn. Deep green from the recent showers, the lawn beyond the tree stretched to the dense hedge that separated the Grantman property from its neighbor. The hedge was a long way off.

She and Kylie were leaving in the afternoon, and Camryn didn't intend to leave without speaking to Paul and trying to settle things between them. He was Kylie's granddad, always would be. She would not take Kylie and run off like a kidnapper. She wouldn't run. Period.

Unlike Dan Lambert.

After spending some time with Kylie following yesterday's meeting, he'd packed and strode out of the house without another word. It made her think that on some level, he might be pleased he wouldn't have the burden of raising someone else's child—that most of his concern was his rigid idea of responsibility. Maybe Holly recognized that, and with the marriage as rocky as it was, decided to leave Camryn's guardianship in place.

Or maybe, Camryn, you're rationalizing, trying to get rid of the persistent gnaw of guilt and confusion you've had since Maddox handed you those papers.

Camryn hadn't pegged Lambert as an uncaring man, but, then, her pegging score for men left a lot to be desired. Shaking off that miserable thought, she said a silent thankyou to the Man Upstairs for the gift of innocence he'd given to children. Because of it, Kylie, barely three, was blissfully playing with the new doll Lambert had left with her, unaware of how her life was about to change.

Telling herself to get this face-off with Paul over with, she walked toward him, determined to say something, anything, to ease the situation between them.

"Paul."

He stiffened, but he didn't turn to look at her, nor did he speak. What he did was rub the lines in his forehead.

She walked to his side, waited a moment, then said, "We have to talk, you know. We can't leave it this way."

"We have nothing to talk about—considering you're stealing my granddaughter." He turned to her then; his eyes were hard, glassy—as if he'd been crying.

Camryn's heart lurched. "I'm not stealing her—"

"You're right. It's more like borrowing. I've already started the necessary legal proceedings, so I'd suggest you don't get overly attached." He gave her a stark, irritated look. "And given that, if you were smart, you'd leave Kylie here with Erin and me until the legal issue is resolved."

Camryn looked at him, what sympathy she had seeping away. "I'm not going to do that."

"I didn't think so."

She took a calming breath. "There's no point, Paul. Holly entrusted Kylie to me. Not you and not Erin." *Particularly not Erin.* She touched his arm. "I'll take good care of her—you must know that. And I'll love her as my own." *I already do.*

"I bet." His tone dripped sarcasm, and his cold gaze turned hot. "A child is not a commodity that someone can will to another, Camryn. That girl is my blood. Holly had no right to name you as guardian. No right at all."

"She was Kylie's mother. She had every right in the world to make her feelings known, and that's what she did. She didn't want—" She stopped. No way did she intend to mention the letter she knew was enclosed with the will. It must have killed Paul reading that letter, hearing his daughter's reasons for her choosing a friend to care for her child rather than her father . . . and Erin.

"You know about the letter," Paul stated, his gaze riveted to hers.

Damn! "Yes."

"You know what's in it."

"Yes."

He looked away, his chest heaving, then turned back to her. "If you're counting on it for backup in court, you're making a mistake. Her allegations about Erin are completely untrue."

Camryn had no intention of arguing for or against Holly's opinion of Erin. To go there now would be incendiary. "I came looking for you in the hope we could work this out," she said. "And to tell you I won't keep Kylie from you." She paused. "This needn't be a court issue unless you make it one. Holly and I were like sisters—you know that. I've been helping her with Kylie since the day she was born. I already love her like my own, and I'll give her a good and loving home." *A home where she'll be safe.*

He faced her, put his hands on his hips, and stared at her for a long moment. "You want her because you're unable to have your own children. You're barren, Camryn—or as they say these days, infertile. So, please, spare me your altruism. Your motive for taking my granddaughter is no higher than your own self-interest."

She froze in place. *How did he . . . ?*

She couldn't ask because her mouth refused to open. She'd spent years struggling with her inability to bear children, the pervasive disappointment and pain of it, but she'd never thought that failure would be used as an emotional bludgeon, a means to make her love for Kylie appear selfish and egocentric.

"Holly told me part of it," he went on. "I followed up. I always follow up. You've spent enough time in fertility clinics in the past few years to earn a degree in gynecology." His mouth tightened. "Obviously with no results. Which is probably why your husband walked out on you."

Whoa . . . Camryn took a deep breath, unclenched hands

that had turned to fists at her sides. She'd always known Paul Grantman was a shark, that he had a reputation as a street fighter in boardrooms and businesses across the continent, but she'd never seen it first hand. Never quite believed her father. *God, poor Holly.* "None of which is your business."

"Holly naming you Kylie's guardian made it my business. Holly was my daughter. I loved her, but she was foolish and soft-hearted. I'm neither. Her way to deal with an issue was to slide around it. From my point of view, the fact that you can't have children of your own is not a reason for you to be *given* my only grandchild. I suspect the courts will feel the same, forced to choose between awarding Kylie to a single mother struggling to support herself, her deadbeat father, or—all this." He lifted a hand to indicate his house and grounds.

You manipulative bastard . . . "And who should be 'given' your granddaughter? Your alcoholic, cocaine-sniffing trophy wife?" She paused, crossed her arms. "Holly didn't think so, and neither do I."

His face reddened. "I won't have you bring Erin into this."

"Let me get this straight. My empty womb is fair game, but your wife's addictions aren't? Well, guess what, Paul? That doesn't work for me." She met his thunderous gaze. "I'm not Holly, Paul. I won't smile, agree with whatever you say, then go and do whatever I meant to do in the first place. And I won't be intimidated."

"How about being bought? I can either pay you, or I can pay my lawyers. Take your pick."

"You're offering to buy Kylie?" *For your dim-witted wife.*

"I want what's mine, and I'll do what I have to do to get it."

Camryn shook her head. "All that 'get what's mine'

stuff . . . it's exactly why Holly did what she did. The answer is no; I won't sell you your granddaughter, because along with not being intimidated, I won't be bought."

"And I won't lose."

"Let's see"—she counted off on her fingers—"so far in this ten-minute conversation you've tried extortion, intimidation, and bribery. Your next move should be fascinating."

"And you won't see it coming."

"I'm breathless with anticipation." She stopped, took a moment and settled herself—somewhat. "But I'll say again, none of this is necessary. So when you stop playing the role of spoiled rich man, stop thinking win-lose, and start thinking about what's good for Kylie, let me know."

She turned her back on him and headed toward the French doors leading into the house. She had nothing more to say to Paul Grantman. The next move was his. All she could do was wait for it.

And take Kylie home.

The plane left on schedule, and within half an hour in the air, an overexcited and very tired Kylie was asleep in the center seat next to Camryn's by the window. Fortunately, the aisle seat was empty, so the airline pillow propped on the armrest wasn't bothering another passenger. Thinking the plane's air conditioning might be too cool on the child's shoulder, Camryn gently covered her with a blanket. Kylie stirred, nuzzled deeper into the pillow, and continued sleeping.

Camryn couldn't stop staring at her, her feelings an unsorted jumble, half warm, half cold. Only love stood front and center—love for this child and her mother.

Oh, Holly, you've given me such a gift—and such a challenge. I won't let you down, my friend. No matter what, I won't let you down. And I won't let Kylie down. I love her, Holly. I love her with my whole heart.

The tears that seeped to Camryn's lower lashes were as confusing to her as her feelings. There was sorrow that she'd lost her dearest friend, elation at having Kylie—another life to concern herself with, a child to love—then a sick regret and guilt that the cost of such a gift was Holly's life. Dear God, if she could change that, she would, but she couldn't.

It's all about Kylie now, she reminded herself, and that's how Holly would want it. She brushed the tears away, leaned her head back on the seat, and closed her eyes.

She couldn't wait to get home. She'd called her father this morning, told him what had happened—that she was bringing Kylie home, but it was as if he'd barely registered what that meant. Just asked how "Grantman took it." But he did say he'd be there to help her until she got things settled and got herself a good nanny. That "until" surprised her; it was the first time he'd indicated he was thinking of leaving. But as she still had a business to run—even though it was from home—her dad helping out for a short time would be welcome.

She hadn't called Gina yet and honestly wasn't looking forward to it, given Gina's current . . . strangeness.

"This seat taken?"

She recognized the male voice immediately.

Dan Lambert!

Chapter 11

"What are you doing here?" She blurted out, "and where in hell did you come from?"

He gestured forward to first-class, then took the aisle seat, sliding in carefully so as not to wake Kylie. When he was seated, he touched the little girl's soft hair, his big hand surprisingly gentle. What he didn't do was answer her question; instead, he posed one of his own.

"How did it go with Grantman?" His eyes, disturbing and unreadable, rested on her.

"Not well."

"I'm not surprised." His lips twisted briefly, into what was either a knowing grin or a curl of aversion.

She turned, as much as she could considering the confines of her economy-class seat, and fully faced him. "I'm guessing about as well as it will 'go' with you, considering you're no more pleased by Holly's decision than he is." She didn't intend to sound combative, but she did.

"Me?" He looked down at Kylie, smoothed some of her fine blond hair over the pillow. "Don't know what you mean."

His remark and his face appeared guileless, but her gut said otherwise, and Camryn always trusted her instincts. "Paul sees me as some kind of kidnapper, and, as you obviously expected Kylie would be with you, I'm guessing you feel much the same way."

"I do." He raised his remarkable eyes to hers, and a shaft of light came through the plane's window, amplifying their greenish-gray color to a sharp silver, but his expression was relaxed when he added, "But if you were going to steal Kylie, stealing her from Paul and Erin Grantman is the lesser of two evils."

"And what would be the first?"

"Stealing her from me." His gaze never wavered from hers. "She's my daughter, Camryn. I don't intend to lose her."

"What do you intend?"

"I haven't quite figured that out yet."

"Well, when you do—"

"You'll be the first to know."

Having no answer to that, Camryn turned her head and looked out the window. The silence between them filled with airplane sounds; a child crying, the odd hiss of air being forced through the cabin, trays being loaded onto a cart somewhere behind them. She didn't want to argue, but she did want to set a few things straight—if anything could be set straight in this morass of a situation.

When she turned to face him again, he was still watching her—as if he'd been waiting. *A quiet man,* she thought, *one who doesn't waste words.*

"Look," she began. "You care about Kylie. I understand that. Appreciate it. But you're her stepfather; there's nothing in place giving you any legal rights over her. Why take on a fight you have virtually no chance of winning?" *Walk away. Please walk away. Paul Grantman is enough to handle.*

"When Kylie wakes up, she'll call me Daddy. It was the first word she ever said—and she's been saying it for over two years. Two thirds of her life. Now that may not be legalese enough for you, but it works for me. There's one other thing. If Holly had lived, had kept her appointment with Maddox, you and I wouldn't be having this conversation."

"But she didn't, and we are having this conversation. And while we're on the 'if' track, how about this? *If* Holly had lived, you might be facing another kind of battle—in the divorce court. What would happen to Kylie then?"

Those eyes of his went quiet again. Scarily quiet. "How much do you know about my marriage, Camryn?"

She saw the flash of anger in his eyes, a hint of pain, and a lot of hard-jawed determination. "Enough to know I might have been naive to buy into your loving-father scenario at first blush. Certainly enough to know you've been out of Kylie's life, virtually an absentee father, for the last three months—and that maybe that was at Holly's request."

He looked at her a long time, then said, "As they say, a little knowledge is a dangerous thing."

He was wearing gray slacks and a fine white cotton shirt, no jacket, and she saw his chest expand and contract, heard the rasp of his indrawn breath. Then without a word, he flagged down the flight attendant before again turning his attention to her. "Would you like a drink?"

Camryn ignored his question. "What I'd like is to get things straight between us."

The flight attendant arrived before he could answer. He glanced at her. "I noticed you drank a merlot at lunch yesterday. Will that do?"

"I do not want a drink."

"Merlot," he said to the attendant. "Times two."

When she left, Camryn rounded on him. "If you won't talk about Holly, then we'll talk about Kylie."

He cocked his head.

"Can I expect you to challenge my guardianship? Will I be seeing you in court along with Paul and Erin?"

"Yes, to the first question," he said. "And no to the second. I'm not a fan of lawyers. I prefer taking the shortest distance between two points." Kylie shifted and stretched between them.

"Which means?" Camryn asked, careful to lower her voice.

When Kylie frowned in her sleep and rubbed her nose, Dan again touched her tousled hair. And when one of her pink-socked feet straightened out and dug into Camryn's thigh, Camryn lifted it to rest more comfortably across her knees.

For a split moment, man, woman, and child were connected.

"Whatever it needs to mean," he said, lowering his voice as she had hers, so as not to wake the sleeping girl between them. The attendant brought their wine, and Dan handed her one of the glasses. "But for now, I suggest we let Kylie sleep. We'll sort things out later."

She didn't like his smugness, and she didn't like the wariness seeding in her chest. She didn't like the idea that Dan Lambert might prove to be more of an adversary than Paul Grantman.

"We have nothing to sort out," she said, determined to set him straight. "And you should . . . go back to your own seat."

"I prefer sitting with my daughter." He gave her an odd half-smile, opened the book he'd brought with him, took a sip of wine, and ignored her for the rest of the trip.

Gina jerked awake, as if she'd been sleeping for hours and was late for a life-and-death appointment. In truth she'd been sleeping for less than fifteen minutes and dreaming . . .

Her body was overheated, slick with a sheen of perspiration, and her vulva pulsed with need. The dream was too raw, too erotic, and it had been too long since she'd had sex, too long since she'd been touched.

She closed her legs, swallowed.

Adam was still here. In the room below hers. Her heart

thumped in her chest, wild and excited, terrified. Her heart was insane. . . .

He'd have to go, of course. Last night and tonight were enough. Maybe the torrid dreams would leave with him.

She would give him what money she had. Send him away. So far she'd stayed away from him, but if he didn't go and soon, she might weaken. No!

Her fingers curled around the sheet's border. Letting him in was crazy—hiding him from Delores crazier still. But she'd hid him because if Delores saw him, she'd want him. She'd play with him to make Gina mad. Madder than she already was.

And Sebastian would kill her—or Adam.

She tossed back the down comforter and swung her legs to the side of the bed. She had to get rid of him. Get him out of the house. Out of her life—where he'd been since she'd lost his baby. She hated him. She had to remind herself of that. She put her hands to the sides of her head, pressed.

I hate him, I hate him, I hate him. . . .

Better. That's better.

She stood, her heart drumming hollowly in her chest, an echo in a shadowed cavern. She headed for the east window. Her room, essentially the attic with two gabled windows and an open-beamed ceiling, had the original wood floors that came with the hundred-year-old house, and her steps across it took her off the rug her bed sat on to the roughness of oak plank floors.

When she was ten and her mother had bought the estate, Gina fell in love with the strangely shaped attic room, had sensed its ability to keep secrets, and loved the idea of there being an entire floor separating her from her mother's lavish suite on the second floor. She'd fought Sebastian for the attic room and won and had relished its quirks and seclusion ever since, leaving it only for college and her brilliant but short-lived legal career. A career frozen in another time, another place.

Immediately after Delores moved into the house, she'd begun renovating: floors, walls, windows, and aging rooms had fallen under the relentless hands of a series of decorators. Delores wanted to "update the ancient heap of lath and plaster" as she called it, to her version of posh livability—all thirty thousand square feet of it. It had taken upwards of two years to turn classic into gauche, chic into tawdry. Delores had a knack.

When Gina, with uncharacteristic stubbornness, had fought to save the attic and the generous welcoming window seats under the gabled windows, her mother, in an equally rare mood of conciliation, had given way, saying she'd never be in the "goddamn attic" anyway, so she didn't care. Gina often slept on the padded window seat as a child, dreaming and watching the moon and sun cast their unique colors across the lake.

Her mother said she'd bought the house for its lakefront location and had agreed with the designer that the entire house needed "refocusing." The result was a renovation catastrophe on a scale only big money could buy, a sprawling, ugly testament to her mother's ego and terrible taste.

Sitting now in the window seat, Gina pulled up her knees, hugged them. She looked eastward over the lake for a sign of morning and worked to ignore the ache stirring in her head. For the hot, clamoring need wracking her body, she could do nothing.

She'd come home to nurture her hatred for Adam Dunn. But even in this she'd failed. Had she succeeded, learning about his affair with Holly wouldn't have felt as if her heart was torn from her breast.

Adam had moved from Gina's arms to Holly's with the ease of a snake slithering through spring grass. Her face heated, her lips went dry.

I do hate him! I burn with hate for him!
I burn for him.

Loathing that truth, she turned her face to the window. Clouds now darkened the path of early light, delaying morning.

She closed her eyes against them, leaned her head back against the window seat wall, and stretched out her legs. She ran her hand down her belly to the throb at their apex and stroked herself through her thin cotton nightgown.

I burn for him.

"Lift the gown, baby. So much better that way."

She froze, sat like an abandoned doll, back to the wall, legs straight and open. "What are you—"

He stood in the dim light, tall, shadowed, wearing nothing but jeans. His feet were bare, his thick, silky hair roughly shoved behind his ears. He was Adam. He was beautiful.

"Doing here?" he finished for her, stepping close enough to block her from leaving the window seat. "Nothing nearly as interesting as you are."

When he looked pointedly at her hand, she snapped it back to her waist, closed her legs.

"Don't stop on my account. You know how I love watching you." He sat on the edge of the seat, faced her, and closed his hand around her ankle, shackling her with warmth and strength. "Remember that time we booked into that Roach Motel—off I-Five somewhere?" he said, his eyes smiling into hers. "You sat on the edge of the bed— wearing that black satin slip I liked. No panties." He inhaled unevenly. "I pulled up a chair and watched you make yourself come. Didn't touch you. Not once." He moved his hand up her leg, stroked under her gown. "Jesus," he said, his voice a low growl. "I damn near came out of my skin. But you wouldn't let me touch you. That was your game. You remember?"

She swallowed, said nothing, and tried to force the heated image from her mind: her laughing at her own game, taunting him, then sitting on the edge of that awful sway-backed bed, knees apart . . . masturbating while Adam sat inches away watching her. His vivid blue eyes had turned almost black with need. And he'd kept telling her how beautiful she was, telling her what to touch, how hard he was getting. . . .

A woman would pay to have a man look at her like that. And in the end she had paid, with her pride and with her heart. Adam had ruined her. He had betrayed her, over and over again. And he'd ignored their child. Adam was dirt.

But in this darkened room, with the heat from his hand warming her long-cold flesh, none of that mattered. Nothing mattered except his being here in the hours before morning with his fingers trailing over her skin.

"God, you were hot that night. I was going crazy wanting to fuck you." He smiled, a smile she sensed rather than saw. "And that's exactly what you wanted, wasn't it? To make me crazy—like you're doing right now."

The dark closed around her, and Adam's voice, the heat of his hand, stopped her breathing. "I don't think—"

"Good. Because this isn't a time for thinking." He slid his hand under her gown, up her outer thigh. She didn't move, couldn't move. Then as if of their own volition, her knees, until this moment, locked flush and tight to each other, eased open. A blur of thought followed. Why not? Why shouldn't she use Adam to cool the boil, ease the rage. It's what he'd do.

She hated him. She loved him. . . .

"I don't want—"

"Yes, you do. You definitely do, Gina. You want the same thing I want—and I'm going to give it to you." He pressed an open palm against her inner thigh, let his fingertips lightly brush her pubic hair.

She remembered. She remembered every engorged vein and muscle in his body; his long, expert fingers. . . . Fire rushed up her throat and she gasped.

"That's it," he said when her legs eased looser. "Now sit back, and I'll take care of you. I'm here, Gina. And all I want to do is make you happy." His hand moved to her inner thigh, again grazed her pubis, and skirted upward over her belly. He found a nipple, circled it with a slow finger, then leaned to kiss it through the thin cotton of her gown.

She drew in a breath, moistened her lips with a tongue too dry for the task. He'd play with her now. Make her wait. She loved to wait, loved that place before coming.

Abruptly, he pulled his hand back. "Get naked, Gina," he said. "I want to see your breasts in the moonlight."

He didn't help her, instead he sat back, watched her brief struggle to nudity. When she'd tossed the loose cotton shift to the floor, he scanned her body. "Nice. Very nice. Fuller than I remember. Lush." He touched the tiny birthmark over her right breast, leaned down to kiss it softly, before running his tongue over her nipple. His tongue wasn't gentle, it was rough and quick, and she gasped from the sting of it. She touched the nipple he'd stroked; it was a small, aching stone. "Stretch out, baby. Open your legs." He smiled, and his teeth glittered white in the growing light of morning. "A man needs room to work."

She wanted to resist—she did! But she obeyed, her traitorous body on a deeply disturbing level craving him to oblivion.

She was enraptured by the idea of Adam, the memory of Adam, of what his hands would make her body do.

She wanted to see him in the same way he saw her, naked

and open to her. She ran her hand up and over the hard swelling below the undone top button of his jeans and pulled down his zipper. No briefs. He shifted his hips and his erection sprang free. He was hard, long, and magnificent.

Her searing dream come to life. Hers for the taking. She started to pant, her lungs unable to fill, unable to empty. "I remember . . ." she whispered, too hot to talk.

"It's all yours," he answered, his words silky. "Anytime you want it." He bent over her, licked her lips, then claimed her mouth. His tongue, hot and demanding, took hers, while his hands roamed her body with softness and care, as if he were reading her skin. The contrast of soft hands and plundering mouth made her body pulse and jerk.

She curled her hand around his erection and felt his stomach contract. He lifted his mouth from hers, took her face in his hands. "It's been too long, baby. Much too long."

She squeezed his length, and he closed his eyes.

"Hm-m . . . that's good," he murmured. "Very good."

Gina took her hand from him, waited for him to open his eyes, saw they were as glazed and crazed as her own. Adam might use sex for his own ends, but he also enjoyed it, and he let it show. She ran her hand over his clean-shaven face and breathed in his expensive musky scent. Something in her registered: no briefs, clean-shaven. The bastard came to her ready . . . absolutely sure she was his for the taking.

She didn't care. She was pathetically grateful.

She stared into his eyes. "Fuck me, Adam. Like you used to." Was that breathless, needy voice hers? Was it really her asking . . . begging for sex from Adam Dunn, the man she'd spent almost a year hating?

He put his hand on her pubis, cupping it lovingly, then moved a finger until he located her clitoris. Circling it slow and easy, then stroking it luxuriously, he leaned to whisper in her ear. "My pleasure."

No. The pleasure was hers, all hers. Adam made sure of it.

She might hate herself in the morning, but she'd hate Adam even more.

Chapter 12

Camryn's first thought when she woke was Kylie. Her plan was to make them both breakfast and take some quiet time to explain, as best she could, why Kylie would be staying with her Aunt Cammie from now on, a subject that she'd avoided—for more than a week.

So far, because Kylie had stayed with Camryn before, often for days at a time, she was at home here. She hadn't felt anything strange about her extended stay. She'd just been her usual happy, joyous self.

Camryn honestly didn't know where to begin, how to tell a three-year-old girl her mother was never coming back. She knew Paul had told her, "Mommy is away," but that wasn't nearly enough. Then there was her insistent—and increasing—questions about when "Daddy?" was coming. Obviously, Camryn had underestimated the bond between Dan and Kylie, or subconsciously denied it. Either way, today she'd at least try to explain the changes in Kylie's young life.

A glance at the clock told her it was seven-thirty. She got out of bed and reached for the robe she'd draped over the baseboard the night before.

She found Kylie and Trent sitting at the kitchen table, Kylie with toast in her hand and peanut butter on her face, her father with coffee and the morning newspaper. Kylie scrambled from her chair and rushed at her like a small, very excited tornado.

"Aunt Cammie," she said. "I got toast with Tent."

"Trent," her dad corrected, then looked up at her. "Morning."

"You fed her," she said. It came out sounding like an accusation, or her disappointment showed. So much for her plan.

"I was up. She was up. Seemed logical."

Of course it was. "Thanks," she said.

He put down his paper, got up. "Get your coat, kiddo. We might as well check out that park now. Before it rains—again."

"I need my brella." She looked at Camryn with a question in her eyes.

"It's in your closet, sweetheart. In the back. You'll have to look."

"I'll find it. I'm a good finder." She rushed off, barefooted, hair uncombed.

"Get your boots!" Camryn yelled at her retreating back. "They're in there, too."

"Okay."

And she was gone. Camryn turned to her dad. "I'm sorry you mentioned the park. I was planning some alone-time with Kylie. I need to talk to her."

"What about?"

"Everything. Her mother particularly."

"I already did," he said.

"What?" Camryn, who'd been pouring herself a coffee, spun, coffeepot in hand.

"I spoke to her yesterday and again today. Did the usual thing." He shrugged. "I said her mommy was in heaven with the angels, and that someday—if she was a really good little girl—she'd see her again. As for the rest . . ." He paused, rubbed at his chin. "What she doesn't know won't hurt her."

Considering Kylie was so young, he was probably right, but it didn't make Camryn less irritated at his cavalier taking-over of what she saw as her role. "And what's that philosophy? The world according to Trent Derne? Bury the truth and throw away the shovel?"

"There's worse ways to deal with a problem, Camryn."

Camryn dialed back on her impatience, set the coffeepot back on the counter, and turned on her father. "I didn't ask you to speak to her, and I wish you hadn't."

"Why the hell not? The sooner the better, and the simpler the better. The girl is three years old. A month from now she'll barely remember her real mother. You'll be the mother of record. It's you she'll remember." He gave her a quizzical look. "That's what you always wanted, wasn't it? To be a mother?"

Mother of record . . . God, the phrase made Kylie sound like a land parcel. "Of course, but—"

"Got it, Tent," Kylie barreled into the room carrying her umbrella. "And socks, too. I put socks on." She lifted a foot; it was encased in a yellow boot with bumblebees on the toe guard. "Can we go?"

"Sure, honey, but give me a kiss first."

Kylie wrapped her arms around her and kissed her soundly on the cheek. That done, she leaned back, still holding Camryn tight, and said, "Tent says Mommy's gone to heaven for a long time."

She didn't pose it as a question, but Camryn took it as one. "Yes, she has, sweetheart."

"She should've tooken me."

"She couldn't do that, because one of the really big and important angels said you have to wait here for a while."

"That's mean." She sealed her lips. "I'm going to tell my Grampa. He'll get mad."

"Grampa already knows, Kylie, and he is mad—very mad, but that angel won't talk to him."

Kylie's face soured even further, then brightened when another idea lit up her thinking. "Then I'll ask Daddy to talk to the angel. He's a real good talker." She thought a minute, then instructed, "You call Daddy, okay?"

Before she could come up with an answer to Kylie's latest plan, Trent interrupted. "Let's go, kiddo." He made a show of looking out the window; the day was clear enough, but the sky held the usual October cloud. "Looks like you were a smart girl," he said, "getting that umbrella. It's going to rain for sure. We might have to share. Okay?" Her father gave Kylie one of his rare smiles, which sent an odd, soft jolt through Camryn's heart. She didn't remember him smiling at her in that way; she remembered him as distracted and preoccupied—and leaving, always leaving on one of his endless business trips. Now, he was here enjoying Kylie— much as he would his own grandchild. If she could give him one. That stupid errant thought, the first step on a nonsensical guilt trip, had her mentally giving her head a shake. What was, was. And she'd spent the last three months accepting it. She wasn't stumbling back to Pity City now.

"Okay, but I hold it," Kylie stated.

"Fair enough," Trent said and reached for her hand.

Camryn kissed Kylie's head, then pulled up her hood. "Run along, sweetheart. We'll talk later."

She watched them walk up the long driveway toward the street. The park, with its large beach area and colorful playground, was about three blocks away.

Although Camryn's house was on the lakefront, her shore area, rimmed with tall grass, was small and rocky; a dock jutted into the lake with not so much as a canoe tied to it. But the old Craftsman-style house on the property was a jewel—and a work in progress. Its state of disrepair, and the strange fact that the house, constructed with its porch facing away from the lakefront, hadn't been built to take advantage of its waterfront location, gave it a price she could afford. It wasn't a large house, but the upper floor, about half the size of the main floor, provided her a private bed and bath and loft with enough working space to run her business, and she adored its wide eaves and exposed rafters.

She'd have to make some changes to the main floor for Kylie's sake, but that would be a joy. She watched her dad and Kylie walk the long path to the street, holding hands.

She was about to close the door behind them when she saw a FedEx truck turn into the driveway. Pulling her robe tighter against the morning chill, she waited. Probably it was that purchase order she'd requested from Holland's Antiques for the Lalique "Serpent" vase. Maybe even a check. "Camryn Bruce?" the man said.

"Uh-huh."

She signed for the envelope and went back into the house, determined to finally get that cup of coffee.

Coffee in hand, she sat at the table and opened the envelope. Her breath caught in her throat and she immediately put her free hand at its base and told herself to get a grip. This wasn't unexpected.

The papers in the envelope—all Washington-state legal— told her she was a free woman. Craig had taken care of everything, as he'd said he would. The divorce was uncontested, neither of them wanted anything from the other, and Washington, being a no-fault divorce state, simply acknowledged the "marriage was irretrievably broken."

All Camryn had to do was sign and she'd erase five years of marriage. Too bad she couldn't do the same to her guilt and sense of failure. She'd hurt Craig, used him, and she still felt lousy about it. He was right; she'd wanted a child more than she'd wanted him. She'd been unfair to him and unfair to their marriage vows.

I have my child now, not in the way I'd planned, but as precious as if she'd come from my own womb. But I'm sorry I hurt you, Craig. You were my . . . friend.

She was brushing tears from her eyes when the doorbell crackled. Or buzzed. Or whatever. There really wasn't a description for the sound, other than aurally painful. She kept meaning to have it fixed—but somehow it stayed low on the list of things to do. She got up immediately to stop whoever it was on the other side of her door from ringing it again.

She looked through the glass, frowned, and again tugged at the belt on her robe, pulling it even tighter. God, she hadn't even brushed her hair!

It was Dan Lambert, carrying a very large bag.

If Camryn hadn't known what to say to Kylie about her mother and all the changes she could expect, she was even less sure what to say to the man Kylie hadn't stopped talking about since she'd brought her home.

The man threatening to take her away, and a man who had a troubling effect on Camryn's logic and determination—and something else she couldn't, or wouldn't, name.

She opened the door. "I don't remember telling you where I lived," she said, at the same time registering how relaxed and confident he looked standing outside her door at a too-early time in the morning. And while he looked rugged and ready for the day in jeans and a tan windbreaker, she looked frowsy—probably irritated, which she was—and incapable of thinking past downing her first cup of coffee.

"You're in the phone book."

"Yes, along with my telephone number." She eyed him. "I thought you'd gone back to California."

"I did. Now I'm here."

"Here, where?"

"A motel in Kenmore—for the time being."

She let out a breath, because other than a curse, it was all she could come up with.

"We have things to settle," he said. "I thought it best we do it face to face." He looked past her. "And I'd like to see Kylie. I brought some of her things from the house. She'll want them."

"She's with my father. At the park." She didn't open the door. "You can leave them with me. I'll make sure she gets them."

"This is only part of it. The rest of it—the bigger toys and some clothes—are in the truck. And her car. She loves her car." He waited, and it was obvious he intended to wait for as long as it took.

Damn! She opened the door wider. "I'll take that." She reached for the bag. "You get the rest."

He handed her the bag, turned without a word, and went back to the black Navigator he'd parked in her driveway.

He made another trip, then Camryn helped him stack Kylie's worldly treasures—which included a pedal-operated pink truck, a miniature replica of the one her daddy had parked in Camryn's driveway. The pink one was now in her kitchen, along with the man who carried it in.

"Thank you," Camryn said, tightening her robe again and stuffing her hands in her pockets. "Kylie will be happy to have her things."

He nodded, glanced at the coffeepot. "Do you mind?"

"I—"

He poured himself a cup, leaned against the counter, and studied her over the rim of the mug, looking as cool and casual as a Sunday shopper. He didn't look as if he was in any hurry to start talking. He looked sharp, all shiny-clean, and focused. He wasn't here to drop off Kylie's toys. He had a purpose. The last thought made her frown.

"You wanted to talk," she finally said, tilting her head, increasingly uncomfortable in her robe and ratty slippers.

"How much do you know about Holly and I? About what was going on between us?"

She didn't know what she'd expected, but it wasn't a discussion of his marriage. Damn, she should have kept her mouth shut on the plane. Then she remembered Sebastian's accusation after the funeral, and her stomach tightened. Better he was here to talk about her smart-mouthed comments than to ask about Adam. She did not, would not, talk about that scumbag. "Nothing." She turned, picked up her abandoned coffee mug from the table, and poured the cold dregs into the sink.

"That's not what you said on the plane," he said.

"I was . . . out of line. What happened between you and Holly is your business, unless—"

"Unless it affects Kylie."

"Yes."

"Fair enough." He sipped some coffee, held it in both hands. "But it still doesn't answer my question."

"Look . . . for a while after you and Holly married we kept in touch, but—and I feel bad about this—I hadn't seen much of her for close to a year. Holly's choice, not mine, and I sensed something was very wrong."

"And when you heard we were separated, you assumed that 'something' was me. Or is that what Holly told you?"

"Holly wouldn't talk about it, but she didn't have to." She took a step toward him. "But my guess? Holly—and Kylie—needed more than an absentee husband and father." She met his level gaze with one of her own. "You were never there. That much I did know."

His jaw moved, and he looked away, took a breath.

"You're right. I traveled a lot. That's my job. But that was about to change. We'd agreed on it." He sent the last of his coffee to join hers in the sink. "Holly didn't wait for that to happen."

"What do you mean?"

He looked as if he had broken glass in his mouth—and broken pride in his eyes. "Your friend Sebastian was right. She had someone."

Damn Sebastian anyway! Why hadn't he kept his jealous paranoia to himself? "You can't take what Sebastian said as fact. He's obsessive when it comes to Holly." She considered her choice of words conservative, knowing 'maniacally addicted' would have suited better.

"He loved her." Dan set out the words and waited.

She hesitated. "Yes. Since high school."

He nodded, then said, "That said, he didn't tell me anything I didn't already know."

Camryn's stomach sank, and her breathing went shallow. "I don't believe that. And neither should you."

"You don't want to believe it. Me? I don't have a choice. My source is impeccable."

"And that would be?"

"Holly."

"Holly told you she was having an affair?" She wanted to sneer at his allegation, but something in his face stopped her.

"Yes."

"She wouldn't! Absolutely would *not* do that." The words shot out of her in a burst of appalled disbelief.

"You actually believe I'd make something like that up?" He rubbed at his jaw, then abruptly dropped his hand, adding, "You believe that a man—any man—wants to admit his wife preferred someone else's company in her bed?"

Camryn's legs suddenly weakened, so she went back to the table and sat down.

Dan followed her, took the chair across from her, and

folded his hands in front of him. Big hands that looked strong and capable, like the man himself, and, like him, deeply tanned.

"Why are you telling me this?" she asked.

"Because I want you to tell me everything you know about this Adam guy."

"That wouldn't be much." Her mind was trying to absorb the idea of Holly and Adam. No! *It couldn't be Adam. It couldn't! Holly wouldn't . . .* But when she thought about the past few months, how Holly had avoided her, it made a crazy kind of sense, because if Holly were seeing him, she'd avoid Camryn—not want to face what she knew would be her shock and disapproval. *But, Adam . . . again!* Surely Holly wouldn't be that stupid. That reckless.

Dan stared at her, his gaze narrowing. "I don't believe you."

"Believe whatever you want. But anything I know about Adam is old news. *Very* old news." Camryn did *not* want to go there—that mean and ugly place Adam Dunn had created in her life, in all their lives. It was sordid and humiliating. After Kylie was born, she, Gina, and Holly had agreed to emotionally bury Adam, dump him and the pain he'd inflicted on each of them into the past and vow to leave him there.

Obviously, Holly had changed her mind.

Camryn hadn't. "Look, even if I believed that Holly had an affair with Adam Dunn—which I honestly can't imagine—what's the point of dragging it up now? She's . . . gone. Why not let it go."

He let out an irritated gust of breath. "How about this for a reason? He's a likely suspect in her murder."

Camryn's eyes shot to his, and shock constricted her chest. "No. No way. Adam might be an amoral opportunist—but a murderer?" She shook a vehement negative. "No." Even as the words crossed her lips, Camryn wondered why she was so certain of them, but she was. "He would never hurt Holly. Never. He'd have no reason to."

"How about if she was dumping him, because she wanted to make things work between us." He watched her face. "Would that be reason enough for you?"

"You think that's true?"

"Holly and I had talked a few days before she was killed. Both of us wanted what was best for Kylie. So, yes, I'd say that's where her head was."

She thought about it, shook her head again. "No. Not Adam."

"Dunn was in Boston when Holly was killed. Did you know that?"

That got her attention, but it didn't change her mind. "Here's a better question. How do *you* know that?"

"I work in the oil business. Security. We check everything about everybody who comes near our sites—who does what, with whom, where they do it, and why. When your buddy Sebastian supplied me with a name. I ran a check on it."

She hesitated. "That's . . . creepy."

"So is being murdered." He twisted his lips. It was as if he were chewing on his patience. "So I repeat, tell me everything you know. If you won't tell me, I'm guessing Gina Solari will."

That brought Camryn to her feet. "Gina has nothing to do with any of this." Camryn didn't know what was wrong with Gina, but sure as hell something was. She was already depressed, lonely, and a life-inch away from a complete breakdown. She didn't need an avenging husband on her case talking about Adam Dunn, of all people, after what he'd done to her in college. She wasn't sure Gina had ever really got over that. "You have to leave her out of this. She's not well."

Dan Lambert eyed her as if she were seeping gray matter. "She's well enough to be entertaining Dunn."

Chapter 13

Paul Grantman put down the phone and carefully scrutinized the surface of his desk and his open briefcase. If he had forgotten anything, he'd have Maury, who was leaving a day behind him and Erin, bring it along.

"Paul?" Erin said from the doorway. "The limo's here. Are you ready to go?"

"Yes. More than ready." Anxious was a better description. Now that Holly was gone, he'd sell this damn place. He'd only kept it for her, because it reminded her of her mother, but Jeri-Ann was gone—and now so was Holly. *Damn,* he wouldn't think about that.

Erin looked at the briefcase, her eyes a bit too bright, but—this morning at least—clear and focused. "Is that for the plane? I was hoping . . ." She let her hope trail off. Either that or she'd forgotten what it was.

He stood, snapped his case shut. "Hoping what, darling?"

"That you wouldn't work . . . just this once." She sniffed, touched her nose with her knuckle, the gesture slow and delicate.

Paul came around the desk, took her by the shoulders, then used one hand to lift her chin. "Are you all right?" Her face, although perfectly made-up, was a shade too pale, made paler by the fine rope of rubies and diamonds blazing around her slender throat.

She leaned into him, nuzzled her face into his neck. "I'm fine, been fine for weeks now. You know that." She wrapped her arms around him, pressed herself close. She was wearing the perfume he'd brought back from France last month, and he drew the sweet scent in, enjoying the way it mingled with her own. He ran his hand down her long blond hair, loving the silk texture of it.

They'd been married six miserable, chaotic years, and she still took his breath away.

"Is Maury coming with us to Seattle?" Her question, spoken against his neck, came with breath and heat.

He held her closer, then said what she wouldn't want to hear. "Yes. Tomorrow."

Her body tensed against his. "I don't want him, Paul. And I don't need him."

Because she hadn't pulled away yet, he stroked her hair again. "I know, but it's only for a while. A very short while. He keeps you safe—"

"He spies on me!" When she straightened as if to pull away, he tightened his grip on her. "I can keep myself safe," she said. "I told you that."

He rubbed her back, making slow, circular motions. "I know, and I believe you, but I want you to go to Leeside and—"

She jerked back. "I don't need another rehab. I won't go. I promised, everything would be all right—for Kylie. And it will be." Her eyes were brighter now, both stubborn and pleading.

Her panic transferred to Paul's chest, and his heart fluttered. If he pushed her, she'd run . . . like she had before. She was gone for days before he found her in that awful hotel room. He held her hands, rubbed his thumbs over the soft skin covering her knuckles. "Why don't we talk about this later, sweetheart. When we're settled in the lake house."

"I don't want—"

"Shush now, everything will be okay. Didn't I promise you I'd fix things?"

She swallowed and nodded, but stubbornness clung to her as surely as the French perfume she wore.

"And that's what I'll do. Fix *you*. But you have to help me. It's more important than ever. You want Kylie, don't you?" He kissed her forehead, confused again about his feelings for this broken young woman. He was rich—too rich by most people's standards—reasonably fit, and not bad-looking. He could have any woman he wanted. Why did he only want this one? Again he tilted her chin up. "It's all about Kylie now. We have to focus on her, on bringing her home. If you don't stay straight—If you don't get things right, all the lawyers in the world won't be able to help us."

She nodded jerkily. "I know that."

"No missteps, my darling. Not one."

When she looked away, he turned her head, determined she meet his eyes. "Camryn knows about your problem."

She looked resigned, chewed on her lower lip, then said with no emotion, "Holly, I guess."

"Yes." Paul stepped back and leaned against his desk. "Camryn will fight us for Kylie. She made that clear. And she's a lot tougher than I thought." He paused. "It won't be pretty if she decides to repeat what Holly told her in open court, during a custody battle." He hated to phrase it that way, knew it would hurt her, but Erin had to understand what was at stake: the Grantman name—and Kylie. Paul didn't intend to lose either one—or his beautiful young wife.

"Camryn's . . . nice. She won't do that."

"She will. Erin. She'll do anything to keep Kylie." Paul had been surprisingly unsettled by Camryn's vehemence, and he recognized a worthy adversary when he saw one. He wouldn't underestimate her. He added, "Just as I'll do everything within my power to make sure Kylie comes back to us, where she belongs. But you have to help."

Erin nodded, and her eyes filled with tears. "I'm so sorry, Paul. God, I'm such a fuck-up." She hugged herself, opening and closing her fingers on the blue cashmere covering her upper arms. "I don't know why you put up with me."

He replaced her hands with his. "That's easy. I love you." He smiled at her, then pulled her close. *Christ, if she only knew how much.* "And to prove it, that briefcase you spotted will stay locked until we get to the lake." He'd read most of what was in it anyway—a couple of acquisition proposals, a snapshot legal opinion by Jason on the Kylie custody issue, all maddeningly inconclusive. Nothing that couldn't wait.

This whole business was going to be messy and time-consuming. From what he'd read so far, everybody had a case. Camryn, because she'd been chosen as Kylie's guardian by Holly. Lambert, who wouldn't be the first stepfather to be awarded custody based on "best interests of the child" precedents. And himself, the grandfather, based on blood ties—and money. Lots of money.

Shit, all they needed now was for Kylie's asshole father to turn up and stick his oar in the water.

"Paul?" Erin said.

"Uh-huh?" He pulled himself out of the legal quagmire, looked at his wife.

"I want Kylie. I really, really do," she murmured, fisting her hands in the cotton of his shirt. "I love her, and I'll make her a good mother. A very good mother," she said, her tone slightly high with desperation.

"Of course you will. You'll be a wonderful mother." Paul didn't know whether he was lying to her or himself, but it didn't matter. Certainly it wouldn't hurt for Erin to see herself as taking on the care of a child. She needed a goal, something to hang on to. Caring for Kylie would give her that.

She stepped away from him and gave him a sad but determined look. He'd seen that look before, many times; it was the lead-in to a promise. "I'll do it. I'll stay clean. I'll do it for you, and I'll do it for Kylie." She stopped. "But no rehab. Not again. I can do it alone. I promise."

Paul stifled his disappointment, knew pressuring her was useless. "You'll have her. Don't worry." Not that he intended to trust her with his only grandchild. The world was full of nannies, after all—and there was always Maury. He hoped the illusion of motherhood would be enough to keep her on track—while he raised Kylie the way she should be raised.

"Now, how about we get moving. Riesman has filed his flight plan. No point in his having to do it twice because we're late."

"Most of my things are already in the limo. I'll get my coat and bag."

When she was gone, Paul chewed on their conversation. He wished he felt as sure of himself as he let on. He shrugged off the negative thinking and picked up his briefcase.

This custody thing was merely another game to be played, and when an opponent in the game had something on him, a smart player did what was necessary to neutralize that advantage. The still incomplete files in his case were the beginning of that process.

With Lambert, the absentee-father thing would play against him in court. Perfect.

But Camryn . . . He scratched a brow. Damned if he hadn't come full circle. Years ago he'd ruined her father, and here he was about to repeat the exercise on the daughter. But Trent Derne was a born loser: greedy, dishonest, and possessed of a supersized ego. The daughter—as the saying went—was a different kettle of fish.

But everyone had either a past they wanted hidden or a weakness to be exploited. All he had to do was find hers.

Going back to Seattle was the first step. He'd start working on step two when he got there.

Adam was bored shitless.

He'd been stashed away, limited to the far end of the second floor in this decorator's psycho ward for too damn long. Jesus, Delores must have been on crack when she did this place. Big, bizarre, butt-ugly—and ripe for a reality-show cleanup job.

And Gina was treating him like her very own dirty little secret, insisting he stay in his room until she "sorted things out"—whatever the hell that meant. He'd been a good little boy so far because he needed to keep her happy, but damned if he wasn't burning up with cabin fever.

Not to mention running out of time.

He stood by the window, looked at the lake, and thought about the running path that started somewhere near the Solari property and connected to the park two, maybe three miles away.

He sure could use the fresh air and the workout. So far the only thing getting any exercise was his dick.

He'd forgotten how fucking insatiable Gina was.

Not that he was complaining. Hell, he'd take all the sex he could get—but he hadn't come here to be stowed away in a room for on-demand stud service.

Trouble was, he wasn't in the mood to have his face rearranged either, so he'd stayed low to keep out of good old brother Sebastian's way. That asshole had hated him since college, and Adam was never sure if the loathing was because of Gina or Holly or both. Gina said he'd been "unbalanced" since Holly died, and that he'd blamed Adam for her death. Shit, as if he would ever hurt Holly. Jesus, the words "deranged" and "delusional" were created for Sebastian Solari!

But fuck! He was going stir crazy. As for that "unbalanced" thing Gina mentioned, Adam figured it must run in the family. Lots of brainpower, but more than a few misfiring neurons scattered among the Solaris.

He ran a finger along the top of an ugly lacquered bureau edged in chipped gilt. He was in what Delores called her Harem Room—which in her skewed universe meant beads, fringes, some kind of filmy drapery, and camels, lots of camels. Even the bedspread had camels. He brushed the dust from his hands. Sticky dust, the kind that had been here for a while.

Surely old Delores had enough coin for a goddamn maid. Hell, there'd been a time she'd been rolling in it— thanks to some lucrative marriages and her own savvy business sense. Gina said she'd blown most it, took living beyond her means to a high art, then funked out after her last husband left and took her for a bundle.

Adam understood the "living beyond the means" thing, which gave him and Delores something else to share—along with those few nights of bonking some years back. Back then the mother was even hotter than the daughter, with the added bonus of experience. He smiled. He'd learned a lot from Delores Solari.

But shit . . . this place, every decoratively mangled square foot of it, was depressing. It'd take a crew of five, wielding high-powered blowers for a week, just to get rid of the dust.

He paced away from the window, then back to it. Stuffing his hands in his pockets, he stared outside. The lake glittered a silvery yellow under the morning sun. The old boathouse was still there, listing left now, and tied to it was a half-sunken rowboat. On the dock, a faded red canoe lay bottom up on the cedar planking.

The day was very fine. . . .

To hell with it. He was out of here. He dressed quickly in a sleeveless tee and nylon running shorts, sat on the bed, and pulled on his Nikes.

He glanced at his watch. Almost nine A.M. If he didn't get out of here right now, Gina would arrive for her morning fuck, which he'd be obliged to provide, considering she'd finally—and grudgingly—agreed to "look into" his problem for him. And, God, hadn't that conversation been ugly. Seemed Gina wasn't too keen on the idea of him becoming a daddy at Camryn's expense. What got her interested was when he got her thinking about his staying close by, needing her help with Kylie. *As if.* But at least she'd called Camryn, got some info, and got the ball rolling.

Camryn.

Holly had left her as guardian, never changed a thing. Old Grantman must be having apoplexy, but, according to Gina, it didn't hurt Adam's case one bit. Might even make it easier. It turned out Grantman had already offered Camryn cash for Kylie—which meant Adam's plan was doable. All he had to do now was get his daughter back from Camryn, then give old moneybags a call. Gina said she would take care of everything. What she couldn't take care of was Lando. Lando—and timing—were Adam's problem. So, damn it, he was here for the duration, playing hide and fuck games with Gina.

Camryn . . .

He sucked up some air and stood away from the bed.

That woman was probably the best thing that had ever happened to him—until Holly—and probably the only woman who'd never let him in her bed again. Although it might be fun to try her on. He scratched his chin.

Heading for the door, he decided to take the back way out, a detour around Delores's room. Christ, he was thirty-five years old, and he felt like a goddamn teenager sneaking out for a sixpack.

But he needed the run, and the running path, as luck would have it, ran very close to Camryn's place.

Chapter 14

Camryn pulled her chair to her desk, held the vase closer to the light, and reexamined the markings. Definitely Tiffany. About 1915 was her guess. Under the lamp the vase gleamed to life, its pattern, olive-colored leaves curling upward to wrap gracefully around the vase's neck, looked silky and rich. When she ran her finger over its opalescent surface, she got that tingle; the one she always got when she held something rare and beautiful in her hands.

The vase was a rarity, having come in as a consignment piece from an estate sale along with three unexceptional dinner services. She suspected the Tremblay family had no idea of its value and would be both surprised and pleased.

She should be pleased, too, given the nice commission the vase would earn for her, if only she weren't dreading Dan Lambert's return visit, which could come at any time. The man was determined to resume the conversation so abruptly aborted yesterday when Kylie and Camryn's dad had come back to interrupt it. Camryn really didn't want to talk to Dan Lambert again until she'd talked to Gina. She went cold thinking about what Dan had said. Adam was at Gina's house—Delores's house! It couldn't be!

She picked up the phone, *again* keyed in Gina's number. Nothing. Not even voice mail, because Delores didn't believe in it. She looked at her watch, then at the top of her desk, and let out a frustrated breath. She made a decision: she'd get the Tremblay inventory entered into the computer, do her tax remittance, and head over to the Solari estate. She'd stand at the gate and ring the damn bell until someone answered.

God, Gina could hardly plead agoraphobia and not be home.

"Cammie, are you up there?"

"Yes, Dad." Phone in hand, she stood and went to the top of the stairs. Her dad, his fingers curled around the newel, was at their base. "What is it?" she asked.

"I'm making a snack for Kylie and me. Want one?"

"No, thanks. I'll be up here a while yet." She hit REDIAL for one last try. "You okay with Kylie for a while?" She put the phone to her ear. It was still ringing. Damn it, she'd let it ring. Maybe if it got irritating enough, someone would answer.

"Sure," her dad said. "We're going to watch that kid's program, right after we eat. The one with the pink gorilla? Seems our girl has a thing for pink."

Camryn smiled. Her dad's devotion to Kylie continued to surprise her. She didn't remember getting the same treatment, only a void where a father should have been. But she didn't have time for little-girl jealousy now. She was too grateful for his help. "Thanks. I won't be long."

He waved and left the bottom of the stairs.

"Hello?"

Camryn had forgotten the phone in her hand was still ringing, and the voice startled her. "Delores?"

"No, it's the queen of England."

Camryn rolled her eyes. "This is Camryn, Delores. Can I speak to Gina, please?"

"What about?"

Camryn set her jaw, determined to be pleasant. With Delores it was an ongoing challenge. "Nothing you'd be interested in, and it'll only take a minute. Can you call her . . . please?" She sure as hell wasn't going to mention Adam's name to Delores, and give her more fodder for her nasty grist mill. That would only make Gina's life more miserable than it already was.

"No. She's in her room. Third floor, you know. She *says* she's sick. Barely seen her for days. Can you believe that? And me in this chair!"

Camryn didn't intend to attend Delores's pity party. "I'll come over then. In about an hour. Will you tell her that?"

"It won't do you any good. She won't see you. She won't see anybody. I had to make my own lunch, for God's sake, and me a cripple." The sound of chewing crunched down the line. "I might as well be living with a ghost."

Camryn gave one desperate look at the piles of work on her desk, then made her decision. The tax remittance could wait. "If she's that sick, I'll come over right now."

The line filled with silence.

"Delores?"

"You don't get it, do you?"

"Get what?"

"She's got some guy with her. Hell, you can hear the rocking and rolling all the way to the main floor."

Camryn swore her heart stopped. "What do you mean 'some guy'?"

"Jesus, Camryn, where have you been, under a cabbage? *A guy!* You know, one of those superior beings with the appendage that lets them pee in the woods." She hung up.

Camryn stared at the dead phone, her heart, which seconds ago had stopped in her chest, now thumped so hard it hurt her ears. *It can't be Adam, it absolutely can't be. Gina wouldn't be so stupid! No woman in her right mind would go back for more of that kind of heartache.*

Holly did . . .

Pressing a hand on her chest, she headed for the stairs.

The sound of singing gorillas came from the den. She got a jacket from the hall closet, then went into the den. She kissed the top of Kylie's head, stroked it. "Aunt Cammie's going out for a bit, sweetheart, but I'll be back in time for Kidz-Spot, Okay?" Kidz-Spot was a mother-child preschool play program at the local recreation center. This would be their second day to attend.

"Okay." Kylie got to her feet and, standing on the sofa, gave Camryn a distracted hug and kiss, quickly turning her attention back to the TV, making it obvious her aunt was no competition for apes in pink tutus.

Camryn glanced at her dad. "I have to see Gina. It's important. Do you mind?"

He shook his head, seeming as enthralled by the TV program as Kylie was.

Camryn left them to it and headed down the hall toward the kitchen door. Her car was in a garage she accessed from the lakeside of the house. She was zipping up her jacket as she opened the back door.

Her hand froze to the metal pull-up tab when she saw who stood on the other side, hand raised as if to knock.

"Hey, Cammie, how's it going?"

Adam Dunn!

He smiled down at her, his straight white teeth made even whiter by the contrast to the faint stubble on his handsome face. The face that launched a thousand beds—that's what Gina, Holly, and Camryn had called it before they all started hating him. It was meant to be derogatory, ironic. It was also true. Female heads didn't simply turn when they saw Adam Dunn for the first time; they spun—fast enough to damage their brains. Camryn should know; it had happened to her.

She still couldn't find her voice. He was even better-looking than she remembered. The years had matured his too-pretty face; given it tight, masculine lines; and deepened the color of his sinfully blue eyes. At an even six feet, his body was lean, tan, and muscular. Adam always took care of his assets.

"Surprised?" Hands on hips; thick, silky hair disheveled; his jaw dark with shadow, he raised a brow. "Are you going to invite me in?"

The last place on earth she wanted Adam was in her house, near her dad . . . near Kylie. She gathered up her wits, stepped outside, and closed the door behind her. "Come with me." She brushed past him and headed for the porch stairs leading to the garage.

"Can I have a glass of water first?" He was still smiling when he rubbed his chest. He'd been running, running hard by the look of him. Sweat dampened the front of his sleeveless tee, and his leanly muscled biceps glistened with it. She glanced up at him. His eyes smiled into hers, teased old memories; it was like a sucker punch to the stomach. Even after everything between them—all of it bad—Camryn's body responded and her breathing hitched, and she hated herself for it. Adam Dunn was still a sexual tsunami.

"No." She started down the stairs.

He laughed easily, then followed her.

When they were out of sight of the house, she rounded on him. "What are you doing here?"

He leaned against the garage, one knee cocked so his foot was flat against the old boards. "Being friendly," he said. "You remember you and I being friendly, don't you, Camryn?" He ran his liquid gaze over her, toe to head, his eyes warm and appreciative. The kind of look that made a woman feel ten years younger, ten pounds lighter, and ten minutes away from the best orgasm of her life. "You look good. Better than good. Spectacular."

"And you're not answering my question." When it looked as if he were going to touch her cheek, she took a step back, stumbled.

"You do remember, don't you?" he said, dropping his hand to his side. "The night on the lake, you and I making out on the picnic table." His gaze deepened. "I know I haven't forgotten. What man could?"

He hadn't moved, but the intimacy in his gaze made it seem as if he had. And damn it, his words brought it back— all of it. The hot sex. The love she'd had for him, or thought she had. And the ugliness of it. Like the moment she'd walked in on him and Holly in the aptly named Cozy Inn motel room. Thank God, Gina had told her where they were, encouraged her to see Adam for who he was. "I remember you were a faithless bastard who slept with anything that wore a skirt—or tight jeans."

His smile was easy, confident. "I was much more discriminating than that." He eyed her with amusement. "Although you got the 'tight' part right. Definitely a prerequisite."

She ignored his last words and his sexy smile. "As much fun as it might be for you to review your conquests, can we stick to the matter at hand? What are you doing here?"

"Checking out the latest crop of virgins?"

"Very funny." She folded her arms.

"I thought so," he said, then shrugged easily. "I heard about the Solaris, the shooting. I thought I'd drop in, see how Gina was doing, pay my respects."

She snorted, loud and ingloriously. "You don't know what the word 'respect' means. Try again."

His seductive mouth curved into a boyish grin, and he touched his chest over his heart. "You hurt me, baby, you really do."

"I'm not your 'baby,' and you know as much about 'hurt' as you do 'respect.' I *know* you, Adam. You don't 'drop in' unless you want something."

He shoved away from the garage wall, and his expression turned . . . serious. At least it seemed so. You never could be sure with Adam. He ran his fingers through his tangle of sleek chestnut hair, then looked away from her. "I was in Boston when Holly was killed, you know. I couldn't go to the funeral"—he glanced back at her—"for the obvious reason."

His tragic pose didn't move her. "And what reason would that be? Grantman? Because he'd kill you on sight? Or Dan Lambert? Who'd do the same . . ."—and here she watched him carefully—"because you were having an affair with his wife."

"You know." He was unperturbed.

"I do now." Camryn's stomach clenched, filled up with the ugly truth she could no longer deny. *Oh, Holly, you fool. You complete and utter fool.*

"Holly was never his, Camryn. You know that. What was between Holly and me, it was . . . pure chemistry. She knew it. I knew it. We never really lost touch. Like the song says, Holly was mine from hello—" He stopped, his face tinged with melancholy. "Hell, maybe I was always hers. Who the hell knows."

"You left her fast enough when she got pregnant with your child." Camryn didn't try to hide her contempt.

"Ah, the magic words. My child." He rested his amazing eyes on her. "You wanted to know why I was here? There's your answer."

Camryn couldn't get her breath. She couldn't have heard right. "What are you saying?"

"I'm saying I've come for what's mine. Kylie." He took a few steps away, then turned back. "She's my daughter. I have a right."

Camryn's world went gray, then black, then blazing red. "Right? You have no rights. You gave them up when Kylie was born. Holly made sure of it."

"Under duress. Under extreme duress. Undue pressure."

He looked smooth. Sly. As if he were already in the witness stand, playing the deprived and misused father. As if he were already being coached. She didn't like it, didn't like to think where the coaching might have come from. "Duress you were well paid for, as I recall."

"The money? The legal stuff? All Paul's idea. Holly would never have done it on her own."

"Really? Then why do you suppose she went to Paul— something she hated doing—for his help to get rid of you?" His arrogance overwhelmed her. That, and his utter incomprehension of what he had done. "You walked out on Holly two months before Kylie was born, for God's sake! And you didn't walk alone." She huffed out a breath. "There was a woman, as I remember, but, then, with you, there's always a woman."

He shrugged, untroubled. "I made a mistake."

"You married your 'mistake,' Adam, a week after Kylie was born! Holly was barely home from the hospital."

"Another mistake. Which doesn't mean I don't love my daughter."

"You love—" She stared at him, speechless, all the breath leaving her lungs in one stunning exhalation. Damned if he didn't look as if he believed himself. When she could inhale again, her chest came alive with anger. "You don't love anyone but yourself, Adam. You never have. If you've come back for Kylie, it isn't out of love. But whatever the reason, you'll fail. You can count on it." She dropped her arms to her sides, faced him openly, and spoke very, very clearly. "Kylie is mine now. Holly wanted me to care for her, and that's what I'm going to do."

"I admit I was surprised Holly hadn't changed guardianship. I thought for sure I'd be taking on rich old Grandpa. Jesus, Grantman must have shit himself." He looked amused. "Turns out it's just as well. From what I've learned, it's pretty doubtful that guardianship thing will stand if a biological parent comes forward—full of remorse for his past mistakes and brimming with love for his lost child." He paused. "Like I said. I want what's mine."

Camryn wouldn't let him see her fear, wouldn't let him see her sweat. "It's never going to happen, Adam." *And I'll take Kylie and run before I let you have her.* "Holly did what she thought was best for Kylie. If you were any kind of man, you'd do the same. Which means going back to whoever's bed you crawled out of, and leaving things as they are." Too late, she realized that bed she was referring to might be Gina's.

"That's one plan." His smile deepened as if at some private amusement. "Or you could marry me, and we'll raise the kid together. That'd sure as hell set Paul's teeth on edge." Before she could stop him, he touched her hair, his eyes narrowing. "Hell of an idea, actually. That way I could crawl into your bed—get the honeymoon started."

She blinked at the sudden turn in the conversation. "You really are crazy."

"You going to give me the 'if you were the last man on earth' speech, Cammie?" He bent his head, met her eyes. "Because you and I both know that's not true. You know how happy I can make you when I set my mind—and hands—to it."

Her stomach rolled into a hard, tight snarl. "Get the hell—"

The crunch of gravel made them both look up. Camryn looked around the corner of the garage toward the front of the house. There was enough view for her see a black Navigator pulled up close to her front stairs.

Adam followed her gaze. "Who is it?"

"Dan Lambert." She looked back at Adam, gave him a blank gaze. "Care for an introduction?"

The sound of her awful door buzzer poured out the open kitchen window.

"I'll take a pass on that," he said.

"I figured you would." She stepped up to him, put her face inches from his, and met his eyes. "Go away, Adam." She lowered her voice to a quiet and urgent tone. "If you've got a decent bone in your body, you'll leave Kylie alone, and you'll leave Gina alone. She's fragile right now. She can't handle . . . you. You have nothing to offer either Kylie or Gina."

"You might want to check with Gina on that 'nothing to offer' idea of yours," he said, and before she could stop him, he took her face between his hands and kissed her hard, moving his mouth over hers as if it belonged there. Then, holding her, their faces so close she could smell his clean, mint-scented breath, see the heat in his eyes, he whispered, "You still taste good, Cammie—exactly like I remember."

Breathless, she jerked from his grasp. "Get the hell out of here. And don't come back."

He touched her cheek with the back of his hand. "I'll be in touch—or rather my lawyer will." He paused, and his expression darkened. "I'm going to claim my daughter, and it'll take a lot more than a paltry hundred grand to change that." With that he stepped behind the other side of the garage and disappeared into the trees and tangled brush on the vacant property next door.

Camryn put her fingers to her mouth, then the back of her hand, determined to rub the sense of him from her lips, the scent of him from her nose.

Dear God, he's come back to claim Kylie.

And he was at Gina's . . . Gina, who'd sworn she'd never see or speak to Adam Dunn again, was helping him.

Under her disappointment, her fear of what might happen now that Adam was back, she felt betrayed, and stupid that she'd been so incredibly naive in underestimating his attraction.

Camryn turned to face the calm waters of the lake. Her

mind and her heart in turmoil, she tried to sort things through. *But, God! First Holly, having an affair with him, and now Gina* . . .

It didn't make sense.

Gina, whom Adam had humiliated in high school, used in college, and walked out on without a word. Adam was always Holly's bad-boy lover—the boy/man she'd used as a freedom ticket to get away from Paul's control, but when it came to dealing with him, she always gave as good as she got. In many ways they were a matched set, both rash, both . . . self-centered. When Adam walked out on her and Kylie, Holly made certain to protect Kylie's interests. Holly was a fool for love, a thrill-seeker, and she'd chosen to play too close to Adam's flame, but she knew how to take care of herself.

Not so Gina. For her, Adam was a sexual toxin. When Gina first got involved with him, she'd given new meaning to the word doormat. She'd said so herself, when she came to her senses—right after Adam slept with Delores. Camryn shuddered. As low points went, the Gina-Delores episode was Adam's personal best. That was during their third year of college, and to Camryn's knowledge, Gina hadn't seen him since.

She couldn't imagine Gina taking him in, but, then, she couldn't imagine Holly having an affair with him, either. Delores was right: Camryn had been living under a damn cabbage.

But cabbage or not, she knew this was the worst possible time for Adam to come back into Gina's life.

So how could she protect her friend? From herself? From Adam? All Camryn had were words and warnings, while Adam had . . . whatever it was he had that made bubbling oatmeal of women's brains.

"Did I interrupt? A kissing cousin, perhaps?"

She looked up to see Dan Lambert standing on her lakeside porch. Obviously, he'd been there a while, watching her. "No. Nothing." She tried to switch her head from concern about Gina, to what, if anything, to tell him about Adam. She was also trying to figure out why she was glad he'd shown up when he did—and what those wings fluttering in her stomach meant. She headed toward him.

You like him, Camryn. It's that simple—and that complex.

Casually dressed in gray slacks and a black shirt, he was leaning against the post at the top of the stairs. His arms were crossed, and while he looked strong and resourceful, she felt limp and ineffectual, still shell-shocked by Adam's reentry into Gina's life—and hers. Looking at Dan Lambert, the strength and honesty of him, she was baffled all over again at why Holly would risk a man like this for Adam.

"That was Dunn, wasn't it?" he said, when she'd taken the three stairs that brought her to his side.

Her reaction to his words was to step away, get some think time, but he stopped her. Wrapping a hand around her upper arm and fixing his gaze on her lips, he smoothed the corner of her mouth with his thumb. "You need a touch-up."

"Let me go."

He didn't. "When you answer my question." His grip was unyielding.

"Yes. It was Adam Dunn." She couldn't think of one good reason not to tell him. He was going to find out soon enough. She might as well share her misery—her fear. When he released his grip, she pulled a tissue from her jacket pocket and wiped off what was left of her lipstick.

"Would I be off-base if I said you were pretty damn cozy with a guy who quite possibly murdered my wife—your best friend?"

"Adam didn't kill anyone."

"And you know that on the basis of one liplock?" He shook his head, his disgust obvious.

She wouldn't dignify that remark with an answer, nor did she feel compelled to defend herself. Let him think whatever he wanted to think. "But, you're right—he's staying at Gina's."

"Our friend Dunn really gets around." His tone was dry.

Camryn couldn't deny that. "He's no one's friend." She turned, leaned her backside against the rail, and looked at him. "And he wants Kylie." *And I think he's working on Gina to help him.* She kept the last to herself, would until she knew for sure.

He cocked his head and looked down at her, looking puzzled. "Kylie? What's he got to do with Kylie?"

Oh my God! He doesn't know.

Camryn's nerves jumped, her throat closed, and then anger flared. For the briefest of moments she thought that if Holly were alive, she'd kill her herself. What she'd done to Dan and Kylie, with her lies, secrets, and infidelity made Camryn's stomach turn. It was as if she'd never truly known her friend, as if Adam's souring presence in their lives had made them strangers. She remembered Adam's words, "never really lost touch." Camryn hadn't seen, or had refused to see, the extent of Holly's obsession with Adam; she never had let go of him. Like addicts everywhere, she'd simply taken her obsession into the shadows.

"Are you going to tell me what the hell that bastard has to do with Kylie, or do I go over to your friend's house and find out for myself?" Lambert glared down at her.

"I'm sorry." She paused, gathered some composure, feeling much like a doctor or police officer who had to report a death in the family. "I assumed you knew. Adam Dunn is Kylie's biological father."

Chapter 15

When Camryn's words registered, it took only seconds before Dan processed and accepted them. Somehow it made sense of things. His wife's lover was Kylie's biological father. He wouldn't have guessed, but maybe he should have.

His gaze caught and followed a powerboat skimming the lake waters and leaving a silver-white wake; he watched it until his breathing eased. For a time he didn't speak, just let the last few months of anger, confusion, and downright fucking misery roll over him.

He'd come by Camryn's house to visit his daughter and spend time with Camryn, work at getting her to trust him. Instead he was kicked back to his doomed marriage, his first serious attempt at building a relationship. A goddamn fiasco, if ever there was one. The only good thing to come out of it was Kylie.

Camryn, standing beside him, chewed on her lower lip for a moment, then said again, "I'm sorry. I shouldn't have been the one to tell you." She appeared to study him. "You don't look surprised."

"In the last few months, I've been nothing but surprised. I guess by now the expression has a look of permanency." He took his eyes from the lake and looked down at her. Her shoulder-length brown hair, catching the breeze, ruffled around her face. In the daylight her hair was shot with dark gold. He hadn't noticed that before. "I asked her once about Kylie's father. She said he was the biggest mistake of her life, and he was out of it. For good. She said there was no need to tell me anything about him, because he'd never be a part of Kylie's life. She'd made sure of that, she said." He shrugged. "That was it. She didn't want to say more, so I didn't push it."

"Didn't want to know, maybe?"

"Maybe."

A sad half-smile played briefly over Camryn's mouth. "Strange . . ."

He raised a brow, waited.

"Holly pulled out all the stops to keep Adam out of Kylie's life, but she couldn't keep him out of hers."

"Explain."

She pulled her jacket closed and crossed her arms. "After Kylie was born, Holly went to her father—something she rarely did—and asked him to ensure Adam stayed out of the picture. Paul was more than happy to oblige." There was that half-smile again. "You think he didn't like you? He despised Adam. He was ecstatic that Holly had, as he said, 'come to her senses.' Adam's parental rights were terminated based on 'abandonment and parental disinterest.'" She frowned slightly. "I think those are the right words. Paul wrote a fat check to make sure Adam didn't fight it. He didn't. He took the money and headed off into the sunset—with another woman. Paul was happy enough to write the check. He said it 'spoke to character,' and if the 'bastard'—his words—ever came back, that cancelled check would come in real handy."

"He was probably right." Dan moved to the rail, looked across the lake, leaving his back to her. "But you say he's come back—for Kylie."

"That's what he said."

"Why would he do that?" Dan turned to face her. "After all this time?"

She brushed a strand of hair from her eyes, looked uncomfortable—or angry. He couldn't tell. The wind had kicked up and was sending a chill. She hugged herself. "Money."

"He wants his kid so he can make a profit off her?" Something in Dan's stomach curdled even as he thought it was a damn good thing all it would take was cash to get rid of Dunn. "And Grantman would go for that." He didn't phrase it as a question.

"He'd pay what he had to—for Erin."

"Jesus!" As "low" went, Dan didn't know who the hell was worse, Grantman for trying to buy Kylie for his wife, or Dunn for selling her. But as a motive for murder, Dunn's scummy plans might interest the Boston Police Department—more so considering Holly had kissed the guy off days before she was shot. He'd let the police know about it while he did some digging of his own. When he was finished, he'd know the label in Dunn's briefs.

Dan cocked a brow. "Has it occurred to you that you're in the middle of all this? That you're Dunn's latest obstacle—one he didn't expect?"

"Don't worry. I can handle Adam." She shot him a calm glance.

He studied the serious face of the woman standing beside him, impressed by her confidence but feeling edgy, afraid she wasn't taking Dunn seriously enough.

I don't want her hurt.

The thought, coming hard and fast, made his gut tight and his head feel as if it had been invaded by aliens. *What the hell!* And he thought he'd been so goddamn smart: get close, get closer . . . He'd thought it was all about Kylie, keeping his daughter. When the hell had it changed? Become all about this steady, brown-haired woman standing next to him, a woman who looked as if she'd have no problem repelling an assault from an armored tank—but who might also have done a little underestimating of her own.

"You sure of that?" he finally asked.

"Adam's a fool—an arrogant fool. A Peter Pan. He's never been able to see anything through in his whole faithless life. I don't think his wanting Kylie will be any different. It's a whim. The chance of the moment. With a few delays, some boring days, and no instant gratification, he'll get bored, or some other 'chance' will show up in a tight skirt and stilettos. When it does, he'll move on as if nothing happened. As if Kylie hadn't happened." Her mouth tensed. "He's a man with no staying power except in—" She stopped, reddened.

Dan got her drift. Didn't like it, and sure as hell didn't want to think about it.

When he said nothing, she lifted her chin, added, "I know what you're thinking—"

"I doubt that." Hell, he didn't know himself.

She chewed her lower lip a couple of times, then said, "Adam and I have a history. A very ancient history."

"Your business."

"Yes, it is."

He decided the smart thing was to get back to the matter at hand. "So you propose to handle him by ignoring him."

She shook her head, looked at him with determined, very sharp eyes. "No, what I intend to do is make things complicated, difficult, and confrontational. Adam doesn't do any of those very well."

"Sounds risky." *And with no guarantee.* "A lot of time has passed. He may have changed."

"He hasn't changed." She spoke with certainty, again shaking her head. "Men like Adam never change."

Dan didn't have her sense of conviction, and, more than that, he hated the idea of Camryn playing games with Dunn, putting herself at risk. Didn't like it at all. "What makes you so sure?"

"He proposed to me."

Dan's brain darkened, and he pushed away from the railing he'd been leaning against. "Say again?"

"He asked me to marry him, suggested we raise Kylie together."

"You're serious."

"So was he—even if he didn't know it. If I'd said yes, he'd be in my bed—house—right now."

"Not a guy to miss the main chance, right?"

She gave him a clear-eyed, knowing look, and a first-hand view of the fierce intelligence and piercing intuition Holly had told him about. "Yes. Awful, isn't it?" she said, half smiling. "But, then, people stoop to anything to get what they want. Seduction. Sex. Even marriage. Whatever it takes." She paused. "I should know." The last she said more to herself than to him.

"Why am I sensing a subtext here?"

She kept her gaze fixed on him. "I'm not a fool, Dan. And subterfuge isn't your strong point—which I might add is a point in your favor. I've already figured out that the 'shortest distance between two points' you mentioned on the plane means you getting Kylie through me."

Before he could answer—not that he had one—she headed for the door.

"I've got to go," she said, as if she hadn't just nailed his intentions to the nearest brick wall. "I've got work to do before Kylie and I leave for the recreation center. So if you want to visit with her, now's the time." When she was at the door, she turned back, gave him a speculative gaze. "Actually, you and I—and Kylie—as a team against the Grantman fortune isn't such a bad idea. But I've already married once for the wrong reasons. I don't intend to do it again."

"I don't remember mentioning marriage," he said, sounding as dry and stiff as a dusty old book.

She made a soft huff. "Considering it's definitely that 'shortest distance' you mentioned on the plane, I'd say that as a concept, it crossed your mind." She cocked a brow, waited.

He considered his answer. "A lot of things crossed my mind when I met you, Camryn. Most of them inappropriate, considering the situation we were both dealing with."

"Excellent non-answer," she said, "which means we'll need to talk later. We have to clear the air between us—for Kylie's sake." She stopped, seemed to think. "Actually, there's something else we should do." She straightened as if an idea had suddenly shaped to the right form. "Come for dinner tonight. Afterward, we'll go over to Gina's place. It's time you met Adam face to face." She smiled, a smile tinged with wickedness. "Like I told you, he doesn't like complications, and as 'complications' go, you're grade A."

She walked into the house.

Dan watched her go, wondered when the sobbing woman who'd hugged him in the church had morphed into a one-woman assault brigade without his noticing. And a woman who laid all her cards on the table.

His kind of woman.

She'd seen through him as if his innards were wrapped in cellophane. And she wasn't above using him in her game with Dunn. He smiled. Seemed it was a day for underestimating. And she was right, he should meet Dunn.

All he had to do was keep himself from killing the bastard when he did.

Gina opened Adam's bedroom door for about the hundredth time. It was well after lunch. He was there—finally!—lolling on the bed with a magazine. Relief nearly brought her to her knees.

"Where have you been?" Her voice was higher than she would have liked, and the intensity of her feelings at seeing him back where he belonged was too strong for her tired and confused mind. She hadn't slept since he'd arrived, her brain in a constant frenzy of sex-dreams, love-dreams, and terror that he'd leave her.

She swallowed, stared at him. This morning, when she'd come to his room and discovered him gone, that terror had come alive.

She'd thought he'd left. Dear God, she'd thought he'd left her . . . again.

He tossed the magazine aside and sat on the edge of the bed. "I went for a run."

He wasn't lying; running shorts and a tee were on the floor at his feet. "I told you to stay here."

"I needed some air, baby. This place is making me crazy."

"Where? Where did you go for a run?"

"The lake path."

"Did anyone see you?" *Did you see anyone . . . ?* Gina didn't want that. Gina wanted him safe, close, and exclusive. She didn't want other women looking at him, wanting him. She couldn't trust them, couldn't trust Adam . . . She was suddenly hot, and her vision blurred. *I have to keep him here for me. Only for me.*

He shrugged, dropped his glance. "A couple of other runners." He got up from the bed. "Now you're here, I'm going to take a shower." He grinned at her, his even, white teeth a bright flash in the shadow of his unshaven jaw. "I was waiting for you. Hoping you'd help." He started to strip off his jeans.

Gina's lungs stilled, overwhelmed by the sound of his zipper going slowly down. Its metallic scrape filled the room—a hundred-piece orchestra playing the opening prelude for what she craved. She hadn't dressed this morning—

too rattled by Adam's absence—so she was still wearing her robe and nightgown. No panties. Nothing to stop the warm rush between her legs. She tightened them. It was a sin, a sickness to want a man this much. To be ready, always ready—and needing his touch the way a newborn needed its mother's breast.

She was ill . . . she was very, very ill. And the only time she felt right was when she was with Adam. "Promise me you won't go out again," she pleaded.

"Sure, sweetheart. I'll stay right here until we get things sorted out on the custody thing." He gave her a stunning gaze, his eyes hot and narrowed. "Anything yet?"

He was talking about Kylie. Jesus, when he got Kylie he'd be gone. She was sure of it. "I've got some ideas." She lied. In some ways Adam was such a fool. He couldn't see there was no incentive for Gina to settle his affairs. She did that, he'd be gone. And this time she wasn't going to let him go. Ever.

Adam pulled his sleeveless tee over his head, tossed it on the bed. "That's good," he said. "I knew you'd come through." He stopped, put his hands on his hips. "Actually, I've got an idea or two of my own. That run did a lot to clear my head."

Avid, Gina drank him in—no sucked him in: his tan chest with its fine dusting of hair, his open zipper. He was wearing black underwear. She liked black underwear. She liked all of Adam's underwear. But she liked what was under it even more.

He watched her watch him, but she couldn't stop what was in her eyes. When she raised her eyes from the bulge in his pants, he gave her a knowing gaze. "Poor baby," he said, putting his hand out and making a come-here signal with his fingers. "You look as hot for me as I am for you."

She touched herself, couldn't help it. "I'm wet. I look at you and I get wet." She walked to him, put her arms around him, and hugged him hard and close. "I love you, Adam. I'm crazy with it." And that's what she was—crazy, mad, utterly insane to love this terrible, seductive man. She started to cry, didn't want to lift her head, let him see the depth and despair of her need. "I don't want you to leave. Promise me you'll never leave me again."

"I promise."

"You have to love me, Adam . . . a little." She was begging and she didn't care. She had to hear it. Had to believe it.

He stroked her hair, kissed her head, and held her close. "I love you, baby. You know I do."

Liar! "Do you, Adam? Do you really?" She wanted to hear the lie again.

He surged against her, his hardened penis jutting into her softness. "Sure I do. Can't you tell?" He pushed against her again, and her breathing stopped. "And it's a lot more than us being sensational in bed. You're special to me, Gina. You have to believe that. Leaving you was the worst thing I ever did."

His words washed over her, into her. Maybe everything would be all right. He'd stay. They'd get married. She'd look after him forever, be a mother to his daughter—everything as it was meant to be. They'd make love, morning, noon, and night . . . forever. She could make it work. She brushed at her tears.

Voices, shrill and insistent, cried from her mind. *Foolish, foolish woman. He's here because he needs you, not because he wants you.*

It didn't matter, as long as he stayed. She had to make him stay.

"I love you, Gina," he repeated. "Come and take that shower with me, and I'll show you how much." He slid his hand between them, touched her wet heat through the silk of her nightgown. His hot breath seared her neck.

She gave him one last desperate embrace, forced herself back far enough to look into his beautiful face.

He smiled down at her; the smile was crooked, his eyes were filled with sex and seduction.

His mouth was smeared with lipstick.

Chapter 16

The night was black, enveloped in cloud, and threatening rain when Dan arrived at Camryn's door. He was met by her father, Trent, who, as usual, looked none too happy to see him. So far, since their initial introduction when Trent had been board-stiff and cool as the northern country Dan had just come from, the two men had avoided each other. Now, with Camryn apparently not yet home, avoidance wasn't in the cards.

Dan stood outside the door, holding a bottle of wine and a coloring book and crayons for Kylie. Trent, looking paler than usual, stood inside. He smoothed his thinning hair, stood there frowning, as if the decision regarding Dan's entry was his to make.

"Come in," he said finally, fully opening the door. "Camryn decided to take Kylie for a haircut, so she's running late." Even having to offer that bit of explaining seemed to annoy him.

Dan stepped inside. "Where can I put these?" He lifted the wine and gift for his daughter.

Trent jerked his head to indicate the kitchen, then spied the cover of the book. "I got her one like that yesterday. So you know."

Recognizing one-upmanship when he saw it, Dan said, "Then I guess she'll have two." He'd sensed the man's proprietary attitude toward Kylie, but so far he'd let it go. The way he saw it, the more people who loved a kid, the better off they were. The safer they were. No reason those people had to love each other in the process, and getting bent about it served no purpose. Dan headed for the kitchen and was surprised when Trent followed. He set the stuff he'd brought on the table.

"What's your game, anyway?" Trent asked.

Dan turned to see him standing near the counter, his expression hovering somewhere between anger and suspicion. "Game?"

"Kylie's not even your natural daughter, for God's sake. So why do you keep coming around, making trouble about things?"

"Things? Like custody, you mean?"

Trent's pale face turned stubborn. "Kylie's where she belongs, with my daughter. You should stop messing with that. Cammie will be a good mom."

Dan took a second to get himself under control. "I never said she wouldn't."

"So, why the hell don't you hoof it on out of here and leave things as they are? The way your wife wanted them. Holly and Camryn were friends since grade school. Hell, I've known from the get-go how she wanted Cammie to look after her girl."

"That right?"

"I knew about her keeping it a secret from her father, too. No surprise there—if you know anything about Grantman." He closed his lips, moved them tight over his teeth as if to keep them closed.

"I know enough, but it seems you know more. About him, and about something that doesn't concern you."

For the first time since Dan had met him, real color tinged his face. Fusing to his normally gray pallor, it was falsely bright, almost feverish. "It concerns me, Lambert, because Camryn loves that little girl. Any fool can see that. She wants that child more than anything, and I want her to have what she wants. I might not have been much of a father, but I won't stand by and let you take Kylie away from her."

"It sounds to me," Dan said, "as if you care about your daughter, and if that's true, you shouldn't have a problem understanding how I feel about mine."

"Kylie's not your daughter, not your blood. It's not the same. Not even close."

"Have it your way." He didn't bother to remind him Kylie wasn't Camryn's *blood* either.

Enough said, as far as Dan was concerned. He headed to the sink, intending to get a glass of water and drop this conversation in cold storage. More words weren't going to change anything.

None of them—not Trent, not Paul, and not Camryn—were ever going to understand what Kylie meant to him. To them he was an inconvenient stepdad who, if he'd go along with the stereotype, should have been long gone by now and be relieved when some new "daddy" took his place—a thought that hit Dan's heart like a blunt bullet. The thing none of them got was that he loved Kylie, and she loved him. And that love was a promise.

He took a drink of water, turned, and leaned against the counter. Trent's brow furrowed, and his mouth was working overtime. He rubbed at his temple and pulled his lower lip under his top teeth. "You're too damned sure of yourself, Lambert. You think everything's going to go your way." He wagged his head. "Take it from one who knows, life doesn't work that way."

"How does it work?" Dan crossed his arms, one hand still holding the glass.

"When your luck's running, life's a feast. Nothing too

much. Nothing too good. Nothing out of reach. You feel like a god."

"And when that luck changes?"

Trent took a breath. "It's a goddamn battering ram. And it doesn't let up. Pound, pound, pound." He dropped the hand he'd been rubbing his temple with to his side, his expression flattened. It was as if he'd had an energy drain or a sudden mood shift. "You don't always get what you want, Lambert. Remember that. You goddamn don't."

"Maybe not, but by and large, I think we get what we deserve."

"Yeah? Well, if that's true, my Cammie deserves a run of luck, deserves to have the child she wants. You interfere with that, and I—"

"Sorry, I'm late. The traffic was awful." Camryn and Kylie entered the room, Camryn laden with grocery bags and both wet from the rain now pounding outside. Kylie, wearing a yellow rain slicker so bright it made her red hair pale by comparison, trailed behind Camryn, but when she spotted Dan, she went straight for him.

"I got my hair cut, Daddy. In a big-lady place. Look." She bent her head awkwardly to show him the back, where its curly copper length had been trimmed to somewhere below her ears.

"It looks beautiful." He stretched out his arms to her, and she didn't waste a heartbeat before rushing into them.

"Aunt Cammie says you're eating with us. Are you?" she asked.

He swung her up and settled her against his chest. She was so tiny, so perfect, she always made him think of porcelain, fine and precious. "That's right, princess." He glanced at Camryn, caught her eye. "Aunt Cammie was very nice to invite me." She looked hurried, but happy. They'd had a good time, Camryn and his Kylie.

Camryn shifted her gaze to the bags, started removing

groceries. "It's going to be rushed," she said. "A quick chicken-and-pasta"—she looked at Dan—"if that's okay."

"Sounds great." This time when their gazes met over Kylie's fiery little head, they held. For the briefest of moments, it felt as if they were seeing each other for the first time. A good feeling, he thought. A very good feeling. But Camryn was right, they did need to talk. They needed to sort this Adam Dunn thing out. Before Dan called the Boston cops, he wanted every bit of information on Dunn he could get. And he wanted Camryn to see things his way. He smiled, shifted Kylie higher in his arms. "Can I give you a hand with anything?"

"No. It'll be faster if I do it. But you can pour some of that." She gestured to the wine he'd brought, which still sat on the kitchen table. "A glass of that would be perfect right now." Her gaze settled on him, then on Kylie, who'd put her head on his shoulder, and a shadow drifted between them. "Kylie, why don't you go with Grandpa Trent for a while, your da . . . Dan and I need to talk for a bit."

"I want to help. I can cook. I can." The little girl pushed back from Dan's chest to stare him down and make her case. "Tell her, Dadd—"

A blast . . . sharp, clear, deadly. The ear getting it, the brain not comprehending. Yet.

Time coalesced, a second into an eternity.

A shattering . . . the window blown out, pieces flying like crystal through the bright kitchen light.

A searing . . . a branding iron at full heat drawn fast and hard across his bicep.

"Jesus!" Dan dropped, took Kylie with him and tucked her under him, put his hand on her head.

She didn't make a sound.

"Down! Everybody down!" he shouted.

"What the hell?" Trent lunged backward into the hall.

Camryn dropped instantly and curled into a ball, her hands over her head. She was in the open, the easiest target from the window the shots were coming from. Lakeside. Whoever the hell it was had to be standing on the porch.

The second shot hit the open fridge door, where a split second earlier Camryn had been about to put away a quart of milk. The milk hadn't made it and pooled on the floor near her head.

The third shot shattered a jar sitting on the counter above.

A grocery bag fell to the floor, splitting on impact. Three apples rolled across the floor.

"Kylie!" Camryn screamed. "Where's Kylie!" She started scrambling toward Dan.

"She's okay. I've got her. Stay down. For God's sake, stay down!"

The next shot came from the hall.

Dan looked up. Trent stood in the doorway, holding a gun with both hands. He fired twice more into the blackness outside the shattered window.

Silence. Then the sound of rain slamming on the porch roof.

Trent leaned against the door jamb, looking as spent as the gun in his hand. His eyes were closed in a tight grimace.

"Dad, are you all right?" Camryn's words came in an uneven whisper.

He was panting, rubbing his chest. "I'm okay." His voice was weak, hoarse. "I think I scared them off."

Camryn pulled herself by her forearms to where Dan, still sheltering Kylie, was starting to get up.

"Take her," he said. "But stay low."

Kylie dug her fingers into Dan's shoulder as if she'd never let go. No tears, but her eyes were wide as saucers.

"It's okay, princess. Everything's okay." He stroked her hair. "Be a good girl now, and go with Aunt Cammie."

When Camryn took her from Dan's arms, Kylie clung to her with the same ferocity. She started to cry.

"Stay down and head for the hall," Dan said to Camryn. She did as he said, and crawling with Kylie tucked under her, she disappeared into the hall.

Trent, pale as a sheet, still stood in the doorway, an easy target from the kitchen window. Dan moved toward him, grabbed his hand and pulled him down, prodded him to follow Camryn.

"Give me that." He took the Smith and Wesson from his limp hand. "You okay?"

Trent nodded, but he looked anything but okay.

"Stay close to them." Dan jerked his head toward Camryn and Kylie.

"Yeah. Okay." The older man pulled himself a few feet down the hall to where the three of them huddled, Trent like a rag doll, Camryn and Kylie in a tight hug.

Dan checked the gun. Two rounds left. He was damn sure the shooter was gone, but he intended to take a look anyway. He glanced around; except for a couple of decorative panels in the front door, a combination of obscure and stained glass, there were no windows, no sightline into the hall. He went to the phone stand, grabbed the phone, and brought it back and handed it to Camryn. "Call 911."

She nodded. "What are you going to do?"

"Take a look."

"You think that's smart?" Her voice was a little high, he noticed, but nowhere near panic. Good.

"I think it's probably a waste of time. I'm pretty sure your dad's wild-west routine scared them off. But it won't hurt to make sure."

Camryn, hugging a sobbing Kylie to her breast, looked as if she was going to protest but then said, "There's some security lighting between the porch and garage. The switch is outside the door. To your left."

"Okay. Make that call."

To Camryn it seemed as if the police were there in seconds. She guessed they didn't get too many shootings on North Lake Washington in the middle of the week. They were fast enough that they picked Dan up outside the house—with her father's gun dangling from his hand. Her heart had stopped when they'd walked him into the house, guns drawn, while Dan calmly explained the situation and waited for her and her father's corroboration.

"You're bleeding," she said to Dan, feeling numb and sounding stupid. She should have noticed before. His shirtsleeve was soaked with blood. She walked over to him and took his hand; the blood had dripped down to between his fingers.

"It's a scrape. We'll deal with it when this is over."

"We'll deal with it now," she said. "Can you hold Kylie?"

He took Kylie with his good arm, kissed her cheek. "Always."

Kylie, sucking her thumb, something Camryn hadn't seen her do in the past year, put her head on Dan's shoulder.

Camryn shook off her thickheadedness and headed for the bathroom, where she foraged for her meager first-aid supplies. Hurrying back to the living room, she saw Dan still in conversation with the officer. He continued answering questions while she tore away his shirtsleeve. She took a good look. He was right; it wasn't much more than a scrape from the grazing heat of a bullet intended for . . . who? She shuddered, concentrated on the job at hand, and started patching him up as best she could.

"And you have no idea who might have fired the bullets?" the officer asked Dan for at least the third time.

"Nope," Dan answered, wincing when Camryn applied antiseptic, then a bandage on his upper arm.

"Nor you, ma'am? This is your house, I understand. No neighbor problems? Kid problems? Anything like that?"

She shook her head. "I'm sorry. I wish I could help, but I haven't a clue."

He flipped his notebook shut. "Okay." He nodded at Dan's arm. "Best get that looked at. Gunshots, even minor ones like that, can get infected."

Dan nodded, put his hand over the bandage.

"Are you okay?" she asked him.

"Yeah, but I could use a glass of water."

When she handed him the water, she took Kylie from his arms and watched him down half the glass. "Thanks."

The police worked the property for another half hour; she could see their flashlights crisscrossing over her poor excuse for a lawn and farther out along the lake shore.

By the time they left, Kylie had finally fallen asleep in Camryn's arms, and even though her arms ached from her weight, she momentarily resisted when Dan finally came to take her. He placed Kylie on the sofa and put a blanket over her. Unable to let her go, Camryn sat at the other end of the sofa, one hand resting on her tiny, purple-socked feet.

She could have been killed.

Kylie could have been taken from her. Terror, until now submerged by events, rose and settled into her brain. Paralyzed her. Through the open doorways of the living room and hall, she had a view of her kitchen. Her mouth dust-dry, she stared unseeingly through the glass teeth now framing her shattered window and into the darkness beyond.

She grew cold, colder . . . Overwhelmed by the sick, sharp truth that she couldn't have protected her child. There was nothing she could have done to stop the evil beyond the glass. She rubbed her arms, tried to warm them.

Dan picked up a soft napping blanket from the chair

across from Kylie and draped it over Camryn's shoulders, squeezed. "Can I get you something?" He sat on the arm of the chair, put his hand on her upper back and rubbed gently.

"No, I'm fine. Thanks." She pulled the blanket tight, welcomed the warmth of it . . . welcomed his touch. "All I want is for this to be over. Better yet, to have had it never happen." She looked up at him. "Who could have done such a thing? And why?"

"The police think it's a random shooting. Maybe kids on boat coming off the lake, leaving the same way."

"What do you think?"

His face turned hard. "I don't think there's anything random about it."

"You can't— You think it has something to do with Adam." Her mind closed over the idea, but couldn't take it in.

"It's a possibility."

"If that's what you think, why didn't you tell the police?"

"What I think and what I *know* are two different things." He stood. "Morning's soon enough to talk about it."

"You're wrong, you know." Adam was bad news, selfish and arrogant, but shooting into her house, endangering his own child? She couldn't accept that. He was devious and faithless, but violent? No. "You're singling him out because you're still angry about—"

"Him sleeping with my wife?" The look he gave her was intense and unreadable. "You know, whatever that guy's got that makes women shut down their brains and start operating from the same place a man does, I want it."

"That's insulting."

"And your accusing me of irrational jealousy isn't?"

She eyed him. He eyed her.

"Checkmate," she said. "For now."

"Good enough. Because what we believe—or don't be-lieve—doesn't matter. Kylie being in harm's way does. And generally speaking, when someone fires a gun they aim to kill someone." He paused. "And you know the drill, if at first you don't succeed . . ."

Camryn's hand tightened around Kylie's foot, and the lit-tle girl protested with a kick. A wave of nausea threatened, but she quelled it. "You think whoever did this will come back?"

"Bet on it. And you should reconsider your opinion of Dunn. We need to know what he's doing here. Why your friend is harboring him."

She looked at her sleeping child. While she still couldn't visualize Adam Dunn standing outside her kitchen window and firing into her home, for Kylie's sake, they needed to be sure. They needed to find out what was going on in De-lores's sad, forlorn house. "You're right."

"Good to know we can agree on something." He took a couple of steps toward the door, stopped. "Does your fa-ther have a permit for that gun?"

She shook her head. "I don't know." Her father, saying he wasn't feeling well, had gone to his room as soon as the police finished questioning him. When she'd checked on him fifteen minutes later, he was already asleep, still in his clothes, on top of the bedcovers. She'd pulled a quilt over him, turned his light out, and left him. "I didn't even know he had a gun." And she didn't know how she felt about that. She'd been glad enough when he'd used it to get rid of the . . . intruder, but she didn't like the idea of a gun in the same house as Kylie.

"He doesn't. Not after tonight. I'm putting it in my truck."

When he came back, he carried Kylie to her bed, then went to work boarding up the window with some plywood he found in the garage. Camryn stayed with Kylie, woke her enough to get her into her PJs, then sat with her until she was sure the child was deeply asleep.

Camryn was back in the kitchen sweeping up broken glass when Dan came in. It was close to midnight. "I made some sandwiches," she said and gestured to the table. "Do you want coffee?"

"If it's all the same to you, I think I'll revisit the wine." He went to the table, lifted the bottle in her direction. "You?"

"Yes. A much better idea than coffee." She put the last of the broken glass in the trash and took a seat at the table. He poured them each a glass of wine.

The silence in the kitchen was deep and cold from left-over fear. Drafts whistled in around the edges of the plywood.

Dan sat across from her, sipped some of the wine, then leaned back in his chair. He looked relaxed enough, except for the thunder in his eyes. A controlled man, she thought, confident, a man able to hold it all in, deal with it. But impatient, too. Perhaps too quick to rush to judgment. And a man who loved Kylie as much as she did, and whose hands, when they'd placed a blanket around her shoulders, were big, sure, and gentle.

"I want to talk about tonight," she said. "What happened here."

"I don't." He picked up a sandwich, bit into it.

"What *do* you want to do?"

"Eat this sandwich." He took another man-sized bite and another drink of wine, then added, "And go to bed."

"Here?"

"Here."

"And you want to stay here because . . ."

"My daughter asked me to. I promised her I'd be here when she woke up."

"You can do that by going to your motel and coming

back early in the morning," she said, trying on some logic that something in her hoped he'd ignore.

"True. But that would mean leaving you." His gaze drifted over her face. A face she knew was drawn and tired. A face that warmed under his scrutiny. "I don't intend to leave, Camryn." His eyes dropped to her mouth. Stayed there. "And I don't think you want me to." He lowered his head, looked at her across his wineglass. "Do you?"

Chapter 17

With that two-word question, Camryn's kitchen shrank in size, its oxygen depleted by half, and its perimeter blurred. All that remained was a man, a woman, and a razor-sharp awareness, a high-voltage sensual jolt that caught Camryn wildly off guard. She hadn't planned on this, hadn't seen it coming—hadn't seen Dan Lambert coming—over six feet of man and muscle who turned into mush when he looked at the little girl who called him Daddy, yet somehow turned into a potent, seductive male when he looked at her. A male who left *everything* to the imagination.

"I repeat, do you want me to go, Camryn?"

Her breathing, uncertain under his steady gaze, leveled off. She told herself not to forget he had an agenda, like Paul Grantman . . . like Adam. She told herself she was a fool for feeling anything, sensual or otherwise, for a man who'd come here solely to take his "daughter" from her. All these rattling emotions were aftershocks from the evening's events, nothing more. Perhaps he was as opportunistic as Adam and saw her weariness as weakness, a chance to shorten that straight line he was so keen on. She told herself all of that, looked into his quietly waiting eyes, and said, "No. I think you should stay." She swallowed, rose from the table, and picked up her plate and glass. She gave him another glance when she added, "After tonight, Kylie needs all the reassurance we can give her."

"Is there a *but*, at the end of that sentence?" He stayed seated, following her with his eyes as she walked to the dishwasher.

When she'd put her dishes away, she rested her hip against the counter. Her gaze, when it again met his, was level. "Yes, and what follows that 'but' is this—your staying here doesn't mean I want you messing with my head, or my hormones."

He stood and, wineglass in hand, walked toward her. When he was solidly in front of her, he reached around her and set his glass on the counter. He was so close the scent of his clean skin, the lingering hint of his aftershave, musk and cedar, drifted up her nose. All of it man-scent, strong and primal. Even though hemmed in by his size and strength, she had no desire to cut and run.

He trailed the back of his hand along her cheek and followed its path with a reflective, focused gaze, finally smoothing her hair gently behind her ear. "You were right, you know, about my ulterior motives." His eyes met hers, dark green and intense, faintly sorrowful. "I'd do anything to keep my daughter. And I did consider the idea that seducing you might be the way to do that." His lips curved briefly into a smile, but it left his face as quickly as it had come. "I thought it would be less time-consuming, a way to avoid a messy and complicated legal battle, and that Paul Grantman wouldn't stand a chance against the two of us." He rested his hand on her shoulder, caressed her throat with his thumb. The gesture both heated and idle. "But now . . ."

When he didn't go on, Camryn waited, then raised a brow. "Now?"

"Now all I want to do is mess with those hormones you mentioned—without a base motive in sight." He leaned toward her and kissed her, a lingering kiss that touched her lips like a shadow, an inquisitive kiss that slammed those hormones she was so worried about into overdrive. "Well, maybe a little base," he whispered over her lips.

She took his face in her hands, held it, and pulled back to look at him, wanting to see his eyes. "You know all this . . . wanting is caused by delayed stress, don't you?" God, she sounded like second-rate therapist.

His hands, which were resting on her shoulders, slid down to grip her waist, tug her close. "Maybe. But right now I'm more concerned with the effect than the cause." He kissed her again, this time harder, deeper.

And . . . she liked it.

She loved it.

She wanted more. More of his mouth, more of his heat, more of his strong body flush to hers.

She pushed him back, leaned heavily against the counter, and said, as evenly as her shaken nerves allowed, "If we do this . . . thing, we'll regret it in the morning." She swallowed hard, gulped for a deep breath, air enough to fill her lungs, air that had been in short supply from the moment his lips touched hers. When she leveled off, she tried to clear her mind while looking into a face with a hard jaw, a map of unknown lines and hollows, and eyes the color of a dark forest. "God, this is insane," she blurted out. "And so— God, I don't know . . . ill-timed, I suppose."

"Wanting someone usually is."

"Then there's the I-hardly-know-you side of things."

"What's to know?" His eyes narrowed, questioned.

About a million things . . . She put more space between them. "You're not going to give me that 'me man, you woman, and we're both over twenty-one' speech, are you?"

This time he did smile. "I was thinking about it. Would it work?"

"Not tonight, Tarzan."

He studied her a second or two, again ran his knuckles lightly across her cheek. "Fair enough. You have questions. I'll answer"—he took another step away—"but not tonight."

"Because you know they'll be about . . . Holly." Voicing

her unease made her feel lighter, more surefooted in her retreat from this potent man.

"Yeah." He rubbed his jaw. "So, if you'll get me a blanket and a pillow, I'll give your couch a try." He headed for the living room, stopped, and turned back to meet her eyes. He took his time before asking, "Ever make a mistake, Camryn?"

Craig, cramming his clothes into a red sports bag jumped to mind, the initial pain of it . . . but then how quickly the pain had subsided. And there was Adam. Who could forget Adam? She nodded.

His chin dipped slowly, thoughtfully. "So did Holly. So did I."

When he walked out of the room, Camryn sagged against the counter as if she were weighted down with wet sand. When she thought about Dan Lambert—his effect on her—she told herself to leave the thinking for another day. Falling in "like" with a man two minutes after her kitchen window had been shot out was plain dumb. She was never dumb.

What she was, was addled and fuzzy-minded, no doubt from the adrenaline cocktail delivered via gunshots.

Pushing away from the counter, she headed to the linen closet at the far end of the hall. She'd think about Dan, what happened tonight, in the morning when her head was clear, and there was a chance of making sense of things.

In the meantime, she'd get the man some bedding. Not that he'd get much sleep on that old couch; he was a big man, at least six inches longer than her sofa. It would probably fit him like a medieval rack.

She touched her lips, remembered his mouth on hers, and shuddered, suddenly sure her bed would feel the same to her.

* * *

Paul Grantman's eyes jerked open, and he glanced at the thin gold watch on his wrist. Close to two A.M. The fire he'd lit earlier in the grate was in its death throes, a few glittering embers giving little defensive warmth against the miserable rain-filled night. He thought he'd heard her car, the splash of tires on the driveway, but cocking his head and listening brought nothing except the sound of rain hitting the windows and the wind whipping through the tall cedars at the side of the house.

He rubbed one eye and straightened in the leather wing chair, one of two that flanked the fireplace in his wood-paneled study. He was surprised he'd dozed off at all, even though it had been for less than twenty minutes. He seldom slept when Erin was away from home. Always tense and vaguely terrorized by the thought that this time she wouldn't come back, he rarely let her go out on her own. But earlier tonight she'd begged him, and he'd allowed it.

Damn, I'm such a fool. He picked up the glass on the table beside his chair, twirled the last of his cognac, watched it catch a sudden flicker of flame from the dying fire, then downed it.

Yes, a fool. He shouldn't give a good goddamn where she was—he should toss her out on her junkie ass. . . .

Why he needed this uncontrollable, unpredictable woman in his life remained a mystery to him. Her addictions were killing her—killing him. She was his third wife and his biggest mistake, but even in his darkest hours with her, he couldn't imagine her not being in his life.

It wasn't as if any of this mess was a surprise—or it shouldn't have been. He knew what she was when he married her. She'd warned him.

"I have to get well myself, Paul. You can't fix me," she'd told him.

He'd ignored her, made her promise to try, and said he'd do the rest. But so far all the doctors and treatment centers he forced her into had done nothing except buy some tense periods of clean time and smooth over the occasional bump in the road. He was losing the battle, and Paul Grantman hated to lose . . . anything.

After years in the trenches fighting Erin's addiction, he was more and more afraid she was right; he couldn't do it for her. His money couldn't do it. Even his misguided obsession with her couldn't do it.

All he could hope for now was that her having a child to care for would accomplish what he hadn't. She would have that child. He'd see to that.

By a sick twist of fate, Holly's brutal murder was Erin's latest, and perhaps last, chance for survival; it had come down to Kylie.

Paul put his head back, closed his eyes to shut out the pain of losing Holly. He quickly opened them again. Holly was gone, and his moaning wouldn't bring her back. Hell, he didn't even have a lead on her killer despite two of the best PIs in the business working on it.

He rubbed his chin and let out a long, irritated breath. *The mighty Paul Grantman thinks he can play God, control everything and everyone around him.* Holly's words, made especially ironic by tonight's events, because he sure as hell hadn't controlled his wife.

Edgy, increasingly tense, he set his empty glass on the table, stared into the dying fire, then rose to go and poke at it. His thoughts went back to Erin—as they always did— and to her determination to go out alone. . . .

"It's just a dinner with a couple of girlfriends, Paul. I haven't seen them in ages," she'd said. "I'll be fine. I promise." She'd given him a pleading look. "You know how much I want Kylie . . . for us to be a real family. I won't do anything to ruin that chance."

"I don't like it. You're still too vulnerable." He lifted her chin. "You've had three months clean before, remember?"

Wrapping her arms around him, she'd looked up. "I know, but this time is different. I'll be home by ten. I promise." She crossed her heart, adding, "I need to know I can do this—go out on my own, trust myself, with no Maury following me. Okay?"

He'd hesitated at that, but finally, after more pleading, he'd given in to what she wanted. His agreement still lay like dirt on his tongue.

Who the hell knew what she was doing out there, alone, no one looking out for her? When she used drugs, drank too much, she was dangerously unpredictable. Anything could happen. *And I let her go.*

Again he poked at the fire, this time impatiently, then tossed on another perfectly cut log.

He'd started calling her at eleven, but she must have turned her cell off, because all he got was her voice mail.

His chest tightened, and he leaned an arm along the mantel, rested his head on it, suddenly weary, as if beaten down by time rushing fast and heavy over aging bones. Time laced with sins, old and new.

He'd failed with Holly, and he was failing with Erin. Maybe Holly had been right when she'd said in her letter that Erin was "too far gone," that she "wasn't worth loving" and would ruin his life. He closed his eyes. And Holly had said Erin was the "last person on earth" she wanted raising her daughter—along with him, who apparently she loved, but found "overprotective and overcontrolling" and not what she wanted for Kylie. No, she wanted Camryn Bruce, as she'd made clear in her guardianship paper and her letter.

A soft rapping at the door had him lift his head, expectant, hopeful.

It was Maury. "She's not back?" he asked.

"No." Maury was fully dressed, Paul noted, ready to go. Which didn't surprise him; they'd both been down this road before. Paul glanced at his watch. Almost 2:30. The waiting was over, anger elbowed melancholy aside.

"Get a car, Maury. Meet me at the front door, and bring that notebook you found in Erin's luggage, the one you said had phone numbers you didn't recognize."

"Which car?"

Paul thought a moment. "The truck. The one the gardener uses." He had no idea what kind of neighborhood they'd end up in; an expensive car would attract attention.

"Done. I'll be out front in five minutes. If I were you, I'd grab a windbreaker. It's a hellish night."

Paul strode down the hall to his bedroom. "Hellish" wasn't even close.

Chapter 18

"Dan. Dan, wake up!" Camryn put her mouth close to his ear, shook his shoulder.

She was on her knees beside him. The couch had obviously failed the comfort test, and he'd opted for the floor. The room was dark except for the night-light she kept on in the hall. She could barely make out his face.

His eyes snapped open, immediately focused on her face. His hand gripped her arm. "What is it? Is Kylie okay?"

"She's fine, but there's someone at the top of the driveway," she whispered. "Standing there, watching the house."

He quickly got to his feet. He was wearing jeans, but was bare-chested. "Show me."

"My room," she said, "You can see better from there. No trees in the way." Her chest was drum-tight, and her legs were stiff as pegs, but her voice was calm enough. She would not panic—she wouldn't.

Dan followed her up the stairs to her dark bedroom, and she took his hand and led him to her window. Her driveway, maybe a hundred yards long, with only one easy bend, took a gentle slope to her house.

"There." She pointed to where a figure stood to the side at the top of the driveway. "Do you see?"

Dan didn't answer, but she sensed his tension, his concentration as he stared out the window. The night was wet and fierce, the window glass a river of rain. Camryn had installed one decorative light at the top of the driveway, but it functioned as more of a guide light than to provide illumination. At this end of the lake, there was only the occasional streetlight and none directly in front of Camryn's old house.

"There," she said again, pointing. "Across from the light—under the tree on the side of the vacant lot." She didn't whisper this time but did keep her voice low. The shadowy shape hadn't moved from where she'd spotted it a few minutes ago when she'd first looked out the window. Unable to sleep, she'd gotten up for a drink of water and, while sipping it, had taken a moment to look out at the storm.

Her heart hadn't found its rhythm since.

"Got it." He dropped the curtain he'd been holding back and headed for the stairs.

"You're going out there?" She didn't bother to remind him that if it was whoever had been there earlier shooting through her kitchen window, chances were they still had a gun; Dan wasn't stupid. He knew the risk he was taking—but so did Camryn, which had her heart leaping crazily in her chest and a knot of panic constricting her lungs. "Maybe it's . . . nothing. Nobody. Maybe—"

He cut her off. "If nothing else, I'll get close enough to get a visual. There's lots of cover along your property line." He headed for the door, made it in a few long strides. "While I check it out, you know who to call."

Camryn nodded, but before heading for the phone to call the police, she glanced back out the window. "Wait!" She pulled back the curtain again, gave him a come-here gesture with her hand. "Look."

An old-model truck had pulled up close to the specter standing so chillingly still at the top of her driveway, the only movement around its form a long coat billowing in the wind. As Dan came back to her side, two men got out of the truck and strode to where the figure stood. They each took an arm and led the person quickly toward the truck. While Camryn was certain enough by their walk and bearing that the new players were men, she still couldn't make out whether the raincoat-clad shadow who'd been looking at her house was a man or a woman.

"Shit!" Dan said, not taking his eyes off the trio now getting into the cab of the truck.

"Whoever it is, he—or maybe she—isn't resisting," Camryn said. "I think they all know each other." She barely got the words out before the truck drove away. Not with a screech of tires, but slowly, quietly, as if not wanting to attract attention.

For a few seconds she and Dan stood there, saying nothing. When relief suddenly eased the stiffness in Camryn's legs, weakening her knees, she gripped the windowsill, then took the few steps to the plump, overstuffed reading chaise she'd placed near the window. She often read here when the house was quiet and her work was done for the day. A neat stack of books sat on a table beside it. Sitting down, somewhat awkwardly, she knocked a couple of them off the pile.

"Are you okay?" Dan asked, turning from the window.

"Fine. I just needed to sit down," she said, ignoring the fallen books.

"Can we have a light on?"

She fumbled for the reading lamp beside the chaise, switched it on low, and was surprised to find her hands were cold—and as untrustworthy as her legs. Dan stood over her, shirtless—a lean, hard-jawed giant, who, with his hands planted on his hips, looked both angry and frustrated. She knew he hated that they were gone, that he couldn't do anything. But she was relieved.

Bringing her hands together, she rested them in her lap, forced herself not to wring them or grip too tightly. God, she was acting—make that overacting—like a young extra in a horror movie—except for the screaming.

Camryn didn't scream, Camryn held on. Camryn held

things together—persevered. Camryn was strong, a rock. Isn't that what her mother always said? Responsible, independent . . . tough. It's how her mother saw her, and it had become how she saw herself. But the truth was suddenly more complex than a mother's skewed vision, which had somehow become her own. The truth was she'd never been tested—until she'd faced gunshots in her kitchen and ghosts in her driveway. Now all she felt was a gnawing fear.

Dan's eyes bored into her. "Will you be all right?"

"Yes, or will be when I catch my breath."

He knelt in front of her and took her chilled hands in his warm ones. "You're trembling. Sit back." He reached around her and grabbed a pillow, put it behind her. "And put your feet up," he ordered, lifting her bare feet from the floor and putting them on the lounge. He drew the blanket she kept at its base up to her waist, then sat beside her, one hand resting on her knee. "You've had a hell of a night."

Not about to acknowledge that, she said, "Could you see anything? Get any idea of who that was?"

He shook his head. "A woman. That's all I got."

"How can you be sure?"

He shrugged. "Can't. But the way she moved, the outline of her, that's my guess."

"Maybe it was nothing, nothing at all," Camryn said, her voice rough, as though the words had scratched her throat on the way out. "Maybe it was a neighbor or someone who lives close by waiting to be picked up by friends. I probably panicked for no good reason." She knew her words were nearer hope than truth.

"You didn't panic." He shifted his hip on the chaise, rested his palm on the other side of her knees. "And even if it was someone waiting for a ride . . . doesn't matter. You did right coming to get me."

She noticed he didn't bother pointing out that the chances of a woman standing in a miserable storm on a dark street

WITHOUT A WORD / 185

miles from anywhere, waiting for a ride, were remote. He didn't have to. Her stomach acid hot, her mind suddenly on spin cycle, she realized that any sane person would figure the truth out, and one truth led to another. She forced herself to calm down, get a grip, however meager, on the events of the evening. The shooting had been bad enough. To think they were being watched—for whatever reason—made her half crazy with fear. She couldn't wrap her mind around any of this, but one thing was very clear: Kylie was at risk—and all her positive thinking and stupid denials wouldn't change that. The thought that she couldn't protect Kylie made her soul ache. She had to do something, and she had to do it fast.

"I'm afraid, Dan," she said. "Not for me—for Kylie." She paused, a thought coming, a way out of this sitting-duck kind of morass they were mired in. "Paul Grantman is back at the lake by now. His place is four, maybe five miles south of here. I think we—*I* should ask him to take Kylie until this situation, or whatever it is, is resolved." She felt him stiffen.

"We don't need Grantman's help. I can take care of my daughter." Pause. "And I can take care of you."

She ignored the last, not wanting to go there. "You might not need him, or like him, but this isn't about your ego or his. It's about Kylie. She'd be safe there. His estate is gated and has enough security to fend off a SWAT team. If Kylie were there, she'd be safe." She swallowed. "It would leave us free to find out what's going on around here." She didn't stumble over her use of the word "us" because it felt right—comfortable.

After another long silence, he said, "It could work against you, you know. Asking Paul for help is saying you can't handle things. He could use it in court. And he would."

"As could you."

He twisted his lips as if that fact didn't sit well, but he had no comeback.

Camryn went on. "I know the risks," she said, adding a new fear to the mess of them in her heart. "But I want Kylie safe. I know you want that, too. Right now, she'll be safest at Paul's."

He was quiet for a long time, then said, "We'll call him tomorrow."

"Good." Camryn visualized Kylie secure behind wired gates and alarm systems and felt instantly lighter. More in control.

"After that we'll drop in on Dunn—and that friend of yours, Gina."

Camryn blinked. "You can't believe she had anything to do with this."

"I don't even know the woman. But I think that relationship she has with Dunn makes her worth looking into—and that was definitely a woman at the top of your driveway."

Everything in her rebelled at the thought of Gina having anything to do with this nightmare. Gina was her friend; she had stood by Camryn during her struggle to have a child, always sympathetic, always there when things got tough.

Not Gina. Never Gina.

But Gina with Adam . . .

Camryn ignored the prickles along her nape that came with the image of Gina together with Adam, and the rush of heat to her face. "Gina had nothing to do with this," she said. "I won't have you thinking that way."

At her overreaction, he lifted a brow, studied her for a moment. If he wanted to take issue with her vehement defense of Gina, it didn't show. "Fair enough," he said, his tone mild. "We won't go there . . . tonight."

He lifted her hand to his mouth, turned it, and kissed her palm. The heat of his kiss rushed up her arm, warmed her chest. "But if I'm forbidden to think about your friend, that frees up a lot of head space . . . a lot of time." He closed her fingers over her heated palm where his mouth had burned moments before, then kissed her wrist, up her arm, to the inside of her elbow.

Not only did the lounge not provide room enough for her to pull back from him, she didn't want to. What she did was tighten the curl of her fingers over the kiss in her hand. Dan lifted his head to look at her, and their gazes met and locked. "Dan I—" She dropped her eyes along with the dropped sentence, tried to get past her traitorous stomach, the fullness between her thighs.

He bent his head, "You know what I want," he said, lifting her face so their eyes again met.

Her thoughts, whatever they were, contracted . . . reduced to the now, what he could give her in the privacy of the night, in the dark bedroom while the rain pounded the old roof, and the fear and danger remained outside the water-slicked windows.

And time stopped.

"I want *you*, Camryn," he said, his hand resting on her shoulder, his thumb rubbing the skin over her collarbone. "I want us"—he moved his head to indicate her bed—"in that big bed doing all the right things to each other."

Her breath stopped. Her mind refused to. "This could be one very big mistake. And it's so . . ."

"Soon. After Holly's death." His thumb stopped moving over her skin.

She nodded. "One good reason."

He looked away, then back, his gaze dark but direct. "You're going to have to trust me on this, but it's not 'soon.' There's no way to make this come out right, but I'll say it anyway. Holly and I were . . . apart for months."

"You mean sexually."

"I mean in every way there is to be apart. When I did

come home, it was to see Kylie." He rubbed his jaw. "Before I left for Canada—after she told me she was seeing someone else—I stayed in a hotel. I'd like to think the whole mess was Dunn's fault, or Holly's, but it wasn't. A lot of the blame was mine. You were right about that. My job took me away for periods of time. Holly hated that." He shook his head. "Hell, even Grantman weighed in on that issue." He stopped, let some quiet in. "I was working to fix that." He stopped again. "But what I couldn't fix was that I got married for all the wrong reasons—because I thought it was time, because I wanted a family, and because"—his face was grim—"Holly and I were having fun in bed at the time. I figured we had as good a chance as anybody else of making things work. For Kylie, if for no other reason."

"What about love?"

"Didn't believe in it. Didn't think it mattered all that much." His chuckle was rueful. "And neither did Holly—or so she said when I leveled with her." He shifted his weight on the chaise.

"You told Holly you didn't believe in love, didn't love *her*, and she married you anyway?"

He shrugged.

She studied the lines of his solemn face, the darkness of his thick, sleep-disheveled hair, the corded muscles of his arms. The shadows of regret in his eyes. It saddened Camryn how little she'd really known her friend—how much she was learning since her death. "And now. What do you believe now about love?"

He looked at her for what seemed forever. "I'm not sure." He leaned closer. "All I'm sure of right now is that I want to *make love* with you."

Camryn let silence linger, then pulled her hand from his. He'd been honest with her; he deserved the same from her. "You should know that I haven't 'made love' in a very long time." She picked at the blanket still covering her knees.

"What I've done is . . . have sex. Pretty boring sex, actually."

He frowned. "Explain."

She took a breath. "I'm saying you're not the only one who married for the wrong reasons. I married my . . . friend, because my biological clock's alarm went off. I loved Craig—just not in the right way. I wanted kids more than I wanted him. And because of that"—she chewed over her next words—"he walked out on me."

This time Dan left the room to silence, then gave her a crooked smile and said, "Looks like we're a matched set of fuckups."

Everything about what was happening between Dan and her was wrong, yet so right, so real, that its presence was a solid force in the room. If being with him was a mistake, it wouldn't be her first, and she'd make it with wide-open eyes. A smile took root in her heart and blossomed on her lips. "Looks like," she finally said.

He stood, held out a hand.

Hesitating, she looked up at him, then let her eyes skim the taut muscles of his chest and powerful biceps, the fullness at his groin. Her breathing skipped. "No promises," she said, having no idea where this night would lead, and at the moment not wanting to know.

He nodded slowly. "Not past tonight."

Anticipation growing, she took his hand, rose from the chaise, and walked with him to her bed. Bedside, she took off her robe and let the regret—a brief but eternal everywoman moment—that she wasn't wearing a Victoria's Secret silk nightgown slide with it to the floor.

Soft cotton would do—and a hard man. Her ears filled with the sound of her own breathing, the pound of her own heart. It had been so very, very long since she'd *wanted* like this.

Her skin warmed. Pulsing heat, long forgotten, burgeoned low in her belly, lower still, and when she looked in Dan's eyes and saw the same heat reflected there, every sinew in her body curled and tensed—strung tight with the need for sex.

Heart-stopping, time-stopping sex . . . and a long, lingering coming. She tried to remember when she'd last felt this powerful an urge, last rode the rough wave of sex to its crest. Not with Craig. Never with Craig. Her fault. Her lousy love life, along with a million other things, was her fault. It had come with her stubborn refusal to accept the truth.

Tonight was sex for sex's sake. Nothing more and nothing less. She liked Dan Lambert. Desired him. It would be enough.

She inhaled deeply, prepared to slip the narrow straps of her cotton gown from her shoulders.

"Uh uh. My job." He took her hands and placed them at her sides. "All you do is stand there and let me look at you."

She swallowed. "Easy for you to say."

He smiled, shifted the straps of her gown low on her shoulders, and kissed her throat and neck. His hands skimmed under the straps and released them, letting her gown drop to the floor and join her velour robe. His gaze wandered her body, deliberate and intense. Appreciative. "Beautiful," he said, adding, "Perfect," in a whisper before pulling her close and taking her mouth in a kiss . . . to seal their bargain.

No promises, past tonight.

Camryn, pulled flush to Dan's naked chest, was okay with that, okay with not thinking past the urges of her body or his, urges made clear when he ground his lower body against her pelvis and murmured into her ear. "We'll be good together, Camryn. I'm sure of it."

When his mouth moved from her mouth to her throat, and his teeth tugged on her earlobe, she sighed and relished a new truth: despite worry, fear, lurking strangers, and gun-shots, she'd never felt so safe, so absolutely right in her life.

Tonight she'd be the Camryn she hadn't been in years, the Camryn she needed to be, wanted to be.

She slid her hands around his taut, narrow waist, pulled him close. Closer.

Tonight she'd let her heat burn them both.

Chapter 19

Dan couldn't get enough of her, couldn't slow down. Her mouth on his, opening for his tongue, letting him play, then playing right back, set him to crazy.

He was so hard, so goddamned much in need, he was in sexual pain. He didn't like pain. He liked smooth. He liked hot, and he liked to take his time.

And Jesus Christ he liked this woman—wanted this woman!

Using every ounce of willpower he had, he pulled back from her and said, "Much as I hate to ask, can you wait a minute?"

Thank God, she didn't look as if the idea of waiting thrilled her.

"I've got protection, but it's"—he filled his lungs—"in my truck." Which at the moment might as well have been Outer Siberia.

Her confused expression turned to one he couldn't quite read. "What?" he said, dipping his chin to better catch her eyes.

"Nothing, but . . . Oh, damn. Might as well say it." She moved from his arms, sat on the edge of the bed, and pulled the quilt over her lap, and up far enough to half-cover her breasts. He could see her jaw moving, then her setting it to determined. Whatever the lady wanted to say, it wasn't coming easy. "Are you . . . healthy?" she finally asked, with only the slightest tremor in her voice. "Sexually speaking, I mean."

"Perfectly," he said. More than healthy, considering the hard weight behind his zipper.

"So am I," she said. "So you—we—won't need protection."

She rose from the bed, let the quilt drop, and as much as he wanted to get back to where they were, he hesitated, planting the hands he'd planned to have all over her on his own hips. "There's other reasons for using protection." Okay, so he was stating the obvious, but it had to be said, because when it came to having kids, either by the old-fashioned way or any other, Dan didn't take chances. He'd let his guard down with Kylie, let her into his life. He'd made promises to her that he damn well intended to keep—wanted to keep. That didn't mean he wanted any more kids. Two were enough—especially when he'd already lost one and was having trouble hanging on to the other.

Camryn raised her eyes to his; they were strangely defiant. "Not with me. I can't have children."

This was a first, and he wasn't exactly sure where the hell to go from here. He had sex on his mind, not procreation, and he was having trouble making the shift. He tried. "And not your call, right?" he asked, remembering her father's mumbled words about her wanting a child.

"Right."

"You're sure?" he asked, more to satisfy himself than her. He didn't think for a moment she'd lie, which gave him a moment's pause, because it went solidly against his usually cautious approach to women.

"Three-doctors sure, and . . . personally sure." She looked a bit grim but didn't add anything else, nor did she look as if she wanted him to ask more questions.

"Then I'm sorry."

She nodded, the gesture terse, prim. "I thought you should know."

He wasted a few seconds wondering why, but couldn't stay focused on anything but the pale skin of her shoulders, the long column of her throat, her breasts pale in the dim light and waiting for his hands. If there was a word for Camryn's body it was *delicious*.

Maybe this issue had to be explored, but not tonight. Tonight was about a man and a woman exploring each other. "Now I do know." He reached for her and brought that delicious body to his. Camryn was lush—narrow in the right places, full in the others. Curves, not angles. She fit him perfectly. "And it doesn't change the way I want you. Need you."

He kissed her again, pulled her hard to where he wanted her the most; the kiss was long, deep, and hot—and in one fiery instant it took them back to pre-confessional mode. Exactly where he wanted to be. And judging from the heat and pulsing in Camryn's body, so did she.

"Lie down," he whispered against her throat, loosening his grip, sliding his hands over her buttocks, then thrusting against her before releasing her. "I have to get out of these jeans. Unfortunately, I'm not the Incredible Hulk."

She stretched out on the bed and smiled at him. "Ever notice, during all that muscle-bulging, fabric-ripping, and seam-splitting, he never did burst from his pants?"

"Yeah." Dan unzipped. He sure as hell didn't have that problem. "Poor bastard."

He stripped, jeans and briefs, and stepped toward the bed.

"No. Wait." She shifted to bedside, stared at his erection, and moistened her lips. "Whoa . . . Just stand there for a moment."

"Easy for you to say," he said, echoing her earlier words.

Her turn to smile. "Impressive."

Christ, she was moving closer, reaching for him. He clamped his jaw closed. If she touched him, chances were good his last few months of celibacy would have him erupting like Vesuvius, but damned if he'd stop her. Hell, he couldn't wait to feel her hands on him.

She slid her hand between his thighs, took the weight of him in her hands . . . squeezed.

Dan's breath left him in one long, harsh groan. He spread his legs for balance and ground out, "That's probably not a good idea." He knew he was beading, knew he wouldn't last. He had to move. Couldn't move.

She closed her hand around him, looked up into his face, which, sure to God, must have looked like a slab of granite, and said, "You're beautiful, too." She leaned in as if to kiss him . . .

He lifted her by the shoulders, tossed her back on the bed and covered her with his body, a body hot and hard enough to stall his brain. All he wanted was in, one long, deep plunge into female heat . . . Camryn's heat.

Too fast, way too fast.

He rolled over, pulled her on top of his thighs—back from the danger zone—took her face in his hands and kissed her hard. She let him, digging her nails into his shoulders and squirming up his body until her softness met his steel—until his mind blanked and his cock pounded like a runner's heart. How he'd thought having her on top would slow him down, he couldn't figure.

"Okay, okay," he muttered. Holding her back from him, he sucked up some air. "Shit, this is going to be worse than I thought." He lifted his throbbing erection to her mound, nestled it in the damp heat of her curls. Her pubis tight to him, he held her there, not moving, striving for control.

She leaned over him, her hair, where the dim lamplight caught it, turning to gold at the tips. He couldn't see her face, but he could hear her exhale—the raggedness of it. He smelled the sharp scent of her toothpaste before she bent her head to his neck and nipped him. "I'll take that as a good thing." She reached a hand down and between them, lifted herself enough so she could touch him.

He closed his eyes, prayed to some godforsaken sex god to intervene with a dose of patience. "You keep doing that, and I won't—" he stopped when she stroked him gently, almost idly. Applying pressure, taking it away.

"Won't last the night?" Her words lashed his feverish skin.

Before he could answer, she said, "What makes you think I want you to?" She lifted herself, positioned herself at the tip of him. "Give me what you've got, Dan. All of it. Now!"

"Fuck!" He gripped her hips, thrust up, and buried himself as far and deep as nature allowed. But he held on.

She moaned, threw her head back, wriggled enough to envelop him, shroud him in her heat, slick him with her juices. He thrust again, held her buttocks, got lost in a series of powerful flesh-grabbing pulses, heard her gasp, then moan long and low.

He did some deep breathing, held on, and placed his hand on her stomach, felt it spasm at his touch. Running his palm up between her breasts, he chose a nipple. It was pebble-hard, a long jut from her firm breast and easily caught between thumb and forefinger.

It wasn't enough . . .

"Lean back," he ordered, and she did—exposing what he needed. He found her sweet spot, heard her intake of breath, then as skillfully as a man could who was breaking apart, he thumbed her clit. Easy. Hard. Around it until the delicate extension sat exposed.

He rubbed. Stroked.

"Oh, God!" She lifted to his tip, came down again.

Her final rush was liquid fire, a deep inner clenching.

Gripping her hips, he held her down, thrust up and released into her desperate frenzy.

She shuddered, and her body clamped his length one last time, squeezed as if for the final drop; her head fell back. After some long, hard breathing, she lowered herself to his chest, sprawling over it like a rag doll.

Nestling her face close to his neck, she murmured, "That was . . . amazing."

"That was crippling."

She lifted her head, then a hand to brush his sweat-dampened hair off his forehead. "Meaning what? You're not up for seconds?"

"I'm up for all of you I can get." He ran his hand down her slick back, stroked her ass. "But I need a minute." He liked this particular minute after sex, two bodies lax and fused by the juices of sex.

She put her face back to his neck. "Me too." She murmured something he couldn't hear against his cooling skin. He was certain she'd laughed.

He touched her hair. "What was that?"

She rolled off his chest, away from his body. She propped her head in one hand and rested the other on his chest. "I was thinking how true that old bumper sticker really is."

He arched a brow.

"A hard man is good to find."

He smiled. "So is a hot woman, one who knows what she likes—and goes for it."

She made a circle with her index finger in his chest hair, then stroked it flat. "Scare you?"

"Yeah, right!" He looked at her, frowned. "You're not kidding."

"Not completely." Silence. "I generally take my time, think things through before I make a decision, finally go for something. But when I do, I tend to, uh, overfocus. As in not knowing when to quit."

Dan shifted to his side, wedged his leg between hers. She was still warm, still wet, and she smelled like sex and roses. She moved to riding position on his thigh, rubbed herself against his leg. Jesus! He put a hand on her face, met her gaze—a gaze honestly concerned. "Then I'm glad you turned that focus on me, because quitting is the last thing on my mind."

"Glad to hear it." She kissed his ear, then nipped his earlobe. When her warm breath touched his ear, his chest contracted.

Okay, he might have to wait a minute or two for old dick to rise to the task, but that didn't mean he couldn't fast-forward things for the lady in his arms.

He pulled his leg back, rose up and over her. Running a finger along her jaw and down her throat, he stopped at the top of her breast, then cupped her fully, bent and took her nipple into his mouth. He tongued and suckled a bit before looking at her again. Her eyes were already glazed, her breath already ragged.

He was one hell of a lucky man.

"But this time," he added, bending again to draw on her nipple, "we'll take it slow. Real slow." He glanced toward the still-dark window, then smiled at her. "Hell, with your focus and my determination, we should be able to last until first light." He ran his hand down her stomach, spread his fingers over her pubis, then slipped one into her crease. "Hell, there's parts of you I haven't even kissed yet." He pressed on her clit.

She inhaled sharply. "Can't have that."

"We won't."

First light, Camryn thought, her brain dimming as his mouth moved over her, down her . . . *if I survive Dan Lambert long enough to see it.*

Chapter 20

A rough, careless hand shook Gina awake, and the barest of light filtered through her half-opened eyes. When they opened wider, she saw Delores glaring at her, her face mere inches away.

"What the hell is the matter with you? What are you doing down here?" Delores said.

"Nothing, I—" Gina couldn't think clearly enough to finish the sentence. She squinted, tried to orient herself. She was in the living room, but it was cold and damp, and the wet wind was rushing over her exposed skin, coming in from the open patio doors. Her very bones were frigid, and the smell of sweat and dirt filled her nostrils. Some non-essentials registered: Her mother was in her chair, maybe a foot away. She wore a pink top—dark pink—and black slacks. And makeup.

"For God's sake, cover yourself up," Delores said.

She looked at her mother, saw her jerk her head toward Gina's chest where her naked breasts spilled from the torn front of her nightgown. One of her breasts was scratched, a sodden brown leaf adhering to the edge of the scrape like a misplaced Band-Aid. She peeled it off, looked at it, and closed her eyes to catch a memory. Her mind flitted like a bird, thought to thought, until . . .

Adam . . . Where was Adam?

Adam was why she was here.

"What time is it?" There was no trace of light outside.

"Almost six."

Focused now, she sat up, so quickly her brain ached, and pulled the remnants of her gown to her chest. Eyes wide and dry, she looked around. She had to be careful; she'd almost voiced her question about Adam. That wouldn't be smart.

Delores knew Adam. Delores had fucked Adam. Delores couldn't be trusted. She didn't know Adam was here, or that he was going to stay. Forever.

"Your feet are bleeding." A pause. "All over my carpet! Get up. Get a towel. Do something!"

Gina looked at her feet. They were mottled with blood and soil. Staring at them, the events of the evening came back.

It had started with a smear of lipstick. They'd fought. Adam had told her to get the hell out of his room, accused her of being irrational, "stupidly jealous," and said if she didn't trust him, wouldn't do what he wanted, he'd leave. Find someone else to help him.

Someone else . . . the words hit her like shrapnel.

She closed her eyes against what happened next. Her going back to his room, begging forgiveness, pleading with him to make love to her. But he'd refused. He wouldn't touch her. All he could talk about was getting custody of his daughter and about Camryn. . . .

First Holly, now Camryn. She couldn't bear it. Hated him for it. Hated them even more.

Her brain boiled, its putrid contents bubbling, swelling, threatening to spew, overwhelm. She forced herself to concentrate, to remember. After she'd left Adam, she'd gone to her room, then she'd . . . She rubbed her forehead.

She'd got the gun from the top of her closet!

"Where were you, Gina? I want to know," Delores demanded. "Speak up, girl, for God's sake, or this will take all night."

"I'm not . . . sure. I must have been sleepwalking." Frantic, she tried to remember where she'd left the gun. She remembered it in her hand, but what did she do with it? *What!*

"Whatever the hell you've been doing, you're a mess, and you're ruining my sofa—not to mention that silk pillow you slept on."

"I'm sorry." She wondered vaguely why Delores cared about the carpet. Delores never cared about anything except herself.

The pillow! She slid her hand under it, let out a relieved breath. The gun. The gun was there! She pulled her hand back and got to her feet, waited for her knees to steady.

"Get off my goddamned carpet!" Delores spit out.

Gina looked down at Delores, her venomous face, and an old loathing chilled her, froze hard in her throat. Then just as quickly she warmed, calmed. She didn't hate Delores, not anymore. She didn't have time to hate her; she didn't care anymore. Delores was nothing more than a pest, an irritant she'd set aside. She had more important things to think about. Gina breathed deeply, straightened her shoulders. It was as if a sodden quilt had been lifted from her shoulders.

She had Adam now, and her focus needed to be on him.

And getting rid of Camryn Bruce.

Tonight she'd lost control of herself, made a mistake. She wouldn't make another one. What she had to do now was think things through. Develop a plan. To hell with Delores. As long as she didn't find out about Adam—didn't make trouble with Adam—she was safe.

"I'll clean up, don't worry. Go to bed, Delores." Her tone was mild, perfectly controlled. She stepped off the carpet, padded to the kitchen over the cold tile, and spun some paper towels off the rack over the counter. She was wiping her scraped and dirty feet when she heard her mother's wheelchair roll up behind her.

"Go to bed? That's it? No explanation about where you've been. Who you've been with?"

"I'm a little old for that kind of inquisition, don't you think?"

"Not while you live in my house, you're not."

Gina kept working on her feet. "I told you I must have been sleepwalking."

"Never heard of those people doing that."

Gina tossed the dirty toweling in the trash can under the counter. "And what '*people*' would that be?"

"Agoraphobic-type people." Delores smirked.

Gina got herself a drink of water, then, sipping it, braced a hip on the counter. "You mean like people in wheelchairs who can walk—if they want to. But won't if it serves to keep a daughter feeling guilty enough to fetch and carry for the rest of her life?"

"What the hell are you trying to say?"

"Stating a fact, Mother. Sebastian was right. You can walk when you want to walk. I've heard you often enough—in your room, that ugly 'parlor' you spend most of your day in. Saw you once, too. Standing at the fridge. Your chair was on the other side of the room. The way I see it, about the only thing you can't handle are the stairs."

"Think you're damn smart, don't you?"

"No, I think you're the smart one—swindling the insurance company into giving you those disability payments." Gina shrugged, set her glass back in the sink. "But don't worry, your secret's safe with me."

"Guess so, considering I'm supporting you with those ill-gotten disability checks." Delores pushed herself out of the chair and started toward her. Her limp was ugly; one leg was twisted and shorter than the other, causing her to lurch awkwardly, as if every step were a precursor to a fall. Gina's bullet had done some of the work, her tumble down the stairs afterward had done the rest. "Not to mention I look a hell of a lot better in a wheelchair than like this." She took one last step and stood beside Gina; she was taller and looked down on her. The accident may have crippled her regal walk, but it did nothing to take the imperiousness from her gaze.

Gina looked at her mother, shook her head. "Sebastian was right. You're a liar, along with all your other faults."

"And you're a simpering, pathetic woman who'll do anything to have Adam Dunn's hand down her pants."

Gina iced up, stilled to alert.

"You honestly didn't think I'd find out he was here," Delores said with a sneer. "You really are a fool, Gina."

"But the stairs—"

"Yeah, you're right about them. Haven't managed more than two or three, no matter how I try." Delores paused, no doubt, for dramatic effect. "But Adam can. And Adam did."

"Adam came to you?" Gina stepped away from the counter, fisted her hands at her sides. She didn't like this. Didn't like the sound of Adam's name on her mother's lips.

"Yesterday"—again a pause—"he came to visit me in the parlor, walked right in, but, then, that's our Adam, isn't it? We had a real nice talk." Delores, who'd placed a hand on the wall for balance, pulled it back and leaned her shoulder against the fridge.

She stood framed there, the white of the refrigerator a perfect backdrop for her raven hair. She wore it down this morning, not roughly tied at her nape as she usually did. She'd put on makeup, styled her hair. She'd fussed over herself, and she looked . . . beautiful. She'd done it for Adam! Through the blood rising in her veins, obscuring her vision,

Gina fixed her gaze on her mother and asked, "What did you talk about?"

"You, mostly."

"What did he say?"

Delores's expression turned cunning. "He said you're helping him with some legal issues—to do with getting his daughter back. Holly's kid, apparently. Something I didn't know but probably should have figured out. He says she's with Camryn?"

Although her last words were more question than statement, Gina didn't answer. What Delores had told her wasn't all of it, Gina was sure. Her mother always kept the best until the last. Gina waited.

"Why didn't you tell me you lost his kid?"

"He told you that?" Gina's belly clenched, then softened. *Damn you, Adam!*

"Yes, he says he feels pretty bad about it. Although with Adam it's hard to tell how much of what he says is the truth—like the pious crap about how getting his daughter back will fill 'that void' in his life. Fill his pockets is more like it, I suspect. But that's our Adam."

Gina sifted through this new information, pressed a hand to her stomach. *Did he tell you he disappeared a week after I told him I was pregnant, that he didn't return my calls after the miscarriage?* She shoved the thoughts aside— all they'd do is weaken her resolve. Adam was here now and they'd have Holly's daughter. There was justice in that. That was all that mattered. "What else did you two talk about?" she asked, calmer now.

"Nothing." Delores crossed her arms. "To tell you the truth, I had other things on my mind." She sighed noisily. "Jesus, that man has gotten better with age. That heavy, silky hair. Those amazing blue eyes. I mean, even as a kid, he was a sexual knockout, but now . . ."

Static, crackling and electrical, started interfering with

Gina's hearing. "You didn't . . ." She couldn't say it, couldn't bear thinking it.

"Have sex?" Delores ran her tongue over her lips. "No." She turned her gaze full on Gina. "Fucking your boyfriend already put me in a wheelchair. A second go with him might net me a pine box." Her arms still crossed, she tapped one finger, smiled. "Although after seeing that gorgeous piece of beef again, it might be worth it."

"I didn't shoot—" Her denial came by rote.

The older woman's expression hardened. "Stop it, Gina! We both know what you did. It takes a cheat and liar to know one—and damned if we both don't qualify. Willing to do whatever it takes to get what we want—and keep it." She gestured to her wheelchair. "I use that chair and falsify medical questionnaires for the few bucks it brings in. You plead agoraphobia so you can stay home and nurse your depression—and obsession for Adam Dunn—and keep the world out while you do it. In the end, we all do whatever the hell works for us. And we don't give a shit who we hurt in the process. And that includes your precious boyfriend up there." She gestured with her head to the upper floors.

"But you," she went on, her tone lower, more thoughtful. "You've got something else going on in that too-smart head of yours—you and your brother. Me? I fuck the world, and win or lose, I move on, but you and Sebastian"—she shook her head—"you don't do that. You never move on. You live in a goddamned time warp. What you do is grab on and never let go. Sebastian to his Holly, you to your Adam. You never let go." She stopped. "Add to that you've both got long memories and a taste for revenge." Her expression accused, her eyes were unyielding. "You shot me, Gina, and you shot to kill."

Gina took a couple of steps toward her mother, then said, "You're right, Delores. I did shoot to kill."

Delores's eyes narrowed, but she looked neither surprised nor relieved at finally hearing the truth, even though she'd been angling for it for months.

"Hell of thing . . ." she said.

"There's something you should know."

"Let me guess, you're going to tell me how sorry you are. That it was all a *horrible* mistake."

"No, I'm telling you that you're right. I don't let go. Ever. So stay away from Adam, or I'll do it again. And this time no last-minute jolt of conscience will make me lose my aim." Stillness, an utter calm, the grace of certainty, came to replace the last of her doubts. She could do it. She could walk over to the sofa, get the gun, and kill her own mother. And because she knew she could do it, she didn't have to— didn't even want to. Knowing was enough. She was comfortable and strong. For the first time in her life, she knew who she was, what she was capable of.

It was as if the truth, evil though it was, had raised its ugly face to the sun and was drawing on its power.

Delores's mouth moved as if she were going to speak, but she said nothing.

Silence, welcome but ungodly, filled the room, and Gina let it lie. She didn't care what her mother thought, wasn't afraid of what she'd do. She was done with her. Done with everyone—except Adam. Adam was her world now. Nothing else mattered. Locked into her own thoughts, at first she didn't hear her mother. The laughter.

Delores, now chuckling, was settling herself back in her wheelchair.

Anger, stabbing short and hard into her chest, unsettled Gina's newfound calm. She reclaimed it. "You think it's funny that I shot you, Delores? Or you don't believe me?"

"Oh, yeah. I believe you . . . but seriously, daughter mine, you think for a minute that gold-plated stud up there could get it up for this?" She waved a hand over her lower half. "Hell, I should be complimented, I guess." Her eyes, filled with laughter and tears, lifted to Gina, then went hard. "But damned if I don't feel bad for you. Because if anybody's going to die around here, it's you, baby. That man will tear your heart from your chest and spit on it."

"I can handle Adam." She couldn't stop from adding, "He loves me. He said so."

"And to have him say that . . . you'll do anything, won't you?"

Gina lifted her chin.

Delores pushed herself to the door, then spun her chair around to face Gina. Morning light shafted into the room, an errant early ray of sun peaking out before the start of the endless bad weather predicted for the coming week. The light caught her mother's hair, illuminated the gray streaks. "In my day, when I had my looks—and money—I could have managed a type like him, but you?" She shook her head, her expression pensive. "Not a chance. Adam Dunn is too hot for you to handle, Gina. He's playing you, and you're letting him. You're trying to put lightning in a bottle, and he'll never let that happen. And he'll never keep that beautiful dick of his in his pants, either—not for you or any other woman." She spun her chair again, gave a backhand wave, and disappeared through the door.

Gina closed her mind against her mother's parting shot. She wouldn't let it reach her or weaken her resolve. But something else Delores had said resonated.

"*. . . put lightning in a bottle.*" She tossed the paper towel she'd been using for her feet into the trash and stayed in the kitchen long after she'd heard the parlor door close.

Yes, that's exactly what she needed to do. She shuddered, rubbed her arms. If she'd been successful tonight, if she had . . . eliminated Camryn, it would have been a disastrous mistake, giving Adam a clear shot at getting his daughter.

He'd have no further use for Gina Solari's body or her law degree. He'd leave. She wouldn't be able to hold him.

Her heart hammered in her breast. She would not allow that to happen.

What she needed to do was put Adam in a bottle.

She walked to the sofa and retrieved the gun.

Chapter 21

Camryn woke with a start and immediately glanced at her bedside clock. A digitally presented 7:07 A.M. was her answer. Her first thought was that she was late. Her second was, she was naked.

She heard a pot bang in the kitchen. That would be Dad, starting breakfast.

Closing her eyes again, she lay very still, not sure how to feel or what to say to the man in her bed, a man she'd made love with, whose arms she'd fallen asleep in. Her only thought, and it came through loud and clear, was that she wasn't sorry. She plumped the pillow, opened her eyes on the day, and lazed in this easy, warm moment, savored the softness in her body, the sense of . . . "wellness" was the only word that fit.

She smiled into her pillow. Hale and hearty, that's exactly how she felt. That and well-loved, in the physical sense. None of which made the morning-after necessity of rolling over and looking into Dan's eyes any less nerve-wracking.

But roll over she did . . .

He wasn't there.

Her hale and hearty feelings shriveled a bit, as she put her feet on the floor and reached for her robe.

In the shower, the incongruous events of last night filtered back, gunshots, stalkers, making love—and her plan to call Paul Grantman. Get Kylie somewhere safe. She pushed aside the sexual afterglow. In another time, another place, she might have basked in it, but right now she didn't have that luxury.

She was on the bottom step when Dan came out of the downstairs bathroom. His hair was damp, and he was buttoning up his shirt, leaving her a last glimpse of a chest she'd come to know intimately in the small hours of the morning. Her breath caught, and that afterglow she'd beaten back began to pulse.

When he saw her, his hands stilled on the last button. "Hi," he said, his eyes covering her as deftly as his body had done last night. "Sleep okay?"

She caught the knowing glance, the pleased look of male arrogance—which, damn it, he was entitled to—and gave him back a raised brow. "No. I had the most terrible dream."

He instantly sobered, the arrogance replaced by a probing look of concern. "What?"

She looked around; the hall was clear. She moved closer to him, whispered, "I was having spectacular sex with this . . . love god. It was absolutely incredible, then"—she sighed noisily and waved a hand—"he was gone, just when things were getting interesting."

He smiled. "That's the thing about love gods. Never can trust the bastards."

"Daddy, you're here!"

His smile expanded, and he swung Kylie into his arms, kissed her. "Said I would be, didn't I?" He touched his cheek, turned his head, and she kissed it soundly. To Camryn the exchange had the look of a ritual, making her feel warm—and left out, until Kylie said, "You, too, Aunt Cammie." When she put her arms out, Camryn moved closer and offered her cheek to get a clone of the damp spot just above Dan's jaw.

Her morning loving done, Kylie put her arms back around Dan's neck and looked at him. "Tent's making wuffles," she said. "You want some?"

Dan put her down. "Sure do. You go ahead and tell 'Tent' I'll be right there." When the child was gone, he looked again at Camryn. "And won't he love that!"

"He won't mind. He'll understand why you stayed. As for the rest? Our business."

He nodded. "Getting back to my departure from your bed, and that love-god thing—"

"Don't let it go to your head, Lambert," she said, arching a brow, barely managing not to paste a smile wide as a clown's on her face. God, it felt good, looking at him, having him within touching distance.

He grinned at that, then added, "I left because I thought my staying the night in your bed might not play well with your dad—maybe confuse Kylie."

She took a step closer, kissed where Kylie had. "You did the right thing, cowboy."

He looked down the hall, saw they were alone, and pulled her close. His back against the wall, he tugged her against a, sadly, unusable morning erection. His kiss was a hell of a lot more than a peck, leaving her breathless and wanting more. "What happened to the 'love god' thing?" he asked, brushing her mouth with his thumb.

"I'm a woman of many fantasies," she said, then pulled back. "Unfortunately, making out in the hall while my dad makes 'wuffles' isn't one of them."

They took the few steps down the hall together, but before entering the kitchen, she put a hand on Dan's arm. "About Kylie. I'm going to call Paul right after breakfast."

His expression darkened. "I hate the idea, but I agree. Kylie will be safe there."

"Then I'll call Gina, tell her we're coming over."

"Now, there's a woman I can't wait to meet."

Camryn gave him a sharp look. "She hasn't done anything, Dan."

"She's got Dunn under her roof, hasn't she? I'd say that makes her—as the cops are inclined to say these days—a person of interest." His tone was flat, darkly wry.

She decided not to push it. When he met Gina, he'd see for himself what a good person she was. Adam being there wouldn't change that—although getting him the hell out of there wouldn't hurt. "And, Dan?"

"Hm." He looked down at her.

"Let's not tell Dad where we're taking Kylie." She hesitated. "He and Paul have a history, and it's not a good one. It'd be easier if we told him after Kylie is safe at Paul's. For now let's just say we're taking her for a walk. Okay?"

His intelligent eyes filled with questions, but he left them unsaid. "Your play. Your way."

"Thanks." She stepped into the kitchen, hoping to God her *play* was the right one.

Paul closed the bedroom door and headed for his study. He had no doubt that Erin would sleep until noon—possibly longer. So far he'd learned nothing. When they'd picked her up last night, it had been purely by chance, her being only minutes from home and standing outside Camryn Bruce's home. What the hell she'd been doing there, he had no idea. And maybe he didn't want to know.

He'd barely sat down at his desk in the study, when his phone rang. Maury was out, but the maid would screen it.

Seconds later, his line lit up.

"Hello."

"Mr. Grantman, there's a Delores Solari on the phone, she says it's urgent."

Paul rolled his eyes. Jesus, he never came back to the lake that he didn't hear from that damned woman. You'd think he had a damned GPS up his ass. He'd paid a steep price for a few nights of sex too many years ago to count—proving beyond a doubt a man's dick not only doesn't have a conscience, it often doesn't have any taste. His ill-fated bedding of Solari had cost him both a wife and a pile of cash. He'd been paying ever since.

What she had on him was small potatoes by today's standards. Hell, three in a bed, a few lousy snaps. Nothing. But he was still paying. He was an important man, a visible man; he didn't need old dirt being thrown at his name. It was easier to pay, and Delores was smart enough never to ask for too much, and she never wheedled or begged; she abraded, until you paid to get her the hell out of your face.

He huffed out a breath. Delores Solari was the last person on earth he wanted to hear from, especially today.

He'd hoped the call was from Steve Bork, the investigator he'd hired to run a background on Camryn Bruce. Nobody was totally clean, all the time, and if there was anything he could use, Bork would find it. Jason would take it from there, and Kylie would be as good as his—and Erin's.

He tapped his fingers on his desk.

"Tell her I'm busy," he finally said and prepared to hang up.

"She said she knew you'd say that, and that if you did, I was to tell you—and I was to use these exact words—that her call 'wasn't about the same old crap.' She insists it's urgent. She says she'll set her phone to autodial if you don't talk to her."

Shit! "I'll take it, Anya, thank you." He hit line one on his phone with more force than necessary.

"Delores," he said, gritting his teeth. "How are you?"

"I'm impressed, Paul. You actually said that as if you gave a damn." "But I'm all right—thank you very much— now that I've got through your palace guard."

Oh, yes, it was the usual darkly sarcastic Delores, he'd

known and fucked—to his unending regret. He forced a laugh. "Hardly that."

"Humph!"

Paul took a breath for patience. "What can I do for you?"

"You can send a car for me, tonight, eight o'clock. And make sure it's something big enough to handle this wheeled metal contraption I'm trussed to."

"Excuse me?"

"We need to talk. And I can't do it from here."

No way. No way was Paul letting this hellish spider of a woman in his home. "I'm sure whatever you want can be handled over the phone, Delores."

"Not this."

"If it's more money—"

"Screw your money, Paul. I said we need to talk—face to face."

Paul's temper flared. "I don't have time—"

"You have the time all right. Because, as it turns out, I have a houseguest you have a particular fondness for."

"What the hell are you talking about?"

"I'm talking about Adam Dunn, Paul. You remember him, don't you?"

Jesus! He dropped the receiver from his ear. *What the hell . . .*

He heard a low laugh filter through the line and put the phone back to his ear. "Got your interest, have I?" she said.

"What's going on, Delores?" He steadied himself.

"You mean other than Adam's plan to fuck his way to getting your granddaughter, and my too-stupid-to-live daughter's determination to help him? Nothing much."

"You don't know what you're talking about. I don't have my granddaughter. Camryn has."

She laughed again, enjoying herself. "Yes, I know. I think that's where the fucking comes in."

"Is this some kind of sick joke?"

She went on as if he hadn't spoken. "By the way, I take back that 'screw your money' comment. After what I tell you, you'll be taking my calls for the rest of your rich, pampered life. Eight o'clock. I'll be waiting." She hung up, but must have fumbled with the phone, because he heard a second click.

Paul frowned at the dead phone, hung up, and tried to make sense of whatever it was Delores had just told him.

The doorbell rang. So did the phone—again. When it kept ringing, he figured Anya was getting the door, so he picked up. "Paul Grantman."

"Steve Bork, Mr. Grantman. I said I'd get back to y—"

He steadied himself. "What do you have?"

"How about I bring it over?"

"Give me the digest version." The call from Delores had him rattled. What the hell did she have on Dunn? On Camryn? He forced himself into the moment, the words coming through the line.

"The woman looks sterling," Bork said, sounding irritated. "No criminal record. No bad company. No drugs. No booze. Nothing. Married. Divorced—one of those no-fault, uncontested deals. Easy all round. No kids. Can't have 'em, judging from how much time she's spent with gynies. Runs a business from her home. Successful with it. No major personal debt. A few credit cards. Nothing over the top. About forty grand in savings. Involved in a couple of orgs, both legit, a women's shelter, a place called Mayday House a few miles south of Seattle, and a kid's—"

"Has she been seeing anyone lately?" The sound of paper rustling came down the line and fed into Paul's growing frustration.

"If you mean of the opposite-sex variety, nope. Not since her husband left."

"You're sure?"

"I'm sure."

"Send that report over, then start running a check on a man named Adam Dunn. Maury will tell you where to start. Call him in an hour—and I'd like everything you can get before eight o'clock tonight."

Bork was sputtering as Paul hung up. And he'd barely done that before there was a soft rap on the door. Rattled, he cursed, ran a hand along his nape, and snapped, "Yes. What is it?" He stayed at his desk.

"Mr. Grantman, there are some people here to see you." It was Anya, the housekeeper.

"Who?"

"They said to tell you, Dan and Camryn. They've brought your granddaughter."

Paul got to his feet. Of all of the morning's surprises, this one topped them all. First off, Lambert and Bruce together—with Kylie. Not a good thing. And second, the three of them arriving on his doorstep. He thought about that a minute and figured it could only mean one thing: they wanted something. But, then, who the hell didn't?

"Bring them in, Anya. And go wake Mrs. Grantman. She'll want to see Kylie."

Anya nodded, stepped back, and closed the door. Seconds later she opened it again, and Dan and Camryn stepped into the room.

Chapter 22

Gina watched Adam get out of bed, watched his flaccid penis sway between his strong runner's legs as he headed toward the bathroom.

Idly, dreamily, she wondered why he didn't ask her to run with him, like he had Camryn, then Holly. He'd started them both on the running kick. Even after he'd left, they'd kept at it. All those ugly lonely miles . . .

It was the one thing he'd given them that she didn't envy.

Sexually sated, she stretched, long and luxuriously. What flowed through her muscles and threaded along her senses was the rightness of things. Bliss and certainty that finally . . . finally she had who and what she wanted. She ran her hand down her belly, cupped herself, and closed her eyes, imagining Adam's hand there. Adam's mouth.

Staring at the ceiling, softly stroking her pubis, she neared ecstasy. Now half closing her eyes, she opened herself, imagined her fingers to be Adam's fingers, imagined her soft moans to be Adam's breath against her heated skin. In the years alone, waiting for her time with Adam, while she watched him first with Camryn, then Holly, and particularly in the months after he left her, she'd become skillful at pleasuring herself. She'd accepted long ago that her body, her passionate nature, demanded constant physical release. There'd been other men, nameless, faceless men, used out of desperation, but none of them were Adam.

But now, being with him again, despite her learned skill at easing her clamoring body, her ministrations were a distant second to his touch—nothing but the weakest of preludes. But until he came back, was ready for her again, she'd make do with her own hand.

She found her clitoris, closed her eyes.

"What the hell are you doing, Gina?"

Her eyes opened, her hand stopped. "I'd think that was obvious."

"Jesus, don't you ever get enough?"

Gina denied the pulsing of her body, pulled her hand back, and studied Adam's annoyance. A few days ago, it would have bothered her, panicked her. She'd have been terrorized at the thought she'd displeased him, that he would leave. Not anymore. And never again. It was satisfying, empowering, to at last have a plan. "I thought you liked watching me get myself off. That it turned you on." She slid naked to the edge of the bed, made no move to cover herself, and played with her nipples.

Adam studied her, his laser-blue eyes simmering, but not sexually. *Anger,* she thought, but was undisturbed. "Not twenty-four seven, Gina. That's goddamn eerie. Hell, *you're* goddamn eerie."

She spread her legs, and her breathing hitched when cool air touched her heat and moisture. "I'm anything you want me to be. You know that."

"Yeah, don't I just." He looked away briefly. "Why don't you throw a robe on. I'd like to talk a little business. Deal with this Camryn thing." He took a step toward her, stopping far enough away so she couldn't touch him, take him in her hands. "You said you had an idea. Let's hear it."

Gina would rather get him back to his warm bed, delay cold, hard decisions. She wanted him. God, she always wanted him. She swallowed, wet her lips, and closed her legs against the throbbing between them, told herself to hold on.

Adam scanned her nakedness, her tightly closed legs, and shot her a knowing look, as if he understood she couldn't tolerate too long of a wait before he fucked her again. That's what it had become between them: fucking, hard, fast, and so hot their sweat mingled, a searing adhesive that locked them together.

Still, she couldn't get enough of him. It was as if, since he'd come back, a sexual switch in her had flicked to ON and set there.

He cocked his head, his expression shifting to curious. "You've got a real problem, don't you, baby? Too hot there"—he nodded toward the apex of her thighs—"too damned often, right?" He looked bemused. "You know some people get help for that, go to those sex-addiction meetings."

"I thought that's what we just had." She stroked the sheets of his bed, still rumpled from their lovemaking. "Besides, you're all the help I need." She looked at him. "I need you, for this"—she touched herself—"and you need me to get to Grantman's money. So, the only meeting I'm interested in we can take in this bed. If that doesn't work for you . . ." She managed a shrug and to tamp down the quick shaft of terror that her implied threat would make him leave. But she had no choice; she had to take control.

The trace of humor left his face, and for a time he didn't speak.

"What are you thinking?" she asked, studying his too handsome, unusually thoughtful face.

He took his time. "I'm thinking about that old saying about being careful what you wish for, you might get it."

"Which means?"

"You. Christ, you're ready for me all the time. Wanting all the time. Like a goddamned wet dream on constant replay. Hot ass, twenty-four seven." He glanced away, and she saw his brows knit. He rubbed his jaw, looked back at her. "You're right, I do need you, but I think you need my cock even more." He reached to stroke her cheek, gently, then trailed a finger down her throat, over her breast, to her nipple. When he pinched her lightly, she jerked, and a smug grin briefly tilted his lips. "Don't worry, I'm not about to waste that greedy body of yours. I'll get to it, but business first. Okay? You said you had an idea. Let's hear it."

"Okay, business it is." Disappointment shivered through her, a hint of shame, but she resisted it. Adam was not in charge; she was—something he'd find out soon enough. But for now, he was right; it was time to talk business. Past time. She reached for the short satin robe she'd worn to come to him earlier and slipped it on, not bothering with the tie at the waist. When she stood, Adam's heatless gaze skimmed the strip of her skin, bared to him by the gaping robe.

Telling herself to be careful, very, very careful, she met his gaze. "My idea, Adam, is to kill Camryn."

She spoke the words clearly, exactly as she'd practiced them, strongly, and with utter conviction. She'd always excelled in court, and she'd use that skill to bring Adam to heel.

Let the game begin.

His mouth slackened, then he shook his head. "Fuck! I've been screwing your brains out for days—and you make a damn joke," he said. "You're not getting it, baby. This is serious shit for me. Dangerous shit. If I don't come up with some cash, I'm a dead man. Don't you get that?"

"What I 'get' is that the most expeditious way out of your 'shit' is a dead Camryn Bruce."

It was the first time she'd seen Adam stunned to silence. He was letting the reality of his situation take hold. Good.

"You're running out of time." Gina tied her robe, picked

up the glass of water from his bedside table, and donned her legal persona. "Which is why my idea is so brilliant." She drank the water, straightened her shoulders—like she used to do in court before summation. "There are two ways to deal with Camryn. By the rules, which means fairly, legally—and slowly—with no guarantee of success. Or"— she shrugged—"get rid of her, which will get you what you want, painlessly and quickly." She met his gaze.

"You're serious." He still looked stunned, but there was something else in his eyes. Calculation. Respect.

"Deadly serious—if you'll excuse the pun." She took a step away. "With Camryn gone, you become the resident thorn in Paul Grantman's side, and the custody issue will be blown wide open." She quirked her lips. "Paul doesn't like thorns; he tends to pay them off." His tidy little loans to her mother proved that point. "With Camryn out of the way, as Kylie's biological father you have a shot at getting her back. Paul will know that, and if he doesn't, his lawyer will quickly correct his ignorance. It will be father first, grand-father second. Of course, you'll have to do the responsible-dad routine. I can help you with that."

She looked him up and down. "Yes, I'd say, as thorns go, you'll measure up nicely. There isn't a judge in the universe who won't hear you out—they're bound to." She paused. "You'll have Paul scrambling from day one. My guess is he'll pay a lot of money to avoid that scramble. And, of course, it helps that he hates you, which means he'll pay even more to ensure you don't get custody of Kylie. Play it right, my love, and you'll avoid that judge altogether."

He arched a brow and frowned at her. "How's that?"

"Call it 'settling out of court' for want of a better de-scription."

"Like extortion."

"Pretty much what you had in mind all along, isn't it?"

He said nothing.

She went on. "When Camryn's out of the way, you simply have a quiet conversation with Paul. You tell him how he can avoid the hassle of a legal challenge—that all it takes is money." She rolled the water glass in her hands. "My bet is he'll pay whatever you ask, and you'll never see the inside of a courtroom."

"But kill Camryn . . . Jesus!" Adam repeated, his high forehead creasing to a frown. When he looked at her, his gaze was densely speculative. "She was my first—" He stopped, seemed to reconsider his words "She's your friend . . . and you can suggest this?"

"You're my only *friend*," she said. "You're my everything." She didn't need to be reminded that Camryn was Adam's first . . . attraction, that back then he'd been true to her, despite all Gina's efforts to get his attention, until Holly came back from Europe and took him under the sheets in that motel room where they'd spent endless hours. After that it was all Holly, all the time. Except for one brief time out—his interlude with her. And Delores.

The look he gave her was indecipherable. Then he shook his head as if to clear it before turning his back on her and walking to the window. He stood, staring out, with his hands on his hips.

Looking at him caused her heart to jump, her sight to dim. Her thoughts turned to Camryn—the woman who'd let him go. . . .

Righteous, smart-thinking Camryn. Forgiving Camryn. Naive Camryn. Trusting Camryn.

When Gina had told her about Adam and Holly, those long years ago, about what they were doing in that motel, Camryn dropped Adam cold, never looked back. She'd even forgiven Holly when she and Adam split from each other a few months later—a split that turned out to be number one in what was to be a series of breakups and make-ups in their messy, obsessive relationship. It was a relationship Gina assiduously kept track of and Camryn knew nothing about until Kylie was born and Holly came clean.

Even then Camryn had stood by Holly, attended her delivery, believed her when she said she was through with Adam. Oh, yes, Camryn had stood by. "That's what friends are for," she'd said, "to be there, when you needed them."

Everybody loved Camryn.

You shouldn't have kissed her, Adam, and you shouldn't have joked about proposing to her—or gone to see her. You shouldn't have fucked my mother—or Holly. You shouldn't do anything except be with me. Only with me. Always with me.

Gina swallowed and pressed a hand to her throat when something sharp and bilious rose from it to coat her mouth—the acrid taste of jealousy. The bitter food of the discarded woman.

Adam turned and faced her. His expression was sober, unsettled. Their eyes met, held, and her stomach fluttered as if a thousand butterflies were testing their wings.

She forced her mind to what had to be done, her next step. He was too quiet, too indecisive. "You wanted my advice on how to solve your problem," she said. "I've given it to you. You could at least comment."

"Okay, here's one. I came here looking for legal advice, not a how-to primer for spending the rest of my life rotting in prison."

"Nobody will go to prison."

"I'll bet there's dozens of guys shuffling along death row who've heard that pickup line."

"There's no risk. Not if it's done right."

He shook his head, but she could see he was thinking, beginning to see her logic. When he started to pace the room, Gina walked to the bureau, opened the bottom drawer, and took out the gun she'd put there earlier. She went back to where Adam now stood beside the rumpled bed and held it out to him. "Take it," she said.

He looked at the gun as if it were an ingot fresh from the furnace.

"It's not loaded. Here." Holding on to the barrel, she offered him the grip. "Take it," she said again. "See how it feels." Powerful. Potent. Deadly.

He looked at her hand, at the innocence of the dimpled metal grip, and took the gun.

Yes!

He studied the cold steel, enclosed the grip in his hand, then abruptly tossed it on the bed. He turned back to her. "I'm not a killer, Gina." he said. "I'm a lot of things, most of which I'll take hell's heat for, but killing . . ." He shook his head. "No."

She nodded, glanced at the gun on the bed. "All right, then I'll do it for you." She met his stormy gaze. "It's another way for me to prove how much I love you."

She saw the faint glimmer of acceptance in his eyes, saw how the idea he wouldn't have to dirty his own hands made the difference. His argument, when it came, carried no passion. "There's another way," he said. "There has to be."

"Shush, darling." She touched his mouth with her fingertips, then replaced them with her mouth. Pulling away, she said. "Leave it to me. I'll take care of everything. When it's done, you'll have what you want. All the money you'll ever need." Again she glanced at the gun on the bed, the gun with his fingerprints on it.

And I'll have you . . .

Camryn might have been your first, and Holly might have been your second, but I'll be your forever.

Camryn entered Paul's spacious study first, holding Kylie's hand. Dan followed, wishing to hell he was anywhere but here. Right now northern Canada in the dead of winter seemed preferable to this warm, oak-paneled room where Paul Grantman stood in the center of the room, as cool and hard as a cement gargoyle.

God, he was going to love this. . . .

"Go see your grandpa, sweetheart," Camryn said, releasing Kylie's hand. One thing was sure, by the look of her, Camryn was as reluctant to be here as he was.

She hadn't been reluctant last night. She'd been hot, willing, a sexual storm in his arms.

His gut tensed. This wasn't the time to think about last night, whatever the havoc it had wreaked on his "cool" quotient. Later. He'd think about it later—when he had her in his bed again.

Kylie ran to Paul, her enthusiasm undimmed by the tension in the room, and he lifted her in his arms. She hugged him as if he were a god, then took his face in her hands and kissed him square on the mouth. "My grandpa," she said and put her head on his shoulder. And while Paul got a queer smile on his face, Dan had an irrational stab of jealousy; he shoved it back. The man was Kylie's grandfather, nothing would change that. Too bad he wouldn't settle for that without having an ulterior motive.

Paul put his hand on her head, her silky, little-girl hair. "How's my best sweetheart?" he said. There was a hell of a lot more warmth in his eyes when he looked at Kylie than at any other time.

"I had wuffles," Kylie announced. "Tent made them. And lots and lots of sirp."

"Sounds good." Continuing to stroke her hair, Paul looked over her head to where Dan and Camryn stood, his gaze one big question mark. When Kylie wiggled, he let her down; she went immediately to his desk.

"She'll make a mess," Camryn said, but made no move to stave off the coming havoc. She looked amused, as if introducing their pint-sized house-wrecker to Paul's organized study provided a sliver of comic relief in what was a grim situation.

Paul was quick. "Here, honey. I'll get you some pencils and paper. Okay?"

When Paul had Kylie settled, busily creating scribbles at his desk with a five-hundred-dollar Mont Blanc pen, he looked at Camryn. "What's this all about?"

Dan heard Camryn take a deep breath. "I want you to keep Kylie for a few days," she said.

Paul's gaze sharpened. Dan could damn well see the wheels turning. "A few days," he repeated. "Considering I'm on your least-favorite-person list, the question begs to be asked. Why?"

"We've had some trouble," Camryn said. "And we think it's best Kylie be away from the house until we settle things."

"There are two key words in that sentence. 'We' and 'trouble.' " He went behind his desk, again put his hand on Kylie's head, bent now over her drawing. "I take it the 'we' is the two of you." He looked at Camryn and Dan in turn, but his eyes lingered on Dan. "You sure as hell didn't waste your time grieving, did you?"

"My grief, my business," Dan said. What Grantman thought of his reply, he didn't care. He glanced at Camryn, but her expression was set to cool. If what Paul said troubled her, it didn't show.

Paul's expression chilled even more. He went on, "Then let's get to the 'trouble' part of the equation. Particularly as it affects my granddaughter."

Before either of them could respond, the door opened and Erin walked into the room. Dan eyed her, noted the weariness in her eyes, her pallor. She looked as if she hadn't slept or wasn't feeling well. He knew how much Holly had hated her peer-age stepmother. She'd called Erin her "junkie mini-mom." But his opinion of Erin, since meeting her, was less harsh. She struck him as tragic, both delicate and flawed.

She was extremely beautiful, even in the jeans and outsize tee she wore.

Erin's glance, accompanied by a quick smile and a "Hello," immediately flew to Kylie. "Hi, little girl," she said and held out her arms.

Kylie rounded the desk and did her hug thing. Erin had dropped to her knees to make it easy. His princess loved everyone, it seemed, and would until life taught her caution and how much of that love she could risk.

"Can I take her for a while, Camryn?" Erin asked, her tone soft, somewhat shy. She was still on her knees. "I've got some dishes for her and a new doll. They're in the living room. We can have a tea party."

Kylie's eyes widened, and she took Erin's hand. "Can I, Aunt Cammie? Can I?"

Camryn studied Erin, then glanced at Paul. She seemed reluctant to let Kylie leave her sight. Which, considering why they were here, didn't make a hell of a lot of sense, but Dan understood the feeling.

"Sure, honey," she finally said. "You go with Erin. Have fun."

When they were gone, Paul got straight to the business at hand. "What kind of trouble?" He gestured toward the sofa and chairs grouped around a fireplace. They sat.

"Someone shot out my kitchen window last night," Camryn said.

"Jesus!" His gaze went to Dan. "You were there?"

"Yes."

"And Kylie?"

"She was there, too. Dan was holding her," Camryn said. "But she's okay. We're all okay. One of the bullets scraped Dan's arm."

"Your arm? And you were holding my granddaughter?" Paul leaped to his feet. "Jesus," he said again. "And you have no idea who did it?"

To Dan, the man looked tight as a bow. More so than usual. "No, but Camryn was the target, not Kylie."

"We don't know that for certain, Dan."

"Whoever it was shot three bullets, two of them in your direction. That's 'certain' enough for me," he said.

Camryn shook a negative. Stubborn woman. "The police think it's possible it was kids, coming in from the lake, their idea of a prank, but—"

"But . . . ?" Paul looked at Dan.

"I think it might have been Dunn," Dan said, seeing no reason not to. "He's at the Solari house."

"I know." Paul's gaze shot to Camryn.

"You know?" Camryn echoed.

"Delores called me—not a half hour ago."

"I see."

"Glad you do, because I sure as hell don't. I thought I'd seen the last of that lowlife bastard Dunn when he took my check." He shook his head. "God knows Holly wanted no more to do with him."

When Camryn glanced his way, Dan said nothing. "If you know he's here, then you know what he wants," she said.

"He wants Kylie." He paced a few steps. "Or to be more accurate, he wants me to pay him to go away again. But you know that, don't you?"

"Yes."

"Which means you're in his way."

Dan had to hand it to him; the man was quick.

"Which does *not* mean he shot out my window." She stared at each of them in turn. "Adam doing something like that is completely out of character."

Dan let out a quiet breath; maybe he wasn't as *up* on Dunn's *character* as Camryn, but he sure knew a motive when he saw one—and getting Camryn out of the way qualified big time.

Paul wasn't so quiet. "Perfectly in character, if you ask me." He got up, went to stand in front of the fireplace. "And while I take care of Kylie, where will you be?"

"The Solaris," Camryn answered calmly.

"Why in God's name would you do that? Risk that? If it was Dunn who shot at you, what's to stop him from doing it again?

Camryn looked ready to snap, and Dan already knew her answer. "Number one, it wasn't Adam who did the shooting, and number two, there'll be five people in the house—a small horde of witnesses—hardly the opportune time to try and kill someone." She rolled her eyes.

Paul shook his head. "I think you're crazy."

"Think whatever you want. All we're asking is that you take care of Kylie. Will you do that?"

"Of course." He looked at Dan, his expression flat. "And you go along with this?"

"You look after Kylie. I'll look after Camryn." He looked at her, saw her frown. "And until things are sorted out, she's right, Kylie is safer here."

"Neither of you is stupid. You know I'll turn this ridiculous . . . escapade—and your asking me to protect my granddaughter—to my advantage, don't you?"

Camryn looked him square in the eye. "You're boring me, Paul. And not telling me anything I don't know. But Kylie—if you haven't figure it out yet—comes first."

He didn't look cowed, but he did look at her with a new respect. "You're stubborn, Camryn. I'll hand you that. Not that it will do you any good." His gaze whipped between them. "When are you going to the Solari place?" he asked her.

"We're on our way there now."

"Hold off until tonight."

Camryn frowned. Dan asked the obvious question, "Why would we do that?"

"Because," Paul said, his tone crisp. "Delores will be here shortly after eight, which, by the way, will seriously cut into that 'horde of witnesses' you mentioned, Camryn." When he got no reaction from her, he shook his head, went on. "When Delores called me earlier, it was to tell me she had information for me about Dunn and her daughter . . . what's her name," he said. "You should know what that information is before you head over there."

"Why would you want to help us?" Camryn asked, not masking her suspicion.

"I don't particularly. But, as you said, Kylie comes first, so for the next few hours, we'll be in this together." He didn't look as if the thought pleased him, more like he was chewing old leather. "If Adam Dunn had a hand in firing a gun anywhere near my granddaughter, I want to know about it." He headed for the door, opened it, and stood waiting for them to leave. "You know what they say, information is power, so if I were you, I'd wait for my call."

Chapter 23

Ten minutes later they'd said good-bye to Kylie and were outside the security wall that enclosed Grantman's lakeside estate.

As Dan cleared the driveway leading from the lake and pulled his Navigator onto the road, Camryn looked over her shoulder at the closed gates.

"Don't worry. She'll be fine. And when this is over, we'll have her back," Dan said.

She faced front again, then faced him. "You don't have to 'look out' for me, Dan," she said, echoing the words he'd said to Grantman.

"No, I don't."

"And you've been using the word 'we' quite a lot. You probably shouldn't get used to it."

"And you probably should." He turned at the next corner. "I'm hungry. I spotted a restaurant when we drove in, about a mile from here. You up for some food?"

She nodded. "It will give us a chance to talk . . . settle a few things."

"That us-we thing?" He smiled at her.

"You think it's funny," she said, narrowing her eyes.

"I think it's inevitable. Have since last night."

She rolled her eyes. "One night of sex and you're into inevitability. Is that how it happened with Holly?"

"Cheap shot, Bruce." He'd given a lot more thought to making that mistake than she gave him credit for.

"Maybe. But great sex aside, we definitely have some trust issues to work on."

"How about you tackle the issues, while I tackle a burger."

"Food first, communication second." May I be very trite and say that's just like a man?"

"You may," he said.

She huffed at his terse answer and looked out the window.

The restaurant was less than ten minutes away. He found a parking spot, turned off the motor. When he looked at her, she was staring straight ahead, a slight frown creasing her brow. He turned her face to catch her gaze. "Any questions you have, I'll answer. But before we go any further, you should understand this. I screwed up with Holly, and I'll regret that—for her sake and mine—for a very long time. But that has nothing to do with what's going on with us. Another thing, I'm not putting our 'great sex aside.' Not for a second. Now . . ." He leaned across her and opened her door. "Can we eat?"

She didn't move, continued to sit there looking . . . studious, so he got out and went around to her door and opened it fully. "You coming?"

She got out of the car, squared off on him. "Only a man can say food, sex, and inevitability in one breath—*and* get pushy about them at the same time."

"It's a gift." He took her by the elbow and steered her toward the restaurant door. "Makes up for God taking away our clubs and animal skins."

When they were settled at the table and had ordered their lunch, Dan the burger he craved, and Camryn a chicken Caesar, she took her cell phone from her bag.

Dan sat back in his chair, idly rotated his water glass, and cocked his head in question.

"I'm calling Gina," she said, "to tell her I'll be later."

"Didn't know you'd called her to set up a time." He frowned. "Have you considered our purpose in going there would have been better served by surprise?" He took a drink of his water and set hot, questioning eyes on her.

His eyes were intelligent, warm, and even in daylight disturbingly sexy. Camryn refused to think deeply about last night, refused to deal with the insane sense of disloyalty she felt about sleeping with her best friend's husband. God, she hoped it hadn't been some Freudian, adolescent maneuver to get back at Holly for Adam! She wouldn't think about that, wouldn't think about any of it until her head was clear, which, thanks to a shooting, accusations about Gina, and a bout of wildly exciting lovemaking, it definitely was not.

"You arriving on the Solari doorstep will be surprise enough, trust me," she said. "But, as it turns out, I didn't call. Gina called me—before we left for Paul's. She said she and Adam wanted to talk to me, that they wanted me to understand. She also said she has a big surprise for me." Camryn keyed in the telephone number but didn't push SEND. "But if she hadn't called, I would have had to anyway, because you *do not* drop in at the Solari house." Camryn had a pretty good idea the surprise Gina mentioned had to do with her and Adam's relationship. *Oh, God, Gina, you can't be that stupid. You can't!*

"Why not?"

"The house runs by Delores Solari's rules. And one of them is visits by appointment only."

"She won't be there, so why does it matter?"

She looked at him, blinked. "I forgot. She'll be with Paul."

"I'm curious, though, what happens if you break the rule?"

Camryn pushed the SEND button. "You could be Prince Charles and you wouldn't get past the front gate, let alone in the house."

"You're kidding."

"Nope. And so you know, if Delores was there, my sneaking you in would get me banned for life. Inhospitable and eccentric don't begin to describe the venerable Delores Solari."

"Sounds charming."

"If there's an antonym for that word, you've got it." And throw in whacko and narcissistic, she thought, as well as bone-mean and more than a little freaky. Camryn was relieved she wouldn't be there, for her sake and Dan's. Every man Delores met was judged as if he were raw meat, and every woman—even her own daughter—was considered competition. Delores was unadulterated ego, pure and uncut. A woman impossible to like. There'd been a time when Gina stood up to her, but not anymore. Not since she'd come home, a ghost of the woman she once was.

The Solaris were a complicated family.

Still holding the phone to her ear, Camryn heard someone pick up. "Gina? . . . Uh huh . . . Me too. . . . But, I can't do it now. . . . It'll be better for me after Kylie's in bed," she lied and grimaced. "I was thinking tonight, say nine-ish?" She listened, then shot a glance at Dan, who was listening intently to her side of the conversation. "Wine? Sure, I can bring a bottle. . . . All right, see you then."

She clicked off the phone and slipped it back in her bag.

"Everything set?"

"Hm-m." She picked up her napkin. Gina had sounded cheerful, almost jovial. *Because she's having sex with Adam. That makes most women cheerful.* The thought soured her mood.

"You okay?"

"She's my friend. It doesn't feel right, not telling her about your coming." She looked up in time to see the waiter bearing down on them, lunches in hand, and welcomed the interruption. The business with Gina was complicated, lunch was not. So she decided to concentrate on her salad.

As if Dan sensed her unease, he remained silent, but midway through lunch, he leaned forward. "Look, chances are your friend had nothing to do with the shooting, but she's playing host, and maybe a whole lot more, to the man who might have . . . a man who wants to take Kylie away from you—and me."

"If that was an attempt to make me feel better about duping Gina, it didn't work." She gave him a level stare. "I don't like game-playing for any reason. I'm no good at it." She dug into her salad, then just as quickly put her fork down and added, "Besides, if anyone's in danger here, it's Gina. If she's playing with Adam Dunn, she'll get hurt. It's what he does. He uses people and he hurts people."

"Not to split hairs, but he uses *women*. And they let him." His face was hard. And a brief flash of pain—or anger—showed in his eyes.

"I didn't mean . . ." Camryn knew he was thinking about Holly, that she'd opened a wound. *Damn!*

Dan sat back, looked seriously puzzled. "What the hell has that guy got, anyway?"

"Let's drop it." No way on earth could she explain Adam to a man like Dan. They were polar opposites . . . except in bed.

"Let's not." He leaned forward, and something shifted in his eyes, making them the eyes of an interrogator. "I'd like to know why a man who made love to three best friends, and went on to screw half the female population of Miami, is welcomed back to a woman's bed as if his fucking around

on her was no more than a brief and well-earned holiday."
He sat back, his hard question resting between them like a
headless snake. "Is he that good in bed?"

When the hand holding the fork started to shake, Camryn lowered it to the table and met his gaze. "Yes. He's that
good."

He drew in a breath, and his jaw hardened.

"You want to know about Adam," she said. "I'll tell
you. There wasn't a girl in college who didn't lust after him,
not because he was brilliantly handsome—which he was,
and is—but because he had what we called the s-e-X *factor,*
a kind of magnetism, indescribable really. But it worked
every time. You could almost call it a gift."

"Most men would," he said, his tone ironic.

She looked away from him a moment, faintly embarrassed at telling such an intimate truth. But he wanted to
know, so she'd tell him. "Whatever it was, Adam smiled
into your eyes and he had you. It was . . . primal. As if he
were elementally sexual in nature." She shrugged. "Back
then, which is when Adam and I were . . . together, he had
something else. A complete lack of ego. If you complimented him, he actually blushed. It was as if he didn't know
how good-looking he was, the power he had over women."
She paused, ran her finger along the handle of her fork.

"I'm guessing he figured it out."

"Yes, and when he did, he cheated on me with Holly, on
Holly with Gina, on Gina with her mother—and I don't
know how many others." She looked at him again. "And
most all of them would take him back. Time and again."
She paused, a touch of regret softening her words. "Even
Holly, I guess."

"Jesus."

Dan looked disgusted and confused; neither reaction surprised her.

"I honestly believed Gina would be the exception," she

said. "I mean it's one thing when a man cheats on you with another woman, but with your own mother..." She wanted to defend her friend, but didn't know how. She certainly couldn't dispute the fact that Adam was in the Solari house again despite all the pain he'd caused.

"They took up with each other a year or so ago. It seems he took a short break from my wife to mess with your other 'best friend,' Gina.

Camryn looked up, shocked. "No. I don't believe you. She'd have told me."

"That's where you're wrong, Camryn. You'd be the last person either Gina or Holly would talk to about Dunn." He paused. "They knew how you felt about him, that you were the only one who saw through him—and the only one who walked away from him and never looked back—or worse yet, took him back." He smiled, but it contained no mirth. "Neither my wife, nor your friend Gina were that smart. My guess? What self-respect they had stopped them from telling you how vulnerable they were to Dunn." He stopped. "Something else Gina might not want you to know was that Dunn left her about the time she was facing charges for poaching funds—considerable funds—from her firm's trust accounts, most of which probably ended up in his wallet."

Camryn covered her mouth, her heart aching. *Oh, Gina, this can't be true. It can't. Not for Adam.*

"She also miscarried. About a month before she came back here."

"Adam's baby?" *Stupid words.*

"Did I run DNA? No. But they'd been tight for months. From what I learned, she wasn't seeing anyone else."

Camryn closed her eyes, remembered their long-ago Barbie vow, three twenty-something women vowing never to let a man—any man—come between them, particularly Adam Dunn. She let out a slow breath. Yet another lesson learned; your friends might not lie to you, but they did withhold. While it hurt to admit it, she knew Dan was right when he said neither Holly nor Gina would would have told her that they were seeing Adam again. She'd have reeked with disapproval and concern, and they'd have hated that. Knowing all this, she was more afraid for Gina than ever. She had to talk to her. Had to.

"And you know all this how?" she asked after a long silence.

"Like I said, my business is security—and whether we like the idea or not, our world is one big disk drive."

And connections, she guessed. Lots of connections. She nodded, picked up her fork, and poked at her half-eaten salad, all trace of appetite gone. She looked around the increasingly crowded restaurant. "Let's get out of here." She reached for her bag.

Dan gripped her arm. "There's more."

"It can wait." She took another breath, stood and headed for the door. She had to get out of here, get some clean air. She was aware of Dan tossing some bills on the table but was at the car before he caught up with her. He gripped her upper arms, held her, and forced her to look at him.

"You think I'm going after Dunn because of Holly." His fingers tightened. "That might have been true in the beginning, but now it's about you and Kylie. Dunn is desperate, and desperate means dangerous. He's in trouble, Camryn. Big trouble."

"Adam's not new to trouble." She was tired of defending him. If Dan wanted to believe he'd killed Holly, there was nothing she could do about it. Or him. That would be up to the Boston Police.

"It was a woman—" he started.

"Surprise, surprise."

"A widow, maybe twice his age. He took her for a lot of

money, then skipped. Turns out the woman was somebody's mother, a guy named Lando, one of the biggest and most ruthless drug dealers on the southeast coast. Lando, very unhappy that his mother was ripped off, is on Dunn's ass."

"To pay back the money."

"Still think he's a lover, not a fighter, Camryn?" Dan's question was straight, his tone wry.

"I don't know what to think. Can't think." And it was true. Carefree Holly, serious Gina, even Adam—once a shy charmer—they were all new to her, as if she were meeting them, uncovering them, for the first time—and not liking what she found.

"Dunn was your first, wasn't he?"

She felt the heat rise over the skin of her throat. She ignored it. "Yes. College. I was what you'd call a late bloomer."

He ran his hands down her arms to her elbows, then reached behind her to open the car door. His face was so close she could feel his breath over her cheek. When his mouth touched her ear, he said. "They say a woman never forgets her first lover, that she compares every man that comes after to that first hot taste." He pressed his lips, lightly, quickly, against her ear. "I guess I've got my work cut out for me."

Adam closed his bedroom door behind him, quietly, then glanced at his watch. Almost four, and he'd been in the sack with Gina since noon, when she'd poured herself into his bed and started working him up. Generally, he'd say that was one hell of a way to spend an afternoon, but . . .

He rubbed his face with one hand, clutched his running sweats and shoes in the other.

Fuck! He was exhausted. If anyone had told him there was such a thing as too much sex, he'd have said they were nuts. Gina put the lie to that. The woman was a nonstop sex machine. Rubber Betty on hormones. Hell, if he didn't get out of the house for a while, give his overworked dick a break, it'd never forgive him. He needed a shower, fresh air, and a good, long run.

And in that order. No way was he hitting the running trail sex-slicked and reeking of that perfume Gina doused herself in. He wanted the smell of his own sweat.

But if he wanted to escape without Gina's bat ears hearing him and her plying him with a million questions, he'd best use the downstairs shower. He listened. There was music coming from Delores's room, so downstairs would definitely be his best bet.

He also needed to think, because he was having one hell of a time recasting himself as a murderer—or an accomplice to one. He wasn't a fan of violence. He'd done a lot of crap in his life, but, hell, he'd never so much as hit a woman, let alone kill one.

He'd come here prepared to make Gina happy and get some free legal advice in return. Fair trade, he figured, and a long way from pointing a gun and blowing someone's heart apart. *Camryn's heart*. At that thought, his own heart thumped fast and hard. The thing was, he had to admit Gina's way would cut down the waiting time to get the money. Camryn dead created a direct chute to the cash.

It wasn't as if she gave a damn about him. She'd made that plain enough. And there was Lando out there, waiting, tracking.

A half a mil. I need a half a mil—yesterday—or I'm a fuckin' dead man.

Even having said it over and over in his mind, the amount staggered him, paralyzed his thinking. He'd counted on Holly and lost. Now there was only Gina.

Gina had it all figured out, said she'd do all the dirty work.

The bloody work . . . Yeah, he needed to think all right.

Not something he was good at. He padded barefoot down the hall. His room was at the far end of the second floor where a second set of stairs led to the kitchen. He headed for those.

Other than the front parlor, the main floor was a huge cavern consisting of kitchen, a family room of sorts—the idea of the Solaris having a family room had him shaking his head—and a mammoth living room with whatever furniture there was shrouded in dust covers—covered in dust. There was a time Delores had entertained, and when she did, she'd done it lavishly—one hundred was a short guest list. The main floor also had two more guest rooms at the far end. He headed for the one farthest from the parlor in case Delores showed up. No way did he want to run into the black widow again. Gina freaking him out with her bizarre murder plan was more than enough to handle. God-damn Delores the Dreadful on his ass would put him over the edge.

He opened the door to the bedroom; it creaked as if it hadn't been open in years. "Jesus . . ." he muttered. The room was tar-black, and the fine grit of disturbed dust hit his nose, made him sneeze. He flicked on the light switch beside the door, but all he got for his effort was a gray casting from a light bulb set behind a grate recessed in the center of the ceiling. This room was some kind of—he looked around, frowning—cave thing. The walls were an undulating rough gray plaster, and the bed, a four-poster, looked as if it had been mounted on stones like an altar. The windows were draped in black silk. What had once been a waterfall or fountain of some kind took up most of one wall. Beside that was a human-sized cage and a hooked rack with stuff hanging from it.

He moved closer: chains, leather straps, handcuffs, a couple of riding crops, dog leashes and collars, and . . . a latex body suit. He recoiled. Shit! He didn't even want to go *there*.

He squinted through the gloom at some lettering above the bed. LOVE CAVERN. He again shook his head. Love *prison* more like it. There wasn't much about sex that Adam didn't like, wouldn't try, but leashes and leather—with a Solari woman? Not in this lifetime.

He spotted the bathroom door and headed toward it—fast. One minute later he was naked, soaped down, and had his face lifted to the hot surge of water coming from the shower nozzle. If he didn't need a run so badly, he'd stay here until the water ran cold. But this time of year the light left early, so that luxury was out of the question.

He forked his fingers through his hair, slicked it behind his ears, and opened the shower door.

He immediately closed his eyes and blew out an irritated breath. *What the hell . . . ?*

"Well, well, what a pleasant surprise. My own private Chippendale." She looked pointedly at his crotch. "Well, maybe not so private." Glancing up at him, she leered. "You've, uh, matured, Adam." She paused but didn't take her eyes off his cock. "Nice. Very nice."

He had to walk around her to get a towel, which he did in three easy strides. Securing the terry around his hips, he said, in as neutral a voice as he could muster, "While I appreciate your . . . appreciation. I have to ask. What are you doing in here, Delores?" He put his hands on his hips, forced a smile, and reminded himself it wouldn't be in his interests to alienate Delores until he had his current problem resolved.

"It's my house. I'm 'in' wherever I choose to be." She set her elbows on the armrests of her wheelchair and locked her hands on her lap, welded them tight to each other. "At the moment this bathroom is a hell of a lot more interesting than any other room in the house."

Adam leaned against the pedestal sink, eyed the woman in front of him. Hell, wheelchair be damned, she was still one good-looking . . . broad. Yeah, that was the word for Delores. She reminded him of one of those padded-shoulder types from an old movie; skinny eyebrows, hard eyes, and even harder mouth—with a gangster boyfriend. And she sure as hell was in charge of what went on around this creep joint. "You enjoy the show?"

"Could use a rerun."

Chapter 24

Adam studied her.

Christ, women were all the same . . .

He loosened the towel, smiled, and watched her face.

Her breath caught, and her tongue came out to moisten her lower lip. She nodded and looked up at him. "You're a devil, Adam Dunn, but a damned beautiful one."

He retied the towel. "My guess is you came in here for more than just a look at my . . . male attributes. What can I do for you, Delores?" He turned to the sink, picked up a comb, and drew it through his hair, watching her reflection as he did so. This game was important; he didn't want to screw up.

She loosened her hands, took a breath. "Well, now, one good look at you and I almost forgot, didn't I?"

"You don't forget anything."

A smile briefly lit her face, before sliding off like greasy lipstick. She reversed her chair a few inches. "You're right. I don't."

"So?"

"I want to know what brought you back, sniffing around my Gina."

"Gina's a fantastic woman. Why the hell wouldn't I be 'sniffing around'?"

"Not only are you as handsome as sin, darling, you're a

smooth liar. Which makes you an interesting, but very dangerous, man."

Adam slid her a gaze from the mirror, then did another long pull of the comb through his hair. "Would you rather I say I came for the sex, because your daughter's the hottest lay I ever had?"

She laughed, a cold and brittle laugh that fit perfectly with the cavern on the other side of the bathroom door. "And you've had plenty to compare her to, no doubt." Her face constricted, got tight and angry. Then sad, or something close to it. "Including me."

He cursed inwardly. *Stupid!* Obviously all that sex he was having with Gina had killed some very necessary neurons, because if there was one thing he'd learned with women, it never paid to talk ratings. Hell, with Delores it could be fatal—but fixable.

Adam turned from the mirror, took the two steps that would put him in front of her, and stroked her hair, rich and thick like her daughter's. "That was a long time ago." He ran his fingers down her face, cupped her chin, bent and brushed his lips over hers. "Maybe you need to refresh my memory."

When he pulled away, she gasped for breath, exhaled loudly, then looked at him a long time. When he thought she wasn't going to answer, she gave him a speculative look, and said. "I think you and I had best get down to business and leave that ancient memory alone . . . for now."

He raised a brow. "My loss, baby." Relieved, he dropped the towel and pulled on his sweats, then sat on the edge of the grotto-inspired tub to put on his sneakers. "But I don't know what business we have to talk about."

"How about the I'll-kill-my-best-friend-for-you business you're involving my daughter in."

Her words slammed into his gut like a fist. *Fuck! How the hell . . . ?*

"You two actually think I wouldn't find out?" She sneered, shook her head. "Gina might be a smart lawyer, but she's a stupid woman. If a fly dies in this house, I hear its last breath. Even you should have picked up on that, 'baby.' "

Adam couldn't find a reply, so he concentrated on tying his shoelaces and buying himself some think time. His fingers fumbled with the ties.

"You listening to me?"

"I'm listening."

"Well, listen harder. You want some of Grantman's money? I can get it for you—and the downside is a lot less bloody than Gina's harebrained scheme. And a hell of a lot less risky for you—unless you *like* the idea of being ass-up in a grimy cell block for the next fifty years." She studied him, smiled. "Somehow I don't think that's *you,* Adam."

"Look, I don't know what you think is going on here, but—" *Lame. Seriously lame.*

She went on as if he hadn't spoken. "I'm seeing Grantman tonight, so I can get the ball rolling—in our mutual direction. All you have to do, lover boy, is not do anything stupid until I get home. And stay away from Gina."

"You've got things all wrong, Gina and I—"

Suddenly Still, she ignored him, and stared at her hands, grinding them against each other in her lap. "She shot me. Did you know that? She shot her own mother. And all because I fucked you, all those years ago. She never forgot, and she never forgave." She shrugged, loosened her hands, put them on the chair rails. "Not that I would have, either, I suppose. Trouble with Gina is she's her mother's daughter." That seemed to amuse her, and she appeared to drift away a moment before snapping back. Her tone was low when she added, "She saw her moment that night, during that stupid argument I was having with Franco, and she took it. If I hadn't turned—"

"She told me—"

She waved a hand. "Doesn't matter what she told you. Gina's a mess. That brain of hers is roaring in her head like a thousand-piece orchestra without a conductor. She's losing it, has been since you screwed with her that last time in Seattle."

He rallied. "The screwing was mutual. Very mutual."

"With you, it always is, I suspect." She lifted a hand. "But I don't care. I don't want to hear about it."

Adam stood, loomed over her, forced her to look up at him. "What exactly do you want?" He had a sinking feeling in his gut that he already knew. He was already sorting through her idea, considering what was in it for him.

"First, I want Gina out of my house. It's getting tiresome living with a woman who wants me dead." She glared up at him, her face lined with purpose. "As for you, I'll get you your money, take care of those people you owe, and in return, you'll stay here and take care of me."

"Take care of you how?" He watched her from under lowered eyelids, his innards coiling, waiting for the inevitable.

She smiled. "In all ways, Adam. In all possible ways." She turned her chair and headed for the open bathroom door. When she was on the other side, she wheeled her chair around and faced him. "It's either that or I'll make sure you and Gina are put away for a very long time. And in your case"—her gaze crept over him, rested where it had lingered over his naked groin minutes before—"that would be a terrible waste of talent."

Adam watched Delores push herself through the gloom of the Love Cavern, his gut stone-hard, his head a sump hole. Black and turgid.

God, Holly, why did you die? Why did you leave me?

He sealed his eyes closed and leveled his shallow breathing. Holly was dead. He couldn't change that, and whining about her wouldn't do him any good. He needed to survive, which meant a long run while he decided on the lesser of two evils.

The man, very pale, and walking as if every step might be his last, neared their meeting place, the St. James Cathedral Chapel. Father Frank Moore had no doubt it was the man who had called him this morning, a man who'd refused to give his name and had insisted they meet at "Father Moore's earliest convenience. He'd thought the man wanted an unscheduled confession, but he was assured not.

"No. I want to talk to you about a gift to St. James—a gift with strings."

In Frank Moore's experience, most gifts had strings of some sort, so he was untroubled by the caveat. But he was troubled by the man himself. He studied him as he walked over the black-and-white marble floor toward the chapel. The dress was respectful: suit, tie, and shined shoes. The man carried a large brown bag and a thin folio. His steps were unhurried and his chin down, indicating he was either reluctant or burdened. Most probably both.

The church, other than for a half dozen prayerfully meditating souls scattered among the pews, sat in silent expectation—at least that's how Father Moore always thought of such quiet times, times he relished. St. James was to him a place of patient waiting, a place for peace, and a place to find answers—or at least the right questions. It was, as he sadly knew, also a place of last resort. He glanced up, wondered, as he often did, at what whispers of sin and repentance this sanctuary had absorbed in its hundred years.

The well-dressed man stopped at the altar, hesitated, and lifted his head to look up at the domed skylight directly above it, then he quickly skirted the altar on the left, neither crossing himself nor genuflecting.

New to St. James, Father thought, *and perhaps new to God. Possibly not even a Catholic.*

No matter. Distressed souls were his vocation and heavy hearts his specialty; whatever this man's reasons for walking through the doors of St. James today, they were borne by a troubled soul.

The priest rose to greet him and offered his hand. "Frank Moore," he said. "*Father* Moore, if you've a bent toward it."

"Thank you for seeing me." A hand was offered but not a name. The man straightened his shoulders.

"Shall we?" Frank gestured to the chapel behind him and let his visitor walk ahead of him. They took seats just inside the chapel doors, and Frank watched as the other man scanned the room absently massaging his temple as he did so.

"You're not a Catholic," Frank said, when they were settled.

"Not anymore." The tone was firm, without apology.

Definitely not here for confession. "That implies a few drops of holy water and a first communion somewhere in your distant past." He smiled.

"Very distant past—and I'm not here to revisit it."

Frank knew not to push. "What are you here for, and how can I help?"

"I want to give you this." His nameless companion set the bag on the floor and pulled a letter from the folio. He handed it to Frank. "It's everything I have."

Frank's eyebrows shot up. Two hundred thousand dollars! "This is a lot of money," he said, stating the obvious. "Who do you want sent to hell?" He smiled at his own joke; his visitor did not, so he added, "The bank is Swiss."

"Yes. And the transfer will be done this afternoon, if you agree to my terms."

"I gather one of which is complete anonymity."

"Yes, but don't worry, the money is ready, willing, and legal. That much you can check with the bank. There's a telephone number there. On the bottom. They'll take care of any concerns you might have."

"I see." Frank didn't see, didn't see at all. He rested the document on his lap, looked hard at the man sitting in the chair next to his. "And in return for this?"

"I want you"—he dipped into the brown bag he'd carried in—"to plant this in the courtyard."

It was a plant, maybe a foot high. "Holly? You want me to plant a holly tree?" He frowned. "That's it?"

"That's it. Do you accept? Will you plant the tree?"

"If everything is as you say it is, yes. We have some outreach programs in need of funding. This money will go a long way."

"Good." He put the tree back in the bag at his feet and shoved it toward the priest.

"There's something else I'd like to do before you go," Frank said.

The man tilted his head; his eyes took on a wary look.

"I'd like to hear your confession." He paused. "That's why you came here, isn't it? Atonement? Perhaps forgiveness?" He lifted the document outlining the details of the wire transfer. "This won't do that, you know." Frank knew he'd taken a shot in the dark, but years in the priesthood had fine-tuned his guilt detector—and guilt lay over this man like a shroud.

For a time silence rested between them, broken finally by a cough coming from somewhere in the heart of the church. Frank's seatmate got to his feet. "I thought about that, but I'd rather not add hypocrisy to my list of sins." He turned to go, turned back. "You'll plant the tree? See that it's tended?"

Frank nodded and rose from his seat. "And I'll pray over it."

"Good."

"Are you sure about that confession?"

"Yes. I'm sure." The man hesitated. "But if I was going to pray on something, it would be that I've been right about at least one damn thing in my life."

"Which is?"

He looked away, appeared to lose his train of thought, then he said, "That what you don't know, can't hurt you."

He walked out of the chapel and didn't look back.

Between rows of empty pews and under the melancholy gaze of its lost saints, the body walked stolidly toward the cathedral's front doors, even as the soul wept and demanded to linger. Weakening with every step, the body carried its spirit across the sanctuary, over the black-and-white marble. Opening the heavy door, feeling the chill and bluster of the air, the body paused, then spoke: There's no going back, no redemption except in death and the silence of the grave.

Outside the church, Trent took a couple of pain-killers, and with not enough strength left to walk, he hailed a passing cab.

"Canston Arms," he said. His fleabag hotel was maybe ten minutes away.

The end of the line.

No more treatments. No more hospitals. Just plain no fucking more!

Just a long good-bye, and as waiting rooms went, the Canston Arms would do. "A matter of months," the doctor had said, "if you take care of yourself." And a matter of weeks if you don't.

It would be weeks. As few as possible.

Maybe, before he took his final sleep, he'd understand why he did it.

Why he'd killed Holly Lambert . . .

He closed his eyes against the image of that day, that autumn path, those sightless eyes he hadn't had courage enough to close.

Was it hatred for Grantman, an act of revenge for everything he'd taken from him, or was it an act of love for Camryn, the daughter he'd ignored while he'd chased his failed dreams? The daughter he'd sought out when his time was gone. The daughter he never really knew—and the daughter he'd never see again.

Was the killing a way to take away from Grantman, or to give to Camryn what she wanted so badly and could never have? A child.

He opened his eyes, stared out the window. Hate or love? He couldn't separate them, and the tumor crowding his brain didn't help.

Not that it mattered. He'd find out soon enough.

The devil would surely know. . . .

Chapter 25

When Camryn and Dan arrived home after lunch, they found a note on the kitchen table. Camryn picked it up.

Cammie, I waited until the new window was put in, then headed for Seattle. Got some business there, not sure when I'll be back. I'll call. Dad

She frowned as she read it.

"Something wrong?" Dan walked to the newly installed window, ran a hand along the sill, looked back at her when she didn't answer right away.

"No. Not really. He's disappeared like this quite a bit since he came here. All very secretive." But, then, Trent Derne was a secret. She'd never really known him, as a man or as a father. Still, in the time he'd been with her, her father had been more relaxed, less driven, less . . . egocentric than she'd ever seen him. Certainly, when she was a child the opposite was true. Age had mellowed him, she suspected, maybe brought introspection and acceptance enough that he could let go of some of his bitterness, accept his losses. For years he'd attributed those losses to Paul Grantman, endlessly talking about revenge. But lately, he'd even given up on the blame game.

Maybe it was the mellowing that came with the passing of time that had him show up in her life in the first place—after so many years away from it.

"Are there some calls you can make? I can make?" Dan asked.

"No, he said he'd call. I'm sure he will."

"You sure?"

"I'm sure." She set the note back on the table and walked to the island in the center of the kitchen. The house felt strangely quiet. No father, so no television; no Kylie, so no banging toys and little-girl screeching. The place had a lull about it. Soft time, she thought, before the sharp and unpredictable hours ahead of them at the Solari house.

Restive, she asked, "Would you like something to drink?"

"You know what I like. And you know what I want." His gaze raked her, and her tummy did a quick clench.

"Unless that's an oblique reference to a roast beef sandwich, I assume you mean me."

"I definitely mean you."

"Not one for mincing words, huh?"

He shook a negative.

Because she didn't know what to say, what she did was cross her arms and study the man who had no problems making his desires known while she struggled with hers—and her conscience.

There was a narrow bench seat under the lakeside kitchen window, and Dan, after his inspection of the window, had sat on it, stretching his legs out in front of him, looking for all the world as if he belonged in her kitchen and had no intention of leaving it.

It seemed the only man intent on leaving her had been her husband. She was still unnerved by how easily she'd let him go. Still wrestled with what that said about her. She'd hurt him; she should hurt, too. But she didn't. What she was doing was aching for the man sitting under her kitchen window.

Camryn had a solid idea of how she felt about Dan Lambert, at least in the physical and hormonal sense; her body made it perfectly clear, as did her heart, which pounded a jungle beat every time he walked into a room. Like it was doing now. It was the mental gymnastics, her moralistic mind, she was having trouble with. Whatever was happening between them had her strangely agitated. Not only was her divorce so recent it had barely scabbed over, Dan was the husband of her best friend—her *late* best friend. The man who'd admitted he'd come on to her solely to keep his daughter. No matter how she looked at it, there seemed to be a serious lack of . . . old-fashioned good taste in this whole scenario. And still she couldn't stop herself.

She walked toward him, stood in front of him, and looked over his head out the shiny new window. "I've been thinking—"

He gripped her by the waist, pulled her to him, and looked up at her. "How about we table the thinking thing. Go to bed."

She put her hands on his hair, then combed it with her fingers. "Are you always so direct?" She liked it—his honest approach, his unconcealed impatience to make love to her.

"Yes." He smiled. "I figure the shortest distance to a good thing is a straightforward question."

"That wasn't exactly a question. More like a proposition." His hair was thick, slightly curled and dusted with sunlight. When she brushed it back from his forehead, he took a deep breath and closed his eyes.

"I like your hands on me. Did I tell you that?"

She touched his ear, traced its shape with her index finger. "And did I tell you I think this relationship of ours should get a speeding ticket?"

He took her hands in his, kissed each palm. "You're right about that, but when a guy gets into a Ferrari for the first time . . ."

"I'm not too sure how I feel being compared to a car. Although, if you must, a Ferrari is a fine choice." She smiled.

He stood, ran his hands along her arms, up to her shoulders. Everything he touched warmed, glowed. "And you're a damn fine woman." He paused. "And—after last night—a hell of a lot more than I bargained for."

"Dan, don't—" There it was, that sense of speeding again, this time through a downhill tunnel. "That could have been a mistake. I was scared . . . Maybe it was nothing but fear and adrenaline."

"Three times?" He cocked his head, and for a moment it looked as if he would smile. "Nobody's that scared." He took her face in his big hands and brushed his lips over hers, until the pounding in her heart, the lusting heave between her thighs shut out everything else. "We've got a few hours before we head over to the house of horribles," he whispered in her ear. "It would be a goddamn sin to waste them." He kissed her hard and deep, and she folded into him, heard him add, "And if I'm going to sin, I want to make damn sure it's worth my while." He ran his hands down her back, gripped her buttocks, and pressed her to him. Steel against cotton.

With the hard length of him flush against her, her own heat turning liquid, she thought of only one thing to say: "And mine, Dan Lambert. Don't forget about me."

"Impossible." He took her hand, and together they headed for the stairs to her room. At their base he stopped and turned to her, his expression stern, uncompromising. "Let's leave everything here, okay? All the second-guessing, the exes, recriminations, shoulds and should-nots." He jerked his head toward the top of the stairs. "Up there, in that bed, there's only you and me. Us. You good with that?"

She nodded, her heart in her throat—or was it tears? For God's sake! Tears. "Just us," she agreed after a deep swallow.

Dan was tearing off his clothes before they hit the door. Seconds later hers joined his in a lumpy pile on the floor, and she was stretched out on the bed.

With only the darkening late afternoon lending its light, her room was dim and chilly. Camryn felt the cool against her exposed breasts, a draft of even colder air prickling along her upper arms.

Then his hands came, rubbing her arms, gentle friction pitting heat against the frost. He kissed her hair, her face, her mouth, the column of her throat, before his lips took in the icy peaks of her breasts—first one, then the other—his tongue a flame licking at her nipples, his mouth a blaze sucking lavishly on the same hardened nubs.

She couldn't breathe, couldn't speak, didn't want to do either. She closed her eyes and lifted her breasts to his mouth, breasts reduced in sensation to tip and areola.

He raised his head, his eyes forest-dark and intent on her. Only her. Watching her, he pressed a thumb against the nipple his mouth had deserted, securing tension and suspended need. "You have magnificent breasts," he whispered. "And these"—using the pads of his thumbs, he circled her nipples—"these I could suck on for hours."

She gasped, her stomach knotting and curling; his words and the sensuous movement of his thumbs connected mystically to every sinew in her body, pulling and releasing, pulling and releasing. . . .

Feeling the heat and hardness of him against her belly, she reached between them, wanting to feel him, stroke his steeled silk.

"No," he said. He grasped both her hands in one of his and positioned her arms over her head; his fingers locked around her wrists. "This time it's all about you." He loosened his grip. "Keep your hands above your head. Can you do that?"

She nodded.

"Promise, no matter what I do, keep them there. And don't speak—let me read you."

"I—"

"Shush. Quiet now." He bent his head again, lightly blew on her nipple, then kissed it. "Whatever you feel . . . pull it inside. All of it."

Her mouth dry with expectancy, she nodded again, sealed her lips, not so sure of her promise when her hands ached to touch him, feel the heat of his skin, the depth of muscle in his arms, and the throbbing erection he bucked intermittently against her mound. She lifted her hips to his hard and heavy penis, savored his need, his control.

Stretched before him, the whole of her open, available, and unconcealed, she quivered—waves of heat and chill rolling under her skin, sensitizing her exposed flesh, goading her body to writhe, crave to the point of breathlessness.

She locked her hands together above her head, and, eyes tightly closed, she imagined red silk scarves securing her wrists, binding her to Dan's male power, binding her to what he could give her. He shifted away, and starting from between her breasts, he ran his hand down, over the curve of her waist, her clenching belly, the rise of her hips. Finally, he cupped her pubis, squeezing it with an easy and gentle hand.

Oh, God . . .

Her hands demanded to touch, her throat ached to moan and swallow, but she did neither. She was bound by her promise and by her imaginary silk, bound and ready. As if on an altar for . . . a smile floated in her mind when she remembered how she'd teased him this morning . . . a love god. She pulled her knees up, opened for him—for herself.

He groaned, muttered heated words against her skin.

Wanton, overwhelmingly aroused by her bold and vulnerable position, by his hands now resting, hot and big, on her pelvic bones, she was stunningly aware of each of his fingers against her trembling flesh, each tic and pressure contained in their barest movement.

"Camryn?" His voice came low and rough to her ear.

At the sound of her name, she let the red silk ties drift from her inner vision and opened her eyes.

He was positioned over her, on his knees between her legs, and his eyes, their true color lost in the dim light, glowed with the black light of sex. "I'm going to look at you, look at all of you."

She started to speak, to say what, she had no idea. But he silenced her with a kiss, before sliding down her body to that part of her that was plumped and weeping with need of him.

He put his hands on her inner thighs, pressed on them insistently. "Open for me. More."

Applying light pressure on her thighs, he waited for her to spread her legs. When she did, his gaze dropped to her sex, and she heard him breathe deeply.

"Beautiful—amazing," he murmured, not taking his eyes off her, gently running his index finger along her crease.

A sexual torch, barely there, all promise and fire.

"Dan, I—"

"I know." He drew another line on her labia, deeper into her lips, this time watching her face with hot, glittering eyes.

She wanted more, more from his expert hands, more from his . . . mouth. And she wanted it deeper. She spread her legs wider, lifted her pelvis. Inviting, greedy . . . breath stalled and thick in her lungs, her hands grinding into each other above her head. Her message to him was implicit, deeply carnal, and he didn't miss it.

Running a finger through her cleft, he spread her lips wide, exposing her slick burning nub to the cool room. He circled it with his finger, pressed it down, then teased it up again, while she kept her shuddering hips lifted to him in avid demand. When he thought her seconds beyond ready, he bent his head and found her clitoris smoothly and unerringly.

One touch of his tongue, the teasing urgency of his mouth, and her shuddering body gave way, melted back to the bed. He slipped his hands to her buttocks, held her to his mouth, feasted on her, whispered against her wild and swollen flesh, until the first fast-licking flames of her coming. She held back, needing to stay in this place, until . . .

She brought her hands down, lifted his head with shaking hands. "Come . . . with me, Dan. In me. . . ."

He slid up, and, holding her face, looking into her eyes, he thrust in, his eyelids drooping briefly, his body holding straight and hard as she contracted around him. He thrust again and again until she contracted around his length one last time, until they fused

Cataclysm. Her fingernails clenching his muscled back.

Then a whirling, pooling dark.

Furnace-hot, sweat-drenched, and emptied. One into the other.

A falling inward, an ecstatic ache grasping for a final spasm. Not wanting to let go, not wanting to fall into the afterglow. Not yet.

Dan held her until their breathing notched down, stroked her damp hair from her forehead, and rolled off her.

On his back, he rested his forearm over his eyes, breathed heavily.

More breathing, easier breathing. The coolness in the room coming back to claim its place. But an outer coolness, because Camryn was absolutely certain, with Dan in her bed, inside her body, she'd never be cool again.

Chapter 26

Camryn shifted to her side, propped her head in her hand, and pulled the quilt up and over Dan's depleted sex, and her own rapidly chilling rear end. She smiled. "I'd say that's a wonderful way to spend a gray afternoon."

He lifted his arm from his eyes. "I'd say you're right." He touched her hair, smoothing a couple of damp tendrils behind her ear. "Do you know why it's so good?"

"Are you angling for love-god status again?"

"Hell, no. That's a given." He grinned, but it didn't stick. "Try again, Camryn." He ran his index finger down her cheek, along her jaw, his own set hard, too sober and serious.

"A shared orgasm?" she quipped. "Rare things, those."

"I'll admit that was damn good, but"—he shook his head—"still not it."

No, that wasn't it. . . .

Camryn was afraid the real "good" between them was something else entirely, something that had arrived unbidden—and far too early. Like an inconsiderate guest. She refused to give it a name. That would encourage it, and she didn't know yet if she could handle it, was even ready for it.

She kissed him quickly, then rolled to her back and stared at the ceiling, invisible in the dark afternoon. A gust of wind batted the window, and the scent of sex, clean sweat, and Dan's musky aftershave perfumed her nose.

When she didn't answer, he said, "Okay, I'll say it for you. The reason we're so good in bed together, Dan, is because there's something going on between us outside of it. Something I'm not ready for." He raised himself, and the last of the light made his head a shadow on her breasts. "That about cover it?"

He'd spoken her very thought! Which, oddly, made her more confused than ever. She took a breath but didn't look at him. "You're right, I wasn't expecting . . . someone like you, and I'm not ready."

"Why not?"

She turned to face him. "Because the timing couldn't be worse. It's too soon, Dan. You know that."

"Not too soon for great sex, but too soon to talk about anything that might happen beyond it. Is that what you're saying?"

She squirmed inwardly, admitting it didn't make sense. It's the sex that should be on hold . . . not the feelings around it. God, he'd made her illogical. She was woman enough to know what that meant. "Come to think of it, it's too soon for the sex, too."

He cocked his head. "I'd leave that where it lies, Camryn." He bent to lightly kiss her, and her breath caught. "There's no going back on that decision. That horse—as a wise man once said—is miles away from the barn. . . ."

He was right again, but she wasn't about to tell him that, especially while he was tracing her nipple with an exquisitely deft middle finger. "We could stop. This could be the end of it, right here." *And elephants could fly . . . or was that pigs?* She couldn't remember. The soft abrading by his slow and easy finger had erased the image.

Leaning down, he kissed the nipple he'd been torturing to a newly hardened peak. "You think?"

She closed her eyes, did some erratic breathing, stopped

even that when he ran his hand down under the quilt to tor-
ture another part of her oversensitized anatomy. "Unfair,
Lambert." She sensed his smile against her ear.

"There's no 'fair,' and there's no right schedule, Camryn," he said. "But if you want to wait to talk about what's
next—after what we've just had—that's fine with me. I'll
find ways to amuse myself." He nuzzled her throat, played
in the curls at the apex of her thighs. "Besides, I already
know what I needed to know."

"Which is," she choked out.

"You trust me."

She stayed his hand, opened her eyes to see his gaze focused on her. She knew her own eyes were questioning.

"You trust me that this—you and I in bed together—is
about us and not—"

"A premeditated seduction on your part to get your
daughter?"

He nodded, and for the briefest moment looked uncertain.

Camryn touched his face. "You're right. I do trust you.
What I don't know is what to do about you."

"The timing thing again?"

When she nodded, he nodded, then kissed her. "There's
no politically correct moment for what's happening between us, Camryn. No right time for people to . . . get interested in each other. And there's no such thing as bad
timing." His hand caressed her breast, the indent of her
waist. "But speaking of timing, we have a couple of lonely
hours left before we go to the Solaris'. Got any idea how we
might use them?" He pulled her closer.

"Yes," she said, kissing him. "I believe I do." She ran her
hand over his flat stomach, through crisp pubic hair, to
where he wasn't so flat—and cupped him, toyed with him.
Anticipated his return to hard, throbbing need. Delighted
in it.

"I like the way your mind works," he said, his breath turning ragged.

"And I like this." She encircled him with her hand.

"Hm-m."

And I can't think of a better way to put off today what I'll have to think about tomorrow. Dan Lambert bursting into her comfortable, workaday, logical life was like a meteor hitting the desert. The attraction was rash, thoughtless, and totally unexpected. She needed to think about it. What it might mean to her and Kylie's future—or if there'd be one.

Paul Grantman started back from the lakeshore, first crossing a stretch of manicured lawn before his grass-dampened feet hit the softly lit, inlaid-brick path leading to his house. Other lights illuminated a pair of tall cedars at the side of the property, and the evening mist gathering at their base.

It was almost time for Maury to pick up Delores, so in less than an hour, the miserable woman would be on his doorstep, and he'd be kissing her cheek and pretending they were old friends.

He hated to admit it, but, damn it, on some vague level the woman frightened him. She was such a bizarre mixture of shrewdness and bone-mean, you never knew what the hell she'd pull.

He told himself none of that mattered; all he wanted from her tonight was information about Adam Dunn, and what his intentions were toward Kylie. Simple enough. Then she was out of here.

If that scheming two-bit asshole was after his grand-daughter, he'd be the sorriest son of a bitch to have ever walked this earth. Paul would make sure of it.

He looked up the path to see Erin coming toward him. She was dressed in jeans and wearing a white lacy top that bared the rise of her breasts, enough that his breathing faltered. She smiled softly, and as she neared him, put her hand out toward him. His heart, as it always did, tripped in his chest.

It struck him he was afraid of Erin, too. Afraid of what he felt for this sad, sick nymph of a woman, a woman too young for him, too much trouble for him; a woman whose life continued to spiral out of control and threatened to take his with it.

No fool like an old fool, he sighed to himself.

He took her hand. "What are you doing out here? Have you abandoned my granddaughter? Who, by the way, I'm convinced you love more than me."

"Kylie's sleeping, and Anya's there, and I wanted to talk to you."

"Then let's go inside." He nodded at her gauzy top, one that would barely stop her from tanning, let alone stay the autumn breeze coming off the lake. "You'll catch your death." He took off his windbreaker and draped it over her shoulders.

"I'd like to stay out here." She breathed in the night air, seemed to savor it. "Where the air is clear." She added the rhyme and smiled.

"Okay."

"Thanks for this." Holding his jacket by the lapels, she stood on her tiptoes and kissed him. "But that 'catch your death' comment makes you sound like the dad I never had—which you definitely aren't."

She looked up at him, her face pale, more . . . serene than he'd seen it in months. "I love you, you know. Or are you sick of hearing me say that?"

He hugged her close and whispered into her hair. "That's something I'll never get tired of hearing."

"Even when I'm an old woman and—"

"I'm an even older man?" He shook his head, then kissed

hers. "No. You're who I want. Who I've always wanted. The day I met you, I quit looking at the calendar."

"Except to count my clean and sober days." She pulled away and gave him an odd, shaky smile. "You've used the calendar for that—and so have I."

Paul frowned. It wasn't like Erin to bring up her problem, and it certainly wasn't like her to smile when she did. He set her away from him, so he could see her face. "What's going on, Erin?"

"I've, uh, made a decision . . ."

"And?"

She tightened his jacket around her and lifted her chin. "I've booked myself into rehab. I arranged it this morning. I'll be leaving the day after tomorrow."

If she'd told him she'd decided to skydive without a parachute, he couldn't have been more shocked. They'd battled over this for months, and she'd resisted his every effort to get her in any of the best drug and alcohol rehabilitation facilities in the country. "It isn't that I'm not happy—damn it, I couldn't be more so—but why now? I don't understand."

"It's Kylie." She took a few steps away. "I love her. So much. I hate the thought she can't stay, but—"

"A temporary situation. I'll fix—"

She lifted a hand and shook her head. "No. I'm not here for that. I don't want you to fix anything. Not anymore. Next month I'll be thirty-three. And after last night, I think it's time I started fixing myself." Before he could reply, she took his hand. "It's starting to rain. You'll get wet. Come with me." She led him to the gazebo that sat between the tall cedars, taking them out of the rain and away from the wind.

Erin sat on the bench that circled the inside of the gazebo and pulled him down beside her. "Last night? Before you found me outside of Camryn's house?"

He nodded.

"I had dinner with my girlfriends—like I planned, but when I left them . . . when I was alone . . ." She let out a breath. "I went to buy cocaine."

"Oh God, Erin . . ."

"No, it's okay. It didn't happen." She stopped. "It wasn't meant to happen."

"Go on."

"The closer I got to downtown Seattle, the more scared I got. The more confused I got. I thought about you, about Kylie, about what you were going to do to get her—for me. I thought about what a mess I was. How I'd gone out that night intending to go to dinner with friends, and now I was in my car pointed to the nearest drug dealer as if I was on autopilot."

Paul was holding her hands in his. When they trembled, he tightened his grip on them but didn't speak. He waited.

"Most of all I thought about what a seriously fucked-up woman I am. It's like I have an . . . animal caged inside me, and when it breaks out, I never know what it's going to do." She raised her eyes to his; she was crying. "It got out again last night. All I could think about was getting high. Then . . . I got scared—really, really scared."

"Oh, baby." He pulled her head to his shoulder, stroked her hair.

She let him hold her a few moments before pulling away. "That's when I did a U-turn—and on the I-Five, the highway that never sleeps, that's not easy—"

"Jesus!"

"I did a U-turn," she repeated, "and I headed home."

"You stopped at Camryn's. Why?"

"I don't know that, anymore than why I was heading to that drug dealer." She looked away. "I just did. I never intended to go in. I don't know what I intended. My head was a jumble of wanting drugs, wanting Kylie. . . . But while I was standing there, I remembered Holly and the one time we had any kind of conversation. It was about Camryn and how much she admired her for always being so strong, so caring. How she'd been there when Kylie was born." Erin paused. "She said Camryn was the kind of person you'd trust with your life."

Paul was getting it now, knew where Erin was heading. "And you're not."

She shook her head. "No. I want to be, but I'm not. And if I can't trust myself, I can't ask Kylie to do it either—or you." She touched his face. "Kylie belongs with Camryn. It's what Holly would want."

"Are you saying—"

"I want you—us—to let go. Leave things as they are."

"But I—" he felt he should protest because not to felt like a defeat of some kind, but she moved her hand to his mouth, covered it with her fingers.

"No 'buts,' darling. It's the right thing to do."

"She's my blood, Erin. I won't let her out of my life."

"Somehow I don't think that will surprise Camryn as much as you dropping the legal challenge. I'll want to see her, too, as often as I can, and spoil her rotten when I do." She hesitated. "That will be all right with Camryn, won't it? My seeing her, I mean."

"I'm sure it will be." *And if it isn't I'll make sure it is.*

She nodded and stood. He stood with her, and they locked hands. "Let's go in, see that our granddaughter is asleep," she said.

"And then?"

"We'll make love." She looked away, then back into his eyes. "It's been a long time."

"Yes, it has. A too-long time." He leaned and brushed a kiss over her lips, and his body tightened, his heart kicked up its beat. It had been almost two months since they'd made love. Night after night of Erin wandering the house at night, battling her demons, as she'd called them, and in the process remote and untouchable.

She took his hand. "Then let's not waste any more of it."

Walking to the house, anticipating the warmth of his big bed with Erin in it, feeling renewed hope for the first time in months, Paul's mood suddenly soured at the thought of seeing Delores.

But if the woman had something to say about that bastard Adam Dunn, he'd hear her out and then get rid of her. In the meantime she could cool her heels for a time—until he made his wife happy.

When Gina walked into Delores's vast, overstuffed room, she saw her mother's wheelchair sitting empty outside her bathroom door. The only illumination came from a bedside lamp and the rivulet of light seeping along the carpet from the half-open door. Steam formed a gauzy, shifting ghost above it. The sound of the shower gushed into the room, inharmonious with the soft strains of cello and violin coming from the stereo. The stereo sat under the lakeside window; its surface covered in newspapers, CDs, and bulbous African carvings. As with any room Delores spent any time in, it smelled of dead cigarettes and gardenia.

Delores's African-themed suite, like the rest of her decorative efforts, was the usual sorry joke. A wooden giraffe, its brown and white mosaic coat barely visible under a long, uninterrupted fall of dust, took up most of what Delores called the "feature corner," along with Ugandan goatskin drums, some bamboo stakes, and a series of solemn masks—bad copies, of course—set against a batik curtain.

There was another spot of light; a candle set into the back of a carved elephant flickered dully along the underbelly of the giraffe.

Gina shuddered. *Awful. Beyond awful.*

Still, this was the finest room in the house, the most spacious, and the one with the best view of the lake. She ran her hand down the smooth ebony of one of the bedposts. Gina had already decided she'd never leave this house. With its somber privacy, perimeter walls, and secluded lakefront, it was ideal. She and Adam would be happy here—after she renovated. Perhaps they'd take this room. Yes, Adam would like it here.

She set the roll of duct tape she'd brought on top of the cluttered stereo. It was instantly camouflaged by the mess.

She walked to the window, peered out. A hint of mist building on the lake clung precariously to the shoreline. Already dark, and with the clouds coming in, soon it would be rain-sodden black. Adam was downstairs; she'd decided to let him have his run while she made her plans, so she didn't have much time. She knew he'd take a nap, as he always did after his run, but if she had trouble here, she risked waking him. Or Delores did.

No. She'd hurry, because she much preferred waking Adam her own special way. She squeezed her legs together at the thought, waited for the pulsing to stop.

Adam said he was tired of waking up with her hand wrapped around his cock—but she knew it wasn't true, because his cock told her so. She smiled.

Still, she intended to keep this Delores business quiet, because her beautiful lover was jumpy enough about her plan for Camryn; she didn't want to add to his uneasiness, make him do something stupid. She wanted him to . . . well, she just wanted him. Period. Everything was for Adam. Or because of Adam.

This was really his fault.

He should never have talked to Delores or listened to her stupid promise to get money from Paul Grantman. That's when she'd known what she had to do. That's when something eely and slick had oozed through her, then congealed to a deadly resolve.

He should never have dropped the towel, let Delores see what belonged to her. Only her.

Perhaps when she was finished with Delores and Camryn, she would punish him. But not until she was certain he couldn't leave her.

The rush of the shower stopped abruptly.

Gina's heart didn't quicken, it hardened. She looked around the messy room, took in the unmade bed, the bottles of pills, books, and papers on the bedside table. She picked up the bottles, three of them, and shook her head. Pain-killers, sleeping pills, and vitamin B. She put the vitamin pills back, studied the others.

Possibly . . .

The bathroom door opened, and Delores, holding the doorjamb with one hand and the doorknob with the other, walked unsteadily into the room. Busy reaching for her chair, she didn't see Gina standing in the shadows near the window until she was settled in it.

Gina noted her mother's shock, quickly covered, when she spotted Gina.

"What the hell are you doing here?" Delores tucked her bathrobe awkwardly over her knees and glanced toward her bed where a dress was laid out. A red dress. Her shoes sat on the floor below it.

Gina, smiling, walked toward her. "I thought I'd check in on you, see if there's anything you need before you go to bed."

Delores eyed her warily, then rolled herself toward the large ebony vanity beside the window. She flicked on a lamp. It might as well have been a candle for all the light it cast.

Her vanity was a mass of carvings: elephant trunks, lion heads, all swirled into tall grass. The mirror frame simulated a series of drums and huts. Hideous.

"Are you crazy? It's not even eight o'clock." Delores said to Gina and rolled her chair so she could see herself in the mirror. She picked up a fat jar of cream and lathered her face and neck with it. "What do you want, Gina? As you can see, I'm busy."

Gina could see her mother watching her in the mirror, so she strolled to the bed and fingered the dress, a soft combination of silk and velvet. A black velvet jacket lay beside it. Beautiful and expensive. Delores never had shortchanged herself. Gina knew her closet was full of clothes like this. From her days of wine and roses, her mother always said.

"You're going out?" she asked, careful to keep her voice neutral. She didn't comment on the rarity of the event or remind Delores she hadn't set a foot outside in months, just as Delores hadn't commented on the rarity of Gina coming into her room. As always, there was more unspoken than spoken chilling the air between them.

"Yes. As a matter of fact, I have a date."

"Hm-m." Gina risked a glance at the duct tape, put her hand in her sweater pocket, and fingered the long silk scarf she'd taken from her bureau. The scarf that would cut off her mother's unending supply of ugly, hateful, hurtful words. Forever.

She'd have used the gun, but it was noisy, and she'd risk ruining Adam's prints.

Delores spun her chair, enough to meet Gina's carefully impassive face. Her expression was taut, irritated. "What? You think you're the only one around here who can get a man? Well, I've got news for you, Gina. All it took was one call." She smiled then, and looked pleased with herself, nothing at all like the traitorous bitch that she was. "Not that it's any of your goddamn business, but Paul Grantman is sending a car for me. We're having dinner." She turned her chair again, maneuvered it back so she could face the vanity, and picked up a brush, started drawing it through her heavily silvered dark hair. "Now, if you want to do something useful—before you get the hell out of here—you can bring me my dress."

Gina took the few steps necessary to stand behind her mother. Their gazes met and caught in the mirror. "Actually"—Gina pulled the soft silk from her pocket—"I don't feel much like being useful, mother dearest. And I don't think you'll be going out . . . ever again."

Chapter 27

"I'm going to call Paul," Camryn said, heading for the phone. "He said after eight-thirty. It's past that already, and we've got to go."

"Go for it," Dan said. "I'll get our coats."

The phone rang as Camryn reached for it.

She answered Dan's questioning glance with a nod, then listened. "Did you phone? . . . Yes, I know. They let it ring. No voice mail. . . . Okay. . . . Yes, we'll call you tonight." She clicked off.

"That was short. What did he say?"

"Delores didn't show. So we're on our own."

"Exactly how I like it." Dan hadn't been comfortable snuggling up to Grantman, anyway.

"He wants us to call him, let us know how it goes with Adam and Gina." He held her raincoat, and she settled into it.

"I'm sure he does." Typical Grantman, not prepared to show his hand but wanting to see theirs.

"Oh, I forgot the wine." Camryn disappeared into the kitchen, reappeared waving a bottle. "Got it." She headed for the door.

Wine . . . as if this little get-together of theirs was a regular Saturday-night party of four. Well, a party wasn't what Dan had in mind.

His mood darkened. Hell, this whole thing with Dunn was probably a waste of time. He'd already forwarded everything he'd learned about the guy to the Boston police; if he were smart, he'd let them take it from there. But damned if he didn't want to meet the man face-to-face—the man who had most likely murdered Holly and who was now messing with his daughter's life. The thought made his mouth bitter and his chest cold.

He opened the door, and he and Camryn both stepped onto the porch. At the top of the stairs, before he could take the first step down into the rain and toward the car, Camryn put her hand on his arm.

"One question, one suggestion," she said.

He pulled up the collar of his windbreaker. "Shoot."

"My mother says, when you go into a meeting, you should always know what you expect to get out of it, so you can measure your progress when you leave, know whether you gained or lost ground."

"Good advice," Dan said.

"I think so, too. So my question is this. What do you expect to get out of . . . whatever happens tonight?"

Dan eyed her, wondered how honest he could afford to be. *Hell* . . . "Nothing. I expect nothing. Other than everyone 'making nice,' pretending all's right in their tight little worlds and skirting any issue that might change that."

She cocked her head. "You're cynical."

"That surprises you?"

She took the first step down, then turned back. The porch light lit her face, making it the only bright thing in a world of gray and rain. "No. Nothing about you surprises me. Not anymore."

He touched her hair—he loved her soft hair. "Good. I guess that's one benefit, among many, to our sleeping together."

She clasped his hand. "I'm serious."

"So am I." He turned her hand in his, kissed her palm, and let go. "But the truth is I expect more from myself than Dunn."

"Like?"

"Like not giving him a new face the second he steps in front of mine, then seeing how well he answers a few direct questions about what the hell he's doing hanging around my daughter."

"What if he doesn't show? Once he knows you're in the house, he might make himself scarce—and that house is huge."

"As the saying goes, he can run, but he can't hide. I'll find him if I have to search every room in the house. That asshole and I are overdue for a face-off." He stepped off the porch to the first step, level with her now. "What about you? What do you expect?"

She opened her mouth to speak, then stopped. "Now that I think of it, pretty much the same as you. Except, my concern is less with Adam than with Gina. I want to know if she's . . . all right. Maybe talk some sense into her." She lifted a hand, brushed at her hair. "She's my friend, Dan, and she's hurting. I don't want her hurting anymore."

Dan, from what he'd learned about the Gina-Dunn affair, figured Camryn was going to fail big time, but he also understood why she felt she had to try.

He took another step down and offered her his hand. "Then we're on track—ready to measure our progress, like your mother said." They walked down the stairs and got into his truck. Before turning on the ignition, he slid a glance at her. She was more tense than she admitted. "But if that was the question, what was the suggestion?"

Her mouth twisted into a brief smile. "That you restrain yourself from 'giving Adam a new face.' "

Dan chuckled.

At the end of the driveway, before they turned onto the road, she said, "There's something else you should know."

"I'm listening."

"I called Sebastian and asked him to be there tonight."

Dan's eyebrows shot up. *This should be a real love-in.*

"I thought he could help with Gina," she went on, "He didn't say he'd come, but . . ." She glanced at him. "If he does, are you okay with it?"

"Did you tell him Dunn would be there?"

"No."

Dan could only shake his head. "This is going to be a hell of a party." He turned the truck onto the road.

In less than ten minutes they were at the Solari gate, and two minutes after that, they were at the front door, and Gina and Camryn were hugging each other with the affection and fierceness of an airport reunion. But when Gina spotted Dan over Camryn's shoulder, her eyes went cool as ice picks.

"Who's this?" she said, stepping back from Camryn and eyeing him as if he were an alien life-form. There was no fear in her face, though, only calculation. He had a flash: he didn't like Gina Solari.

He had to hand it to Camryn; she didn't miss a beat. "This is Kylie's stepfather, Gina. I'd talked so much about you, and when you told me Delores wasn't going to be here, I thought I'd bring him along to meet you in person." Eyes wide, she added, "You don't mind, do you?" She looked around. "Delores is out, isn't she?"

Camryn was damn smooth. If Gina didn't want him and said so, she'd look as crazy as her mother, which, according to Camryn, Gina would never admit, considering the mother was straitjacket material.

Nice family.

He offered his hand. "Good to meet you, Gina." She ignored his outstretched hand.

"Hm-m." She eyed him with a gaze both hot and cool at the same time. Her eyes were brown, deeply intelligent, yet strangely bright; they made him think of pinwheels. She was a lush woman, curves in all the right places, with a head of thick black hair, and a chest that would make a Hollywood starlet proud. He wouldn't call her a pretty woman, no softness anywhere. No warmth. She still hadn't said a goddamn word. All she did was stare at him, her hands stuffed into the pockets of her bulky sweater. She looked as if her brain were shuffling out-of-order paperwork. Then, suddenly, as if she'd filed her last folder, she smiled at him. Barely. "Odd we've never met, because I've heard a lot about you . . . from your dead wife."

Okay . . . not the best turn of phrase; it caught him off guard. When he looked at her, saw the faint upward twist on one side of her mouth, he knew she'd intended it to do that and was waiting for his reaction. He gave her nothing.

He looked around. "Interesting place you've got here." *And a goddamn mess.* He tried not to look judgmental, but even a sweeping glance told him that was the only sweep this place had had in years.

"We like it. Mother and I." She hooked her arm through Camryn's. "Let's go into the parlor," she said.

"Delores's parlor?" Camryn looked surprised.

"Why not? She won't be home for"—she waved her other hand—"hours. And hours."

"Where is she?"

"She has a date. Very mysterious."

"Really," Camryn said, frowning.

Dan knew she was thinking about Grantman's call, about Delores being a no-show. "If you're sure, then."

"Not to worry." Gina smiled again, and those pinwheel eyes of hers spun to Dan. "I'm so sorry you won't get a chance to meet her. My mother is what most people would call a real piece of work. A rather nasty piece, but entertaining at times."

When Dan didn't reply, she took the wine from Camryn's hand and gave it to him. "Can you handle this?" He took the wine but couldn't stop looking around.

They were standing in a poorly lit room off the kitchen, a room large enough to host prom night. Dark, scuffed hardwood floors, furniture at odd angles, a dozen or more long-dead potted plants, more mess than he'd found in the roughest and most remote camps he'd worked in, and the ugliest pink and silver draperies he'd ever seen, some of them off their hooks. Everything upholstered in the room was pink in one shade or another, and all of it was beat-up. Cobwebs shadowed the corners.

"It's mother's take on a bordello waiting room. Like it?" Gina asked, her mouth, tightening, told him she didn't.

"Creative," he said, looking at her, then lifting the wine bottle. "Glasses? A corkscrew maybe?"

"Over there." She gestured toward an enameled bar in the corner of the garish room. "When you're done. We'll be in there." Another gesture toward a door a few feet away. Delores's parlor, he presumed.

"How many glasses?" he asked.

Gina eyed him, then looked at Camryn. Defensively, Dan thought. "Four. Adam will be down in a few minutes." She upped the wattage in her sharp eyes. "And he's the one you're *just dying* to meet, right?" She smiled then, as if what she'd said was in jest. The woman was a definite nut job.

"Four it is." He crossed the room, opened the wine—a decent one thanks to Camryn—then joined the two women in what could only be described as a dark, furniture-packed pigsty of a room that faced the lake.

"Could use some light," he said.

"Mother likes it this way. Sorry."

He shrugged, set four glasses—none too clean from what he could see—on the coffee table next to a couple of heaping ashtrays. He poured the wine for the three of them.

Camryn, who'd been standing by the window when he came into the room, walked toward the settee. She shoved some magazines aside so she could sit down, but before she could sit—

"No!" Gina said. "Don't sit there." Holding her drink in one hand, she pointed toward two chairs, and, as if she were directing a stage play, said to Dan, "You sit there," nodding to one, "and you there, Camryn," gesturing toward another chair, directly across from the settee and in the opposite corner from Dan. The room was long and somewhat narrow, so it seemed their hostess wanted them as far apart as she could get them. *Damned strange,* thought Dan.

Gina went on. "While you settle in, I'll go up and see if I can hurry up Adam. Oh, and I've got some cheese and crackers. I'll get them, too." She set her wineglass precariously on a stack of books that sat beside the ugliest sofa he'd ever seen. "God," she babbled on, her voice a pitch higher. "We have so much to talk about. It's been ages. Absolute ages." She shot a look toward him. "You won't mind listening to some girly catch-up talk, will you, Dan?"

"Not at all." From here on in—at least until Dunn showed up—he'd happily let Camryn carry the ball.

When Gina was gone, Camryn, aghast at her friend's odd behavior, turned to Dan, "God, I didn't know . . . Something's not right with her. I could feel it the minute we walked in the door." She tugged nervously on her earlobe. "And where's Delores?"

She was asking herself, not Dan, but he shook his head. "Can't say I'm sorry to have missed her, after meeting the daughter. That woman's more out of it than Erin Grantman on her worst day—and not from drugs." Dan wandered the room, tried a couple of the lamps, but none of them worked. They were left with the light from a gooseneck reading lamp near a chair in the far corner, enough to cast shadows but little else.

"Damn it!" Camryn said, "I should have stayed in closer contact these past months, but she kept . . . resisting it, saying she needed time alone for a while. When I did press, saying I'd come here, she'd put me off." Camryn got up, sipped her wine, and started to pace. "She always blamed Delores and, knowing Delores, I believed her. Damn it," she said again. "I shouldn't have taken no for an answer." The truth was she hated coming here; the unending mess and Delores's withering tongue did not make for a fun time. So she'd decided to give Gina what she wanted. Time alone to work out whatever needed to be worked out. She'd never dreamed it had anything to do with Adam.

"So now you're making this loony bin"—he waved a careless hand—"and its flaky inhabitants your fault?"

"No, but I could have been more sensitive. Maybe helped in some way."

"Seriously doubt that." He jerked his head toward the door, then looked at her, "What's the story here, anyway?" He looked around. "This place is a mess."

She followed his gaze, welcomed the change of subject, used it to ease the gnaw of worry about her friend. "The house has been on a downhill run since Delores bought it twenty-five years ago. Back then everyone attributed it to Delores's"—she rolled her eyes—"decorating taste. But according to Gina, the real problem started after Delores's third husband walked out on her with most of her bank account—maybe fifteen years ago; I can't remember exactly. Gina called it the GDD, the Great Delores Depression, and said she was never the same after that. She fired the cleaning staff, rarely went out herself, and started ignoring the deteriorating condition of the house, wouldn't allow anyone— even Gina—to touch it with so much as a feather duster."

Camryn scanned the room and sighed. She remembered

once hearing Delores describe her decorating style as whimsical. Grotesque was more apt. The dimly lit parlor, with its overladen ashtrays, stained carpet, and ratty furniture, made you want to don an antiviral suit and a gas mask. The smell of stale tobacco and dust was so strong it was like thorns in your nose.

She thought of Gina, losing a baby, coming to this awful place, depressed and alone, and her heart ached for her.

Gina, obsessively neat and organized, had always loathed this place, and to say the mother-daughter relationship was strained was a gross understatement. Gina had once said, dramatically, that if she didn't get out of "Misery Manor" and free herself from the talons of "Mother Dracula," she'd go mad.

Perhaps she had.

Dan clicked his fingers, tilted his head. "Dan to Camryn. Anyone there?"

"Sorry." Camryn pulled herself from her memories. "Anyway, to make a long story short, Gina left for college, then settled in Seattle to practice law. After that, she came to the lake maybe once a year. Her 'guilt visit,' she called it. Even then it was mostly to see Sebastian. He lived here, in a perpetual state of war with Delores, until maybe three years ago."

"What the hell does he do anyway?"

"He's a day trader. A successful one, I'm told," she said absently.

They both heard the sound of a man's voice, then a door slam somewhere in the house. Then absolute silence. No, not quite. Music, barely audible, floated into the room. The same chords repeating and repeating. . . .

Unaccountably, Camryn's heart pounded, and she had the insane desire to run. Her every instinct sensing trouble and pain.

She looked at Dan, who'd taken a pile of paper and mag-

azines off a chair in the farthest corner of the room and settled into it with his glass of wine. He'd leaned forward at
the sound of a door slamming from somewhere in the
house, listened intently for a moment, then leaned back, his
expression calm, his body relaxed.

"Looks to me as if we'll be here a while," he said, not a
trace of impatience in his voice. "You might as well sit
down and enjoy your wine."

She nodded. He might be right about their having to
wait for a time, but instead of drinking her wine, she set it
beside the bottle on the cluttered coffee table and went back
to the seat Gina assigned her, across the room from Dan.
She stared into the blackness outside the window.

And thought of bullets. . . .

Chapter 28

"Shush, they'll hear you," Gina said, closing her bedroom door too quickly and much too hard. At least he'd waited where she'd asked him to. A miracle, considering he'd become less and less obliging lately.

"Yeah, well, I don't give a fuck. You're crazy if you think I'm going down there. That guy hates my guts."

"You have to come. Dan Lambert being here changes everything. I didn't factor him in. I need you, Adam." Gina's voice was calm, but her insides rolled and banged like dropped drums. "There's no risk. None. If we do this right."

"You said you'd do it, Gina. This whole goddamn thing was your idea." He glared at her, his eyes jumping with frustration, refusing to settle on her. He sounded like a petulant teenager.

"I will, my darling. All I want you to do is provide a distraction. Buy me a little time to get the second shot off." She went to stand in front of him, ran her fingers along the soft cotton of his shirt front. She felt high, excited, frustrated, panicked. Wild. More alive than she'd been in months. The only thing that came close was an orgasm à la Adam. At that thought, she moistened her dry lips, rubbed her palms over his nipples, tried to kiss his chin. . . .

He pulled away. "Jesus, Gina, will you stop rubbing

yourself against me like a bitch in heat. Can't you keep your hands off me for five minutes? Give me some goddamn time to think." He ran a hand through his lustrous hair. She loved his hair. . . . He turned his back, took a few steps away, leaving his hand to rest on the nape of his neck, head bowed.

Even from where she stood, a few steps away, she could hear his heavy breathing.

"Whatever you want, Adam," she said, knowing she'd have her hands all over him forever when this night was done. In a way it was perfect—two birds with one stone. It wasn't that Dan Lambert was a threat exactly, but he was a nuisance, determined as he was to keep Adam's daughter. There was always the chance he'd cause trouble, delay Adam's money. Their money. "All I want is for you to come into the room—noisily—about five minutes after I go back down to the parlor—"

"The parlor? You're in Delores's parlor?" He turned enough to look at her, seeming puzzled.

"Yes." She skidded over his questioning interruption. "It's simple enough, Adam. All I need is a moment's diversion, and I'll take it from there. Camryn first. Lambert second. I told you I'd do it, and I will. Then we'll have everything we ever wanted. We'll have this house. Money. We can live here forever, make love, make more love. . . ." She smiled. "Think of it! Your Lando problem solved, and us with the freedom to do whatever we want, whenever we want."

He shook his head. "With two bodies buried in the basement." He sneered. "Nice. Real nice. And who the hell said I wanted anything to do with this shit-house?" He made a full turn, put his hands on his hips, and glared at her. "And where the hell is Delores?"

It was as if her lungs collapsed. "Delores?" she repeated, suddenly feeling slow and stupid. Her mother. Where was her mother? *Oh, yes* . . . She took a breath. She should have expected this.

Adam and Delores. Delores and Adam.

"Delores, Gina. Where is she?"

"She, uh, went out. She said something about seeing Paul Grantman. You must have heard the car."

His direct gaze wavered, but only for a second. "No, I didn't hear a car. Where is she, Gina?" he repeated, his words slow, his eyes narrowed and suspicious.

Gina wanted to turn her back on him, but she couldn't, couldn't look away from his cold eyes. Adam. *Her* Adam. Asking about Delores. She couldn't bear it. "Why do you care where she is?" She kept her voice soft and pushed back at the rage tearing into her chest. She could feel its claws, the heat of it, see its sharp, fatal brilliance before her eyes. "Why do you want to know?"

He hesitated, and she could see his hands shift and tighten on his slim waist. "Because she offered me a better deal—a bloodless deal—and I've decided to take it. I don't want anyone dead, Gina. I especially don't want Camryn dead. You got that?"

The brilliance, grayed, and shattered, letting rage in on a roar, deafening her to her own thoughts. "You love her, don't you? That's what this is all about, isn't it? You still want her. You've always wanted her."

"Jesus, there's a leap. I don't want to kill someone, and you think it's because I want to fuck her."

"You fucked my mother, Adam. And if you'd crawl between her sheets, you sure as hell won't say no to Camryn."

He studied her as if she were a dropped egg, a horrible mess that he didn't want to clean up. "I shouldn't have come to you. Shit! I always knew you were different from Holly and Camryn, but I didn't know you were goddamn crazy."

Why did he have to speak their names, bring them into

the room, like smug, sneering ghosts? There should be only her and Adam. Not Camryn, not Holly, not Delores—not a thousand nameless women Gina hadn't met, would never meet.

Weariness sucked at her, engulfed her, sapped her energy. She'd tried so hard . . . she was finished.

Color followed, the red of surging violence, the gray of disgust for what she was. Despair enveloped her, even as her mind skirted reason.

Adam didn't love her—would never love her.

Through dark eyes she saw him, his excess of gifts, masculine beauty, grace, leanly muscled body, midnight smile . . . the latent consuming power of his sex. His lying words.

I hate him. I hate them all. All who've been given life's unfathomable gifts—to love and be loved. Children.

Small, loving souls. Mine only tissue and blood.

Her brain blanked with the abruptness of a power failure, and the light of her mind, already diffused and dim, went out.

Hatred, bloody and sharp, dried her mouth.

Desolation coated her heart.

I can't—won't—take it anymore.

She stuffed her hands in her sweater pocket, wrapped her fingers around the comfort of death. "I'm different from anyone you've ever met, Adam." She took the gun from her pocket.

Adam's eyes fell to the gun, widened. "Jesus, Gina—"

"Don't worry," she said, calm flowering inside her, lightening her tone. "You're going where you belong . . . to Mother, to Holly." She lowered the gun to his groin. "And you might want to wait up, because Camryn will be along shortly."

As will I. We'll see you in hell, Adam. All of us.

She fired.

* * *

Dan shot to his feet. "What the hell!"

Camryn's head snapped up. They both looked upward to the ceiling. To whatever was beyond it.

The harsh report of the gun coming from the far reaches of the big house had barely registered before the room filled with music: a clash of cymbals, a crescendo of violins . . . what sounded like the onslaught of a hundred-piece orchestra; its rush of sharps and flats, as if herded by the volume at which they were played, tripping over themselves, tumbling down the stairs and into the miserable parlor.

The gunshot attracted the ear. The music, thundering in its wake, filled it, leaving no room to comprehend.

Then . . .

Camryn rushed to the parlor door. "My God! Gina!"

"Stop." Dan caught her arm. "Wait."

More shots! Closer than the first.

The music dying . . . dead. An even deadlier silence.

"Get back." Dan whispered, his voice low, urgent.

"But Gina . . ."

"Back, Camryn." He hadn't let go of her arm, and when she stood as if rooted to the floor, he pulled her, roughly and without apology, and put her behind him. He cocked his ear toward the door. "Listen."

Nothing. Only the wind and the spit of rain against the windows, a dense quiet that rested uneasily within the walls of the big house.

She stepped to his side, took a gulping breath. The air entered her lungs like broken glass, but it jerked her out of panic mode. She took another. "Gina might be hurt. We have to check."

"We will." Dan looked around the dim, cluttered room, took in the small-paned windows, narrow transom openings at their tops, no way out other than the door they'd entered by. "No phone. Damn." He looked at her. "You?"

"In my bag. I left it by the front door."

He cursed, again scanned the room.

Camryn already knew the room provided them no escape. She cracked the door a couple of inches, put her ear to it. No sound. But light, from the family room, what there was of it, brightened the carpet at her feet, adding wattage to the dimly lit parlor. "We have to get out of here." She shot him a look over her shoulder. "We have to find Gina. See if she's okay."

The added light disappeared abruptly. "I'm very much okay, Camryn." Gina gave the door a push, causing Camryn to stumble back, and walked into the room, kicking the door shut behind her. "I couldn't find any cheese and crackers, so I brought cake."

"Cake?" Camryn echoed stupidly. Her mind didn't work fast enough to accept Gina's sudden breezy entrance, grasp what it meant. She was aware of Dan moving into the shadow behind the gooseneck lamp.

"I made it this morning." She smiled, but her eyes were fixed, like tacks in a corkboard. "I didn't think it was for a celebration, but there you are!"

"You're all right?"

"Couldn't be better," she said.

From gunshots to celebration. Everything was so wrong . . . this house. Gina.

"What's going on here, Gina? You must have heard that." Camryn forced herself to a calm she didn't feel, determined to get, if not control, at least a grasp of what was going on here. "Those were gunshots. What happened?"

Gina set the cake beside her abandoned wineglass on the messy table and frowned. "I guess cake and wine don't make a very good combination, do they?"

Camryn strode toward her, grabbed her by the upper arms. "Forget the cake! Answer me. For God's sake, what's wrong with you?"

Gina blinked but the smile she'd walked in with didn't

budge; it seemed frozen on her face. "I don't know what you mean." She pulled back from Camryn's hold and slid her right hand into her sweater pocket. "I told you I'm fine. As a matter of fact, I feel better than I have in months. It helps when things crystallize, doesn't it? When things get clear in your mind." The last was said more to herself than Camryn, then she tilted her head, her too-bright, eyes, studying Camryn as if they'd lit on her for the first time, as if they hadn't been friends for twenty years. "You were always the organized one, Camryn, always the get-everything-right one, so you should know how important clear thinking is. When you're feeling low, get busy, take action—that's what you used to say." She amped up her smile. "You made everything happen, exactly how you wanted it. Except maybe the baby thing. And now you even have that, don't you? You have Adam's child."

"Are you actually saying I had something to do with Holly's death?" Shock took Camryn's breath away.

"Oh no, I know you'd never do that. Not Saint Camryn. She'd never do anything as *ba-a-d* as that." She giggled. "No, all Camryn has to do is wait around, and everything will work out. Adam says you're the last good woman—or his last woman . . ." She paused, looked confused for a minute. "I never really understood what he meant by that."

"I don't know what's wrong with you," Camryn said, "but you're my friend, Gina. All I want to do is help. But you have to tell me what's going on. There were shots . . . upstairs, then you come down acting crazy. None of this makes sense."

Gina's fixed expression ignited. "I'm not crazy! Don't say that! Don't *ever* say that!" She looked through the shadowy room to where Dan stood silently, a large gray blur behind the lamp. "Come out where I can see you, Dan. Have some cake." She smiled in his direction, but Camryn wasn't sure she actually saw him. It was more like she sensed him, the way an animal would its prey. The smile she gave him was crooked, like a slash of carelessly applied lipstick.

Camryn watched her hand, sliding out of her pocket, slowly exposing her wrist, her knuckles—Camryn's chest went drum-tight.

Was that . . . ?

The sound of the front door opening, then slamming shut, snapped Gina to attention, her expression a haze of surprise, confusion, and panic.

"Gina? Delores?" a man's voice shouted. "Jesus, why the hell don't you two turn some lights on in this place?" Heavy footsteps came toward them, the solid thwack of sneakers on the hardwood floor.

Pale yellow light again flickered through the door to color the stained parlor carpet. Gina shoved her hands deep into her sweater pockets. "Sebastian, what are you doing here?"

He ignored her question and tried the light switch on the wall inside the door of the parlor. Click. Click. He cursed again. "What's with the damn lights?" He shook his head, looking irritated, then spotted Camryn; he nodded unsmiling in her direction. "Hey."

"Hey," she said back. With the image of what her friend had in her pocket fronting her mind, Camryn was grateful only a three-letter word was required.

When neither woman spoke further, Sebastian walked to where the bottle of wine sat illuminated on the coffee table. He was reaching for it when he spotted Dan. He went gravestone-straight. "Okay." He swung to look at Camryn. "What the hell am I doing here?"

Gina shot a cold gaze at Camryn. "You invited Sebastian?"

"I thought—" Dear God, she had no idea what she had thought, but she knew what she had to do. She took in a breath. "I wanted him here because I thought he—we—could help you. But now"—she swallowed—"all I want him to do is take that gun out of your pocket."

Gina's eyes narrowed.

"Then," Camryn continued, keeping her voice flat, "I want us to go upstairs and see what those gunshots were all about."

"Fuck!" Gina pulled out the gun.

"What the hell—?" Sebastian froze.

Dan snapped the gooseneck lamp up, shone its light directly into Gina's face. The glare wasn't much, but in the dim room, it was contrast enough that she raised the arm not holding the gun to shield her eyes.

Bolting from behind the chair, Dan made a dash to where Gina, now clearly illuminated by the focused lamplight stood, blinking—the gun glinting and wavering in her shaking hand. But the furniture in the room impeded him, giving her enough time to steady the gun. Aim it at him.

Camryn lunged for the gun. She was fast, but Gina was faster; she fell back, braced her back against the parlor wall, and fired.

The room, the people in it, hit STOP time and locked in place.

"Get back! All of you, get back!" Gina's eyes, as wild as the shot she'd fired, bulged from their sockets. Her back was to the open door now, making her a silhouette, armed and dangerous. "Stay away from me."

She was breathing heavily; Camryn could hear the rasps, and she held the gun in both hands. "Gina, stay calm. Think this through. You don't want to do this."

As if she hadn't heard, Gina waved the gun. "I'll shoot the first person who comes near me." She tossed a quick, scared glance Sebastian's way. "Even you, Seb. I'm sorry. So sorry, but it doesn't matter now. One dead. Two dead . . . a dozen. It doesn't matter."

"Gina, what are you talking about? What the hell is the matter with you?" Sebastian stepped forward. "Give me that thing."

"Stop!" she screeched. "I told you to stop!"

He stopped.

Dan stepped in front of Camryn, and when he spoke, his voice was flat, smooth as soft cloth. "Who's dead, Gina?" He jerked his head toward the ceiling. "Who's up there?"

"Delores!" Sebastian said. "Jesus, no, Gina, fuck no. You didn't—" Sebastian took a step toward the open door. Gina fired. The bullet caught him in the knee. He dropped screaming to the floor and clutched his leg. Blood spurted to the carpet.

"Oh, Sebastian . . ." She stared at him, her eyes moist—and terrified. "I told you not to move. I've got business here. Can't you see that? Understand that? Doesn't anyone understand?" She blinked against her tears and brushed at them jerkily with her left wrist.

Sebastian writhed on the floor, clutching his knee, blood soaking his pant leg. "You're crazy, just like our fucking mother. You're crazy."

"Shut up!" She arced the gun, took another step back, and waved it in a sweeping motion to encompass the parlor. "Shut up. . . . Everyone shut up! I'll shoot again. I will. I'll kill you all." Her voice was pitched high, broke when she looked at Sebastian's blood, the growing stain of it seeping into the ugly leaf-patterned carpet.

Camryn, horrified and achingly sad, stared at her friend. "Gina, why?" she asked, her voice as calm and low as she could manage from her tight throat. "Tell me why."

The room filled with a grim silence. Dan wrapped his hand around her arm, tried to pull her back. "Camryn, move. Get back." She refused to budge, determined to reach her friend in whatever way she could. He loosened his grip but didn't let go.

Gina waved the gun between them, then her mad, dark eyes met Camryn's and held; the moisture of tears burning in their resolve.

And confusion. . . .

"Cammie, I . . ." Her voice trailed off, and for a moment she appeared limp, exposed.

When Camryn took a step toward her, reached for her hand, Gina leveled the gun and shook her head. "No. It's too late." Her lips flattened over her teeth, and her shoulders straightened.

Dan's grip again tightened. He was trying to put himself in front of Camryn. *No!*

"Please, you can't do this! You can't!" Camryn pressed the hand she'd extended to Gina flat over her chest—but it wasn't the frantic beat of her own heart she felt; it was the pounding of Gina's broken one, her aching weariness, and then the racing of her dark and chaotic mind. It was as if her friend's thoughts flew out of pattern, fast, and too heavy and desperate to bear.

Camryn knew this as if Gina had spoken it, had exposed her soul. Her own soul whispered back: *Where are you, my smart, funny, Barbie-doll friend? Where are you? Wherever you are, come back. Come back. . . .*

Their eyes met and held.

Gina shook her head, the gesture one of longing and defeat. "I hate too much." Tears slicked her cheeks and made her eyelashes glisten. "Delores, Adam, Holly . . . even you. I even hate you, Camryn. I hate myself . . . what I feel. What I've done. I'm sick with hate, and there's nowhere for it to go except the grave." She pointed the gun at her face. "Why, Camryn? why does everyone get who they want . . . except me?

"You mean Adam."

"My Adam. He's dead, you know." She half-smiled. "Dead and gone." Pain slashed through her eyes.

"No, Gina. You didn't. You couldn't."

She went on as if Camryn hadn't spoken. "He's mine now. He'll always be mine." She smiled fully then, wistfully. "He didn't want this, you know. He refused to kill you, didn't even want me to kill you for him. But, of course, I have to now. It's the only way." She gripped the gun in both hands, and spread her legs slightly.

Dan tugged Camryn back a step, his fingers urgent, digging pain into her arm. "Camryn, move away." His tone was low, urgent.

She heard him but couldn't react, couldn't take her eyes from the death in Gina's hand.

"For God's sake, get back!" He didn't raise his voice, but he snarled. "Now!"

Gina gave him a sad look. "It won't do any good," she said, her tone as steady and directed as the gun in her hand. "I'm going to kill you all. I have no choice."

Camryn stepped back, as if a few inches of distance from Gina's ugly weapon would add time to her life, and, following the quick shuttering of Dan's eyes, she looked down—and was instantly mesmerized. Her mind clicking through a disjointed series of events.

A body. Behind Gina.

More dead than alive.

A wake of blood and ooze in its tortuous trail.

A red-slicked hand reaching out, unfurling bloody fingers, coiling them around Gina's ankle.

Muscles straining their last. Finger bones locking. A death grip.

Gina's head turning, looking down. Too late. Her slow, blinking eyes. Their widening. Her scream. "No!"

From the floor—the crawling thing, a groan, a heavy rattling breath, a last draw on strength—all as one.

A hard, twisting yank.

Gina stumbling, falling face forward. Her elbow hitting the floor. The gun exploding its evil load . . .

The bullet searing through Camryn's soft flesh, her falling with Gina. Eyes wide. Down. Down. Her head hitting something, an emptying of her lungs. Gasping.

She lay beside Gina, heard Dan curse, saw him kick the gun from Gina's hand, heard it clatter into the far corner of the room. Everything dimming. . . .

"Camryn. Jesus, Camryn, are you okay?" His hands were on her thigh, tearing at her slacks. *Good slacks,* she thought, her thinking woozy, her eyes unable to focus. *These are my good slacks.* She saw Gina's hand, her nails digging into the carpet, crawling.

She reached for her, wanted to help . . . but the darkness denied her.

Chapter 29

Dan had applied a rough bandage to Camryn's thigh. It was a damned nasty wound, but not as nasty as the brother's knee. For both of them he'd had to make do with applied pressure and some hastily grabbed towels.

There was little or nothing he could do for the woman.

Sebastian was sitting on the floor, his back propped against the wall, his mother's head on his lap. He was smoothing her tangled, blood-clotted hair off her face, whispering to her, telling her to hold on, that help was on its way. Her hand lay in his, but it was loose, its fingers lax and splayed. Considering the trail of blood she'd left from the second floor, if she made it to the hospital alive, it would be a miracle.

"Hm-m . . ."

Camryn. His attention snapped to where it belonged. She'd been out for only a few minutes, but it felt like a lifetime. "You're going to be all right. Just take it easy. The ambulance will be here any minute. Everything will be okay." He bent to kiss her hair and whisper, "Thank God, you're going to be okay." It was the closest he'd come to praying in too many years to remember. But prayer or not, he couldn't wait for that ambulance to get here. The wound wasn't deep, but she'd lost a lot of blood.

She seemed ready to lapse into unconsciousness again, but then rallied and said, "Gina. How's Gina?" She tried to get up, winced.

"Don't. Stay still. Gina's fine." He deliberated on his answer. "She's in the kitchen, tied to a chair."

"Oh, Dan . . ."

She didn't have to finish for him to hear a "poor, poor Gina" in there. He didn't feel the same, and didn't add that Gina had slipped from a screaming, babbling crazy woman to a catatonic a few seconds after he'd subdued her. "I made her as comfortable as I could. She has a couple of bruises from when her mother brought her down, but other than that, she's okay."

"Then it was Delores." She swallowed, and it seemed to hurt her. "I couldn't tell. She was so . . ."

"I know." Dan had seen some tough women in his time, but watching that unholy bloodied apparition crawl across the floor and grasp Gina's ankle with enough force to topple her, he knew he'd seen the toughest of them all.

Camryn slid her hand into his, and he squeezed it; it was like ice. "Is she okay?"

"I don't know. She's got at least three bullets in her. She mumbled something about being taped in her chair. About how she'd got out, tried to call Adam. With the music. But Gina came instead." He stroked her hair. "Those were the second set of shots we heard."

"What about Adam?"

"I don't know. I didn't know where to look—and I didn't want to leave you to do it." His attentions taken up by the living, finding a corpse had slipped low on his priority list.

She lifted his hand, kissed it. "Thank you." She smiled at him, but it was a strained smile, and he knew, now that she was fully awake, the pain from the gunshot would kick in.

"You're welcome," he said, turning his hand to cover hers and doing a little kissing of his own. Her hand was so cool. So small in his. Almost gone . . . He sucked up a breath; no point dwelling on the "what if"s. She was here. She was safe. That's all that mattered.

"Find him, Dan. Please. He might be—"

She winced again, couldn't finish, but Dan recognized hope when he saw it. He touched her cheek, smoothed some stray hair back. She wanted to know, and right now all he wanted was for her to stay calm. "I'll check, but don't try to move." He gave her as stern a look as he could, remembering as he did the fear in watching her fall, seeing her blood flow. It had damn near stopped his heart. He doubted it would ever beat steadily again. "*Do not move,*" he said. "Promise?"

"Promise."

"I'll be right back."

Dan headed for the stairs, the sound of sirens—finally—coming to his ear. *Thank God!*

The sooner he and Camryn were out of this hellhole of a house, the happier he'd be. He took the stairs two at a time and strode quickly down the hall, opening doors—there seemed to be a hundred of them—before he discovered another set of stairs leading to an attic room.

Which was where he found Dunn—in a massive pool of blood, with a good part of his lower torso blown away.

Dead. Definitely dead.

Dan set his hands on his hips, let out a long breath, looked away, and briefly closed his eyes. He thought about covering the body with a blanket from the bed but knew it would mess things up for the cops.

He looked back at the ruined corpse, wondered if he was looking at the remains of the man who'd killed his wife.

His chest constricted, in some weird hybrid of anger and pity. Either way, it didn't matter anymore. What was done was done. He guessed now he'd never know if Dunn killed Holly, and while he hated not knowing, one thing was certain, he wouldn't have wished this kind of dying on any man. Even Dunn.

He walked out, leaving the door open.

He met the police and a medic coming up the stairs, shook his head and pointed toward the attic. Let them do their jobs; he was going downstairs to Camryn, and he planned to stay with her—and Kylie—for the rest of his life.

All he had to do was convince her of that.

Chapter 30

"Don't you have a home to go to?" Camryn teased when she walked into the den and saw Dan sprawled on her sofa, shoes off, his long denim-covered legs stretched in front of him. She set the bowl of buttered popcorn she was carrying on the coffee table in front of him and experienced the usual stomach flip when he looked up at her and winked.

She still limped, and she'd have a rather interesting and unlovely three-inch scar on her upper thigh to show off if she ever donned a bikini again, but she couldn't bring herself to care about it. She was alive. Dan was alive. Kylie was safe, and they were together, even if it was an undefined relationship on an uncharted testing ground that neither of them seemed anxious to talk about. It was as if, in the three weeks since the shooting, she and Dan both needed the days of calm, time to gather their breath and thoughts. Be normal.

"I *am* home." Dan said, muting the TV. She glanced at it, expecting to see a game of some sort. It was an old black-and-white movie.

Oh, yes, there were those martinis.

She smiled and sat beside him. He immediately put his arm around her, drew her close, and kissed her temple. "Kylie asleep?"

"Her and a hundred stuffed animals."

"Grantman called a while ago, when you were putting her to bed."

"How's Erin doing?"

"Good, so he says. That's why he called. He's flying down to see her."

"I'm glad. Glad for all of us: Paul, Kylie—it's good all around." She paused. "What about you and Paul?"

He slid her a glance. "What *about* us?"

"Do you talk? Are things okay between you?"

"First off, men don't 'talk.' They form pacts of manly silence. Grunts are optional." He smiled at her.

"That sounds tedious and ineffective."

He laughed. "Both. But it works. I figure in a few years, maybe we'll go to a Seahawks game together. Now, that's bonding."

For a time they watched the movie, soundless. "How's the leg?"

"How about you quit asking me that? Or are you angling to see my scar again?"

He wiggled his brows. "How'd you guess?"

"Maybe because the last time you had me drop my jeans, it went way, way beyond looking." She picked up the bowl, held it out to him. "Have some popcorn."

He laughed again, took some popcorn, and settled back into silence. He looked as though he were watching the muted movie, but Camryn knew he wasn't.

"I called the Boston Police Department today."

Of all the things he might have said, she hadn't expected this. She sighed, knowing their escape to normal was at an end. "And?"

"They didn't say as much, but I think they've put Holly's file on the back burner."

"Nothing? Nothing at all?" The idea of not knowing who killed Holly made her sad, a bit sick to her stomach. It wasn't right that justice would not be done, that there was someone out there who'd gotten away with murder. But, as she'd learned the hard way the night of the shooting, life wasn't always fair—or just—and things weren't always what they seemed or should be. Nor were people.

He shook his head. "Same result from the P.I. Grantman hired. Everything comes up a dead end."

"It's hard to accept, isn't it? Not knowing."

"Yeah."

"You still think it was Adam?"

"Logic said he was a reasonable suspect. He was in Boston at the time. Holly had dumped him. He needed money, and getting custody of Kylie was his way to do that. It seemed to make sense."

"And now?"

"Now, I think your famous"—he narrowed his gaze, showed a hint of stubbornness—"intuition, sixth sense, or whatever it is you've got was probably right."

"Plus, he refused to kill me—even though the same motivation still applied."

Dan nodded.

Again the room fell to silence. Camryn put her head on Dan's arm and closed her eyes. She thought of Holly, Gina . . . Adam. She thought of herself those many years ago and wondered again why she'd been able to let Adam go and neither Holly nor Gina ever had. She couldn't understand it. Just as she couldn't understand why, of the three of them, she was the one who would never bear a child. At that thought, the usual sliver of pain pierced her heart. She took a breath and worked to let it go. She had Kylie. She was blessed.

As blessed as Gina was . . . cursed.

"Sebastian is moving back in with Delores, did you know that?" she said. The words came out reluctantly because she didn't want to think about the Solaris, their complicated, tragic lives. Or the deeply disturbed Gina, now in

West Seattle Psychiatric, in the "padded room" she'd so often joked was reserved for her eccentric mother. "He said he's going to stay until she's 'out of the woods.' "

"I still can't believe she made it. How many surgeries?"

"Three."

Dan shook his head. "Jesus."

Camryn's heart seemed to slow in her chest. "He got Gina a lawyer."

"That's going to be a tough one." He met her gaze. "And my guess is you'd rather not talk about it."

She nodded. "I'm going to go see her—just not yet."

"Smart." He said nothing more for a moment, then, "Have you heard from your dad yet?" He turned, put an arm over the back of the sofa.

"Yesterday." And damned if it wasn't another topic she'd shied away from, with no idea why.

"You didn't mention it."

"No." She'd talked to Dan about her dad, their long non-relationship, how she'd always felt there was some skewed genes that made it impossible for her to connect with him, but she still felt guilty about it. Whatever was between them had never felt right. She loved him, but always sensed her love wasn't enough, that he was too busy for it.

"Is he okay?"

"He says so." She wanted to believe him but hadn't been able to shake the sense of unease she'd had since hanging up the phone.

"But?" he prodded.

"He sounded strange, and his voice was weak. The flu, he said." She paused. "He's going away for a few days."

"Then he must be okay." He studied her face a second. "He'll be back, Camryn."

"Not permanently. He said when he comes back, he'll be picking up his things."

Dan frowned. "Because of me? Us?"

"No, I don't think so." She ran her hand along his firm thigh, squeezed. "He says it's time for him to move on. To greener pastures, he said. I just hope those pastures don't contain another sour business deal. I'm not sure he can take another one of those."

"He's a big boy, Camryn. He'll be okay—and if he isn't, you'll hear about it."

"Yes." She put her hand on her chest, massaged the tightness there, the odd gloominess she'd felt since her father's call, and told herself Dan was right; if something was wrong, she'd hear.

They rested in quiet for a time, and both of them ignored the popcorn. The TV was still on MUTE. Camryn could almost hear Dan's mind shifting gears, moving in another direction.

Finally, he said, "I do have a home to go to, you know. Or had, at least. In L.A., remember?"

She turned her head enough to look at him. "What are you saying?"

"I put it up for sale. There's an offer on it. A good one." He stopped, pulled his arm from behind her, and picked up the TV remote. He hit the OFF button.

Camryn straightened. Here it was. She'd known damn well it was coming, and while it made her crazy with happiness and expectation, it also frightened her in a way she couldn't define. It was too . . . easy. Which, when she considered the tragedy of Holly's death, Adam's selfish intentions, and Gina's terrible plan, describing their relationship as *easy* made no sense at all. Yet, Dan Lambert had slipped into her casual and well-organized life as if he were the final puzzle piece—as if he'd belonged there all along.

Now, after only a few weeks, she couldn't imagine him not being here. She loved him, and she wanted him in a way she'd never wanted a man. But there were those three little words. Words he hadn't even said to Holly, because he didn't believe in them. Silly, romantic words that shouldn't matter after all they'd been through together, but somehow did matter, more than she cared to admit.

He turned his head, set those seriously green and intense eyes of his on her. "I'm going down to deal with the sale and a few business things. I'm leaving tomorrow. I'll be gone a few days." He stopped. "And when I come back, I'd like to settle things between us."

"Settle things?" If ever there was a vague statement, that was it.

"About Kylie. About us. The custody issue."

"I see." She ignored the ripple of tension on her neck. God, they were back to that. She sighed, told herself she should be glad it was only Dan she had left to deal with, since Paul and Erin had stepped aside and decided the role of doting grandparents would be enough. Unable to sit any longer, Camryn stood and hobbled toward the fireplace.

He stood and joined her there. Putting his hands in the back pockets of his jeans, he stared at the flames. "But before we get to them, there's something you should know." When he shifted his gaze from the fire to her, his eyes still danced from the gold and heat of the flames. Even so, they looked cool . . . sad. He went on, "I had a son. He was killed when he was two years old."

"Oh, Dan. I'm so sorry. . . ." Camryn closed her eyes, a rush of feeling overwhelming her. Surely, the one thing worse than being unable to have a child was to have had, loved, and lost one. "What happened?"

"Billy—that was his name—was what some people would call a 'young man's accident,' the result of a one-night-stand. I was eighteen at the time—and careless. Damned careless." He nodded his head as if agreeing with himself, flaying himself. "His mother didn't bother telling me about him until he was six months old. I hadn't seen her since we—" He shrugged. "When I found out about Billy, I offered to skip college and marry her, but by then she was seeing someone else—getting married. She was decent enough about Billy, though, and we made arrangements for me to see him as often as I wanted. Turned out, I wanted him more often than she did. Her new boyfriend kept her busy, I guess. For the next year and a half, Billy and I were a team. That's what I used to tell him, not that he understood a word." He smiled briefly. "I'd tell him that 'me and him' were a team." He met her eyes. "He was my son, and I made promises to him, and I loved him in a way I'd never imagined I could love."

When he went back to staring into the dancing flames, she said, "What happened?"

He stepped away from the fire. His hands were still in his pockets, but he stood straighter, his jaw firm. "A car accident. An everyday rear-ender, or would have been if Jocelyn had put Billy in his car seat." He spoke tersely, as if wanting the words said and gone.

Camryn put a hand to her mouth, sensing from his rigid posture that an embrace wouldn't be welcome. This grief, this remembered moment, was between him and his son.

"I wanted you to know, so you'll understand how much Kylie means to me, how important it is I . . . look out for her." He took his hands from his pockets and rested an elbow on the mantel. "I made promises to her, too, Camryn. And I love her. Like I loved Billy. I hadn't intended it to happen, sure as hell didn't expect it, but it did—and I'll never walk away from her."

"I wouldn't want you to. I think you know that now." They'd been cohabiting—co-parenting—for weeks; Dan would have to be blind not to take that as her acceptance of him in Kylie's life—and her own life.

"I do. And I'm grateful." He nodded, rubbed an eyebrow, apparently gathering his thoughts. "And then there's you."

Her heart stopped.

He reached out and ran his knuckles along her cheek, lifted her face to his. "You're someone else I hadn't expected to . . . feel this way about."

What way? Just say it. Please, just say it.

Be patient, Camryn, he'll get around to it in man-time. Her stopped heart thumped to life, heavy and warm in her chest.

"We've got a lot going for us." He moved closer. "We like the same wine, we both love Kylie, we're good in bed." He arched a brow, smiled. "Very good in bed."

She managed a smile back. "It helps that you're a love god."

His smile deepened. "And that you know exactly how to stoke up a guy's ego—which isn't too hard to live with."

"Don't get used to it." He was stroking her jaw with his thumb, diverting her, and making it difficult to be flip and amusing. Especially since she'd never been more serious in her life.

With his mouth a breath away from hers, he said, "That's the thing, though. I *want* to get used to it. I want to get used to you, Camryn—for the rest of my life." He kissed her then, one of his soft, haunting kisses that weakened her bones, emptied her lungs, and filled her heart.

He stood back, took her face between his hands, and looked directly into her eyes. "I love you, Camryn. And I'd be honored if you'd give me the chance to prove it—in all ways for the rest of my days and yours."

He'd taken her breath away. Stolen it as if by magic. She absolutely could not speak. She'd never felt this way about a man, any man, and for a brief moment she mourned her failed marriage, what she'd denied Craig—what she'd denied herself. Maybe she, like Dan, had never truly believed in love. If she had, surely she'd have moved heaven and earth to get it, sought it out with everything she had, and settled for nothing less. She sighed. That wasn't how it worked, she supposed. Love came when it was ready, when you were ready—but never when you expected it. Oh, yes, Camryn was ready to spend her life with Dan, with all its uncertainties and fears, all its surprises, good and bad.

She'd never been more ready in her life.

He bent his head, tilted it, and studied her. "You okay with that?"

She nodded against the light pressure of his hands still holding her face. Big hands, strong hands, forever hands. . . .

He lifted a brow. "Somehow, I was hoping for more enthusiasm."

She took both his hands in hers and finally found her voice. "Oh, Dan." She pulled in another breath. "If I was any more enthusiastic, I'd swoon from it and make a complete and utter fool of myself."

"That'd be good." He paused. "So, I'll take that as a yes on the 'rest of my days' thing?"

"Yes, yes, yes. But"—pulling him, she limped toward the door—"if I'm going to swoon, I'd like to land in a soft place."

He stood his ground, pulled her back to his arms. "Uh uh. It's not that easy. What are the magic words, Camryn?"

"Please, Dan." She grinned up at him.

He shook his head.

She touched his face, ran her finger along his hard jaw. "How about . . . I love you, Dan Lambert—with all my heart. And Kylie and I will be honored to have you in our lives—forever."

He pulled her close and kissed her hard and long. "As magic words go, those will do. Those will definitely do."

She smiled at him. "Now can we get to the swooning part?

Don't miss Donna Kauffman's
scintillating read
THE GREAT SCOT.
Available now from Brava!

Erin smiled. "Honestly, I don't know what to think of you. I guess that's why I keep badgering you with questions. You aren't easy to figure out, Dylan Chisholm."

Amusement did shift into his eyes then, and the resulting gleam was no trick of the sun. She swallowed hard. Perhaps it would be wiser not to provoke the playful side of him after all.

And then he was lifting his hands, pushing back the errant strands of hair the car ride had likely blown into a complete rat's nest around her face. Suddenly painfully aware of her looks, or lack thereof, and at the same time exquisitely aware of his touch, almost to the point of pain, she wanted to shrink away, pretend this moment wasn't happening. Because whatever he was thinking behind those dancing gray eyes of his, no way could it be anything that she found herself suddenly hoping, praying, it would be. She didn't attract men like Dylan Chisholm.

Gorgeous, confident, successful men were typically attracted to beauty first, and brains a distant second. Erin was used to falling in the distant second category, okay with it even. When it came to men like the one touching her now, looking at her so intently, well . . . it simply didn't happen. So it had hardly been a problem for her. It would be the epitome of foolishness to allow herself, even for a second, to think this was somehow different.

"I canno' figure you out either, Erin MacGregor," he said, his voice deeper, somewhat rougher, as if . . . as if he were perhaps at least a tiny bit affected by her. Then all rational thought fled, because he was lowering his head toward hers, pressing his fingers into the back of her neck, to tip her face upward to his.

"Ye badger me with yer questions, talk me into abandoning my own home . . ." He lowered his head further until his mouth was hovering just above her own.

He couldn't be, wasn't going to—

"Ye sneak into my dreams, haunt my waking hours. I dinnae understand it. What've ye done to me, lass?

She haunted his dreams? In a good way? "Dylan—"

He made a guttural noise at the sound of his name that had a little instinctive moan of her own escaping her lips.

"I havena felt a hunger such as this in a very long time. Will ye allow me the pleasure?"

He was asking permission? Did he not realize that a second or two more of his heated whisperings and he could have her naked on the hood of his Jag?

He brushed her lips with his. "Perhaps I havena been the most merry of fellows, but if there has been anything to cause me to want a bit of respite from the endless hours of work, it has been you."

"I thought I made you crazy."

And there it was. The smile she'd been waiting for. It was slow to happen, but as it stole across his face, his entire countenance changed, as if he was lit from within. There was fire there, passion. "Aye, that you do. Yer trouble, Erin, with a capital T. Ye plague me."

"A plague am I," she said, but the intended dry sarcasm was somewhat offset by the breathy quality of her voice.

Which served to widen his smile further. "You have refreshing candor, and a smart mouth. You don't seem to care overly much what I think."

She tipped her head back slightly, to look fully into his eyes. "And that's attractive to you? Hard to believe I'm still single with those lovely attributes."

He rubbed his thumbs along the corners of her mouth, making her shiver at the feeling of his work-roughened fingers on her skin. "Hard." Then he slipped his arms around her waist and brought her fully up against him. "Aye, 'tis that."

She barely had time to register the stunning truth, shocked silent by the rigid proof pressing against her midsection. Then he claimed her mouth with his own and any hope of rational thought fled completely.

The hot thrill of being sheltered against the hard length of his body, feeling his hands on her, his mouth on her, swamped her senses. His kiss was insistent and compellingly seductive. Forceful and inviting. An intoxicating combination she had no hope of resisting. Not that she made any real effort.

Where had this come from?

Take a look at Amy J. Fetzer's
spellbinding new novel
INTIMATE DANGER.
Available now from Brava!

When the woman came flying over the gate, Mike couldn't have been more surprised—and disappointed. He'd expected to find his men. One, at least. She dropped to the ground, and he thought, *That's gonna leave a mark.* Then he heard the troops, the gunshots, and didn't think about his decision to help. But she fought him, landing a kick to his shin, and all he could do was drag her.

Out of sight, he gritted, "Stop fighting me, damn it."

Clancy turned wide eyes toward the voice. An American. Where did he come from?

He didn't give her the chance to ask, moving on long legs, pulling her with him, then paused long enough to toss her unceremoniously over his shoulder and grab something off the ground. Then he was off again, running hard, each jolt punching the air out of her lungs and making her want to puke down the back of his trousers.

"Stop," she choked. "Stop!"

He didn't.

So she cupped his rear and squeezed. He nearly stumbled. "Stop, damn it, please!" she hissed. "I can run."

Mike set her on her feet.

Clancy pushed hair from her eyes, then reached out when the world tilted. Her hand landed on his hard shoulder. "That was unnecessary. Nice butt, by the way."

"We have to move."

She met his gaze and thought, *He's huge.* "Who are you?"

"Help?"

"Yeah, well, I was doing okay, sorta."

"If you wanted a bullet in your head, sure. Get moving."

Clancy was about to bitch when she glanced back and through the trees, saw troops. She looked at him. All he did was arch a dark brow.

Great, big, handsome, *and* arrogant? "Lead the way."

He didn't wait for her, and Clancy struggled to keep up. For a big thing, he was agile, leaping chunks of ground while she raced over it.

"They took my jeep," she said into the silence.

He glared at her and thumped a finger to his lips. He waded into the water, his machete in his hand as he turned back for her. She held out her hand. He stared at it for a second and she wiggled her fingers, her expression pleading for help. He grabbed her hand, pulled her the last couple of feet to the shore. She smacked into him, her nose to his chest.

She met his gaze. *Thank you,* she mouthed exaggeratedly, and his lips curved. She had a feeling he didn't do that often. He turned away, kept the steady pace, and she thought, *Somewhere at the end of this better be a bed and a hot bath, and lots of room service.*

No such luck. Just more jungle.

Mike listened for her footsteps instead of looking behind himself. She barely made a sound. What the heck she was doing in jail was something he'd learn later. Right now, getting out of here was essential. He didn't want the notice and pissing off the *Federales* wasn't good any way you looked at it.

When he felt they'd lost the troops, he stopped. She slammed into his back. He twisted, grabbing her before she fell. She was winded, sweating, not unusual in this country, but she looked like a drowned cat. Wisely, he didn't say so.

"Okay, chief, you're gonna have to cut the pace a little." She bent over, her hands on her knees as she dragged in air.

"It was only a mile."

"At top speed when it's a hundred ten out here?" She tried to put some force in her words, but it just sounded like whining to Clancy. She hated whiners. "I run five miles, three times a week for years. But you . . . you'd clean up in the Olympics."

"Keep up or I leave you behind," he said coldly, then frowned at the GPS.

Cute and crabby, who knew? "Well, that would just ruin my day," she bit back.

His gaze flashed to hers. "You want to be a fugitive?"

"No, but I'm still wondering why they wouldn't let me contact the consulate."

"Maybe because the nearest one is in the capital."

"You're kidding."

His frown deepened. "Who arrested you?"

"Some *jefe* . . . Richora?" His features smoothed and Clancy said, "What?"

"You pissed off the wrong guy, lady. He's corrupt as hell."

She'd figured that out easy enough. "Abusive, too."

Mike just noticed her swollen lip. "Richora won't let this go. This is his jungle."

Clancy didn't need an explanation. He owned the people, not the land. Richora ruled, and she didn't doubt that the smugglers who took her jeep handed it right over to him.

His gaze moved over her slowly and she felt, well . . . so thoroughly undressed she looked down to see if her clothes had suddenly melted off.

"If they search you, what will they find?"

She cocked her hip. "Tits, ass, and a gun."

Both brows shot up this time.

"What could I be hiding? They killed Fuad, took my

jeep, and have my good panties and makeup." She wanted
to shout, to really let it loose, but that was just plain stupid.
But whispering at him like a madwoman wasn't helping her
case either.

Mike grabbed her bag, and since it was still looped
around her, the motion pulled her close. He dug in it.

"All you had to do was ask," she said, yet understood
this man didn't ask for anything.

Mike fished and found what he was looking for. He
opened her passport. "Grace Murray?"

"Here, teacher." She grabbed for it.

He held it away, then found her wallet. It was empty except for some cash and a credit card. "No other ID? Who
are you?"

Clancy just tipped her chin up, refusing to answer, and
for a moment she thought he'd given up till he pulled her
close and ran his hands firmly over her body. A little gasp
escaped when his hand smoothed between her legs, then up
the back of her thighs.

"Shouldn't we date before you get this familiar?"

Mike ignored the sound of her voice, but this close, her
words skipped down his spine. His hand slid over her tight
little rear, and his look went as dark as the ocean floor.

"Interesting hiding place."

His big hand dove down the back of her slacks and
pulled out the passport. Inside it was her Virginia driver's li-
cense. He took a step back, examining it, and then only his
gaze shifted. "So Clancy, Moira McRae, why two pass-
ports? CIA?"

"You know, that's the second time someone's asked me
that. What is this area, spy central?"

"Other than intel operatives, people who are dealing in
illegal contraband need more than one passport."

"I'm neither."

He studied both, then waved one. "This is the fake."

She grabbed them back. "How did you know?" And did Phil screw it up on purpose?

"I just do." He inspected her gun, checking the ammo. "Can you even fire this?"

She took it back. "Yes, I can, and lay the hell off." She cocked the slide and pushed it down behind her back. "I'm not your problem."

"You are right now."

And finally, here's Karen Kelley's
CLOSE ENCOUNTERS OF THE SEXY KIND.
Coming next month from Brava!

"Would you like something to eat?"

Eat? Mala had two food capsules prior to leaving her planet, which was enough nutrition for one rotation, but she was curious about the food on Earth. Her grandmother had mentioned it was almost as good as sex. She just couldn't imagine that.

"Yes, food would be nice."

"Why don't you sit on the sofa and rest while I throw us something together." Mason picked up a black object. "Here's the remote. I have a satellite dish so you should be able to find something to entertain you while I rustle us up some food."

She nodded and took the remote, then watched him leave the room and go into another. The remote felt warm in her hand. A transferal of body heat? Tingles spread up and down her arm. The light above her head flickered.

She glanced up. Now that was odd. But then, she *was* on Earth.

Her attention returned to the remote.

Very primitive. The history books on her planet had spoken about remote controls in the old days. You pointed it at the object it was programmed to work with so you wouldn't have to leave your seat.

She pointed it toward the door and pushed the power

button. The door didn't open. She tried different objects around the room without success. Finally, she pointed toward a black box.

The screen immediately became a picture. Of course, television. She made herself comfortable on the lounging sofa and began clicking different channels. Everything interested her, but what she found most fascinating was a channel called Sensual Heat.

She tossed the remote to a small table and curled her feet under her, hugging the sofa pillow, her gaze glued to the screen. A naked man walked across the set, his tanned butt clenching and unclenching with every step he took. When he faced her, the man's erection stood tall, hypnotizing her. It was so large she couldn't take her gaze off it.

A naked woman appeared behind him. She slipped her arms around him, her hands splayed over his chest. Slowly, she began to move her hands over his body, inching them downward, ever closer.

Mala held her breath.

"I want you," the woman whispered. "I want to take you into my mouth, my tongue swirling around your hard cock."

The man groaned.

Mala leaned forward, biting her bottom lip as the man's hands snaked behind him and grabbed the woman's butt. In one swift movement, he turned around. "Damn, you make me hard with just your words."

"And I love when you talk dirty to me."

"So, you want me to tell you what I want to do to your body?"

The woman nodded.

He grinned, then began talking again. "I want to squeeze your breasts and rub my thumbs over your hard nipples." His actions followed his words. "You like that?"

"Yes!" She flung her head back, arching toward the man.

Mala leaned forward, her mouth dry, her body tingling with excitement. Yes! She wanted this, too!

"Do you like French bread, or white bread?" Mason asked, walking into the room.

She dragged her gaze from the television. Bred. That was what humans called copulating. Getting bred. Her nipples ached. "Yes, can we breed now?" She stood and began slipping her clothes off.

"No!" That's not what I meant." He hurried forward and grabbed her dress as it slipped off one shoulder, quickly putting it back in place. Damn, what did Doc give her? This was one hell of a side effect.

"You don't want to copulate?" Her forehead wrinkled, causing her to wince and raise her hand to the bump on her head. "Do you find that I'm not to your liking?"

"Yes, I like you."

"But you do not wish to . . ." She bit her bottom lip as if searching for the right words. "To have sex?"

His hand rested lightly on her shoulder as he met her gaze. "Of course I'd like to . . . uh . . ." He marveled at how soft the fabric felt. His fingers brushed her skin, thinking it felt just as soft. What would she taste like? His gaze moved to her lips. Soft . . . full lips. Kissable.

He jerked his hand away from her shoulder. Anyone watching would think he'd been burned . . . and maybe he had because he certainly felt hot.

He cleared his throat, his gaze not able to meet those innocent, sensuous turquoise eyes. He felt like such a heel. He'd invited her to his home and all he could think about was having hot sex.

How Hot Do You Like It?

 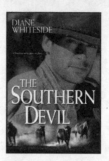